"When it comes to providing fast and furious adventure while making readers snort with helpless laughter, no one does it better than Shearin. It takes serious skill to walk the line that keeps the plotline danger intense yet allows Raine's irreverent humor to shine through, and this perfect blend is what makes this series so massively addictive. Entertainment at its best!" —*Romantic Times* (top pick)

Praise for

The Trouble with Demons

"The book reads more like an urban fantasy with pirates and sharp wit and humor. I found the mix quite refreshing. Lisa Shearin's fun, action-paced writing style gives this world life and vibrancy." —*Fresh Fiction*

"Fans can rejoice as ubertalented Shearin dishes up more hilarious mayhem. Snappy dialogue, great pacing, and two seriously sexy heroes ensure hours of nonstop pleasure. Raine is sassy and irreverent, and this book is an auto-buy!" —*Romantic Times* (top pick)

"If you haven't read the previous books in the series, no matter—you can pick this on up and fall right into the story, but I can pretty much guarantee you'll be looking for the other books so you can go back and enjoy more of Raine's adventures. A book by author Lisa Shearin should come with a warning on the cover or the pages coated in plastic. You are going to laugh out loud." —*Bitten by Books*

"The brisk pace and increasingly complex character development propel the story on a roller-coaster ride through demons, goblins, elves, and mages while maintaining a satisfying level of romantic attention . . . that will leave readers chomping at the bit for more."—*Monsters and Critics*

continued . . .

Armed & Magical

Magic Lost, Trouble Found

"Take a witty, kick-ass heroine and put her in a vividly realized fantasy world where the stakes are high, and you've got a fun, page-turning read in *Magic Lost, Trouble Found*. I can't wait to read more of Raine Benares's adventures."

—Shanna Swendson, author of *Don't Hex with Texas*

"Shearin serves up an imaginative fantasy . . . The strong, well-executed story line and characters, along with a nice twist to the 'object of unspeakable power' theme, make for an enjoyable, fast-paced read." —*Monsters and Critics*

"Lisa Shearin turns expectation on its ear and gives us a different kind of urban fantasy with *Magic Lost, Trouble Found*. For once, the urban is as fantastic as the fantasy, as Shearin presents an otherworld city peopled with beautiful goblins, piratical elves, and hardly a human to be found. Littered with entertaining characters and a protagonist whose self-serving lifestyle is compromised only by her loyalty to her friends, *Magic Lost* is an absolutely enjoyable read. I look forward to the next one!"

—C. E. Murphy, author of *Walking Dead*

"[An] edgy and fascinating first-person adventure. In her auspicious debut, Shearin populates her series with a variety of supernatural characters with a multitude of motives. Following along as this tough and feisty woman kicks butt and takes names is a most enjoyable way to spend your time." —*Romantic Times*

"Fun, fascinating, and loaded with excitement! *Magic Lost, Trouble Found* is a top-notch read of magic, mayhem, and some of the most charming elves and goblins I've ever encountered. Enthralling characters and a thrilling plot . . . I now need to cast a spell on Ms. Shearin to ensure there's a sequel." —Linnea Sinclair

"A friendly romp, a magical adventure story with a touch of light romance." —*Romance Reviews Today*

Ace Books by Lisa Shearin

MAGIC LOST, TROUBLE FOUND
ARMED & MAGICAL
THE TROUBLE WITH DEMONS
BEWITCHED & BETRAYED

Bewitched
& Betrayed

Lisa Shearin

ACE BOOKS, NEW YORK

THE BERKLEY PUBLISHING GROUP
Published by the Penguin Group
Penguin Group (USA) Inc.
375 Hudson Street, New York, New York 10014, USA
Penguin Group (Canada), 90 Eglinton Avenue East, Suite 700, Toronto, Ontario M4P 2Y3, Canada
(a division of Pearson Penguin Canada Inc.)
Penguin Books Ltd., 80 Strand, London WC2R 0RL, England
Penguin Group Ireland, 25 St. Stephen's Green, Dublin 2, Ireland (a division of Penguin Books Ltd.)
Penguin Group (Australia), 250 Camberwell Road, Camberwell, Victoria 3124, Australia
(a division of Pearson Australia Group Pty. Ltd.)
Penguin Books India Pvt. Ltd., 11 Community Centre, Panchsheel Park, New Delhi—110 017, India
Penguin Group (NZ), 67 Apollo Drive, Rosedale, North Shore 0632, New Zealand
(a division of Pearson New Zealand Ltd.)
Penguin Books (South Africa) (Pty.) Ltd., 24 Sturdee Avenue, Rosebank, Johannesburg 2196,
South Africa

Penguin Books Ltd., Registered Offices: 80 Strand, London WC2R 0RL, England

This is a work of fiction. Names, characters, places, and incidents either are the product of the author's imagination or are used fictitiously, and any resemblance to actual persons, living or dead, business establishments, events, or locales is entirely coincidental. The publisher does not have any control over and does not assume any responsibility for author or third-party websites or their content.

BEWITCHED & BETRAYED

An Ace Book / published by arrangement with the author

PRINTING HISTORY
Ace mass-market edition / May 2010

Copyright © 2010 by Lisa Shearin.
Map illustration by Lisa Shearin and Shari Lambert.
Cover art by Aleta Rafton.
Cover design by Judith Lagerman.
Interior text design by Kristin del Rosario.

ISBN: 978-0-441-01872-7

ACE
Ace Books are published by The Berkley Publishing Group,
a division of Penguin Group (USA) Inc.,
375 Hudson Street, New York, New York 10014.
ACE and the "A" design are trademarks of Penguin Group (USA) Inc.

PRINTED IN THE UNITED STATES OF AMERICA

10 9 8 7 6 5 4 3 2 1

Acknowledgments

To Kristin Nelson, my agent. You're always there with invaluable guidance, advice, and support. I'm a lucky author to be your client.

To Anne Sowards, my editor. Thank you for helping me to find and bring out the story inside the story.

To Katherine Shaw, a wonderful fan. The winner of my Name That Bordello contest with "The Satyr's Grove."

To my fans. Your boundless enthusiasm for my books never ceases to amaze and inspire me. I write these books for you.

Chapter 1

I was being chased by a pissed-off naked guy with a knife. A really big knife.

Him being naked was expected since I was doing my ducking, weaving, and dodging down a hall in the Isle of Mid's finest bordello. You'd think that the worst that could happen to me was acute embarrassment and possible death. But this naked guy was possessed by the specter of a three-thousand-year-old evil elven sorcerer who'd turned Mid's red-light district into his personal playground. I'd interrupted recess, and he was mad as hell.

My name is Raine Benares, and I'm a seeker. Tonight I'd found what I was looking for, as well as things I never wanted to see. The men who frequented the Satyr's Grove were here because they had money, not muscle tone. These weren't your finer specimens of manhood. And believe me, I got to see enough manhoods and fleeing pasty white posteriors to last me a lifetime.

Even worse, the sorcerer's specter had picked himself a young, fit, and fast body, not an old, flabby, and slow one. But on the upside, apparently slinging spells was a challenge when wearing someone else's skin. Hence the big knife and bad attitude.

There were screams, shouts, and chaos from the first and second floors. We now had the third-floor hallway all to ourselves. Everyone had either fled downstairs, or barricaded themselves in the bedrooms that lined the hall. Unfortunately, in the Satyr's Grove, the more expensive ladies were on the top floor, and our quarry had decided to splurge. I'd gotten separated from my Guardian bodyguards in the stampede of working girls and clients on the two floors below. I couldn't stop to wait for them. I'd been tracking this specter all week; I'd found him, and he was not getting away.

We'd had a plan, a good plan, but like most plans I'd been involved with lately, it'd gone straight down the crapper moments after implementation. I was upstairs, the specter was upstairs, but the man with the containment box to trap the specter in was somewhere in the chaos downstairs.

"Get him to stand still," shrieked the necromancer.

Yeah, I was sure he'd do that, just as soon as he got close enough to start killing me. The specter-possessed man was chasing me. Sid, the necromancer on loan from the college's necrology department, was chasing the man. At the same time, he was waving around a little drawstring bag of something he'd promised would keep the specter in his host body until an exorcist could extract him. With a choice of a naked guy with a knife versus an evil sorcerer with three thousand years of practice, I was all for the specter staying right where he was. Then it wouldn't matter if the containment box that was downstairs found its way upstairs.

My job had been to find the specter; that'd been the easy part. But judging from the ruckus and outraged upper-class-sounding voices coming from downstairs, Mychael and his boys had caught some of Mid's elite with their trousers down or their robes up. Getting caught being naughty by the commander of the Conclave Guardians and a dozen of his best knights had heaped mortification on top of outrage.

So until Mychael could cut through that crowd with the containment box, it was just me and Sid.

And a dead-end hallway.

Oh crap.

I drew a long dagger and spun to face tall, naked, and pissed—and he stopped dead in his tracks, eyes wide in recognition. He probably didn't know who I was, but he knew what I was.

What he saw was a slender elf with red hair, pale skin probably paler than usual right now, and gray eyes wide with either mere panic or basic terror. But the thing he sensed coiled and eagerly waiting inside of me was what froze him to the spot.

The Isle of Mid was haunted. Not by the chain-rattling, cold spot, moaning sort of specters. This sorcerer and five of his coconspirators had escaped from the Saghred, a soul-stealing stone of unlimited power. They weren't dead, but they weren't exactly alive, either. A couple thousand years ago, this guy had probably tried to use the Saghred to do something he shouldn't, and by some mishap had gotten himself sucked inside.

Through a few mishaps of my own, I was linked to the Saghred. My life's goal had become to find a way to sever that link, but for now the rock and I were locked in a struggle of wills. It wanted me to use its power so it could take my soul or possibly my sanity one nibble at a time, but mostly it wanted me to feed it. And right now, it wanted the ancient shadow I saw reflected in the man's eyes, and it wanted it badly. My link to the Saghred made me the Conclave Guardians' specter-hunting bloodhound. Not only could I sense the specters; I could see them. Lucky me.

No way in hell was I going to be a straw for the Saghred to slurp up stray souls, and I didn't want to kill the host body. That would just force the specter out, and Sid and I were not equipped to handle that alone. Besides, this poor naked bastard had just been looking to get laid, not possessed. I didn't want to kill him, but the specter inside of him didn't share my moral dilemma.

His eyes glittered in the dim light. That was all the warning I got.

He lunged. I dropped into a low crouch, and his knife missed me by an inch and a hair, slashing the scarlet and gilt wallpaper covering the wall behind me.

I hadn't survived my thirty-some-odd years by being squeamish. I twisted my body, going for an uppercut straight into his nuts. What I got was his fist on my back, pounding me flat to the floor and knocking the air out of me. His knife was going to follow his fist. I needed to roll, move, anything, but all my body could manage was a wheezing gasp. Stupid body. I managed to turn my head to the side and sank my teeth into his ankle.

He bellowed in pain and rage, and I felt a thump as Sid the necromancer jumped on his back and began beating him on the head with his drawstring pouch of ghost dust, pixie powder, or whatever the hell it was. I used the distraction to drag, crawl, and finally scramble my way out of knife range. Once I was on my feet, I drew my sword from the harness on my back. The naked guy whirled to face me while reaching back over his shoulder, trying to dislodge Sid. I had to hand it to the little necromancer; he held on with the tenacity of a tick. One thin arm was locked around the man's throat, while the other continued to beat him on the head with the pouch—that is, until the naked guy snatched it away from him.

Oh damn.

Sid's lips began desperately moving in silent incantation. Fast as a striking snake, the man had the tip of his knife under Sid's chin, took a quick step back, and pinned the necromancer to the wall like a bug. A thin stream of blood ran down the blade. Sid whimpered. The fingers of the man's other hand closed around the pouch.

I held out my hands, palms out. "Sid, don't try anything else," I told him, like the necromancer had a choice. I just didn't want to give the specter any more reasons to kill him.

"Listen to her, or not, little human." The elven sorcerer's voice was a deep rasp emerging from the man's throat, the rasp of a voice unused for thousands of years. An amused voice. Amused wasn't good coming from a sorcerer with a couple of millennia of dark deeds and malicious mayhem under his belt. He spoke to Sid, but his gleaming eyes were locked on mine. "It matters not. I am finished with this body for the evening. I can find another. Perhaps yours, *necromancer.*" The last word came out as a lascivious rasp. "I can easily flow from this body into yours." The specter caused the man's lips to curl in a slow grin, and I saw the shadow of the elf's face as if it were floating just beneath the man's skin. His face was gaunt, his lips thin, and his hairline receding. No wonder he grabbed the best-looking body he could find.

"Are you up for an evening of sport?" the elven specter was asking Sid. "There are other establishments we could patronize. What say you, little man?"

My blade was worthless against the sorcerer. He knew it, and so did I. Even if I killed his host body, he would flow into Sid, or through the nearest wall, and there wasn't a damned thing I could do to stop him.

But the Saghred could. It could stop him, take him, and have him for a late-night snack—through me. Though if I used one iota of the Saghred's power to stop him, I didn't think I could stop the power from taking me. It'd happened before with three demons. I vaporized them, and the only way I'd kept myself from sharing their fate was to discharge the surge of power by destroying another demon the size of a small house. I'd squashed him like a wet sponge—right before I passed out. Right now, I was in a building packed with people. I couldn't let the Saghred off its leash, but the sorcerer didn't know that.

I tried to swallow, but my mouth was bone-dry. "You're forgetting the rock." I said it slowly and deliberately. It was the only way I'd keep my voice from shaking. My legs were already shaking. They wanted to run; they had the right idea.

The sorcerer drew the man's body up to his full height. "And you're forgetting your place. The Saghred must indeed be desperate to accept a bond servant such as you." The smile widened into a teeth-baring grin, and the man's eyes went completely black. The lamps in the hall slowly dimmed to mere pinpricks of flame, and the bottom dropped out of the

•

temperature. Two of those flames were reflected in the man's black orbs. It was highly theatrical and spooky as hell. "The goblin has told us about you, the elven seeker who battled the queen of demons. I must admit my disappointment."

It was more like a rolling-around-on-the-floor catfight than a battle, but I wasn't about to tell him that. The goblin he referred to was Sarad Nukpana. Blackest of the black mages. Psychotic for the fun of it. Prisoner of the Saghred until said queen plunged a demonic dagger into the rock and opened the way for his escape, along with five other inmates he'd plotted with on the inside. Now they were all outside with us.

I felt the sorcerer's specter gathering power, probing at my will. The air constricted, tightened, cold and brittle. Too tight to breathe, too cold to bear.

"Yes, you are weak, afraid. You will not take souls into yourself," the sorcerer taunted, the heat of the man's breath frosting the air with each word. He laughed, a hollow, ugly sound. "I'm leaving, and I'm taking the necromancer with me. Attempt to follow me and you will both die."

I had no backup—and no choice.

The sorcerer knew I wouldn't take his soul, but the Saghred had other ideas. The rock was starving, so I let it rear its head. I could handle rearing; rearing wasn't taking. I wasn't firing the cannon; I was merely opening the hatch.

And hunger gripped me, fierce and overwhelming.

I was starving. I had always hungered, never been satisfied, eternally needing, forever wanting. I couldn't remember a time when I hadn't been starving. I had been teased with food, so close, the souls writhing helplessly within my reach, then snatched away, denying me yet again. I would be deprived no longer. Food was here before me, offering itself, teasing, tempting.

Mine.

The sorcerer made a low sound of satisfaction, and the eyes of the man he possessed no longer reflected flame—they were flame. "There you are." His voice was a caressing whisper. "I knew you wouldn't be able to resist coming out to play."

The crazy son of a bitch was talking to the rock.

He was talking to me.

"Yes, we have spent much time together. I know its needs, its desires." He took one step toward me, then another. "It wants me, almost more than it can bear. You feel its hunger, don't you? I know you do. Your eyes burn with its need. As bond servant, the Saghred's desires are your desires." The man's mouth twisted into a smirk as did the shadow lips of the elf possessing him. "Do you want me, servant? There are rooms here in which we may fulfill many such desires. Come to me now and I will allow the necromancer to live."

Take him. Take him now.

I dimly felt my right foot slide along the floor, trying to take a step toward him, wanting to go to him, my need overpowering. My breath hissed in and out between clenched teeth; the muscles in my legs were shaking with the effort not to move. I would not move; I would fight both of them—the specter and the Saghred. But part of me wanted to give in to the hunger, rush forward and take what was mine. Yes. I would feast on the traitorous spirit, the sorcerer who dared to pit his pathetic power against mine. I would take and rip—

"Raine!"

That strong, deep voice turned my name into a command and a lifeline, raw magical power given voice.

My mind instantly cleared. The sorcerer was a specter; the body encasing him was just a man.

I screamed and lunged, the point of my sword going between the man's fingers, puncturing the pouch of Sid's dust, sending a glittering cloud of glowing blue into the air.

"No!" Two voices screamed their denial—both man and specter. The man flung Sid to the floor and brushed frantically at the powder. It stuck to his skin, then disappeared underneath, the blue glow intensifying, consuming, until the man was glowing from the inside. His eyes went blank, his mouth open and gasping. The specter screamed alone, high and keening, as the man he possessed slowly sank to his knees, his eyes closing, his body falling forward.

The lamps along the hall brightened, and I leaned back against the wall, taking one deep, shuddering breath, then another. The man sprawled at my feet was still breathing, albeit raggedly, the sorcerer's specter trapped inside. For now.

A few of the doors started opening, heads tentatively peeking out. They took one look at the hard face of the armored man—the owner of that commanding voice—striding down the hall toward me and slammed them shut again. His armor was dark, sleek steel and custom fit, conforming to his leanly muscled body almost like a second skin. No armorer was that good; magic was definitely involved when it was forged.

Paladin Mychael Eiliesor was the top law enforcement officer on the island, and as paladin and commander of the Conclave Guardians, he was in charge of the most elite magical fighting force in the seven kingdoms. He was a master spellsinger, healer, and warrior, lethally skilled in battlefield magic. What had happened downstairs had constituted a raid, even if it was only a raid looking for the naked man sprawled at my feet. A lot of Mid's social elite were probably climbing out windows right now; some of them may have even remembered their clothes.

I felt the sense of controlled power emanating from him as he closed the distance between us. He was a man with a purpose, and that purpose was me.

Sid sank to his knees, hand clutching his throat. "It worked," he said in utter disbelief. He took his hand away, looked down at the blood, and turned kind of pasty.

I was incredulous. "What do you mean, 'it worked'?"

"I've never used that formula on anything that old. It worked on a six-hundred-year-old poltergeist last year, but I have to admit it was touch and go there for a minute."

A strong hand rested on my shoulder, and I shivered. Mychael's hand was warm and I didn't realize how cold I was.

I turned my head to look up at him. "As always your timing is perfect."

That wasn't all I thought was perfect about Mychael Eiliesor, but I'd been trying to keep those thoughts to myself lately. As a red-blooded, breathing woman, believe me, it wasn't easy. I could tell myself that Mychael was just your basic tall, hot, and handsome elf, but there was a lot more to him than met the eye.

The bordello's hall was dimly lit, but I could see Mychael well enough, and what I couldn't see, I knew all too well. Auburn hair, chiseled features, elven ears elegantly pointed and temptingly nibbleable. His eyes were that mix of blue and pale green found only in warm, tropical seas. Eyes that reflected a razor-sharp intelligence, watchful eyes that missed nothing.

He hadn't missed what had almost happened to me.

"My timing could have been better." I could hear the anger in his voice, aimed at himself, not at me. "You were alone."

He stepped around me and knelt next to the unconscious man and pulled his hands behind his back, securing them with a pair of manacles. I heard the hum when the locks clicked. Magic-sapping manacles. If the man woke up and the specter along with him, neither one would be able to do any damage, at least not of the magical variety.

I took a shaky breath and blew it out. "Well, next time we won't chase a specter into a cathouse while there's an orgy going on. Did you know any of them?"

Mychael stood and chuckled softly. "Just all of them. A few visiting dignitaries, a minor elven royal, and more than a few Conclave officials."

Sid whistled. "That must have been some party."

Mychael grinned. "Let's just say I got to see a different side of our government at work."

I grimaced. "Glad I missed that; I got to see more than enough up here."

"So it appears. Never let it be said that I don't take a lady to interesting places." Mychael glanced down at the manacled naked guy at our feet. "And speaking of having seen enough . . ." He turned and pounded once on the nearest door with his fist. "Blanket, please." The words were polite; the force and the volume demanded a response.

Sounds of scrambling came from inside, and the door opened just far enough for a hairy-backed hand to push a blanket through. The door quickly closed, and at least three dead bolts were thrown. Mychael made good use of the blanket, and the naked, possessed guy was finally covered.

"One down, five to go," I said. "I'm going to take this as a sign that our luck's about to improve."

"Raine, you were going to go to him." Mychael's voice was in my head, his words for me alone. It was a smart way to communicate, considering that where we were standing was about as public as you could get. And for a necromancer, Sid was a nice enough sort, but neither one of us wanted him or anyone else to know the details of what had almost happened.

"No chance." I tried for a quip. *"Neither one of them was my type."*

"Type doesn't matter and you know it."

"Mychael, I'm the only one who can track these things."

"Next time you'll track; we'll retrieve."

I wasn't going to argue with him now. There'd be plenty of time for that later. First, I had to find the next escaped soul—before their ringleader found me.

Sarad Nukpana was an evil that I could almost smell in the air. I glanced at the man on the floor. I could see the faint, dark outline of the elven sorcerer trapped inside. And now the evil could touch me right back. The evil stalking me was breathing down the back of my neck. Not literally, but I could sense the gloating, the anticipation, the eagerness of Sarad Nukpana close to getting what he wanted.

Me.

Nearly two months ago, to keep Sarad Nukpana from sacrificing someone I loved like a brother to the Saghred, I had tricked him into picking up the stone with his bloody hand. In that moment, the Saghred considered him a sacrifice and took him, destroyed his body, and imprisoned his soul. As far as Nukpana was concerned, no body equaled my fault. The bastard would love to take mine.

It had been three weeks since Sarad Nukpana and his allies had escaped the Saghred, three weeks that I'd been hunting him—and he'd been haunting me.

I hadn't even come close to finding him, not yet. The goblin was being smart; he had too much at stake to do anything other than execute his plan. Sarad Nukpana wanted the Saghred and all the kingdom-crushing power that came with it—that and vengeance against me and a number of people I cared about, Mychael included. Our best guess had him holed up in the goblin embassy where there were plenty of magically powerful and politically influential people to possess. Nukpana could take his pick. And even though Mychael was the top law officer on Mid, he couldn't legally set foot in the goblin embassy. If he did, it'd be an act of war. Mychael wasn't holding his breath that an engraved invitation was going to be delivered to his office in the citadel. And with the Saghred in the citadel behind heavily guarded and warded doors, Mychael wasn't going to be inviting anyone from anywhere over for a visit.

We heard booted feet running up the stairs. Vegard didn't even pause at the head of the stairs, but covered the distance to us with long strides. Vegard Rolfgar was a Guardian. He was also big, blond, and human; and as my personal bodyguard, he had his work cut out for him. Let's just say guarding me was a challenge.

"I'm sorry, ma'am," he told me.

"Not your fault, Vegard." I gave him a half grin. "How did you know you were going to get caught in a stampede of screaming, half-naked working girls?"

Mychael scowled. "You wouldn't have been separated from him if you had waited rather than storming up here."

"I wasn't going to lose this one," I said, a little more forcefully than I'd intended.

"Instead you'd rather risk losing yourself," said his voice in my head.

Mychael knew what had almost happened as if it had been happening to him. And in a way, it had. Mychael and I were two-thirds of an umi'atsu bond; an intimate, magical bond that usually linked only two mages, binding them first through their magic, then through hearing, sight, and finally their minds and souls. After that, an umi'atsu bond could only be broken by death. Body and soul become one; magically mated, if you will. The level of magical talent I was born with came nowhere near mage level. Ever since the Saghred had latched onto me like a psychic leech, my so-so powers had gotten one hell of a boost, and no one knew what my limits were. And, in a first as far as umi'atsu bonds were concerned, there was a third mage bonded with us—Tamnais Nathrach, a goblin aristocrat, nightclub owner, and quasi-rehabilitated dark mage. Tam was also a good friend of mine. Some considered an umi'atsu bond much like a marriage, which made my intimate connection to two gorgeous and powerful men more awkward than I wanted to think about.

Vegard handed me a dark cloak. "You dropped this downstairs, ma'am."

I took it and draped it over my arm. "Thank you, Vegard." I'd been cloaked when I came in here, and no doubt Mychael wanted me to wear it when I left. Thanks to the Saghred, I was in enough trouble with a lot of influential people on this island; I didn't need to add to it by being seen leaving the city's most lavish and notorious bordello.

Vegard indicated the blanket-covered man. "Sir, the coach is waiting outside," he told Mychael.

I knew where that coach would take him—a containment room in the lower levels of the citadel, where an exorcist would be waiting for the man and the ancient specter who had possessed him. Fortunately for the poor bastard, he'd only been possessed a few hours ago. If the specter had been inside of him from one sunrise until the next, the possession would have been permanent.

Four Guardians arrived with a stretcher. They put the man on it, securely strapped him down, and started down the hall toward the stairs. I started to follow. Mychael's hand on my arm stopped me.

"Professor," he said to Sid. "Please accompany my men. I'll escort Miss Benares out another way."

Sid nodded solemnly. "It's not exactly a proper place for a lady to be seen leaving."

"No, it's not."

Once Sid and the Guardians were on the stairs, Mychael took my hand and started toward the wall the naked guy had pinned Sid against.

"Uh, Mychael. That's a wall."

A corner of his lips curled in a crooked grin as he ran his free hand behind a wall lamp. There was a click, and a section of the wall opened.

I laughed once and shook my head. "Damn, there *was* another way out." I looked up at his sea blue eyes sparkling in the lamplight. "And you knew about this how?"

He winked at me. "This isn't the first time I've been here."

"You don't say. And you know your way around, too."

We stepped into the darkness. Mychael spoke a soft word, and lamps flickered to life, lighting the way down a narrow staircase.

"I know the floor plan of every bordello on this island," he told me. "It's part of my job."

"And which job would that be?"

"Prostitution is legal here, as is gambling." His smile vanished. "But there are other things that are highly illegal. Many of those acts are committed in places such as these, sometimes with the knowledge of the proprietor, most of the time without."

Mychael's hand tightened on mine to assist me down the

steep stairs, and a familiar surge of energy radiated from that point of contact throughout the rest of my body. I knew from past experience that Mychael was feeling the same shiver of raw sensation. We shared a bond all our own that had nothing to do with the Saghred. We didn't know what it was; we just knew it was getting stronger. But we had bigger problems to deal with. Sarad Nukpana and evil specters first; deliciously tingly and mysterious magical bonds later.

At the bottom of the stairs was a simple wooden door that provided us with a discreet exit to a side street next to a perfectly respectable bakery.

As we neared the main boulevard, Mychael reluctantly released my hand.

Phaelan grinned and his eyes sparkled as he watched the Guard-ians load the stretcher in the coach. "I was right; the old guy wanted to get laid."

I sighed and shook my head.

Captain Phaelan Benares was my cousin by relation, and a seafaring businessman by trade. The Benares family had extensive interests in shipping and finance. That was how the family saw it. Law enforcement in every major port and city in the seven kingdoms called Phaelan a pirate, and our family a criminal dynasty. I walked the fine line of being a member of the Benares family, but not being in the family business. My family didn't understand why; law enforcement didn't believe me.

Phaelan had been the one to come to the conclusion that if a man had spent the past couple thousand years trapped inside a soul-sucking rock, the first thing he'd want to do wouldn't have anything to do with world domination. He suggested checking Mid's brothels and asking the working girls about their clients. Did they have any new ones? Were any regulars asking for something a little irregular? Naturally, Phaelan and some of his crew volunteered for duty.

"Yes, you were right," I told him. "You don't have to be so happy about it."

"Why shouldn't I be? I'm a man proud to do his civic duty."

"By finding a sorcerer in a cathouse."

"By endangering myself for the greater public good."

"By talking to every working girl in the city?"

"And flushing out any new perverts in town. Someone had to do it, and Mychael couldn't spare the men to do the legwork." Phaelan indicated the coach that was pulling away. "And it looks like it went well."

I snorted. "Oh yeah, it was a piece of cake."

A buxom, blue-eyed, blond working girl sashayed by with a come-hither glance at Phaelan, and legwork took on a whole new meaning.

"Speaking of treats," he said, moving to follow her.

I grabbed him by the arm.

Phaelan wasn't particularly tall, but he was dark and definitely handsome. Many of the working girls obviously had working eyes, and were doing their best to give my cousin the come-hither. Phaelan's dark eyes were busy remembering the cream of the crop for later visits.

Once the coach was safely on its way, Mychael came over to where we were. Vegard had been guarding me from a discreet distance. He was supposed to stick to me like glue, but he was considerate enough to occasionally give me a little breathing room.

"I take it you received my bill?" Phaelan asked Mychael once he was close enough.

I couldn't believe my ears. "You *billed* him?"

Phaelan looked mildly insulted. "Mid's establishments aren't cheap. I merely wanted reimbursement for services rendered."

I laughed once. "For services rendered to *you*."

My cousin waved a negligent hand. "Same thing." He beamed with his newfound civic pride. "I believe in being thorough. And I'm only billing him for half. The *Fortune* has been anchored in Mid's harbor for damned near two months. We've never stayed anywhere this long; my men were getting restless, so I footed the bill for half."

"How generous of you."

"I thought so. My men are happy; you bagged yourself a ghost."

"Specter," I corrected him.

"Same thing."

"One's dead. The other is not."

"Whatever. Either way, tonight was a win-win for me and Mychael."

I turned to Mychael. "And you agreed to this?"

Mychael smiled slightly. "It seemed a small price to pay. I've got enough problems; I didn't want to add 'restless' pirates to the list. It kept the peace."

Phaelan grinned wickedly. "And we got a piece."

There was a commotion at the entrance to the Satyr's Grove.

"Stay here," Mychael told me. "Phaelan, Vegard—"

Vegard stepped up beside me. "Keeping her here, sir."

Mychael's eyes met mine. "I'll be right back."

Phaelan's civic-mindedness had helped snare one Saghred escapee, but there were five more out there—and one of them was Sarad Nukpana. The others appeared to be sticking to the goblin's plan; and worse, they were saving their collective strength, or at least they weren't wasting it in bordellos. All that power, millennia of intelligence—and it had a purpose.

I looked around us. At nearly two bells in the morning, the red-light district was a busy place. The entire city was busy, day or night. The Isle of Mid was home to the most prestigious college for sorcery, as well as the Conclave, the governing body for all magic users in the seven kingdoms. Thousands of students and mages, and somewhere among them were the specters of five escaped sorcerers, spirits without bodies. The one tonight had taken a body for fun; the others were stalking bodies for power. Mychael had safety measures in place for the students, though he thought that the students would be safe. The specters were after power, so a teenager sputtering through his or her first spells need not apply.

Mychael had made sure that everyone on the island was aware of the situation. But for the vast majority of those on Mid, it was school and business as usual. Public opinion split between not believing in what they deemed ghosts or believing they were qualified to protect themselves. They practiced magic, yet they didn't believe in ghosts.

The public were idiots.

There was plenty of horse and coach traffic along the cobbled and lamp-lit streets. Many of the coaches clearly cost a small fortune, and no doubt their occupants were shopping for equally expensive company. The curtains on most of the coaches were closed. Rich men or women who couldn't afford—or couldn't risk—a house call didn't want to advertise to everyone that they were anywhere near here.

A gleaming black coach stopped in front of us to allow another coach to cross at the intersection. It was pulled by four sleek, black horses. I didn't particularly care for horses, and they didn't particularly care for me, but I had to admire this team; they were magnificent animals. The coachman was cloaked, his collar pulled up, his hat pulled low.

"Bravo, little seeker," he called out. "You deserve a gift."

I froze. I knew that voice from dozens of nightmares. The coachman turned his face toward me: handsome and smiling.

And solid.

Sarad Nukpana. He wasn't a specter. He was solid.

Oh *shit*.

The coach door opened and a dead body was pushed into the gutter at my feet. The goblin cracked his whip and the horses ran as if the devil himself had their reins. Sarad Nukpana's taunt carried back to me.

"The first of many, little seeker."

Chapter 2

The dead elf on the examination table was more of a dried husk than anything that had once been a living man.

Mychael had the body taken back to the citadel. Considering its condition—but mostly that Sarad Nukpana was probably responsible for making it that way—the body was in one of the Guardians' dozens of containment rooms in the lower levels of the citadel. Wards, spells, and iron-banded doors kept anything inside a containment room from getting outside a containment room. This guy didn't look like he was going anywhere ever again, but considering who and what he had been when he was alive, Mychael wasn't in the mood to take chances. Before something or someone had drained him dry, the man's uniform had probably fit him very well. Identification had been all too easy.

General Daman Aratus was the fourth-highest-ranking commander of the elf queen's army. That he was now a dried husk on a Guardian examination table had turned him from an elven general into a political and diplomatic nightmare.

And it had all happened in two blinks of an eye. Sarad Nukpana and his accomplice inside that coach had been that fast, and the coach had been warded. The Guardians fired at it, pursued it, but it still seemed to vanish into thin air. There were plenty of warehouses around the red-light district. Mychael had all of these searched. Nothing turned up, not even a trace.

Someone had tipped off Sarad Nukpana; he'd known we

were going to be there. He dropped that body at my feet, and he couldn't have made the delivery without knowing my destination. Only a few people had known about the raid on the Satyr's Grove ahead of time. Myself, Phaelan, and Sid the necromancer were the only non-Guardians. Mychael had caught a traitor among his own men a few weeks ago. The young Guardian was the brother of the defense attaché at the elven embassy. The defense attaché had reported directly to the husk on the table that used to be General Aratus.

Mychael knew he had other traitors among his Guardians. I couldn't imagine one of them selling information to Sarad Nukpana, but stranger things had happened. When someone sold out, it wasn't always for money. Mostly it was for money or power; sometimes it was to keep a secret untold—or keep someone you loved alive. I knew from personal experience that there was no limit to what Sarad Nukpana would do to get what he wanted.

I'd seen it with my own eyes, but I still couldn't believe it. "Nukpana was solid. How the hell was he solid?"

I'd asked that question more than a few times already, and I'd probably ask it a few more before I came to grips with the implication of Sarad Nukpana not being a body-hopping specter. The goblin black mage was solid, and he shouldn't have been. When he'd been taken by the Saghred, his body had been consumed, his soul trapped inside the stone. I'd been surprised that the sadistic bastard had a soul to trap.

"I know he was solid," Mychael said patiently, also for the umpteenth time. He was probably just as disturbed about the whole thing as I was, but being the commander of the Guardians—but mostly just being Mychael—he would never show it. I'd rarely seen him as anything other than the very picture of professional calm. "And we're going to find out how he did it."

"For starters, it looks like he took a few things the general won't be using anymore."

"But that doesn't tell us *how* he did it," Mychael pointed out.

And we definitely needed to know how he did it, because Nukpana had told me he'd be doing it again.

The door opened and Vegard stood aside for a robed man to enter. It was nearly four bells in the morning, and Archmagus Justinius Valerian was wide-awake and dressed in the robes of his office. Justinius was the supreme head of the Conclave of Sorcerers, commander in chief of the Conclave Guardians, Mychael's boss, and quite possibly the most powerful mage, period. Since I'd known him, the old man had struck me as the type who didn't give a damn what he wore and when, and what anyone said about it. But after barely surviving an assassination attempt within the past few weeks and the ensuing scramble for power, he wasn't about to be seen as being anything other than fully recovered and completely in charge. Mid was home to some of the most powerful mages in the seven kingdoms, who also happened to be backstabbing, manipulative sons (and daughters) of bitches. As their leader, Justinius Valerian couldn't afford to lower his guard for one instant. Not anymore.

Vegard came into the room and closed the door.

"Well, General Aratus hasn't been seen since mid-afternoon at the elven embassy," Justinius told us.

Mychael frowned. "Why weren't we told he was missing?"

The old man chuckled dryly. "Because the elven ambassador wouldn't admit that Aratus had been missing until I told him he was dead. If the general had been found dead behind the Satyr's Grove with his trousers around his ankles, I could understand the ambassador not wanting to fess up." Justinius looked at the husk of a body with clinical interest, then he looked at me. "So this is Sarad Nukpana's idea of a present."

I nodded once. "That's what he said."

"That goblin bastard did a piece of work on him."

"Couldn't agree more, sir." I avoided looking at my gift. I had the distinct displeasure of knowing what a dead body smelled like. The general didn't smell dead as much as, well . . . leathery. I wore leather; I'd always liked leather. Now I was trying to breathe and not use my nose—and was considering buying a new wardrobe.

"Does Markus Sevelien know?" Mychael asked grimly.

"That little weasel of an ambassador wouldn't tell me where Sevelien was. Said he was 'out.'"

The dried body on the slab also had the dubious distinction of being the middleman between an elven inquisitor, who I knew to be an evil son of a bitch, and an elven duke I had once worked for and trusted. Duke Markus Sevelien was the newly appointed chief of elven intelligence. Markus being "out" could mean anything, but he was never out at this hour unless he was working.

"The ambassador said that he would 'convey the tragic news to the appropriate individuals,'" Justinius told us. "He came here in a coach that looked more like a damned hearse." He snorted, a sort of laugh. "Thought he was going to be taking the general here with him. I told him he could have Aratus's body when we were done with it." He looked closely at the folds of loose skin shrunken against the general's face, and grimaced. "We've got a murderer to catch; Aratus sure as hell didn't do this to himself. Is Vidor Kalta on his way?"

Mychael nodded. "He will be. He's extracting a nest of banshees from the basement of the old Judicial Building. He said he'd come as soon as he was finished."

The old man whistled. "Wouldn't want him to do a half-assed job of that."

"No, sir."

I looked from one of them to the other. "Him having the same last name as Lucan Kalta is just a coincidence, right?"

Mychael lips quirked in a quick grin. "Afraid not. They're brothers. Lucan is the baby."

"A baby what?"

I'd had an up-close and unpleasant encounter with Lucan Kalta within days of arriving on the island. He didn't like me then, and I thought it highly unlikely that he'd warmed to me since. He was the chief librarian of the Scriptorium, a massive repository of nearly every magic-related book, scroll, or stone slab. He didn't like me because I'd defied his authority in front of his staff. The rule I broke was stupid to begin with, so I saw nothing wrong with going around it.

"Is Vidor Kalta a necromancer or a nachtmagus?" I asked Mychael.

"Nachtmagus. In my opinion, one of the best."

"Crap," I muttered. "Like my skin hasn't crawled enough tonight."

Most people thought a necromancer and a nachtmagus were pretty much the same thing. I guess you could say that, if you thought there wasn't much difference between a garden snake and a cobra. Necromancers could communicate with the dead. They did séances, detected hauntings, and could tell you if you had a frisky poltergeist or an ancestor who simply refused to leave.

A nachtmagus could control the dead—in all of their forms. Communicating with the dead was the least of what they could do. I'd heard that given enough time, money, and motivation, they could raise the dead. I never wanted to meet anyone that motivated.

In my opinion, no one majored in necromancy unless they were just plain weird. In theory, the Conclave college had a way to weed out the weirdos. I don't know what that said about the department's graduates. They wanted to work with dead things, but at the same time they couldn't be weird. Had to be the college's smallest graduating class.

"He's an odd bird, and quite frankly a creepy bastard," Justinius agreed. "But he knows his business, and best of all, he's discreet." He inclined his head toward the body. "How many people got a good look at the general here?"

"Few, if any," Mychael assured him. "The section of street he landed in is between lampposts. The shadows helped. Vegard throwing his cloak over the body helped the most."

"Quick thinking," Justinius told my bodyguard.

Vegard nodded. "Thank you, sir. I saw his uniform, and knew nobody else needed to."

"Other than the fact that pure-blooded goblins hate any and all elves, why would Sarad Nukpana . . ." I fumbled for a way to describe what was on that table. ". . . do this or have this done to an elven general? Was Aratus a magic user?"

Justinius shook his head. "Not a spell to his name."

Something occurred to me and I didn't like it at all. In fact, the sudden realization made me a little sick.

I felt Mychael's hand on my elbow. "Raine, are you all right?"

I didn't answer. My mind was too busy running in panicked circles. I thought I'd hit on why Sarad Nukpana had killed General Aratus and then given what was left of him to me.

Mychael's grip tightened. "The air isn't good; you shouldn't be in here." It was his paladin's voice, the one that gave orders I usually didn't take. "Vegard, escort—"

I waved them both off. "I'm fine. Actually, I'm not, but it's not because of him." I indicated Aratus. "Well, it is indirectly, or it could be." I put my palm to my forehead. "Crap. I'm babbling, aren't I?"

Mychael's hand stayed right where it was. "Not yet, but you're getting there."

I looked up at him. "What if this actually *was* some sort of twisted gift for me?" I asked quietly. "*And* a setup?"

His brows knit in confusion. I had a tendency to do that to people.

"Explain."

"There are two elves on this island who we know report directly to elven intelligence," I said, "specifically to Markus Sevelien—and one of them is on that table. The other one is Taltek Balmorlan."

Part of me wouldn't mind seeing Taltek Balmorlan's shriveled body on a table. I'd never liked that part of me, but that part always had my best interests at heart—like survival. Balmorlan was an inquisitor for elven intelligence who had an obsession for high-powered weapons, not the steel and gunpowder variety, but people like me whose off-the-charts magical skills made them weapons. Taltek Balmorlan didn't ask; he just took. He was still on the island, and he still hadn't given up on getting me.

"Think about it," I continued. "Sarad Nukpana dumps the general's dead body at my feet in public and calls it a gift. And in the red-light district right after a raid on a cathouse is about as public as you can get. Balmorlan's been claiming that Nukpana and I are working together."

"Nukpana's been stalking you since the day he met you." Mychael's voice was clipped with barely restrained anger. "Even being inside the Saghred didn't slow him down. I would hardly call that working together."

"Apparently Balmorlan has a looser definition," I told him. "And that's his boss on that table. What do you want to bet, he's going to claim that I'm an accessory to kidnapping and murder? And since I'm an elf, that I should be in elven government custody, which conveniently happens to be him. He gets me locked up, which is exactly what he wants, and Sarad Nukpana gets the added bonus of knowing where to find me when he wants me."

"He'd have to get Markus Sevelien's approval to arrest you," Justinius pointed out.

I jerked my head toward Aratus's corpse. "Right now, I think he'd get it."

Years ago, Duke Markus Sevelien had given me my first big job as a seeker. My new business was struggling. I guess potential clients didn't trust a Benares to find—and then actually return—their valuables. I took occasional assignments from Markus that mostly consisted of finding abducted elves: diplomats, intelligence agents, aristocrats who'd gotten involved in something over their highborn heads. It was gratifying work and I was good at it.

Markus's help got me through the lean years. I liked him;

I trusted him. At least I used to. Now I wasn't so sure. I never thought he'd betray me; but before, I'd never been the only person to wield the Saghred and stay both sane and alive.

Markus had always been up-front and honest with me. And if I'd been standing face-to-face with him right now, he'd probably still be honest—his loyalties were to elven intelligence, not to me. He'd put any friendship we might have to the side as an impediment to him doing his job. And I knew from past experience that Markus would do his job at any and all costs. It wasn't personal; it was business.

It was the Saghred.

And since the Saghred had attached itself to me, that made me his business. I could almost understand that; the Saghred was a weapon that elven intelligence wasn't about to let fall into goblin hands. That meant he couldn't allow me to fall into goblin hands. Hell, I didn't want to be in anyone's hands.

If Markus had to arrest me to make that happen, he'd do it in a heartbeat.

And both Mychael and Justinius knew it.

The old man's blue eyes were hard as agates. "No one is going to arrest you. As long as you're on this island, you're under Guardian protection and mine."

The Guardians were protectors of the Saghred, and since the Saghred and I were psychic roommates that protection extended to me. To Mychael, I had become more than his job.

"Would any of that protection override a charge of accessory to kidnapping and murdering an elven general?" I asked them both.

The old man's silence told me what I already knew.

"Where were you this afternoon?" he asked.

"On the *Fortune* with Phaelan. So I've got a fine alibi—a Benares pirate vouching for an accused Benares murderer." I snorted. "That'll carry weight in court."

Right around my neck.

•   •   •

Nachtmagus Vidor Kalta's pale, long-fingered hand hovered above the dead man's lips. "His memories were the first thing taken, then his conscious mind, his soul, and finally what little remained of his life force. The ritual . . . the act that resulted in this is called cha'nescu, and the victim was conscious and fully aware while it happened."

"Shit," Vegard muttered from behind me.

Kalta nodded without looking away from the body. "Quite." The nachtmagus regarded the general like a lab project. "A complete absence of life," he murmured as if he were the only one in the room. "Not one flicker remains. It's as if he never lived. Grisly work, yet truly astounding in its complexity."

I remembered Nukpana's "bravo." Kalta's comment was just as chilling.

Vidor Kalta was tall, thin, and seemingly born to wear funeral black. His dark hair was cropped close to his head. I guess when you chased down ghouls and banshees for a living, short hair was a safety precaution. Kalta's features were sharp, and his face had the pallor one would expect of someone who worked mostly nights. But it was his eyes that gave him away. Black and bright as a raven's, Vidor Kalta's eyes were a reflection of a quick mind, a keen intellect, and, if what I felt coming off of him was any indication, an incredible power. Power that was all the more impressive because of his restraint. It was like the man had Death on a leash, and it was following him around like a puppy.

"Do you know how it was done?" Mychael asked.

Kalta nodded. "Everything was consumed that made General Aratus who he was." He took a small towel from beside the table and carefully wiped his hands. "Once the entity that did this began the process, it continued to feed until there was nothing left. Pausing at any point would have negated the ritual."

My stomach did a slow, nauseating roll. "Feed?"

"Not a pleasant procedure—nor painless. Though the act itself is said to be done through mouth-to-mouth contact."

That did it; I was going to be sick. "A kiss?"

"Not one you would ever want to receive, Mistress Benares. Or be able to survive."

"What or who could have done it?"

"Greater demons are the most common culprits."

"What are the uncommon culprits?"

"A nachtmagus with enough power could have done this." Vidor Kalta smiled at his macabre joke in a flash of small teeth, white and even. "But considering Mid's present predicament, I believe the response you seek is a spiritual entity—one of those previously imprisoned in the Saghred, perhaps?"

"We have a suspect," Mychael told him. "Could a spirit have done this?"

"That would depend on who the spirit was in life, and how long they had been imprisoned inside the Saghred." Kalta's bright, black eyes were on me. "From what Mistress Benares reported from her most enviable journeys inside the stone, most of those inside would have been too weakened to perform the ritual. Do you know the ages of the escaped spirits?"

Mychael hesitated a moment before answering. "We do. The youngest is approximately forty years old; the eldest is more than four thousand."

"Fascinating. Since you have only captured one, may I ask how you know this?"

"We have a source."

"May I ask—"

I spoke. "Sarad Nukpana took my soul inside the Saghred not long after he was imprisoned. Generally villains only share their evil master plan with you when they don't think you'll be getting away. He told me who his allies were; I gave the names to Paladin Eiliesor."

And I'd just given Nachtmagus Vidor Kalta a bald-faced lie. Hell's hounds could have been snapping at my heels and I wouldn't have told anyone that a seventh soul had escaped from the Saghred.

Our information source was my father. A Guardian and

protector of the Saghred since its capture from the goblin king almost nine hundred years ago. Nearly continuous contact with the stone had stopped my father from aging. About a year ago, the Saghred had turned its protector into its dinner, imprisoning my father's soul inside the stone with the thousands that had been previously consumed by the Saghred, or sacrificed to it. Now his soul occupied the body of a young Guardian who had been killed by the demon queen moments before she opened the Saghred.

Dad was also still a wanted criminal. He had fled Mid nine centuries ago and had taken the Saghred with him to keep the stone's power out of the hands of some of the Conclave's top mages, but as far as the Conclave was concerned, there was no statute of limitations on Saghred stealing. If he was discovered, he'd be executed; it didn't matter whose body he was wearing.

"Our primary suspect had only been inside for a month," Mychael told Kalta.

"You refer to Sarad Nukpana."

"I do."

"Last winter I had the unique opportunity to meet him. The high priest of the Brotherhood of the Khrynsani. A most ancient and—among the goblin aristocracy—a most venerable order. Being a human, I do not share their belief that goblins are the superior race and all others should be subject to their whim and rule. But I valued the chance for an extended discussion with their leader. A most prodigious intellect, eager to learn, to experience. Not surprisingly, he expressed a keen interest in my calling."

"The Sarad Nukpana I saw tonight wasn't an entity, spiritual or otherwise," I told him bluntly. "Could doing that"—I indicated the corpse—"help Nukpana . . . regrow his body?"

"You said he was wearing a cloak."

"Yes, and a hat."

"Did you see his hands, or was he wearing gloves?"

I gazed at a point on the far wall, recalling the street, the coach, the horses, and the hands of the coachman who held their reins. "Gloves. Only his face was exposed."

Kalta's eyes flickered with what looked like doubt. "It was dark."

"It was light enough," I snapped. "I couldn't see through him. And he had enough of something in those gloves to control four horses."

"I don't dispute your account, Mistress Benares. I am merely attempting to gauge the extent to which Sarad Nukpana has regenerated."

The bottom dropped completely out of my stomach. "It's possible, then."

"Oh, yes. Most of my colleagues still consider such an accomplishment to be theory. But a very few have actually witnessed the phenomenon; unfortunately, I was not one of them." He flashed his teeth in an anticipatory smile. "It appears that's about to change."

"If you ran across Sarad Nukpana now, I hardly think he'd want to chat over drinks."

Mychael's expression was hard. "If he's not completely regenerated, how do I stop him from going further?"

I spoke. "Better yet, how can we make him go back?"

"You can kill him, Mistress Benares," Kalta told me point-blank. "According to the notes of one of my colleagues, Sarad Nukpana will become almost corporeal every time he feeds. But as his regenerating body absorbs the life force of his victims, he will fade again."

"Feeding and digesting," Mychael concluded.

Kalta nodded. "And then hungering once again. Though each time he feeds, the fading will become less, until he has consumed enough life to qualify as a living being himself. Only then will you be able to kill him like any other mortal."

Mychael glanced down at the general's corpse. "Nachtmagus Kalta, I can't wait until Nukpana gorges himself on the citizens and guests on this island, so there's enough of him for me to kill."

"You may not have long to wait for that opportunity," Kalta said. "If he has been free for nearly three weeks, and was strong enough to drive a team of horses, then General Aratus was hardly his first victim."

"To get the strength he needed to kill someone like General Aratus, he probably began with people he thought wouldn't be missed," Mychael surmised.

"A correct assessment, in my opinion. A weakened predator consumes whatever it can to become strong enough to go after the larger game it truly desires."

I snorted. "People whose deaths would cause an inter-kingdom incident."

"You said that Sarad Nukpana consumed the general's memories," Mychael said.

Kalta nodded. "That is correct."

"Would Nukpana retain those memories?"

"His memories, as well as his abilities and talents."

Oh hell.

That meant Sarad Nukpana knew everything a top elven general knew, meaning Aratus's military strategic ability and any secrets he was privy to by being in close contact with elven intelligence. Only now they were Nukpana's secrets. He could use them, or he could share them with the goblin secret service. Their highest-ranking officers had been arriving on Mid along with their counterparts in elven intelligence. Give it another week and Mid would be seething with spies.

All of them wanted to get their hands on me. Any of them would be perfect victims for Sarad Nukpana.

I blew out my breath, steeling myself for what I knew I had to do next. "Mychael, I know I'm stating the obvious here, but we have to find him. Now."

I looked down at General Aratus. He used to be an elven general. Now he was all that was left of one. He was an object who had been killed in one of the most repulsive ways I'd ever heard of. As a seeker, I could pick up impressions from inanimate objects touched by someone I was looking for.

I grimaced. Yep, the general was about as inanimate as you could get.

Mychael knew exactly what I was thinking. "Raine, no. If he intended the general's remains as a gift, it's almost certainly a trap." His tone said no arguments.

I had to give him one. It might be the only chance we had.

"He probably left something for me, but it's not a trap. Nukpana's just starting his game; he's not about to end his fun before he's even gotten started. And Nukpana touched the general for . . ." I turned to Vidor Kalta. "How long does this ritual take?"

"An hour, probably longer."

Shit. Sarad Nukpana sucking your life out through your mouth for an hour or more.

"Yes, it would be quite appalling," Kalta said.

I told my body to stop shaking. It almost listened to me. "That's a lot of contact, leaving a lot of residue."

"I forbid it," Mychael said. "There are other ways we can do this."

"Name one."

Mychael couldn't and we both knew it.

"Believe me, the last thing I want to do is touch that thing," I assured him. "Yes, he used to be a person, but right now, he's a thing—a really disgusting thing. But if there's any chance that I can find out where Nukpana was when he turned the general into what's on this table, I have to take that chance."

"It's exactly what Nukpana wants you to do."

"Maybe, maybe not. A dead elven general tossed at my feet is trouble enough; maybe that's all the trouble he needed to cause. Mychael, we've got the elven ambassador parked outside with a hearse, and his boss is 'out' somewhere in the city right now. If we don't have trouble already, it's brewing. The quicker we find out where Nukpana did this, the closer we could be to finding out where he is now."

Whatever Nukpana had done to him, any magical residue would be gone soon, if it wasn't already. The goblin said he'd be doing this again, and I believed him. Oh yeah, I definitely believed him. That meant I had to touch his handiwork.

On the lips.

I grimaced at the thought. "You're here. Vegard's here. Nachtmagus Kalta, will you help pull my ass out of the fire if necessary?"

"Of course." The inquisitive sparkle in Kalta's eyes told me he'd love to see something bad happen just for the academic interest.

I turned to Mychael. "I'm as safe as I'm going to get."

Mychael's sea blue eyes narrowed in disapproval. I took that to be a "yes" but under extreme protest. Protest noted. And if what I was about to do worked, that protest wouldn't matter. Unless, of course, it was a soon-to-be-fatal trap, in which case it still didn't matter what Mychael thought because I wouldn't be around for him to yell at.

I quickly muttered my personal shields into place. Get shielded and get it done. If I truly thought about what I was going to touch, I'd probably run screaming from the room. Touch him, find out what you can, and get the hell away from him. I was going to do this. I might be sick afterward, but I was going to do this.

I laid my hand across the corpse's mouth.

The connection was immediate, but not what I expected. It certainly wasn't the type of connection I usually got. I smelled musty air that had been closed up for way too long. Traces of mold . . . and something else. Something familiar. I'd smelled it before, but couldn't place it now. I stood absolutely still, doing my best to block out that I was getting this from my hand on a corpse's mouth.

That was all I got. Smells. No noise, no screams, no final moments of life about to be extinguished, no sense of General Aratus or Sarad Nukpana. No life at all. None. I breathed in and slowly out, trying to relax, to open myself to whatever was there.

Nothing.

The corpse's hand snatched my wrist in an iron grip.

I shrieked. Mychael's magic flared behind me and Vegard drew steel.

"No!" I told them both. I sucked air in and out through my teeth. The corpse's grip tightened, dry and cold. I shivered all the way down to my toenails.

"It is but a programmed response, Paladin Eiliesor," I heard Kalta say. "A message. The corpse is but a vessel."

Dried eyelids drew back to reveal empty sockets, and the jaw dropped open in a sick parody of speech. I heard a squeak; I think it was me. Then Sarad Nukpana's silken voice filled my head. No sound came from Aratus's leathery lips. Nukpana's words were for me alone.

"I knew you could not resist, little seeker. As you can see from General Aratus, I have taken your enemies as my enemies." His voice dropped to a low purr. *"And I very much want to take your friends. I will meet all of them one by one, and I will grow stronger with each one I take. Their knowledge shall become mine, as will their power."* The goblin's onyx eyes appeared to glitter in the depths of those dead, empty sockets. I knew it wasn't real, just another illusion, a really sick one.

"Remember the promise I made to you when you refused to help me escape the Saghred?" The goblin's voice was as hard and cold as the corpse's withered hand that clutched me, and just as unyielding. *"I always keep my promises. You betrayed me, seeker. I warned you what action I would take, but you chose to ignore me. You will ignore me now at your peril. Attempt to find me. Use all of your skill, all of what you call cunning; I will stay one step ahead of you. And while you're hunting me, I'll be hunting those you love. And after I've taken them all, and your pain and loss has become too much for you to bear, then I will come for you. And when I take you, your soul and the Saghred's power shall be mine."*

Chapter 3

The corpse's hand went limp, severing the link between us. The contact break was too quick, and the room spun around me, bringing a wave of disorienting nausea. I snatched my hand from the corpse's grip and tried to remember how to breathe. I thought my lungs knew what to do, but apparently they didn't. I was gasping, but I wasn't getting any air. A dim corner of my mind calmly informed me that I was about to pass out, like I didn't already know that.

Mychael's arm went around my waist, lifted me off my feet, and carried me out into the hall. There was air in the hall, blessed air, cool and fresh, and best of all it didn't smell like dead elf general. Mychael set me on my feet and I bent over, hands on my knees, gulping air in great heaping lungfuls.

Mychael kept his arm around my waist and put his other hand on my back, and I could feel the pull of his healer's magic as he helped my lungs pull in air and blow it out. My head started to clear.

"She'll be fine," I dimly heard him tell the Guardians posted on either side of the door.

No doubt they thought that I was one of those women who couldn't handle being in the same room with a dead body. I could deal with dead bodies just fine; it was the ones that grabbed me that I had a problem with.

A shudder ran through me, ending with a tingling on the back of my neck that felt like the featherlight touch of a certain goblin psycho.

"Well, that shot my . . . concentration . . . straight to hell," I managed and went back to gulping air.

Mychael didn't say, "I told you so," but he didn't have to and he knew it. A lot of people would have called what I'd done stupid and/or suicidal. I called it the risks of doing my job. A lot of people would call my job stupid and/or suicidal, too.

"You're damned lucky he didn't do more than taunt," Mychael said.

I froze. *"You heard him?"* I said in mindspeak. There were a lot of things those two Guardians didn't need to know.

"Yes," Mychael responded. *"The words were for you; the message was for me as well."*

The umi'atsu bond we had with Tam, or the other even more powerful link that only Mychael and I shared. One or both had let Mychael hear everything. Good. When a corpse grabbed your hand and a phantom goblin whispered sick nothings in your ear, it was good to have company.

"Ma'am?" came Vegard's concerned voice from behind us.

"Fine . . . I'm fine." I swallowed and stood up slowly. If I did it too fast, I'd be right back where I started from. I glanced up and down the hall. There was another pair of tense Guardians stationed by the stairs. Their keen eyes were focused on us, hands on sword hilts, and those hands and hilts were glowing with deadly spells at the ready. All they were waiting for was word from their paladin that there was something inside that containment room that needed killing.

What needed killing wasn't in that room. I didn't know where Sarad Nukpana was, and what I'd gotten from General Aratus hadn't given me much of a clue.

Or who he was going after next.

Even with only four Guardians, the hall was way too crowded. To Mychael, they were his trusted men. To me, they would be witnesses to questions I needed to ask out loud, but didn't want them to hear.

"Is there somewhere we can talk?" I asked him.

"My office."

It was private, warded, and had a well-stocked liquor cabinet. I wanted all three.

"Perfect," I told him. "I could use a—"

The bottom dropped out of the temperature, and bone-numbing cold flowed up through the stone floor. The long muscles of my legs convulsed with cold; the shock of it sent a spike of pain through my body.

I'd felt it before.

"Oh no," I managed through chattering teeth.

Mychael knew what was here; he'd fought on enough battlefields, seen more than enough men die.

And knew that Death always sent Reapers to collect.

I'd never seen a Reaper, but I'd felt one before. I'd been attacked by one. In the pitch-dark tunnels under Mid, it had come for me and for once I'd been grateful for the dark. What I'd felt was horrifying enough without having to look at it, too. The Reaper had attacked me, but it had wanted to go through me to get to the souls the Saghred held prisoner, using me as a straw to slurp them up. The Reaper had come too close to getting what it came for, with my soul as a bonus. Reapers were indiscriminate diners. The dead, the dying, and those who shared their bodies or minds with more than one soul— we were all fair game to creatures who acted more like a pack of starving wolves than anything else. Prey was just food they hadn't eaten yet.

I was most definitely prey.

"Vegard, get Raine out of here," Mychael ordered. "In my office, behind the wards, and seal them."

"Yes, sir."

I didn't move. I felt the cold flowing down the hall on one of the floors below, flowing away from us. "It's not after me." I focused my will and found them. "Two Reapers, one floor below."

"The mage's ghost," Mychael growled.

Damn. The exorcist was working to separate it from the body it had possessed. One body, two souls, both weakened. Would the Reapers be able to tell which one belonged? Would they care?

A scream from below said they didn't.

Mychael shouted commands and the Guardians stationed at the stairs charged down them, Mychael and Nachtmagus Kalta right behind them.

Vegard's hand locked around my arm.

I didn't have time for this, and neither did the man downstairs. "Vegard, let me go." I tried to be reasonable, but I was prepared to be violent.

"Not this time, ma'am." He'd been there for my first run-in with a Reaper. He knew how close I'd come then to being taken.

Shouting joined the screaming, and I felt more cold spots blooming below.

"There's more coming," I said urgently. "They're outnumbered down there." I could have done any number of things to get Vegard to let me go, but I was counting on his loyalty to Mychael, not to Mychael's orders. If Mychael tried to stop those Reapers from feeding, they'd turn on him like a pack of wolves. "I can help him. I can sense Reapers, so I can probably see them."

And probably no one else could. Just like the specters. I didn't need to say it; Vegard knew it.

"Dammit," he snarled, releasing my arm. "Not three feet from my side. Not. Three. Feet."

We got downstairs and at first glance there were only four Guardians in the hall. I didn't have to look much closer to see what else was there.

I could see them. Hellfire and damnation, I could actually see the things.

"Raine, get out of here!" Mychael shouted.

"I can see them," I said. "And there aren't two of them." An insubstantial form slipped through the stone wall not ten feet from Mychael as if the wall wasn't there. "Now there're five."

Nachtmagus Vidor Kalta stood utterly still in the middle of the hall, as if listening to something no one else could hear. "With more on the way."

The terrified screaming continued from inside the containment room. It ended abruptly.

"Clear!" Mychael's hands were glowing incandescent white, and I felt a tightly focused, controlled surge of power as he put his hands on the door.

And the door—four-inch-thick wood, banded with heavy iron—simply vanished.

I felt something cold closing in behind me and spun to face it. "Make that six."

A Reaper floated there, mere steps away, watching me. At least I assumed it was watching me; the thing didn't have any eyes.

An up-close look at a Reaper was something I never wanted.

Vegard took up a guard position in front of me, his glowing sword waving slowly back and forth. "Where is it?" He obviously couldn't see it.

"Right in front of us." I didn't move; I didn't want to give the thing any ideas.

Vegard's pale blue eyes darted back and forth, seeing nothing, but alert to anything. "What's it doing?"

"Waiting for something." I knew we didn't want to find out what that something was.

Reapers were only visible to the dead or dying. My connection to the Saghred made me a special case. The rock held thousands of disembodied souls that were not truly alive, not entirely dead. To Reapers, they were shining beacons, irresistible lures, prizes they had been created to capture. As the Saghred's bond servant, souls could pass through me to the Saghred, so souls could pass out of me into a Reaper—and my own soul would probably be taken right along with them.

Slurp. Gone. I didn't know for sure, and I sure as hell didn't want to find out.

I'd heard that if you saw a Reaper, you saw what you expected to see, what you thought the agents of Death would look like. Personally, I wanted to see little, fuzzy pink bunnies, but apparently my subconscious visualized tall, scary, and skeletal. My subconscious and I needed to have a long talk.

Roughly man height and shape, the Reaper had the translucence of a jellyfish, with filmy tendrils flowing gently around it like the ragged edges of a long, tattered robe. I knew from experience that those tendrils turned into constricting coils when they touched you. Yes, those tendrils could be soft and soothing, but a Reaper was also death in its purest form, eternal cold, and I do mean eternal. Its touch made you want that cold more than you'd ever wanted anything, to step into it with open arms, eager to embrace the darkness. Reapers used that lure to draw the souls of the wandering dead into themselves.

Like the souls in the Saghred.

I dimly heard Mychael and Vidor Kalta shouting orders.

The Reaper in front of me wasn't getting any closer; it just hovered there. This many Reapers weren't here to collect just one wayward specter. A few weeks ago when I'd escaped the Reaper in the tunnels under the island, I knew that it would be back, and when it came it would bring reinforcements.

Dad stood at the top of the stairs, not even twenty feet away.

"Run!" I screamed at him.

Dad knew the danger. From the expression on his face, he wasn't running from anything.

Dammit.

Anyone who had died and been brought back to life was fair game for a Reaper. If you had only been dead a few minutes, you were still theirs. The young Guardian whose body my dad's soul inhabited had died. As far as the Reapers were concerned, coming back to life was my dad's problem, not theirs.

He ran toward me, darting around the Reaper. A tendril snapped out, lashing Dad across the back. His breath hissed out in pain, but he kept coming until he was at my side.

I couldn't believe him. "Are you insane?"

He flashed a crooked smile. "I've heard that question a lot."

To everyone watching, he was a twenty-year-old Guardian either brave or stupid enough to tangle with a Reaper. To me, he was a dad trying to protect his newly found daughter.

"I've dealt with them before." His words came quickly and in near silence.

I caught a flash of another face under the young Guardian's skin, that of Eamaliel Anguis, my dad. I knew it was an illusion—at least I thought it was. Dad's elegantly pointed ears marked him as an elf, a beautiful pure-blooded high elf. His hair was silver, and his eyes were the gray of gathering storm clouds. Eyes identical to my own.

Eyes that could see the Reapers just as clearly as I could.

Sudden movement caught my attention. Vidor Kalta. I didn't think he could see the Reapers, but he knew exactly where they were, surrounding us. Then he saw my dad and his black eyes widened in realization and disbelief.

Oh no. He knew.

The body that housed my dad's soul had been murdered, dead for only a few minutes, but dead was dead and Kalta knew it.

The Reapers were coming out of the walls. I felt two of them rise from the floor behind us. Dad went back to back with me, his entire body suddenly aglow with the same incandescent white power that had covered Mychael's hands.

He was going to fight.

"Tell me what to do," I asked as my eyes tried to look everywhere at once. The Reapers were too damned fast.

"Tamp down that rock!" he growled. "They can't eat what they can't find."

"I'm standing right here," I snapped. "It's not like I can—"

"Just do it. Leave the rest to me."

"How are—"

Dad took my hand and his thoughts instantly passed to me.

My mouth fell open. "You're kidding?"

"It's worked before. Take care of the rock and leave the beasties to me."

No doubt my dad had plenty of experience keeping Reapers away from the Saghred, nine hundred years' worth. But as far as these Reapers were concerned, I *was* the Saghred.

And his idea of fighting them was to sing them a children's song.

It was a nursery rhyme sung by children at bedtime to chase away things that hid in closets and under beds. Those were imaginary monsters; these were real.

These were hungry.

My dad, Eamaliel Anguis, was a master spellsinger. Arlyn Ravide, the young Guardian whose body his soul occupied, was not.

His first note confirmed that with sickening certainty.

Arlyn Ravide couldn't carry a tune in a bucket. The Reapers were getting closer but Arlyn's off-key tenor kept right on singing. It wasn't just awful to hear; it was going to get us killed.

Then magic spun from that note-cracking voice. He was doing more than singing the words; he was believing them, and that belief gave them life and substance, but most of all it gave them power, pitch be damned. I could feel it and so could the Reapers. This actually might work. Arlyn repeated the verse again, and then again, and each time the words took on a new certainty, a defiance. The Reapers didn't back off, but they didn't come any closer. At this point, I considered that a victory.

Until the souls inside the Saghred began to struggle.

"Stop them!"

Dad's urgent plea came inside my head. I wanted to answer

him, I wanted to stop the souls that were surging up inside of me, but I couldn't. I couldn't speak; I couldn't breathe. The Saghred was in a guarded and warded chamber five floors below, yet I felt it as if I were holding it in my hands, feeling the souls writhe inside. Their terror was mine and so was their desperation.

One soul broke away, then another, and yet another, trembling with eagerness. They weren't inside the Saghred.

They were inside of me.

Inside of me and struggling to get out, to go to the Reapers, to embrace and be embraced by Death. They wanted it with an intensity that stole my breath and froze my body. They were coming out; the Reapers were drawing them out.

Through me.

I gasped with shallow breaths, the shouts and screams of the men around me dying away until my own panting breath was all I heard. I looked down in horror as a twisting, curling ribbon of light as thick as my arm emerged from my chest, the cold vapor of a wraith, a captive soul that was captive no longer. In a flash of light it was gone, snatched by the nearest Reaper. Another wraith followed the first, then a third, and a fourth.

I couldn't breathe. I couldn't scream, and I desperately needed to do both. I was blacking out. Pain dug with white-hot claws into the center of my chest. It felt like my insides were being ripped out, and I was helpless to stop it.

I raggedly dragged air into my lungs and screamed, an agonized wail of unbearable pain.

The wraiths inside of me stopped.

And the Reapers rushed us.

Vidor Kalta shouted something and ran forward, a spell spreading a black nimbus over his long-fingered hands like a shield. He used it like a battering ram between two Reapers. The things jerked away from him as if burned and he closed the distance to us. The nachtmagus turned his back to me, putting himself squarely between us and any Reaper who tried to get past him.

Vidor Kalta was defending us.

Three Reapers darted back and forth mere inches from the nachtmagus's extended hands, looking for a weakness, determined to find a way to get past him. Kalta's already pale face blanched further under the invisible onslaught, beads of sweat forming at his temples and running down his face, his breath harsh and ragged. He couldn't hold on for much longer.

What felt like a whip made of ice lashed itself around my wrist, jerking my hand from Dad's grasp. He disappeared into a knot of Reapers.

"No!" I screamed.

A roar tore its way out of my throat as I shielded myself and charged into the Reapers. Tendrils that a moment before had looked thin and filmy lashed at me like the stings of hundreds of jellyfish. My legs went numb with cold; coils whipped my throat, face, arms. One wrapped like a weighted chain around my waist and dragged me down. Coils of soul-numbing, burning cold grabbed at me, stabbing, slashing, looking for a weakness.

Finding a way in.

I screamed in terror and pain. I struggled to think, to fight back. I was covered in Reapers, panicking, their coils weaving their way around me like a shroud. I'd denied Death before; I would win again. My scream turned into a snarl, channeling my rage into a white-hot fury. I had to fight them; I had to get up. They would take me, and then they would take Dad.

A flash of impossibly bright light pierced the cold. An avenging angel, blazing with rage and savage strength, beautiful and deadly.

Mychael.

The coils and tendrils loosened, retracted. I could feel my legs and arms burning as if lashed with fiery whips.

A pair of arms wrapped around me, warm and strong. I blinked slowly, trying to focus. My vision cleared and I looked up into eyes younger than my own, but haunted with nine centuries of life.

I dimly felt my lips twitch in a smile. "Found you," I croaked. My throat was raw from screaming.

Dad's hands were cool on either side of my face. "Raine!" His shout came to me as if from the top of a deep well.

I dimly heard Mychael shouting commands, then he was by my side. He spoke quickly to someone I couldn't see; his voice was forced calm, but his words had an urgency that scared me.

I looked down at myself.

My hands and arms were covered with red lashes. My shirt was in tatters; the raw welts slashed my chest, back, and legs. I tried to move and pain blazed from every burn as I fell into darkness.

Chapter 4

I drifted.

And dreamed.

Impossibly soft, sun-kissed sand, heated and firm against my back. Gentle waves and ripples flowed over me, caressing my bare skin with tropical warmth as I lay in the shallows, my long hair flowing loose around me. Soothing, calming.

Healing.

The waves receded and the dream slowly shifted. Large, warm hands roamed over my body, caressing, lightly brushing, barely touching. Strong, skilled fingers soothed painful aches, aches that were determined to drag me awake.

I wanted to stay right where I was, warm, cradled, held.

Held?

My mind's brief flutter of concern was outvoted by eyelids too heavy to open, too content to move. I sighed and shifted, rolling over on my side, snuggling back against the source of that warmth.

Warmth whose breath tickled my ear, followed by a low, masculine snore.

Huh?

I forced my sleep-sticky eyelids open. Disoriented and confused, my groggy mind tried to remember where I was. I didn't recognize anything.

I was in a bed, a big bed with a canopy and curtains. A lightglobe glowed on a bedside table, and I could just make out a desk piled with papers. I dimly heard the crackle of a fireplace, but seeing it would mean moving or at least turning my head. Neither one was going to happen. My head felt like it weighed a ton; I couldn't lift it off the pillow, and I didn't want to.

My eyelids closed and I drifted some more, deliciously lethargic. I knew I should move; something about moving was important, really important. Not just moving—running. I needed to run from . . . from what? Why would I . . .

Reapers.

Shit! I gasped and my eyes flew open. No Reapers, just a strange bed. And a warm, hard . . . whoa . . . very male body pressed firmly against me. A muscular arm slid lazily around my waist, his hand stopping just below my breasts, pulling me even closer, lips nuzzling the back of my neck.

My mind screamed fight; my body muttered sleep.

"Raine?"

Mychael's voice was deep and rusty with sleep.

I tried to speak, even one word would do, but my throat was dry; nothing would come out. I looked down where Mychael's hand was and the word I was trying to say came out as a squeak.

My breasts were bare and so was the rest of me.

I was buck naked, wearing nothing but a sheet—and Mychael.

I swallowed and managed to get some words out. "Uh . . . uh, Mychael?"

"Mmmm?" He nuzzled closer.

"What are you doing?" Better yet, what had we done? The last I remembered, I was covered in Reapers. Now I was covered in Mychael. This went beyond not making sense.

Mychael sighed and shifted, and it was all too obvious that he wasn't wearing much, if anything.

"Healing you," he rumbled drowsily.

"Naked?"

"Bare skin works best."

"For who?"

It took a few seconds, but Mychael propped himself up on one elbow and gazed down at me. His auburn hair was tousled with sleep and his face was darkened with his morning beard. His hand slid from the base of my breasts to the flat of my stomach. The sensation of heated tropical waters swirled and spiraled down from his hand into me, soothing burned skin, aching muscles.

Healing what the Reapers had done to me.

"Better for both of us," he said.

Through his hand, the ebb and flow of magic spread from Mychael into me and back again, like the tide, like the waves in my dream. Soothing, healing.

Connecting us. Bonding.

I tried to sit up, but Mychael's hand on my stomach held me still, gently, but firmly enough that I wasn't going anywhere. Damn, I was still weak as a kitten. I did manage to pull the sheet up to restore some semblance of modesty, though he'd already seen—and probably touched—everything I had, so I didn't know why I bothered. Maybe I was still delirious.

I took enough of a breath to get the words out. "Your bedroom?"

"It is. I brought you here because it's better warded than almost any other room in the citadel."

"You carried me here?"

"I did."

"And undressed me."

A corner of his lips quirked upward. "I certainly wasn't going to let anyone else do it. Now, lie still." His voice lowered. "I'm not finished healing you yet."

Firelight gleamed on his smoothly sculpted chest and taut stomach—and on several dark, angry stripes running from his shoulder to his ribs. I instinctively reached out, but Mychael's hand around my wrist stopped me.

"Try not to move," he told me.

"Reapers did that to you?" My voice was barely a whisper.

Mychael nodded once.

I frowned at him. "Because of me."

"No, because I wasn't going to let them take you."

"Still my fault."

"You didn't do it; they did."

"You know what I mean."

Mychael smiled, very slightly. "I do and I'm ignoring it. I'll heal you, but if you want to argue, you'll have to do that by yourself."

My hand reached his chest before he could stop me. My fingers tentatively touching, gently tracing the burn across his chest. My hand tingled at the contact, and Mychael went utterly still.

"Who's going to heal you?" I asked quietly.

"I can heal myself now that you're out of danger."

My fingers stopped. "How much danger?"

Something flickered in his eyes that I'd never seen in them before. Fear. "More than I ever want you to be in again."

Fear of losing me.

If I'd been close to death, I really didn't want to know how close. Regardless, Mychael had obviously drained himself to bring me back.

"Thank you," I said simply. My voice was raspy and raw. I dimly recalled screaming while covered in Reapers. Mere thanks wasn't nearly enough, didn't even begin to be enough for all the sacrifices Mychael had made for me since we'd met.

He sat up and leaned over to the bedside table where there was a pitcher and two glasses. He poured me a glass of water. I winced and eased myself up on the pillows, pulling the sheet up with me.

"Careful," Mychael cautioned, gently holding the glass to my lips. "Drink slowly."

I took a sip. The water was cold, nectar-of-the-gods cold; I resisted the urge to gulp.

When I'd finished, Mychael took the glass and turned to put it back on the table.

That was when I saw the lash on his neck. It was worse than the ones on his chest, much worse. Dammit. He could claim otherwise, but if it hadn't been for me, none of those burns would have been there, and his very life wouldn't be in danger from mages who not only wanted him removed as paladin; they wanted his head removed from his shoulders.

And every last bit of it was my fault.

Mychael had stood steadfastly by my side from the very moment the Saghred had sunk its figurative claws into me. While nearly everyone else wanted to kill me or lock me up, Mychael had fought to save and protect me. He knew who and what I was—the Saghred's bond servant and a Benares, a name synonymous with criminal. He was the top lawman in the seven kingdoms. I was trouble of the worst kind for him in more ways than one. He knew it, and he didn't give a damn.

He was willing to take that risk, take it and not look back. Saving my life more than proved it.

Mychael and I had a link, a magical bond of the most intimate kind. Just over a week ago, with a single touch of his hand, Mychael's magic had merged with mine. My magic had surged forward to meet his, matching him, and for a few intensely intimate, breath-stopping moments I had been keenly aware of his every pulse, every muscle, the surging of blood through his veins. Two people with one body, and magic pulsing like a single heart that we shared.

He had been just as aware of me—all of me. We didn't know what had caused it, and right now it didn't matter.

Not with what I was about to do.

"Mychael, healing me . . . like this. What did it do to our link?"

"Probably made it stronger."

That was what I thought. "Is that a good idea?"

"I think it's the best idea."

"I don't see how that could possibly be good—especially for you."

"The Saghred has nothing to do with our bond," he told me. "I think that the closer you are to me—and the closer we are to each other—the better you'll be protected from the Saghred."

"Or the better the Saghred can get its hooks into you." I hesitated. "Mychael, right now I am the Saghred. I don't want to hurt you."

"And you won't."

Mychael regarded me with calm, confident eyes. He had no doubts, no fears. He didn't need any; I had enough for both of us.

"Raine, I've only felt myself being drawn closer to you. I haven't sensed the Saghred at all."

"Nothing?"

"Whatsoever. Just more of you." In the firelight, his eyes had darkened to the blue of ocean depths. "And I think that's a very good thing."

Protecting Mychael from the Saghred was an even better thing. The stone's presence had been like a weight behind my breastbone since it'd bonded itself to me. I didn't know if it was Mychael's healing, the Reapers' attack, or something else entirely, but right now I had no sense of the Saghred at all.

If I was going to do this, I needed to do it now. My pulse quickened at the thought of what I was about to attempt. No, not attempt. Do. I didn't know how it would affect me, but I wanted to do this for him.

Mychael noticed a burn remaining on my right shoulder. He reached out once again, to touch me, to heal.

I caught his hand in mine, quickly curling my fingers through his. The power he held in readiness to heal me thrummed through my skin and raced up my arm and into my body. I gasped with the sheer strength of it. I took one deep breath, then another, holding his magic tightly inside of me as my own awakened and responded, spiraling upward from the deep core of me where it ran like molten heat.

Mychael knew what was happening and tried to pull his hand away, but our magic had already fused us.

"Raine, no." Mychael's voice said no arguments.

For once I wasn't going to argue with him.

I was going to heal him.

"I can't do them all, but I can do one."

"Raine, you're not—"

I gave him a small smile, confident and sure. "I'm stronger than you think." My voice dropped to an intense whisper. "Mychael, please let me do this for you. Your knowledge, our magic. I don't want you hurt because of me any more."

I didn't wait for a response. I placed my hand on his neck, my palm flat against his pulse point. Our combined power surged out of me and into him, and now it was Mychael's turn to gasp.

I felt the burn beneath my hand—not just felt it; I became a part of it, flowing down through the layers of damaged skin and muscle, the touch of my hand absorbing the heat and pain, and sending cool, healing magic in its place.

Mychael's strength, my will. Our magic.

But it didn't stop there. The power that coursed through me into Mychael surged through him and slammed back into me. Hard. The flow of magic was like water released from a dam, barely controlled. It picked up speed as it went from me into Mychael and back again, a breath-stealing, stomach-clenching cyclone of power.

As quickly as it caught us up in its current, the magic slowed, receded, then left us both in a cool rush. I kept my fingers clenched through his until the last tremors of magic between us faded. I didn't think I could have let go even if I'd wanted to.

I didn't want to.

Mychael's hand dropped from mine and I fell back against the pillows. Mychael was leaning against the bed's headboard. Both of us were breathing heavily, but I didn't feel exhausted, not in the least. I was exhilarated.

Mychael looked at me and laughed low in his throat. "I would ask if you're all right, but it's obvious that you are."

I was a little light-headed, but in a very good way. I glanced at his throat. The burn was gone. My eyes were drawn down to his chest. Smoothly sculpted and muscled—and no trace of the burns that had marred it minutes before.

"The burn on your shoulder is gone," Mychael noted.

"We do good work," I managed between pants.

"You shouldn't have risked that."

"I wanted to."

He hesitated, not quite sure how to respond. "Thank you."

"My pleasure."

His eyes gleamed. "I can tell."

There were two polite taps on the door.

"That would be breakfast." Mychael took a shuddering breath and blew it out, then he laughed, warm and deep. "Let's see if my legs will hold me up long enough to get to the door."

Mychael rolled out of bed and padded barefoot to the door. From what I could see, his long, leanly muscled legs were holding him up just fine. He wasn't naked, though with what little he was wearing, he may as well have been. Silken sleep pants were tied low on his hips, leaving almost nothing to the imagination.

He opened the door and accepted a tray from someone on the other side, and exchanged a few words, their murmurs too quiet for me to make out what they were saying. Mychael had brought me back from death, and if that coffee was as strong as it smelled, it'd bring me the rest of the way back to life and beyond. Though I didn't know how it could possibly improve on how I felt right now. When my nose told me what was on that tray, my stomach growled in approval.

Mychael stood over me, his eyes sparkling. "So you've worked up an appetite, too."

I flashed a grin. "I think I can put a respectable dint in whatever the kitchen sent up." I sat up and the sheet fell down.

Oh crap, my nipples were hard. It was the cold air, definitely the cold air, though Mychael wouldn't believe that; he'd probably think that I . . . because he was . . . because we had . . . Dammit.

I sighed and just left the sheet where it was. No use bothering now. "You wouldn't happen to have something I could wear, would you?"

Mychael winked and sat the tray down across my lap. "Got just the thing." The silk sleep shirt he retrieved from the back of a chair was the match to the pants he was wearing. He held the tray while I put it on.

I buttoned the shirt. "Perfect."

Mychael grinned crookedly. "Now you can eat, retain your modesty, and prevent any *cold*-related . . . issues."

I tucked the sheet around my waist, and lifted the cover off one of the two plates on the tray. There were eggs, bacon, cheese, fried potatoes, bread, and butter. "And my appetite would like to thank you in advance. How did you know when to have food brought?"

"I asked that it be brought in ten hours."

I stopped with a fork of eggs halfway to my open mouth. "We've been in bed together for ten hours?"

"The minimal length of time for healing injuries as severe as yours is seven hours. I allowed another three for sleep for both of us."

Meaning I'd been naked in Mychael's arms for ten hours—and during seven of those hours, his hands had been all over me.

Since that image struck me pretty much speechless, I stuffed a forkful of eggs in my mouth.

Mychael pulled the nightstand over next to him and put the second plate on it. He had the same breakfast as mine and dug in with gusto. I imagine healing a naked woman all night and half the morning combined with what we had just done would give a man one hell of an appetite.

Mychael scowled at me between bites. "I know the answer

I'm going to get, but I have to ask. What possessed you to throw yourself into a nest of Reapers?"

"Those things went after Dad. I—"

"A man who has been protecting himself against Reapers for centuries. Your father's had plenty of practice. You, on the other hand, have not."

I stopped chewing, and the fire crackled in the silence.

"So I tried to save someone who didn't need saving," I finally said.

"Someone who was trying to save *you*. That you're still alive after what you did is nothing short of a miracle."

I just stared at him. He didn't know. If he couldn't see Reapers, that meant he didn't see the souls that tore their way out of the Saghred through me.

"Mychael, when I started screaming . . . did you see what was happening?"

"You were surrounded by Reapers."

"You could see them?"

"No, but I could sense them."

I took a breath and slowly let it out. "Mychael, four souls from inside the Saghred . . ." I stopped, my food suddenly like a rock in my stomach. "They came out of me and went into a Reaper."

Mychael froze. "The Reapers took them out of you?"

I shook my head. "No, the souls wanted to go. They were . . ." I fought down the sensation that I'd felt, could still feel. "Squirming inside of me. They wanted to get out. They ripped their way out; it was like someone grabbed a handful of my guts and pulled." I put my fork down, and made myself take another breath. "When they were out, the Reapers took them. I couldn't stop them from going or the Reapers from taking."

"Vidor Kalta told me he'd seen something moving between you and the Reapers, but he didn't know what it was."

Fear seized me as I remembered Kalta looking at my dad, recognizing what he was, what he'd been. "Kalta knows about Dad."

"Vidor is the finest nachtmagus I know; I fully expected him to know your father for what he is."

"You don't sound concerned."

"And you shouldn't be, either. I've spoken with Vidor and he understands the need for discretion."

"You trust him?"

"Without hesitation. Your father and Vidor are fine; you however are not. I've had Vidor ward this room against Reapers. There's nothing strong enough to keep them out, but Vidor's discouraged them. Just because you appear to be healed doesn't mean that you are. You need sleep. I don't want you leaving this bed for at least the next day, and this room until I have located and dealt with Sarad Nukpana."

I sat up, sloshing coffee on the tray. "Not without me, you don't."

"Raine, you're hardly in any condition—"

"Neither are you."

"I wasn't the one buried in Reapers."

"You heard Nukpana; he wants me *last*. For the first time in my life, I have a dad." My voice caught. "I never knew my mother. I'm not going to lose him." I felt the sudden sting of tears in my eyes. "And I'm not going to lose anyone else I care about, either. Sarad Nukpana won't stop until he takes every person I love. He said it, and I believe him. I will not lie here in this bed while that happens."

"He won't act on that threat immediately," Mychael assured me. "Remember what Vidor said? After Nukpana fully absorbs the life force he got from General Aratus, he'll become incorporeal again."

"Meaning not solid."

"Exactly. Nukpana will want to build up his power before he comes after one of us. He can't risk failure. He's issued his challenge; he's knows we're hunting him. He won't act openly until he's strong enough."

"Which means there's going to be more bodies," I said, a

lump of dread sticking in my throat. "Or 'gifts,' as Nukpana calls them."

Mychael nodded grimly. "Magically powerful victims, probably with nothing less than mage-level talents. I've made Justinius aware of the danger to our senior mages. Whether they take the threat seriously is another matter. Our more powerful mages are known for thinking themselves invulnerable to attacks of any kind."

I snorted. "If Sarad Nukpana gets hold of one of them, their thinking days are over."

"True."

"If we don't stop Nukpana soon, no one will have enough power to stop him."

"Except you, Raine," Mychael said quietly.

"You mean the Saghred."

"You and the Saghred are essentially one and the same." Mychael's eyes were intent on mine. "The Reapers know that and so does Sarad Nukpana. If he were to take you, he wouldn't just have you; he would have the Saghred's power."

I knew what Mychael meant, and it scared me more than anything had ever scared me before. If Sarad Nukpana absorbed the life force, knowledge, and magic of enough mages, he would be unstoppable.

And if he took me and the Saghred, Sarad Nukpana would be a dark demigod with the world at his mercy.

So much for my appetite.

Chapter 5

When I woke up, Mychael had already gone, and I was determined to be dressed and out of here in half an hour.

I had to find Piaras.

Piaras's last name was Rivalin, not Benares, and we weren't related by anyone, anywhere; but I loved the kid like a little brother, so in my book, that made him family.

Family that I knew was near the top of Sarad Nukpana's kill list.

Piaras needed to know it and I needed to assure myself that he was safe.

I was two steps away from the bed when I remembered that the Reapers had shredded the hell out of my clothes. Damn. Well, I'd help myself to Mychael's wardrobe. I just needed to get out of here, not make a fashion statement.

Then I spotted a familiar duffel bag leaning against his desk, and the shoulder harness holding my brace of swords was hooked over the back of Mychael's chair. I grinned. If Mychael had wanted to keep me here, he'd just made a grave tactical error. For the past two weeks, I had been staying on the *Fortune*, so Phaelan must have sent along a few things, and Mychael had left them for me. An intricate knot tied the canvas bag closed. Definitely Phaelan's work. He did it to let me know that he'd packed my bag himself, and that the knot was still intact told me Mychael hadn't gone snooping. Good. If there was one thing my cousin knew how to do, it was pack for a quick getaway—or a jailbreak. No doubt everything I needed to get out of Mychael's bedroom, his apartment, and the citadel was in that bag. Phaelan liked to be thorough.

I opened the bag. My set of midnight blue leathers was on top: boots, trousers, and doublet. Two shirts were below that, and then the contents got fun: various small and easily concealable weapons, lock picks, and even a small grappling hook and rope. He tossed in the latter I guess in case I felt the need to go over the wall.

I left the grappling hook but took everything else. I had no intention of going over the wall. Piaras was a Guardian cadet; he was in the citadel.

But before I could step one foot into the hallway, I had to negotiate my release with the Guardian on duty at the door.

I knew that would be Vegard.

When I was dressed and armed to my satisfaction, I went to the door and tried the knob. Surprisingly it was unlocked. I opened the door. Not surprisingly, the space on the other side was filled with a big, blond, overprotective Guardian.

"Afternoon, Vegard."

My bodyguard nodded once. "Ma'am. Aren't you supposed to be resting?"

I glanced down the hall. There were two burly Guardians at the other end. Not an easy escape scenario, but I could get past them if necessary.

I knew the drill. Mychael had ordered Vegard to keep me here. When confronted with familiar tactics, go with the direct approach. If that didn't work, then I'd come up with something sneaky.

"I'm plenty rested," I told him. "Where's Piaras?"

"It's two bells; he's finished his morning lessons, so he should be in the gym." Vegard looked at me with a combination of concern and guilt, but mostly guilt. I knew he felt responsible for what had happened to me. When would everyone accept that my own trouble was my own fault?

"How are you feeling?" he asked.

"I'm fine. Really."

His expression was carefully neutral. "I'm glad to hear that, ma'am."

"Vegard?"

"Ma'am?"

"What happened wasn't your fault; it was mine. Yes, you're my bodyguard, but I'm a big girl with a mind of my own . . . a stubborn mind of my own."

At least that made him smile a little. "Yes, ma'am, you are. You're also my responsibility, and—"

"Vegard, I—"

"Ma'am, please let me finish."

I shut up. Yes, it's possible.

Vegard's pale blue eyes were steady. "If you had been killed, I would have never forgiven myself. It's my job to keep you not only alive, but safe. It's become more than my job." He clenched his jaw and looked away, but not before I saw a faint glisten in his eyes.

Way to go, Raine. You're about to make a grown Guardian cry. Maybe I should have taken the grappling hook and gone out the window.

"If someone kills you, they might as well cut a big chunk out of me while they're at it." His words came in a rush. "Or hell, just finish me off. I don't have a sister, but I'd like to think if I did, she'd be like you."

Oh great, now I was going to cry.

I laid my hand on his forearm. "Okay, Vegard, I'll make you a deal. At least I'll try really hard. I can try to stay away from trouble, but trouble's not going to stay away from me."

"I know."

"Actually, trouble's chasing me right now, a lot of it. Hell, there's a line."

"I know that, too. But ma'am?"

"Yes."

"All I ask is that you let me be at your side when it catches up to you."

I squeezed his arm and bit my lip against my own case

of the misties. Vegard gently covered my hand with his huge paw.

"Deal," I managed. "If it's in my control, you'll be with me. We'll get slaughtered together."

He grinned. "A man can't ask for more than that."

"Now, which way is the gym?"

The grim Guardian was back in spades. "Oh no, you don't, ma'am. The boss told me you weren't supposed to leave this room until he came back."

"Where is he?"

"Meeting with the archmagus."

"And when will he be back?"

"Since it's with the old man there's no telling."

"That's what I thought. Vegard, the gym is in the citadel. Mychael has deemed the citadel safe for me. Isn't the gym filled with Guardians working out with weapons?"

"Yes, ma'am." He knew his argument was crumbling faster than a Nebian trader's morals.

"Then how much safer could I be? I need to talk to Piaras. I'm not the only one in danger."

The big Guardian sighed in defeat. "Follow me, ma'am."

I smiled up at him and linked my arm in his. "How about at my side?"

Piaras was a Conclave Guardian cadet. He'd go from cadet to squire, and eventually be knighted as a full Guardian. And from the way he was going, the kid would probably set a speed record for achieving knighthood.

Before the Guardians accepted a young man into the brotherhood for training, they assessed his skills—both martial and magical. They had to have both. When it came to future Guardians, those skills covered a lot of unusual ground.

Piaras Rivalin was a spellsinger, possibly the best of his generation. He'd also apprenticed with his grandmother as an apothecary. Tarsilia had taught him more than mixing poultices. The kid knew the nastier blends—potions, drugs, poisons, and the antidotes to them all. An elven teenager probably wouldn't need to whip up an antidote on a moment's notice, but a Guardian just might. And last, but definitely not least, due to being under Sarad Nukpana's psychic influence a few weeks ago, Piaras also had the full measure of the goblin's deadly skill with a sword.

Like I said, the kid was on the Guardian fast track.

The Guardian's gym smelled like sweat and worn leather and steel with the coppery tang of blood thrown in for good measure. It was also hot and noisy.

Piaras was in a fighting ring with a Guardian trainer and looked like he was having the time of his young life.

Piaras had come to apprentice with Tarsilia Rivalin when he was eight years old. Phaelan and I had decided that it just wasn't right for a kid to spend his days only learning about a bunch of dried plants. Not that that wasn't a good thing to know, but we felt he needed to know more, especially if he was going to live in Mermeia and, most important, stay alive in Mermeia. Tarsilia agreed. I taught him defense and evasion, and Phaelan took care of offense and confrontation—and we didn't teach him to fight fair. Piaras was tall and lanky, so if anyone came after him with deadly intentions, the kid better be able to make his first move count or run like hell. I'd made sure he knew that there's no shame in running, only in being caught.

Considering what had happened to Piaras in the past two months just as a result of knowing me and getting tangled up in my problems, I was all for the Guardians furthering his education in every way possible.

And becoming a Conclave Guardian was the fulfillment of Piaras's lifelong dream. He couldn't see himself behind an apothecary counter or singing magical lullabies for some noble's bratty children. As a Guardian, he felt he could make a difference.

Piaras wasn't singing right now. He was fighting, the hand-to-hand variety. At eighteen years old, Piaras was plenty tall, but he had some filling out to do.

"How's he doing?" I asked Vegard.

"There are a few rough spots." He shrugged. "But we all have our strong points, and our not-so-strong points. Piaras's should solve themselves once he gets some more weight on him. He's quick; he's got that going for him." He flashed a grin. "If you have to be scrawny, at least be fast."

I smiled. "Is he eating the Guardians out of house and home?"

Vegard chuckled. "He's trying, but we haven't had a cadet succeed yet."

Piaras spotted me and took his attention off his trainer for a blink of an eye. That was all the time it took for the man to administer an object lesson Piaras wouldn't soon forget. I winced. One second Piaras was on his feet; the next he was on the mat, flat on his back.

Vegard whistled. "That one's gonna hurt tomorrow."

Piaras was slowly picking himself up as we walked over to the ring.

"That was my fault, darlin'," I told Piaras. "Sorry about that."

"It was his eyes' fault for wandering," the trainer said.

Piaras finished hauling himself to his feet with no help. Made sense. Your enemy sure as hell wasn't going to help you up on a battlefield or in a back alley.

His trainer spoke without turning to look at him. "Distractions are deadly, Cadet Rivalin."

Vegard grinned. "It's not always good to let a beautiful woman catch your eye."

"Lesson's over, Piaras," the trainer told him. "I don't think the lady's here just to see you sprawled on your back."

Piaras took off his head gear, exposing dark, curly hair; though now it was dark, damp, curly hair. The kid had a pair of big brown eyes that could have gotten him any coed on the island. He was taller than me and still growing. Piaras had potential written all over him, and I was going to do everything in my power to make sure we were both alive to see how he turned out.

Piaras took out his mouthpiece, blew some apparently much needed air in and out of his lungs, then tried some words. "Thank you, sir," he said to his trainer. He looked at me. "You didn't come just to see me embarrass myself, did you?"

"No, but I'm not opposed to unexpected entertainment."

Vegard tossed Piaras a towel that was draped over the ring ropes. "Get yourself cleaned up, little brother, and make it quick."

Piaras looked questioningly from me to Vegard and back again.

"We need to talk," I told him.

Piaras headed off toward the locker room, and two expressionless Guardians followed him. One remained by the door; the other went in with Piaras. I recognized them both. They'd been Piaras's shadows since a few days before Sarad Nukpana escaped the Saghred.

Until then, it'd been an accepted fact that the Saghred couldn't be opened or destroyed. It wouldn't be the first time or the last that accepted fact turned out to be absolute fiction. A couple of millennia ago, the demons were some of the first to get their collective claws on the Saghred. Realizing there were tasty souls trapped inside, the king of demons ordered that a way be found to open it. The demons not only found a way to open the rock; they forged the means to do it—the Scythe of Nen, a dagger no longer than my hand. The Saghred didn't like being opened and having its souls slurped out like oysters. The rock slurped back, and the demon king was now a prisoner with the souls he'd been trying to eat.

Two weeks ago, the demon queen came looking for the Saghred and the Scythe of Nen to free her husband. To force me to find the Scythe of Nen first, and free him from the

Saghred, Sarad Nukpana invaded Piaras's dreams, essentially possessing him. That possession plus Nukpana's sword skills had nearly resulted in Piaras committing a cold-blooded murder. There were men on Mid who were just waiting for the chance to lock Piaras up, and they'd almost gotten their wish.

The two Guardian bodyguards were Mychael's idea of a preventative measure to keep Sarad Nukpana from getting back into Piaras's head. Mychael had assured me that Nukpana wouldn't go after Piaras immediately, if at all, but I felt better that he obviously wasn't taking any chances.

My expression must have said that I didn't think two Guardians were enough, regardless of how big and magically talented they were.

"Piaras won't be leaving the citadel until Sarad Nukpana's been terminated," Vegard said. "Every Guardian in the citadel is watching him."

"That's what I'm worried about," I told him. "When it comes to revenge, Sarad Nukpana likes the personal touch. But if he can't get to Piaras himself, he's perfectly capable of getting someone else to do it for him." I hesitated. "And don't take this the wrong way, but Mychael's already had one Guardian turn traitor. In my experience, traitors are like rats; if you find one, there's more in a dark corner somewhere."

Piaras came out a few minutes later wearing his dove gray Guardian cadet uniform, his dark curls now damp from a quick shower. Vegard's and Piaras's heavily armed shadows gave us some privacy and we found a quiet corner near a rack of wicked-looking bladed pikes.

"What's wrong?" Piaras asked point-blank, his large brown eyes solemn.

Like me, Piaras knew that when someone said, "We need to talk," chances were it wasn't going to be something you wanted to hear. Until recently, I would have tried to protect him by telling him only as much as he needed to know, no more. Now ignorance was deadly.

I told him everything, leathery corpses and all.

"Are you having any more dreams about Sarad Nukpana?" I asked, once I'd finished.

Piaras knew what I meant. Dreams that Nukpana may have planted in his head, along with any impulses—like murder.

"No. I've had a couple of nightmares, but I had those all by myself, no help needed."

"Your guards know about them?"

Piaras snorted derisively. "Them and every cadet in the barracks." He gave me a lopsided grin. "But they assure me that I'm screaming like a man, not a girl."

I cringed inwardly. "That's always good." I leaned forward, then stopped myself. It was all I could do not to hug him.

"Hug received," Piaras whispered.

He'd always blushed before whenever I'd hugged or obviously wanted to hug him. This time he didn't. That just made me want to hug him more.

"But thanks for not actually doing it in the middle of the gym," he added quietly.

I had a lump in my throat. "Hey, any one of these men would jump at the chance to have me hug them."

"Any one of these men doesn't scream in the middle of the night and wake up half the citadel. Spellsinger pipes are loud."

"Vegard says you're restricted to the citadel for the duration." I didn't need to say for the duration of what; Piaras knew. When Sarad Nukpana was dead for good, Piaras could set foot outside the citadel's walls.

Piaras scowled. "All my classes are here right now. Paladin Eiliesor has asked my two other professors to come to the citadel, so I'm getting private tutoring."

"You don't sound happy about it."

"Would you be? Locked up here like a . . ." He fumbled for the word that expressed every bit of the frustration and anger he was obviously feeling. "Like a *child*. And worst of all, every cadet in the barracks knows why—the paladin doesn't think I can defend myself."

I could see what had happened as if I'd been there. "I take it the other cadets have been giving you a hard time."

Piaras's silence answered my question better than any words.

"I just want to do *something*," Piaras blurted. "And that the paladin doesn't think I'm good enough to—"

"Stop right there. Mychael doesn't doubt your ability and neither do I. And if any cadets say that you being in the citadel makes you incompetent or a coward, that's not teasing; that's jealousy, pure and simple. What you did in that cave under the elven embassy saved every last one of us. That's public knowledge now. And I don't know how much more public you could have been when you summoned three rampaging bukas out of thin air to take down those embassy guards who were trying to kill you. And just three weeks ago, you fought at the archmagus's side and killed I don't know how many demons." I stopped, thought, and surmised the source of the problem.

"Those other cadets wouldn't happen to be highborn elves, would they?"

Piaras hesitated before replying. "Yes."

That was it, then, or at least a big part of it. Piaras's parents were merchants in Laerin, and they'd done well for themselves. No blue blood, just good, solid business sense and a lot of hard work. No doubt Piaras's background would be looked down on by the young, snobby, rich aristocrats. Piaras had worked for everything he had; those elf cadets just had to be born. I didn't have to tell Piaras any of this; he'd experienced it firsthand over the years.

"Then I know it's jealousy," I told him. "One, they're nowhere near as magically gifted as you. Two, they'd probably crap their uniforms if a demon came running at them. Three, and this is what really gets their collective goat, you're going to make knight before any of them. Some may not even make it to squire and they know it." I sighed. "Piaras, Mychael isn't keeping you here because he questions your competence. He's keeping you here because he recognizes your *poten-*

tial. Yes, you're eighteen; and yes, that makes you a man. But you're also a cadet under the command of a paladin who wants to make sure that you live long enough to grow up to realize that potential. And if it makes you feel any better, even Mychael is having a tough time with this one. Every time he turns around, more bad guys have crawled out of the woodwork. He wants you safe and so do I."

Piaras scowled. "But you're not safe and neither is the paladin. You're both facing all the danger, and I can't make a move without those two." He jerked his head back at the big Guardians trying to loom unobtrusively. "If they were any closer, they'd be in my boots with me."

That image earned him a smile. Everything I'd been through, Piaras had been right there with me. That neither one of us had any white hairs to show for it was a miracle.

"You're here *learning* to face danger," I told him. "Mychael and I want you to get a little more experience under your belt before you have to fight off death five times a day, which seems to be becoming the story of my life." I kept my voice steady, but it wasn't easy. "Promise me you won't try to lose your guards. They're shadowing you for your own good." I lowered my voice further. "Mychael's had one traitor among his men, and it's been my experience that traitors at least come in pairs."

Piaras knew that only too well; that traitor had tried to kill him—and under Sarad Nukpana's influence, Piaras had nearly killed that traitor.

"I promise," he said.

"Thank you. That'll give me one less thing to worry about."

"And I'm watching my own back, too."

"Good. Don't stop there. Watch your sides and your front, and your head and those big feet of yours while you're at it. Right now, there's no way you can be too careful. As paladin, Mychael is your commander. That means you take your orders from him. And if he orders you to stay put, you stay put. Got it?"

Piaras grinned slowly. "I've got it, but obviously you don't."

"What?"

"From what I hear, he ordered you to stay in your room, and here you are."

I gave him a big smile. "I got news for you kid. Mychael ain't my commander."

Vegard and I were leaving the gym when I saw Dad standing in the doorway watching me. Beside him stood a complete surprise and I wasn't sure it was a good one.

Nachtmagus Vidor Kalta.

They made no move to come in, so Vegard and I crossed over to them.

"Arlyn, Nachtmagus Kalta," I greeted them. Kalta knew my dad's soul was living in Arlyn Ravide's body, but every other Guardian in the gym thought Arlyn was just a young knight. They weren't going to find out any different from me.

"We were told that we would find you here, Miss Benares," Dad said. "Nachtmagus Kalta needed to speak with you."

I felt his unease. Dad and I didn't have a bond, at least not of the magical variety, but I guess sometimes a father and daughter can know what the other's thinking, no words needed.

Dad didn't want to be here. But I was here, so he came regardless of his fear.

Fear. That was what I felt from him.

I knew why.

He had died here.

Arlyn Ravide, the young Guardian in whose body my dad's soul lived, had died at the hands of the demon queen only a few yards from where we were standing, the Scythe of Nen plunged through his heart. She'd wet the blade with his sacrificial blood, then stabbed the Saghred with equal ease. My dad's soul had escaped the Saghred and occupied Arlyn Ravide's lifeless body.

"Let's go out into the hall," I suggested.

Dad nodded once, wordlessly.

"Do you remember any of it?" I asked him quietly. He knew what I was talking about.

"Flashes of memory, nothing more."

He was lying. But considering he had bled and died in the room we'd just left, he deserved a little lie. Hell, he deserved all the lies he wanted to tell.

"Vegard, is there anywhere around here that's private?" I asked.

"Yes, ma'am," he said solemnly. "Follow me."

Vegard led the way, Vidor Kalta and I followed, and my dad, as Arlyn Ravide, brought up the rear as a young Guardian should in the presence of a high-ranking guest and a superior officer. That would be Kalta and Vegard. I had no clue where I fell on the Guardian scale of military etiquette.

Kalta broke the uncomfortable silence, bless him. "Sir Arlyn and I were on our way out into the city, and we wanted to see how you were doing."

"Very well," I replied. "No thanks to my own foolishness."

"Bravery, Mistress Benares," Kalta corrected me. "Attacking in the face of certain death to save others is bravery."

Or stupid, if your dad was a super mage and didn't need your help. But I didn't need to say that out loud; Kalta knew. He was just making conversation for anyone who might hear.

Vegard led us down a side hallway, opened a door, and stepped aside for the three of us to enter. He followed and closed the door.

"No one can hear us in here," he told me. "You may speak freely."

I raised an eyebrow. "Are you certain?"

"Positive."

I glanced at Dad, then spoke to Vidor Kalta. "Mychael said that you and he spoke and that you understand the need for discretion."

Kalta flashed a quick smile. "I've always been discreet, even in the face of the most cryptic of comments."

Dad chuckled. "Raine wants to know if you're going to expose me for who I am, but she doesn't want to come right out and say it. She's trying to protect me again. Raine, Vidor knew the moment he saw me with those Reapers that I was an old soul."

"Paladin Eiliesor has explained the situation," Kalta told me. "It's my belief that a man's past, regardless of how extensive, is his own business. I am interested in Sir Arlyn's specialized knowledge in solving your problem."

I bit back a snort. "I have so many. Which problem would that be?"

"My intention was to research a way to break your link to the Saghred," Dad said. "But I believe the continued existence of Sarad Nukpana is a greater danger to you right now."

I felt a chill of apprehension. I knew where he was going with this, or more to the point, who he was going after.

"No," I told him.

"No, what?"

"No, you're not going after him."

Dad grinned boyishly. "I can hardly go after that which I have not found—a situation I hope to change very soon. Raine, I was here nine hundred years ago. The city is only a century older than me. You said you smelled stale air, damp, and mold."

"Yes."

"Sounds like something old, just like me."

"I don't like it."

"You don't have to like it. You're my daughter. I came close to losing you yesterday. I'm doing this so that you'll be safe tomorrow and every day after that."

I met him with silence.

"I know every crypt, ruin, and dark and dank hiding place on this island. I used more than a few of them myself before I escaped the island with the Saghred. Sarad Nukpana needs seclusion. The cha'nescu ritual takes over an hour, and once begun, it cannot be stopped. Sarad cannot risk discovery. He's gone to ground." My dad's smile was fierce. "So I'm going to search every square inch of it."

"Please tell me Mychael assigned some Guardians to go with—"

Dad held up his hand. He knew what I was thinking.

"I'll have a few Guardians with me." He paused meaningfully. "Men he trusts enough to take orders from a junior knight and not ask questions or spread rumors."

I let out a breath I didn't know I was holding. "Good."

Sarad Nukpana knew that my dad had escaped the Saghred and whose body he was living in. There was no statute of limitations on Saghred stealing. If anyone discovered that Arlyn Ravide was my father, Eamaliel Anguis, he would be arrested and tried, with execution being a foregone conclusion.

I closed the distance between us and hugged him, tightly. "Be careful."

"Whenever possible. I know I'm probably wasting my words, but would you please do the same?"

I smiled and glanced at Vegard. "Whenever possible."

Dad's expression was stern. "Raine, souls came out of you and went into Reapers; those same Reapers damned near killed you to get more. And Mychael told me what happened with the mage's specter in the bordello."

"Nothing happened. I stopped it."

"Did you? You are strong, incredibly so, but—"

I knew where he was going. Strong, but not strong enough. "Mychael calls me stubborn," I said to lighten the mood.

"Raine, the Saghred and those Reapers have existed for untold millennia. They know how to get what they want. Have a care, daughter. Please. I didn't fight my way out of the Saghred to watch you be consumed by it—or by those who hunt it." He paused, his solemn eyes on mine. "Those Reapers were coming for you. Yes, they took the sorcerer's specter first. It was easier prey. But what attracted them was you."

Kalta tactfully cleared his throat. "Miss Benares, if I may ask a question."

A question from a nachtmagus probably wasn't a question I wanted to think about, let alone answer. "Go ahead."

"When the souls came out of you, were they struggling against the Reapers . . . or were they struggling against you?"

Kalta knew the answer just as well as I did.

"They were struggling to get out of me." I took a deep, steadying breath. "Nothing's ever hurt me that bad in my life."

He regarded me somberly. "It is the nature of spirits to cross over. Most not only want to; they need to. Only the most angry or confused spirits refuse to go—they either want revenge, or they won't admit, or simply don't know, that they're dead. Crossing over completes the cycle of life into death. It is the natural way of things."

I pressed my lips into a thin line. "Pardon me for disputing the natural order, but what happened sure as hell didn't feel natural to me."

"No doubt. You are the vessel that holds them prisoner." He paused. "You and the Saghred are virtually one."

He didn't need to spell it out for me. I knew. I knew it to the point that I'd given up trying to deny or forget it. The closer the Saghred and I became, the more often the Reapers would appear. Like Sarad Nukpana, they wouldn't stop until they got what they wanted.

Death had all the time in the world.

Mine was running out.

Chapter 6

Mychael wanted me to stay in the citadel. I had to leave the citadel, and I had a good reason.

Like Piaras, I had lessons.

I was learning how to kill Sarad Nukpana.

And today those lessons would have the added bonus of giving me a much-needed outlet for my growing fear, frustration, and rage. Yes, I could have taken it out on a Guardian in their gym, but that wasn't the kind of workout I needed. Well, it was, but I required a specialist. No Guardian was a master swordsman with the long, curved blades favored by goblins.

Tamnais Nathrach was.

So was Sarad Nukpana.

Since Nukpana had oozed his way out of the Saghred, I'd made it my goal to not only know every way that Nukpana, his Khrynsani, or any other goblin could possibly come after me, but have a lethal response ready for each and every one of them.

Tam could help. He'd known Sarad Nukpana at the goblin court, and fenced with him on numerous occasions. Not with deadly intent, but when goblin courtiers crossed blades, blood was spilled. Naturally, it was always an unfortunate accident.

Mychael didn't like it. Not the lethal response part; he didn't like me being anywhere near Tam. Tam was a dark mage; my connection with the Saghred made me a dark mage magnet. The two of us together with the Saghred wasn't just trouble for us; it could be trouble for every living creature, period, not to mention civilization, such that it was.

The Saghred didn't just forge our umi'atsu bond; the rock specifically chose Tam to pair me with.

Tam used to be the chief mage for the royal House of Mal'Salin, the late goblin queen's magical enforcer, and possibly one of the most powerful dark mages there was. The Saghred didn't want to use Tam; it wanted Tam to use *it*. The rock was starving and it wanted souls. And after the escape of those four souls yesterday, it had to be more desperate than ever. There was no way in hell that I was feeding the thing and the Saghred knew it, so it forged an umi'atsu bond between me and Tam. Since I refused to feed it, given enough time and temptation, Tam just might. But that didn't mean the rock was giving up on me; what happened in that bordello was proof.

Like I said, Mychael didn't want me near Tam, but he agreed with me learning to defend myself in every way Sarad Nukpana could possibly attack me. He had just one condition; actually it was more like two dozen conditions.

I was on horseback, riding to Tam's nightclub, surrounded by at least two dozen mounted and absurdly well-armed Guardians. Needless to say, anyone we met gave us a wide berth. It was late afternoon, and the sun was starting to go down behind some of the Conclave's government buildings, throwing most of the city streets into shadow.

I'd sent word ahead to Tam that what had happened with the Reapers wasn't keeping me from my lesson, so the front doors were unlocked and unwarded. The main floor of the theatre was usually filled with small tables covered in crisp white cloths, each with two or four chairs. The second-floor dining suites were like private boxes in a fine theatre. Columns stretched from the floor to the high, vaulted ceiling, carved with mermaids and mermen—sirens that could sing men or women to their doom—or somewhere much more enjoyable.

Today the tables were bare of cloths and most of them were stacked against the far walls, leaving the center of the floor clear and open. Officially Sirens was closed for renovation. In reality, Tam had closed the club until the present situation had been dealt with. Tam had a lot of potentially fatal "situations" other than being in an umi'atsu bond with me and Mychael, and he didn't want running a nightclub to distract him from staying alive, nor did he want some of his clients being killed because they had the poor timing to walk between Tam and someone bent on killing him.

Tam was waiting for me. He was wearing sleek, dark fencing clothes with his black hair pulled back in a long goblin battle braid. His strong hands were bare, and a pair of steel-mesh dueling goggles dangled from his long fingers.

Like most goblins, Tam was tall and leanly muscled, and as I'd experienced on more than one occasion, Tam was also lightning quick. His pale gray skin set off what was a goblin's most distinctive feature—a pair of fangs that weren't for decorative use only. A goblin wouldn't hesitate to use them if a fight turned dirty. Tam wouldn't hesitate to use them if I got within nibbling range.

Tam's black eyes gleamed in the club's dim lighting, lighting he wasn't going to turn up for our lesson. Sarad Nukpana's goblin eyes were at their best in this kind of light. Either I learned to adapt or I learned to be dead.

A table near the wall held an array of bladed goblin weapons. Chances were any fighting I'd be doing would be with magic, but I wanted to be prepared for anything. I'd always considered myself a good fencer; and when the situation called for it, I wasn't squeamish about killing. If it came down to me or them, it sure as hell wasn't going to be me. Survival was a powerful motivator.

Vegard and four other Guardians arranged themselves around the room. The rest remained outside to stand guard.

Tam stood in the center of the dueling circle and made no move to come toward me. "You should be resting."

"I slept for nearly ten hours and stayed in my room for most of the day." I thought I wouldn't mention that "my room" had in fact been Mychael's bedroom. "I've had enough rest. I can't afford to be stiff or slow."

"You can't afford to be hurt again."

"Too late for that. Sarad Nukpana isn't going to cut me any slack, so neither am I. That means neither are you. Tam, you know it as well as I do—either I'm deadly or I'm dead."

Tam tossed me a pair of goggles identical to his own. I was good, Tam was better, and our practice blades weren't killing sharp, but accidents happened. To risk losing an eye in a practice session was just plain stupid. And it'd be careless after what'd happened with the Reapers for me not to warm up first. Even with all the healing Mychael had done, my muscles were still stiff and sore. Tam waited patiently as I stretched out. He'd probably already stretched. Though who was I kidding? Tam and jungle cats—they didn't stretch; they just attacked.

I sat on the floor and started stretching. Tam pulled a chair close to me and sat, his elbows resting on spread knees, his hands clasped loosely in front of him. I groaned silently. I knew what that meant.

Tam wanted to talk. Tam never wanted to talk. He was manipulative, secretive, and you couldn't get a straight answer even if you could choke it out of him, but when Tam wanted to know something, he was relentless.

I didn't need our umi'atsu bond to know what he wanted to talk about. With the closeness of our bond, he probably knew everything that had happened to me. I was about to find out how much "everything" included.

"You nearly died," he said quietly.

"What, no small talk first?"

"Reapers are nothing to joke about."

I stopped stretching and looked up at him. "Tam, if joking keeps me from screaming and curling up in a corner, then I'm going to keep it up. If I joke or think about it as little as I have to, I might not need a padded room."

"Understood. But you shouldn't have attacked them."

I flexed my foot back, stretching my calf, and pain shot up my leg. I winced, and stretched it again, slower. "Yeah, my hindsight works real good. It's seeing into the future that I can't do." I lowered my voice. Vegard was the only Guardian in the room who knew my dad's identity. "I didn't know he could defend himself against those things. He's my dad, Tam. I'm not going to lose him."

Tam was silent. He knew all about losing people he loved. He'd been married while at the goblin court. His wife had been a duchess, making Tam a duke by marriage, a title he retained after her death—murder, actually. Tam blamed it on his ambition; her family blamed it on Tam.

"You don't want to lose your father," Tam said quietly. "I don't want to lose you."

Tam wasn't just talking about a Reaper sucking my soul out.

Until the Saghred was a pile of dust, the rock and I were a package deal. Wanting me would get Tam killed; the Saghred would get him damned. I was determined that neither one was going to happen.

Tam was a dark mage. I knew what that meant, and none of it was good. For a dark mage, power was an addiction, and the more power they got, the more they wanted—and the more they were willing to do to get it.

Like use objects of power such as the Saghred. I'd been resisting its temptations ever since it latched onto me. A dark mage wouldn't have resisted. I'd always told myself that whatever Tam had done while in the goblin court, he'd done it to survive. Maybe. When Tam left the goblin court, he'd gotten help for his addiction. Call it what you will—intervention, black-magic rehab—Tam had fought his way back from the brink. I wasn't going to be the cause of his relapse.

I stood up. "Then let's work on making Mid a safer place for everyone."

Tam moved the chair out of the dueling circle. I put on the goggles and pulled on a pair of padded leather fencing gloves.

I drew my swords and exchanged them for the pair of practice blades Tam had laid out on a table for me.

"What are we working on today?" I asked him.

Tam pulled his goggles down. "The same thing we worked on last time."

"What? I didn't get it right?"

"You got it right twice." He put on his fencing gloves. "You need to get it right on instinct, not thought. Last time I could still sense you thinking—and if I could sense it, Sarad will, too."

I swore softly.

"That's why we're only working on four moves," Tam reminded me. "You don't have time to perfect any more. You've got the first three down, one more to go."

Since I knew my way around a blade and was good at adapting my fighting style to my opponent, Tam was teaching me four down-and-dirty moves using goblin blades. Really dirty moves. Moves that I could throw into a fight and if I was quick enough and lucky enough—and if Sarad Nukpana was solid enough—I just might get to skewer the goblin.

That moment would be a dream come true.

Goblin swords were both stabbing and slashing weapons. Goblins used two blades as naturally as breathing, like extensions of their arms. They were taught from an early age. Elf children played with building blocks; goblins learned to spin blades.

Tam stood facing me, his hands by his side, his blades angled toward the floor. He looked relaxed. I knew better. When Tam had swords in his hands, relaxed meant ready.

In our lessons, Tam always made the first move.

Change is good. Dirty is better.

I sauntered toward him like I was just getting into position to go on guard. Then I lunged, my blades dropped to block his, and my heel came down hard on his instep. Tam hissed and I pivoted sharply to the right, intending to pommel strike his ribs and dart the hell out of range.

Darting didn't happen. Neither did the pommel strike.

Tam's leather-clad arms pinned my arms—and swords—to my sides. His blades were up and crossed entirely too close to my face for any kind of comfort.

So much for striking and darting.

"Well, shit," I said mildly. "That could have worked better."

"My foot thinks it worked quite well." I heard the pained grimace in his voice. "Nicely done." Leather creaked as his arms tightened around me, and his voice lowered to a teasing purr. "The rest of me agrees. This is more than pleasant. Now, how do you propose to get away from me?"

"What?"

Vegard was here, so I knew Tam wouldn't actually try anything, but that didn't mean he wouldn't play with me like a mouse.

Sarad Nukpana would do the same thing.

Tam was right. He couldn't let me go.

"You chose the game, darling. I didn't." His lips were near the tip of my ear. "Escape from me, and feel free to do whatever you have to—" He froze, then inhaled, taking my scent. "Mychael."

My heart did a double thump. Goblins had a predator's sense of smell. "Mychael what?"

"I can smell him on you." Tam inhaled again, deeper. "All over you."

I sighed. I'd really wanted to avoid this. "You said it yourself, those Reapers almost killed me. Mychael healed me. If he hadn't, I wouldn't be alive and standing here for you to sniff."

Tam was silent for a few moments. "Mychael told me that your injuries were quite extensive—covering nearly your entire body."

"So was the healing he had to do."

"I'm familiar with the process." Tam's voice was flat and emotionless. "How long?"

I wasn't going to lie to him. "Ten hours. Seven for healing, three for sleep."

"In bed." He paused. "Together. And bare skin works best."

"Yes," I said simply. "Tam, I—"

"Mychael did what he had to do." Tam's warm breath exhaled against my ear. "I am grateful for his talent—and that he was there when you needed him."

Those were his words. With goblins, it was the meaning behind the words that you had to listen for. Tam knew what Mychael had done—and now he knew exactly how he'd done it. While that knowledge had probably bumped Tam's alpha male possessiveness up a few notches, at the same time he was sincerely grateful that Mychael had been able to save my life, and was all too aware that he wouldn't have been able to do the same.

Tam also knew about the magical bond that only Mychael and I shared—a bond that was drawing us closer every day. Though I didn't know anymore how much of our closeness was the bond and how much was our own growing attraction to each other.

I swore silently. Now Tam was jealous, had a wounded ego, *and* a stomped foot. Earlier, I'd almost made Vegard cry. I was just spreading cheer all over the place today.

"Mychael did his job, and he did it well." Tam's voice was all business. "Now I'm going to do mine equally well. Teach you how to kill a goblin."

He loosened his hold on me.

"No, no," I told him.

"Excuse me?" Tam asked, genuinely confused.

"You're right. I got myself into this; I have to get myself out. Sarad Nukpana wouldn't let me go, so you shouldn't, either. Though what I'd do to Nukpana wouldn't exactly work on you."

"And what would that be?"

"You're a little taller than he is. My head fits under your

chin with about an inch to spare. Though if I jumped up hard enough, I might get the same results."

Tam grinned. "A head butt."

"Nukpana's the perfect height for me. Let my head sag forward a little in defeat, then snap it back under his chin and knock out some of the bastard's teeth."

"Ouch."

"Yeah, I'd enjoy it, too."

Tam snuggled closer. "What would you do next?" he whispered.

Goblins. What other race got excited talking about in-fighting?

"Once he let me go to catch the teeth falling out of his mouth, I'd stab or slit whatever I could reach. I don't think I'd be picky at that point."

While we'd talked, Tam had loosened his hold on me ever so slightly. It might be enough. Only one way to find out.

"Sarad Nukpana's not the one holding you now," Tam said on the barest breath. "I am. So what are you going to—"

I threw my head back as a diversion, then drove my elbow hard into his stomach. After a gratifying "oof" from Tam, I twisted sharply and drove my other elbow into his ribs. I was rewarded with a pained hiss and freedom.

I got the hell out of range and got my blades on guard, balancing on the balls of my feet, ready to move wherever Tam didn't. Sometimes winning a fight just meant surviving.

Tam didn't come after me. He just stood there, his right arm cradling his ribs. I wasn't buying the wounded bird routine. I hadn't hit him *that* hard.

Tam blew his breath in and out, wincing with every inhale. Okay, maybe he wasn't faking it.

"You okay?"

"You bumped a rib I've had broken a couple of times."

Bumped?

"That was damned near my best shot and you call it a bump?" I felt a sudden urge to hit him again, harder this time.

Tam breathed in and hissed the air out. "It never healed quite right." He slowly stood straight. "I'm fine."

"Which rib?"

One side of Tam's mouth curved up in a smile. "What, so you can hit me again?"

"So I know what to avoid, you idiot. I'm not the only one Nukpana is after, so I'm not the only one who doesn't need to get hurt."

"Second rib, obviously the left side."

"Injury noted. I'll avoid it next time."

Tam spun his blades with graceful and deadly efficiency, then flashed a grin full of fang. "Who says I'm going to let you have a next time?"

He circled off to the left, faster and smoother than any mortal creature had a right to move. I moved with him, keeping as much distance between us as possible. Tam lunged, both blades extended, his long legs damned near giving him the reach he needed to skewer me. I parried sharply, pivoted off, and kept moving, quicker now. Tam could circle and feint all day. Sarad Nukpana would do it as long as it was fun, and when he was ready, he'd move in for the kill.

"Raine, you've got two Khrynsani guards coming with more on the way." Tam's voice was sharp, commanding. It was his fencing master's voice; it was also the voice telling me move my ass, do something, and stay alive. There weren't really any bloodthirsty Khrynsani closing in on me, blades drawn for the kill, but Tam wanted me ready for any scenario. At least it was only two this time; last time he'd made it four.

Tam's words were a staccato bark. "Stop running! Fight!"

He was right. I was running, but not from him.

I was running from Sarad Nukpana, from the inevitable. I would meet him, and if I didn't kill him, he would do worse than kill me. I didn't want to get anywhere near the crazed son of a bitch. He scared me. Hell, he didn't just scare me. He terrified me. I didn't just want to run. I wanted to run and hide. The goblin was turning himself into a monster, a monster whose only goal was to consume me and all that I was.

After he killed everyone that I loved.

After he killed them slowly, reveling in their agony, murdering them in the most hideous way I had ever seen.

I saw a dried corpse on a slab, but it wasn't General Aratus, not this time. The image was so clear, too real, the stench of dried flesh too cloying. The slender body lying on that slab wore the pale gray uniform of a Guardian cadet; the face was—

A scream built in my throat, rage fighting for a voice, desperate for release.

"Kill him!" roared a voice I only vaguely recognized as Tam. Then it twisted, the words a phantom echo in my head, taunting, silken smooth, daring me to kill him, laughing that I had already failed.

I had failed to kill him before he killed Piaras.

I screamed and attacked the black-clad goblin in front of me, my blades a blur before my eyes, my movements sheer instinct, my swords extensions of my rage. He fought me, but I forced him back, kicking a chair out of my way, then another, any obstacle that kept me from reaching and killing.

And ending my terror.

I was on the floor, on top of Tam, the full edge of my blade against his throat, one hand on the grip, the other flat against the blade, ready to shove the steel home through his throat.

I drew a sharp breath, horror choking me. I opened both hands and dropped the blade. It fell against Tam's neck. He left it there, his hands closing around mine, holding, comforting.

Only then was I aware of Vegard's hand firmly gripping the back of my doublet at the neck, pulling me back.

"Steady, Raine," Tam said. "It's all right. Breathe. There you go, love. Just breathe."

When I did, Vegard released me. I sat back, breathing heavily.

"Ma'am, are you all right?" Vegard's voice was low and

professional, a Guardian's voice, a Guardian who'd just stopped a killing.

I nodded. My mouth was dry, my throat raw. I dimly remembered screaming like a crazy woman.

"Did I scream?" I rasped.

"Yes, you did," Tam said. "I'm sorry; I shouldn't have pushed you like that, not after what those Reapers did to you."

I laughed, dry and hollow. My throat felt like it was on fire. "*You're* sorry?" The laugh turned into a cough. "I almost—"

Tam's now-gloveless hands were smoothly rubbing up and down my arms, soothing, calming. "Almost doesn't count in a sword fight. Don't worry about it."

"That's easy for you to say; you're not the one who went nuts."

"You didn't go 'nuts.' You tapped your rage is what you did. Cold, hard rage."

"It's okay, ma'am," Vegard told me. "It happens."

"What the hell do you mean, 'it happens'?"

Vegard sheathed his sword. I hadn't even realized he'd had it in his hand. I closed my eyes and forced down a shudder. I'd even scared Vegard.

"My people call it berserker, ma'am," he was saying. "And if you ask me, it's what you're going to need."

"I'm sorry," I told them both.

Tam sat up and put his arms around my waist, pulling me close. "For what—coming after me like a berserker? Rage is your friend, as long as you keep it controlled. Focus your anger."

"Lose control, lose life."

"Precisely. Sarad Nukpana is counting on you to hesitate if you ever get a blade to his throat, or in the Saghred's crosshairs. He knows you're not a killer; but this once, for him you have to be. You have *no choice*." His black eyes were hard, his expression grim. It was the game face of the goblin queen's enforcer. "Raine, if you hesitate, you're worse than dead and you know it. If you're sitting on Sarad Nukpana's chest with your blade to his throat—*finish him.* No hesitation, no mercy."

I took a shaky breath and slowly let it out. "No Nukpana."

Tam nodded in approval. "Exactly."

It would be self-defense, but it would also be murder of the cold-blooded variety.

"You don't have to like it, Raine," Tam said, picking up my thoughts. "You just have to do it. And it's not murder; it's extermination. Nukpana isn't going to give you the gift of time."

"He prefers corpses." And I didn't want the next one to be Piaras.

Or Mychael.

Or Tam.

"I will be fine," he assured me, his voice a bare whisper. "Sarad couldn't take me when he was in his full power. He's still a specter, almost a ghost." Tam's dark eyes glittered with anticipation. "My plan is to make that arrangement permanent."

I tried to get up, but my knees had other ideas. Vegard was there to help. As always.

"Thank you."

A little smile curled his lips. "Always glad to help a fellow warrior, ma'am." There was quiet pride in his voice.

I gave him as much of a smile as I was able. "I like your plan," I told Tam. "Mychael's plan is to lock me up in the citadel. I refuse to sit in a warded and guarded room like some kind of crown jewel while Sarad Nukpana picks off the people I care for." I paused uncomfortably. "Mychael and Piaras are in the citadel . . . and you're here. I don't like it, Tam."

Tam stood, his grin wicked. "So you want me and my crown jewels in the citadel with you?" His grin faded. "I'm not alone, Raine, and I am certainly not defenseless. I am prepared for many forms of attack—as I always have been. I can take care of myself and my son."

Tam's son, Talon, was the result of a relationship Tam once had with an elven woman. That made Talon a half-breed, which in the opinion of the goblin aristocracy made him an abomination. Tam had rubbed their collective nose in it by publicly acknowledging Talon as his son and heir.

"Where is he?" I asked.

"In his rooms. And yes, I'm sure he's there and is going to stay there," Tam said in response to the question I was about to ask. "He was just escorted back from his spellsinging lesson. He has homework, which he'd better be working on right now."

Instead of trying to sneak out a window for an early date.

Tam pulled out a chair for me, and I straddled it, resting my arms across the back. Tam tossed me a towel from behind the bar, then pulled a chair opposite me and sat down, leisurely stretching his long legs out in front of him and crossing his ankles.

His black eyes gleamed. "I found the coach Sarad Nukpana used last night."

Apparently Tam had already dismissed the fact that I'd almost separated his head from the rest of him. I knew I couldn't. I'd be replaying it in my nightmares. I'd just add it to the growing list of nightmare fodder. For now, if Tam wanted to ignore it, I could, too.

"And when were you going to tell me about the coach?"

"I'm telling you now," Tam said. "I told Mychael earlier."

"Well, where is it?"

"A town house on Park Street. It's a rental property. A robe maker has a shop on the first floor and lives on the second; the third floor is being used by a bookseller for extra storage."

"And it has a carriage house."

"It does, and inside is a very nice black coach, covered in tarps, of course."

"What about the horses?"

Tam shook his head. "Just the coach. In his present state, Nukpana would have to have at least one person working for him. Likely it was that person who hired the horses from a nearby stable—and there are at least six stables within acceptable distance. Black horses are common here, Raine. Conclave mages looking to impress their peers on a night on the town would want a matched set."

Or Sarad Nukpana wanting to scare the crap out of me.

"The town house is one of four in the city owned by the Ghalfari family," Tam said.

"Goblins?"

"Even better. Sarad Nukpana's family on his mother's side."

I spat a laugh. "That thing has a mother? Let me guess, she says he's really just a nice goblin boy who wouldn't hurt a fly."

"Actually, she's quite proud of him."

"Figures. And you found which house he was using by process of elimination?"

"That and proximity to one of his hideouts."

I couldn't believe what I just heard. "You know where he is? And you didn't tell us?"

"I know where he *was*. He hasn't been there in over a week."

"And Mychael knows this, too." I didn't ask it as a question; I knew the answer only too well. Mychael knew, I didn't, and he had probably wanted it to stay that way. Mychael and I were going to have a talk.

"Mychael knows. However, Nukpana was no longer there and it was obvious to me that he had no intention of coming back. Mychael stepped up Guardian patrols in that neighborhood. The city watch has the next few streets under surveillance. Sarad is fond of taunting us, but he has come too far to take needless risks."

"How about the other three houses?"

"They're all occupied. Rented, like the first."

"One of those occupants could be hiding him. Or he could be living in the attic or a cellar."

"He could be, but he's not. One is being rented by an elven family whose daughter is enrolled in the college, the second by a pair of human mages, and the third is the home of a college fraternity."

I tried to picture Sarad Nukpana haunting a frat house. "That doesn't mean that he's not there."

"My men and I have checked each house."

"No Nukpana."

"Not a trace."

I wanted to believe that they had missed something, but Tam's men were dark mages, trusted colleagues from Tam's days in the goblin court—or as close to trusted as you could get in the goblin court. If they said Sarad Nukpana wasn't there, then he wasn't there.

"Tam, I need to lay hands on that coach."

He knew I meant that literally. "Absolutely not."

"You said Nukpana hid it well, so it's unlikely he thought anyone was going to find it. If he used that coach to kidnap General Aratus, there's going to be psychic residue all over it; and the more violent the kidnapping, the stronger those images will be. Yes, it'd be great if I could get enough from that coach to track Nukpana, but it might be just as productive if I could find his accomplice."

Tam didn't say a word; he just looked at me. You know the look, the one that said shaved ices would be served in the lower hells before he'd let me get within five blocks of that coach.

"Tam, you said someone had to hire horses for that coach. That same living, breathing, solid someone tossed the general's body at my feet. Nukpana's not fully corporeal yet; he needs mortal, flesh-and-blood help, and his helper was in that coach. If I can get in there, I can get his scent, and I can find him."

The stubborn set of Tam's jaw told me he knew I was right. Tam hated it when that happened.

"When did you find the coach?" I tried to keep my eagerness from showing. Tam knew I'd already sunk my teeth into this one. His sigh confirmed it.

"Just before dawn this morning."

"Did anyone see you?"

Tam gave me another look; you know that one, too.

I raised my hands. "Sorry. Of course no one saw you."

"Momentary lapse accepted."

"So you found all this out—the coach, houses, horses—in less than a day?"

Tam smiled. "You're not the only one who can find things people want to keep hidden."

"I never said I was." I stood. "Now, where is that coach?"

"Being watched."

"That's not what I meant, and you know it."

"I know precisely what you mean, and I'm not telling you where it is. It's too close to dark to risk you going anywhere near there. Nukpana may be planning to use that coach again tonight."

"Yeah, and we can't let him."

"And we won't. Three of my men are watching the carriage house. If Nukpana shows, two will follow him; one will report back to me."

I opened my mouth to protest, and Tam held up a hand. "Yes, Mychael does know; and yes, he has provided backup for my men. If Nukpana or his accomplice comes for that coach, he or they will be stopped. And if we're lucky, we can end this tonight."

Lady Luck had stopped speaking to me; I hoped she was on better terms with Tam. Women liked Tam.

Tam's lips turned into a firm line. "If we don't, Sarad may soon have all the help he needs to regenerate himself, highly qualified help. The best nachtmagus in the goblin court arrived late yesterday on a ship from Regor, sent by Sathrik himself. He went directly to the goblin embassy."

King Sathrik Mal'Salin. Goblin king, Nukpana's boss, mildly psychotic, extremely murderous. But then, this was the goblin royal family; crazy was in their blood. Aside from getting Sarad Nukpana back, he wanted to get his hands on me and the Saghred. When Nukpana failed to deliver me, Sathrik set his royal lawyers on me. As far as I knew, they were still slithering their way through Mid's legal system.

"Would Sarad Nukpana trust this nachtmagus?"

"Probably," Tam said. "It's his uncle on his mother's side— Janos Ghalfari."

"Damn."

"Trust me, something stronger would be infinitely more appropriate. I've seen Janos at work. There's nothing he hasn't done, or at least tried; and if he liked it, he did it again. And when he stepped off of that goblin ship, he had Khrynsani temple guards with him."

"Do you think Sarad Nukpana might have gone to the embassy?"

Tam shook his head. "Not a chance. Until he's fully regenerated, he's vulnerable. Rudra Muralin is still goblin ambassador, and both would like nothing more than to see the other dead. No, Nukpana wants and needs privacy right now. He cannot—"

The door opened and a Guardian stepped inside. "There is a lady here to see you. Imala Kalis. She said that you're probably expecting her."

Tam snarled a curse in Goblin under his breath.

Vegard laid a hand casually on the pommel of his sword. "If she's trouble, I can tell her to go away."

"She's most definitely trouble, but no one has ever successfully made her leave."

Vegard grinned in a flash of teeth. "She's never been persuaded by a Guardian."

Tam's laugh was a short bark. "And you've never met the head of the goblin secret service."

Chapter 7

When we'd arrived, the street outside Sirens had been fairly busy. Now not a soul was in sight—except for my Guardians and an equal number of equally well-armed goblins. Goblins were normally tall; these guys were taller than that, and would probably have looked just as big without all that black body armor. It was way too quiet; we were in the middle of a city and the only sound was the uneasy shifting of horses' hooves on the cobbles and the occasional equine snort. That was just wrong.

Everyone was on horseback except for Tam and me and the Guardians who had been inside Sirens. Rathdowne Street was more of a broad boulevard than a street, but it was still entirely too full of armed goblins for my taste.

The sun was down, leaving only the faintest glow, and the streetlamps had been lit. Damn, I hadn't meant to stay this long. Grim-faced Guardians were alert to any move the goblins made or were even thinking about making. I could have cut the tension with a spoon. Somehow I didn't think that the first move was going to be friendly handshakes.

I counted ten goblins in the street in front of Sirens, with a pair guarding—or blocking—both ends of Rathdowne Street. The same number of Guardians had moved to cover them. Mid was under a dusk-to-dawn curfew, so what would have normally been a crowded street in the middle of the entertainment district was conveniently empty of witnesses for whatever was about to happen.

Guardians and city watch patrolled the city to enforce the curfew. Overhead, periodic plumes of fire marked where Guardian sentry dragons prowled the sky over the city, nimble and quick enough that their riders could land pretty much anywhere they wanted. If anything happened down here, any one of the Guardians with me could instantly conjure and launch a flare. Backup was just a fireball away. One of the goblins occasionally glanced skyward. They knew what was up there. It might be a deterrent; it might not.

One horse and its goblin rider were slightly out in front of the others. Since she was the only woman in the group, I assumed that she was Imala Kalis. Unlike some of her men, she didn't look in the least bit tense; in fact, the goblin was smiling. Her face was half in shadow, but since that smile gave everyone a good look at a pair of tiny, white, and obviously sharp fangs, her intention could have been anything. But it had been my experience that social calls generally weren't made with an armed escort. Imala Kalis could have brought two dozen mounted and heavily armed men with her for protection, or it could have been for persuasion. My bet was on the latter.

"You're not going to invite me inside, Tam?" Imala Kalis's voice was like a silk-covered stiletto.

"You, possibly," Tam said coolly. "Your muscle, highly unlikely."

"You've refused my invitations, so if I wished to speak with you, you left me no choice but to come to your place of business. And considering the present political climate, I could hardly make a social call by myself."

I stepped out of the shadows to stand next to Tam. I was certain he'd prefer if I stayed out of sight, but I wanted a closer look at Imala Kalis—and I wanted her to get a closer look at me. My family doesn't like being intimidated, and while I knew Tam didn't intimidate, I wasn't going to stand in the shadows while the lady played her little games. I'd ditched the fake blades; my own razor-sharp ones were now strapped in clear view across my back. Imala Kalis's guards shifted uneasily at the sign of an armed elf. I didn't hide my magical power; I didn't flaunt it, either. It never hurts to let them know you're packing.

Imala Kalis didn't look uneasy or even a wee bit nervous. Her smile just got wider. "Mistress Benares, I presume."

I bared my teeth to match hers. "Presumption correct."

"I expected you to be taller." She swung a graceful leg over her horse's neck and dismounted, landing lightly on the cobbles.

Damned if she wasn't shorter than I was. The streetlamps gave me a good look at her face. I have to admit I was surprised there, too. The head of the goblin secret service, the agent at the top of the ladder, the lady in the big office was . . . well, cute.

Her face was oval, delicate, and pretty. It'd been my experience that goblin women were tall and coldly beautiful. Imala Kalis was petite and perky. She looked like someone's cute little sister, someone's cute and deadly little sister. And I wasn't the only one packing magic. Imala Kalis had nowhere near the level of talent that the Saghred had cursed me with, but it was obvious that she knew her way around a spell or two. She might be petite, but magically speaking she was no lightweight. Large, dark eyes shone with a keen intelligence and secrets, lots of secrets. One look at this lady told me that she probably had schemes and plots piled on top of motives, and she didn't bother with alibis, or care who she had to kill. In other words, a perfect goblin.

Imala Kalis stepped forward and extended her hand. It was gloved; so was mine. A handshake between mages was more than a greeting. Skin-on-skin contact combined with a quick questing spell could let a mage assess the true power of another. That was one reason when mages got together there was a lot of head nodding and bowing going on.

I took two steps and accepted her hand, and there were hisses, a couple of growls, and one "shit" when I did it. The last one came from Vegard. I shook Imala Kalis's hand because I wanted to and it would be rude not to. I also had three reasons why it was perfectly safe. One, I was wearing thick gloves; two, thanks to the Saghred, I was packing more than enough power to protect myself; and three, if Imala Kalis tried a questing spell on me, I'd be using my fist on her.

She looked in my eyes, and I think she knew all three. Her smile turned into a grin, and I swear the woman had dimples. A cute killer goblin with dimples. Damn.

"You are not what I expected, Mistress Benares." She actually looked happy about that.

"You're not exactly what I envisioned, either."

"I get that comment quite often."

"I'm sure you do." And looking into those sharp, intelligent eyes, anyone would be making a fatal mistake if they underestimated her for one second. I wondered if those dimples had been the last thing some people had seen before being dispatched to their great reward. I shrugged. "What you see is what I am."

"I very much doubt that." Imala Kalis raised her voice to address her men. "Gentlemen, this is the lady who tricked Sarad Nukpana into feeding himself to the Saghred."

The goblins with her grinned; a few chuckled darkly. I wasn't sure if either was a good thing since both involved me seeing a lot of fangs. If a goblin wanted to kill you, they would prefer a single, efficient slash or stab; but like I said, in a down-and-dirty fight, they would use their fangs to fatal effect. I'd seen the aftermath before; it wasn't pretty.

Tam stepped forward to stand at my side, so close I could feel his tense disapproval. He didn't want me here.

"There is no love lost between the secret service and Sarad Nukpana—and his Khrynsani," he explained. His voice was preternaturally calm, which meant that Tam wasn't.

"Not to put too fine a point on it, Mistress Benares," Imala Kalis said without taking her bright black eyes from Tam. "We each curse the ground the other walks on."

I assumed she was talking about Nukpana and the Khrynsani, not Tam, but I wasn't entirely sure.

Tam didn't bat an eye. "It's one of the few viewpoints we have ever agreed upon."

Score one point for Imala Kalis's people, though I wasn't going to be in a hurry to give them any more. Like I said, she hadn't brought that many guards with her because she was afraid of being mugged. This tiny woman didn't get to where she was by being afraid of much, if anything. Tam towered over her by a good foot, and she showed no sign of stepping back; if anything, the lady looked challenged and happy about it.

"It is indeed convenient that you are here, Mistress Benares," she said. "I've been asked to deliver this to you."

She drew an intricately folded piece of parchment out of her sleekly tailored doublet and extended it to me.

I made no move to touch it. "And this is from . . ."

"Ambassador Rudra Muralin." Imala Kalis flashed her dainty fangs. "Excuse me, my mistake—Ambassador Rudra *Mal'Salin*. False identities are so inconvenient to remember."

Imala Kalis hadn't forgotten a thing. I knew it and so did she. Rudra Muralin was a thousand-year-old goblin, the blackest of dark mages who had used the Saghred to slaughter thousands and enslave thousands more.

Rudra Muralin wanted the Saghred. He needed me dead.

Any old death would do just as long as he was the first mage to reach the rock after my untimely demise.

I still made no move to touch Rudra's letter. "It's been opened."

Imala Kalis laughed. "Of course it has. First I had to break the spell, then the seal. It was a nasty one, too."

"Hardly surprising. Then you've read it."

"Yes, it was the most direct way to confirm what else he's up to. The contents are no surprise to me—as I doubt they will be to you. My advice is to read it, burn it, and ignore it. His assurances are lies and his promises poison."

I took the parchment and, after muttering a quick shielding spell, I unfolded the paper, holding it so Tam could read along with me.

Imala Kalis was right; Rudra's letter contained the same demands, though he had made the effort to spin a new, sick twist on them. He still wanted me and the Saghred. And like Sarad Nukpana, Rudra knew about the umi'atsu bond between me, Tam, Mychael, and the Saghred. And the only way to stop him from posting an announcement on the citadel's front doors would be for me to surrender to him.

Come to the goblin embassy alone and your secret is safe. If you come to me, Tamnais and Mychael will not be exposed. Refuse me and you will all die—and I will still get what I want. It will merely take longer. I offer you the opportunity to save Tamnais and Mychael. They would give their lives for you. Would you give your soul for them?

Several weeks ago, Tam, Mychael, and I had used the power we could generate and share through our umi'atsu bond to close a Hellgate that Rudra Muralin and his black mage allies had opened. Imala Kalis had been there in the shadows, watching. She knew what we'd done—and how we'd done it.

My first impulse was to mutter a fire spell and torch the offending piece of parchment. As usual, Rudra didn't sign it, so it was worthless as evidence against him, but Mychael would want to see it, so I folded it and put it in the small leather purse on my belt. No way was I tucking anything Rudra had touched inside my doublet. If I were Imala Kalis, when I went home, I'd take a bath.

As to what I was going to do about it—bottom line was that I didn't like being bullied. When I was a kid, being small meant I'd been a target; being a Benares meant deadly backup was a whistle away. The only thing I hated more than a bully was asking someone to protect me from one. I took on my own bullies, thank you very much—even if they were thousand-year-old, obscenely powerful psychotic megalomaniacs.

"Vintage Rudra," I noted dryly. "I give him what he wants and he promises to kill me nicely." I looked directly at Imala Kalis. "And are you here to tell me the same thing?"

She gazed at me a moment, her expression unreadable. "I am not. I have no intentions of revealing the contents of that letter."

"Don't take this the wrong way, but that's one of those things that I'll believe when I don't see it."

"Considering who and what the two of us are, I expected no less. I'm not asking for your belief or trust; though you will know soon enough that my words are the truth."

"That would be nice, but I'm not going to hold my breath for it."

She shrugged. "Were I in your place, I would do the same." She gave me a small, self-satisfied smile. "And do not concern yourself with Rudra Muralin. The ambassador will be unable to act on any of his threats for at least the next three days."

"Three days?"

Cute turned to fierce. "Rudra Muralin poisoned two of my people. They nearly died. Naturally, I retaliated. Three days is the length of time it takes to recover from a particular intestinal malady caused by a certain tasteless and odorless plant. Several of the ambassador's closest advisors have mysteriously contracted it and are spending most of their time in the privy." She smiled fully. "Whenever the ambassador wants advice, he has to go to where his advisors are. He's quite unused to carrying out a plan without his lackeys. Your secret is safe for at least that long."

Tam laughed. "Rudra forced to plot in the privy. If it weren't for the stench, I'd almost pay to see that."

"Unfortunately, Rudra didn't eat the fish that night," Imala Kalis told him. "I knew I should have put it in the beef." She shrugged. "He has to eat again sometime. If he wishes to avoid an embassy-wide case of the runs, he will come to terms with me."

"Terms?"

"I will accept nothing short of his resignation, then I will personally see him on a ship back to Regor—or to Hell for all I care."

"Didn't King Sathrik appoint him personally?" I asked.

"As head of the secret service, Imala outranks a mere ambassador," Tam informed me.

Nice.

"And Sathrik knows of your botanical activities?" I asked Imala.

The cute smile was back. "It is not my intention to tell him."

"You know who and what and how old Rudra Muralin is, right?" I asked her.

"I make it my business to know my enemies, Mistress Benares—to know what strengths can be turned against them and which weaknesses may be exploited. I think I would refer to that creature as a 'what,' not a 'who.'"

I grinned at her. I couldn't help it. I didn't know why Imala Kalis was here or what she wanted, but I had to admit that the lady had style. "Rudra with the runs; that would be priceless."

"Since he has a food taster whom I do not wish to harm, I've now tainted his soap. He's especially fond of bathing."

"Are the contents of that letter why you're here?" Tam asked Imala Kalis.

I knew he meant her knowing about our umi'atsu bond.

"No." She lowered her voice. "It is not in my best interests, or yours, for the contents of that letter to become public."

"When will it be in your best interests?" Frost rolled off of Tam's words.

"Never."

"I don't believe you."

"I didn't expect you to. I'm here to help you. And if we can stop standing in the middle of the street, I can tell you why."

Tam lowered his voice. "You can tell me right here."

"And if I refuse?" Her words were playful but her eyes weren't.

"Then Raine and I will go inside—and you and your men will leave."

All signs of cute instantly vanished. "This is not a topic you want discussed openly."

"I'll decide that," Tam countered smoothly. "Tell me what—"

There was a whistle and a thump and a goblin guard's eyes went wide in pain and shock. He slid from horse to the street, a crossbow bolt embedded in his back. Two of the goblins posted at the end of the street were next. Then the air was thick with shouts and bolts.

I caught a flash of one of the shooters on a roof across the street. Dark clothes, with a tight, dark hood over his head.

The goblins nearest Imala Kalis instantly surrounded her, forming a goblin and equine shield around their boss. Tam and Vegard moved to protect me. They needn't have bothered. I was in the shadows of Sirens before they could pull me there. I didn't want to be turned into a pincushion, and I did want to know who was trying to make me one.

Vegard's hands glowed incandescent white. The glow turned to white flame, spinning faster than the eye could follow into a whirling ball of fire. One shot skyward, a flare blazing straight up into the night sky. Vegard held the second fireball in his hand and scanned the rooftops. His lips curled back from his teeth in a feral snarl as he hurled it at the roofline of a nightclub across the street. A sniper erupted in burning white light and fell screaming three stories down to the street. There wasn't much left when he landed. A blast of flame from a sentry dragon circling in the skies above the city signaled that Vegard's flare had been seen. A second and a third dragon responded to the call. Backup was on the way, but would there be anything left of us when they got here?

A voice shouted three words from above us, each with its own discordant pitch and vibrating with a power that charged the air like the aftermath of a lightning strike. It was magic—raw, potent, and dangerous.

Talon.

Oh hell, kid. Not now.

I looked up to see Talon leaning out of a window two stories above us, his eyes fixed on a figure in the shadows not a dozen feet from where we were standing.

Shit.

I drew blades and the man didn't move; I mean, he didn't move at all. He had a crossbow, it was loaded, but it was only half-raised. The man was frozen. Not with a paralysis spell; I knew the residuals of a paralysis spell. This wasn't it. It was as if Talon had stopped time for him.

That was impossible.

Tam saw what his son had done, and from the nearly sick expression on his face, I knew it was something Talon had no business doing, especially not with a street full of goblin secret service agents.

Talon nimbly swung out of the window and onto a fire escape ladder attached to the stone wall. The kid wasn't coming down to us; he was running up that ladder to the roof.

Now it was my turn to feel sick. There were snipers up there and Talon was going after them. Alone. Recently Talon had taken on a major demon with his voice, and at that moment I'd known that the kid's spellsongs weren't limited to making Sirens' clientele horny.

This was a deadly skill—and an inexperienced, impulsive teenager who had no clue of his own mortality had it.

We had to get up to that roof.

Two more goblins lay motionless in the street, their riderless horses adding to the chaos. As I watched, a Guardian went down. They had all shielded themselves with war magic so strong it was like a wall between them and whatever tried to get through. Solid work. The bolts passed through like there was nothing there. That meant there was magic of the blackest kind involved.

A hood did more than hide a face; it hid skin color and ears.

"Khrynsani!" shouted one of the goblins.

Tam shot an infuriated glance at Sirens' roof, flung open the doors, and ran inside.

I was on his heels with Vegard right behind me. I sheathed my blades and checked my throwing daggers. I was going to bag myself a sniper. Alive would be good; I had some questions for the bastard, but dead would be perfectly acceptable.

I ran across the theatre floor toward the stage; that is, until Tam's arm went around my waist and snatched me off my feet.

"Just where do you think—"

I twisted in his arms, putting us face-to-face. I pointed straight up. "Same place you're going."

"I'm going to the roof; you're staying here." Tam released me and ran to the bar, reaching behind it to pull out the wickedest crossbow I'd ever seen and a quarrel of bolts big enough to take down a sentry dragon.

I whistled. "Got another one of—"

"No!" Tam stalked past me and leapt to the stage in one smooth move. The stage was nearly shoulder-high on me so I had to run around to the stairs.

"Vegard, keep Raine down here," Tam shouted back without turning. He was headed backstage and to the ladder that went to the catwalk above the stage and to the roof.

Not without me, he wasn't. I think Tam realized that he couldn't keep me from following him and get to the roof at the same time, and Vegard wasn't about to sit this one out. By going up on that roof, he could protect me and get his hands on a Khrynsani at the same time. Tam slung the straps of the bow and quarrel over his shoulders and climbed that ladder quicker than a man could run up a flight of stairs.

"Those sentry dragons are going to torch anything on that roof," Vegard said from behind me. "And if they're Khrynsani, they're goblins, and our men won't be able to tell the difference between them and Talon."

Tam swore and climbed faster.

I couldn't catch Tam, but I could almost keep up. "We need one alive." Though Nachtmagus Kalta could probably have a conversation with a dead one just as easily, and we'd be spared the annoyance of leaving a Khrynsani among the living. But in my family, killing someone you needed information from was just sloppy work. I was going to get a sniper, neat and tidy. He might have a neat hole or two in him, but he'd still be able to talk.

The ladder ended in the kind of door I didn't want to see. It wasn't a door; it was a hatch. It looked metal, and being on a roof meant it was probably heavy. Something or someone could be on top of it or next to it. That meant anyone trying to get through would have their head sticking up for about a split second too long if there was an alert sniper on the other side.

Tam slowed as he neared the top of the ladder, his boots making no sound as he stopped just short of the hatch. I stopped about five rungs below him. If Tam needed to come back down quickly, I'd worry about how to get out of his way then. Tam had the wicked crossbow, not me. It was the roof of his nightclub that a sniper was using as his killing perch—and it was his son up there. By rights, it was his takedown.

I was in the middle of hoping that the hinges had been oiled recently, when the hatch was flung open above Tam's head.

I knew Tam was fast, but damn. One second his crossbow was slung over his shoulder; the next he put a bolt straight up through the opening. A grunt and the thud of a body hitting the roof told me that not only had some idiot opened the hatch; he'd bent over to take a peek inside.

Since stealth had just been shot to hell, Tam leapt out onto the roof, a solid shield of red surrounding him. He just stood there, unmoving, not firing, glowing red, and scanning the rooftop. He held his crossbow ready, but he didn't fire; he also didn't call out the all clear.

"What is it?" I asked Tam in mindspeak. About the only good thing about the umi'atsu bond that Tam and I shared was the ability to communicate silently. That had come in handy recently.

"Talon's got one." Even Tam's mindspeak was the barest whisper.

I knew why.

Spellsong magic was dependent on sound: tone and pitch. Vocal or direct magical interference could negate a spellsong or send it snapping back at the singer. A master spellsinger could block out interference.

Talon wasn't a master. At least I didn't think so.

I shielded myself and scrambled as quickly and silently as I could through the hatch before Tam could think to close it on me. Vegard emerged a split second after I did. From the shouts down below, Imala Kalis and her people were still under attack, but no one was firing on them from Sirens' roof.

Tam hadn't taken cover behind anything because there was absolutely zero cover up here. If we lived through tonight, I was sure Tam would rectify that oversight.

Talon had a sniper frozen, unmoving, unblinking, unaware. With a paralysis spell, the subject had no clue what was happening. Like I'd said, it was as if the kid had frozen time.

Talon was unwholesomely handsome, a slightly smaller version of his father. The only difference was Talon's paler gray skin and aquamarine eyes courtesy of his elven mother.

The kid's voice was silk, descending in tone and pitch until he held a single deep note and then carefully let it evaporate in the air.

I reached for my blades. To stop a spellsong is to stop the spell.

Talon's spell held and the sniper didn't as much as blink.

It should have been impossible, but unless my eyes were

lying to me, it was all too possible, and Talon had done it easily.

With an ease that said it clearly wasn't the first time he'd done it.

Talon sounded pleased with himself. "Don't worry," he told Tam. "I got this one; you got the other. End of problem. It was just the two of them up here."

What Tam was worried and angry about wasn't snipers on his roof, but what his son had just done and who might have seen him do it. Tam's fear was a palpable thing in the air. The only thing Tam had ever been truly afraid of was having someone he loved in danger. I sensed that fear now for Talon.

Tam's voice was a tight, enraged whisper. "I've told you never to—"

"Keep a killer from putting a bolt in your back?" Talon retorted, never taking his eyes off of his subject. Apparently singing wasn't necessary to maintain the spell, but concentration was.

Vegard had a pair of slender manacles in his hands and was quickly but carefully approaching the frozen sniper. Get him cuffed, and Talon could let him go.

"Never to expose yourself needlessly," Tam snapped.

"This wasn't needless."

"In your opinion. Don't you ever—"

"What? Save your life?"

"You just showed the head of the goblin secret service and her top agents exactly what you're capable of—and any Khrynsani who might have seen you."

Talon blanched. "Oh shit."

"Yes, it is," Tam readily agreed. "And you've jumped in it with both feet."

Vegard cuffed one of the sniper's wrists and was prying the crossbow out of his hand. That done, he cuffed both hands behind the man's back. With him frozen like that I'd expected him to be stiff as a board, but his body was still pliant, just staring and unresponsive. Vegard jerked the hood off of his head.

An elf.

Oh hell. Not just any elf. A Nightshade.

Talon just sank in that metaphorical crap heap up to his neck.

Nightshades were assassins, kidnappers, blackmailers, or whatever they had been given enough gold to do. You pay, they'll play. And to get a Nightshade in a playful mood took more gold than could be had outside of either a vast personal fortune—or a government treasury.

The air moved, brushing the skin on the back of my neck.

We weren't alone.

Just because I couldn't see, hear, or smell him didn't mean he wasn't there, watching us. He was; I could feel it. And he had been the entire time.

"A veil." I sent the thought to Tam. *"A good one."* Recently some demons had used veils to hide themselves. Thanks to the boost my magic had picked up from the Saghred, I'd been able to see them just fine. It was night, the sniper was probably wearing black, but he shouldn't be invisible, at least not to me.

A prickling of magic was all the warning we got.

Tam fired a bolt that blazed red like a comet at the spot where the man had to be. Something batted it harmlessly aside with no more effort than swatting a fly.

Then came a laugh, taunting and confident.

And familiar.

Banan Ryce had always been a cocky bastard.

The Nightshade commander dropped the veil and with a tug and dramatic flourish pulled off the hood covering his head. The streetlamps gave me enough light to know it was Banan. I didn't need any more light to remember what he looked like: dark hair, tanned skin, pale green eyes, crooked smile, and the morals of a horny demon with an hour to live.

He had an absurdly large crossbow leveled on yours truly. "Consorting with goblins again, Raine?"

I indicated the bow. "Compensating for something, Banan?"

"Your half-breed spawn is indeed gifted, Nathrach."

Tam controlled himself. I knew it took nearly everything he had not to close the distance between them and rip Banan's head off.

Banan kept going. "My employers are going to be thrilled to know what tricks your mongrel can do."

Talon snapped three words—the same words he'd used on the sniper in the street.

Banan laughed as they bounced harmlessly off of his shields.

"Nice try, boy. If I had a treat, I'd toss you one." Then he smiled like this was the happiest moment of his life.

Then he fired.

And I trusted my backup.

Shooters usually expect you to dive left or right. I did neither, instead diving down and straight toward Banan as Tam and Vegard opened up on him. With our umi'atsu bond, I didn't have to tell Tam what I was going to do; he knew it as I thought it. It was teamwork at its finest.

Banan's shield was solid, but regardless of how strong they were, shields extended only so far. Tam kept him occupied with a blur of magic-spawned red needles while I worked on that shield. I wasn't pounding my way through it; I was going under it, not to attack Banan, but to let my magic eat that shield from the inside out.

We were near the edge of Sirens' roof. Banan had nothing at his back but a three-story drop and at least twenty feet of air between him and the roof of the next building. I didn't sense any warded Nightshade reinforcements. Banan was up here all by his lonesome. I didn't like it, trust it, or really believe it, but I didn't have time to go hunting for what probably wasn't there. Banan first; look for invisible bogeymen later.

Vegard kept up the fireballs, coin-sized and blazing white, and maneuvered to get around Banan and his shield.

In a flash of sizzling green light, Banan's shield wrapped him in a protective bubble, no seams, no openings, no way in.

Dammit.

Impressive work. Too impressive for Banan; he didn't have that kind of power.

He laughed and looked at me—with eyes of red flame.

Oh hell.

Banan Ryce had a guest; and unlike the possessed naked guy, Banan had invited the specter in.

Hellfire and damnation.

Banan chuckled. "Surprise." He shifted and I could see the specter, floating like a glowing reflection beneath his skin. Banan's shield glowed brighter. I felt Tam's power building behind me; he was going to hit Banan once with everything he had. Normally that'd make Banan a greasy spot on Tam's roof, but I wasn't so sure about now. Neither was Tam, but he was going to try anyway.

"I'd like you all to meet my new partner, Alastair Kratos."

Tam spat a single curse in Goblin.

Banan smirked. "Magus Kratos feels much the same way about you, goblin."

The son of a bitch was reading our minds.

"Quite right, Raine, with a little assistance from Magus Kratos. He knows all about you."

I didn't know who the hell Alastair Kratos was, but Tam obviously did. And an instant later, he'd shared the sickening knowledge with me mind-to-mind. With goblins and elves, the hatred and the resulting atrocities went both ways. During yet another war between the two races, Alastair Kratos thought that simply killing goblin captives was a wasted opportunity. He was the chief healer in the elven army. He called himself a healer; history called him a monster. He considered the acts he performed on goblin captives, mostly children, medical experiments. It was torture, gleefully sadistic torture.

"And he looks forward to continuing his work," Banan

told us. He glanced at Talon. "A half-breed so uniquely gifted would provide weeks of study—if he lives that long. Magus Kratos despises goblins, but necessity creates alliances where there would only be animosity. Sarad Nukpana didn't choose Magus Kratos as an ally inside the Saghred because of his sparkling personality; he chose those who were the most powerful, those who, when the opportunity came, stood the best chance of escaping the Saghred. Now that he is no longer imprisoned, Magus Kratos is free to form partnerships more to his liking."

"A sadistic monster and a murderer for hire," I noted. "A match made in Hell."

"Let's just say we share many of the same goals. My men and I didn't come here tonight to kill you or your hopeful goblin lover. Seeing his young spawn at play was an added bonus. Others have plans for you, and for the moment we've been asked not to interfere. For now. I'm here tonight to eliminate one goblin bitch."

As if in response, Imala Kalis's enraged shouts carried up to us from the street. I'd always said that if you needed to do any quality swearing, Goblin was the way to go. Imala Kalis was most creative in her use of her native language.

"An impressive display." Banan admitted. "Apparently her guards were equally impressive. Oh well, we're prepared to make more than one attempt." He flashed a grin. "Time for Plan B."

And he stepped off the roof.

We ran to the edge in time to see Banan land catlike on the street and disappear into the dark of an alley.

Three stories below.

A jump like that should have killed him; apparently being possessed gives you more than just an invisible friend.

Tam spat the same word again.

I couldn't have agreed more.

•   •   •

On the street in front of Sirens were two sentry dragons, and a gratifying number of city watchmen. Chief Watcher Sedge Rinker had his hands full with an infuriated Imala Kalis.

"We come here in peace to speak with our countryman, only to be attacked by elves on neutral ground." Imala Kalis was toe-to-toe with Sedge Rinker. Sedge wasn't the type to back off, but he looked rather taken aback at her cold fury.

Sedge wasn't just Mid's chief watcher; he was also good people. He didn't get to be chief by sitting behind a desk all day. He was a consummate professional, knew his business, and cared about the safety of his citizens.

Tam saw and swore. One of Imala Kalis's guards thought to stop him, then he saw the expression on Tam's face and stepped aside. Sedge spotted Tam and made a quick half bow and murmured a few words to a stunned Imala Kalis. I guess the lady didn't have much experience being cut off in mid-rant.

Sedge met Tam in the middle of the street, looking like a man with bad news. I heard the chief watcher's words. We all did.

"Tamnais Nathrach, you're under arrest for the kidnapping and murder of General Daman Aratus."

Chapter 8

"Sedge, he's innocent and you know it." It took every bit of self-control I had not to scream those words. I wouldn't help Tam if I did something dumb and got myself locked up in the cell next to his.

I had enough trouble on my hands with Talon.

Naturally, he'd insisted on coming with us, and now Vegard was faced with the challenge of keeping both me and Talon out of jail. I didn't want Talon to hear what I was saying and possibly do something even more impulsive and arrestworthy than what I knew he was already thinking. Vegard agreed with me, so he and Talon were in Sedge's conference room next to his office. Vegard had the door cracked so he could see and hear everything going on in the watchers' squad room.

My Guardian bodyguard was getting his eyes and ears full.

Sedge Rinker blew out his breath. "Raine, I've had multiple witnesses report that they saw Tam force General Aratus into a coach. An hour later the general's body was tossed into the street. As chief watcher, I can't ignore that."

I glanced at Tam. He was leaning against the back wall of a cell crackling with wards; the same cell that had held three demons just weeks before. He was leaning back, arms crossed, one ankle crossed over the other, looking completely relaxed. Tam's leisurely pose might have been an act—or it might have been confidence. I'd seen Tam tear through stronger wards before, with a lot nastier magical manpower waiting outside the cell. Tam went in because he was being a law-abiding citizen. For now. But if anyone came near his son, I knew all bets were off and it would be ugly.

And two of those so-called witnesses were standing in the squad room right now.

I couldn't speak to Tam with my voice or mind-to-mind with our bond. The wards prevented both. Tam was doing the cool, confident, and cocky act because he had the men responsible for putting him behind those wards in sight, and a couple rips of those wards would put them within reach. Tam's slight smile told me he was probably entertaining himself with the thoughts of what he was going to do to Carnades Silvanus and Taltek Balmorlan when he got his hands on them. And since Carnades and Balmorlan had waited until Tam was safely locked away before making their grand entrance, the elf bastards knew that fact only too well.

I was in Sedge Rinker's office. It was in the corner of the squad room, and the two walls facing the room were glass. It let Sedge keep an eye on things, but tonight it was also letting people keep an eye on us. I didn't give a damn. I hadn't been arrested, but I'd been asked politely, yet firmly, to come to watcher headquarters to give a statement. Oh boy, was I giving Sedge a statement. The walls may have been glass, but the door was closed and I was taking full advantage.

"Raine, my instincts agree with you; unfortunately, the proof and witnesses say otherwise."

"Proof," I spat. "Some elves saying they saw a goblin shove the general into a coach? One of them even said, 'All goblins look alike.' The moron. Sarad Nukpana is a goblin, and he killed the general."

"Raine, I need proof."

"I saw him driving that coach last night, and I heard his voice through General Aratus's corpse." My voice turned bitter. "But my word is worthless, isn't it? You can't take the word of a Benares and Saghred bond servant, can you?"

"I believe you, Raine."

"Then let Tam go!" I managed between clenched teeth.

"I can't do that, and you know why."

I knew why all right. A handful of elven witnesses under compulsion by a certain high-ranking elven mage. Carnades Silvanus was the golden boy of the Seat of Twelve, the mages governing the Conclave, and he was one step away from being the next archmagus. He'd had the job for a few days recently, acquired a taste for self-righteous retribution, and had been well on his way to becoming a one-man inquisition.

And he had an expert at inquisition and intimidation standing right next to him. Taltek Balmorlan hadn't taken his eyes off of me since he and Carnades had slithered through the front doors.

You could see Taltek Balmorlan in a room and look right past him—which was exactly what the elven inquisitor wanted. The word that described him best was average. His hair and eyes were an unremarkable shade of dull brown. He was of average height with average looks. There was absolutely nothing remarkable about his appearance.

It was perfect camouflage for the predator he was.

One of Carnades's "witnesses" was an elven shopkeeper who said he had seen Tam force the general into a coach. When questioned as to why he hadn't come forward until now, the elf had claimed goblin intimidation. If Tam's life hadn't been at stake, that statement would have been laughable. Unless the elven ambassador had personally delivered an announcement to the goblin embassy—which would happen as soon as flavored ices were being served in the lower hells—there weren't any goblins other than Sarad Nukpana and his accomplice who had even known that the general was dead.

I resisted the urge to hit something. "Pay someone enough and they'll say they saw their mother do it." Another "witness" was a clearly frightened elderly elven mage in shabby robes who stood as far away from Carnades and Balmorlan and as close to the front doors, and escape, as he could. "Or threaten them."

And I had no doubt that the black-silk-and-velvet-robed mage essentially holding court in the center of the squad room would have done that and more to get Tam behind bars and wards. Carnades Silvanus looked like his birthday had come early this year.

No doubt Carnades believed himself to be the pinnacle of elven fine breeding. The elf's shoulder-length hair was the color of winter frost, and his eyes the pale blue of arctic ice. His face was like flawless alabaster, a cold, sharp beauty. He was a pure-blooded high elf and he wasn't about to let anyone forget it.

Carnades had served as Conclave emissary to the goblin court at the same time that Tam had been the queen's magical right-hand man. Something that happened during that time— and knowing Tam, probably more than one something—had made Carnades despise Tam even more than he hated every other goblin who breathed his air. Tam didn't exactly harbor warm feelings toward Carnades, so the animosity was more than mutual.

And from the sound of the charges, Carnades was getting his revenge for any slight or insult, either real or imagined, in one fell swoop.

The elven mage wasn't satisfied by seeing Tam charged with the kidnapping and grisly murder of the fourth-highest-ranking general in the elf queen's army. He was accusing Tam of having fed General Aratus's soul to the Saghred. When asked to explain, Carnades just smiled wider and Balmorlan coolly said that an expert would arrive soon to substantiate the claim. No one other than the rock itself could tell whether it had been fed or not. Carnades and Balmorlan were lying, and soon someone was going to walk through those doors and lie some more. The elf bastards couldn't prove a damned thing; but their smug smiles told me that they'd found a way around that impediment to vigilante justice called the truth, and what I had been dreading was about to happen. Carnades knew that Tam could have only fed the Saghred through me.

Through our umi'atsu bond.

Carnades knew all about it.

He hadn't ratted us out. Yet. The self-righteous elf was saving it for just the right moment—much like Sarad Nukpana's gift of a dried corpse.

From the smug expression on his face, that moment had come.

I knew that General Aratus's soul was inside Sarad Nukpana, not the Saghred. But just as Carnades couldn't prove that the Saghred had been fed, I couldn't prove that it hadn't. And Mychael and I had been the only ones to hear Sarad Nukpana's threats spoken through the general's dried corpse. I couldn't tell Sedge Rinker that. The only way Mychael had heard those threats was through the part of the umi'atsu bond that I shared with him.

After Tam had been arrested, Vegard had ordered one of the Guardians on sentry dragon patrol to return immediately to the citadel and tell Mychael what had happened.

I pinched the bridge of my nose against the headache that was well on its way. Mychael would probably be here any minute, and when he got here, that would put him in the same room with me and Tam. Our proximity to one another would leave no doubt about the bond the three of us shared. Any and every mage in the room would know.

Which was precisely what Carnades wanted.

I wasn't about to leave Tam alone in the same room with Carnades.

The elf mage knew that, too. He also wanted everyone to know what he already did—the paladin of the Conclave Guardians was in an umi'atsu bond with a goblin dark mage and accused murderer, and the bond servant of the Saghred. If it were proven, Mychael would be arrested, tried, and executed; and Tam and I wouldn't be far behind him.

Carnades had seen the proof of our joint powers two weeks ago when Mychael, Tam, and I had worked together to close a Hellgate that had been opened on the island. Phaelan had clubbed him over the head with a rock to keep him from exposing the three of us right then and there. Markus Sevelien had visited Carnades the moment his ship had docked. Mychael had sources in Carnades's household, and those sources reported that Markus told Carnades to stay home and see no one. Either Markus had rescinded that order, or Carnades was feeling rebellious this evening.

And for the icing on the cake, Taltek Balmorlan reported to Markus and now seemed to be Carnades's new best friend. Best friends didn't keep secrets. Balmorlan knew about our umi'atsu bond; I was certain of it. What he was going to do about it remained to be seen, but from his self-satisfied smirk, he couldn't be happier with how things were playing out.

There was a cell waiting next to Tam's that had Mychael's name written all over it.

Or mine.

Dammit. Mychael knew I was here with Tam, yet he was coming down here anyway. He knew it was a trap and he was walking right into it. Mychael was coolheaded and a tactician; I told myself that he would never walk into a trap without a plan to spring it on its maker. I was sure he had a plan, a good one. I'd just feel a hell of a lot better if I knew what that plan was.

If it came down to it, I would do anything I had to do to keep Tam and Mychael from the executioner's block. The Benares in me had a few ideas; the Saghred in me had a few more.

I would do whatever it took, and whatever it did to me didn't matter.

Mychael had told me once that if anyone wanted his head on an executioner's block, they'd have to fight him for the privilege. Sounded good to me.

"Magus Silvanus has requested that I take you into custody as an accessory before and after the fact." Sedge sounded almost apologetic.

"Are you?"

"No. He has no proof or witnesses to substantiate his charge."

I barked a short laugh. "Give him another hour; I'm sure he'll come up with something and someone."

I looked out at Carnades. He must have sensed me and turned toward Sedge's office. Our eyes met. I'd given Carnades the benefit of a doubt ever since I'd met him; hell, I'd even saved his life twice. He was through playing games. Well, so was I. He had lied and manipulated his way into having Tam caged like an animal, and he wouldn't stop until he'd done the same to me and Mychael. Though the one thing he wouldn't be lying about was that Mychael shared an umi'atsu bond with me and Tam. That Mychael had done it to save both of us wouldn't matter to Carnades and his ilk. Once Mychael was proven to be a criminal, Justinius Valerian's political power base would be weakened. He'd handpicked Mychael as paladin; his judgment would be suspect.

Carnades Silvanus had taken the first steps to getting himself elected archmagus. If that happened, he would have the power of life or death over every magic user in the seven kingdoms, and the Guardians would be reduced to his personal enforcers.

It had to stop. Tonight. Now. This was war; my gloves were off.

I gave Carnades a slow, cold smile that told him that and much more. If Tam could act cool and confident, so could I. In reality I was scared shitless and mad as hell, but considering how close I was to a whole row of empty cells, I thought I'd keep that to myself for now. I could always let my rage out to play later. I didn't want to, but if Carnades pushed me too far, I would push back. He'd seen the Saghred's full power in me when I'd crushed a demon the size of a small house, right here in this very room. He knew what I could do, but he thought I wouldn't do it. If he laid a hand on Tam or Mychael, I'd show him just how wrong he was.

I opened the door and walked out into the squad room. I

vaguely heard Vegard order Talon to stay put. Like that was going to happen, though I hoped the kid showed some sense for once and did as told.

Normally Vegard would be trying to keep me from saying or doing anything to Carnades or Balmorlan that I'd regret later. Not this time. He knew that whatever I did, I'd have no regrets. Vegard was as pissed off and fed up as I was. His solid and reassuring presence at my left shoulder told me, without saying a word, that whatever I wanted to start, he'd help me finish. I got a lump in my throat and forced it down. Hugging Vegard would definitely ruin my badass Saghred-wielder act.

I still had my blades, every last one of them. Since I hadn't been officially arrested, Sedge hadn't ordered my weapons be taken. I stopped when I got about ten feet from Carnades Silvanus and Taltek Balmorlan. I didn't trust myself to get any closer. And to tell you the truth, I didn't want to be any closer to them. I'd rather touch a dried-up corpse.

When I spoke, my voice was cool and conversational. "So you boys don't believe Sarad Nukpana has gone on a high-elf killing spree?"

"I believe that he's a convenient scapegoat for the crimes perpetrated by you and your goblin lover," Carnades said smoothly. "You even carry goblin weapons."

"Because they kill better than elf blades." I gave him a tight smile. "I only use the best."

"You've always preferred the company of goblins, haven't you, Mistress Benares?" Balmorlan said smoothly. Hell, even his voice was bland.

"I certainly prefer them to elves like the two of you. In fact, I don't know of any elf who wouldn't."

"You have quite the reputation among several of our agents for succeeding where they have failed," Balmorlan noted. "Goblin prisons are notoriously difficult to break into, some would even say impossible, but you have done it on more than one occasion and made it look almost easy."

"I'm a Benares, remember? Jail breaking is in our blood."

"I don't believe your success was due to skill either as a criminal or a seeker. I believe, as do others, that you had goblin allies inside those prisons. You believe that Markus Sevelien retained your services because of your criminal tendencies, but no doubt he knew precisely what was going on. He didn't care how or who"—Balmorlan paused in contempt—"or *what* got our people back; he was only interested in the results. That it was accomplished through a traitor made no difference to him."

It was like a slap in the face, a knife to the heart of my worst fear—Markus had only been using me. I kept my breathing smooth and steady, my face expressionless. Even if what Balmorlan said was true, I wasn't about to give him any satisfaction.

"And tonight you brazenly meet in the street with Imala Kalis, shaking hands like old friends," Balmorlan continued. "Working for the goblin secret service, Mistress Benares? Or will you simply work for any government with a treasury to pay you?"

"I find your theory . . . interesting." I found the thought of knocking out his teeth even more interesting. "Guardians *and* goblins were attacked by Nightshades soon after what was merely a civil—and *first*—handshake between myself and Imala Kalis. Chief Rinker and his men didn't arrive until after the Nightshades had fled." I turned to Sedge. "Is that an accurate statement, Chief?"

"It is," Sedge replied. "We took no living Nightshades into custody; the only ones left were dead."

I locked eyes with Balmorlan. "It sounds like you were there watching. Did you take a walk down to the entertainment district this evening for a little spying? Or did a Nightshade tell you when he came to collect his pay? Anyone you know been dipping into the elven treasury to pay assassins to attack Conclave Guardians?"

"You *dare* accuse me—"

"I said 'anyone.' If you take offense, maybe it's because you're carrying around a load of guilt to go with it."

"Chief Rinker, I demand that this woman be arrested."

"On what charges?"

"Vicious public slander against an elven government official."

"Inquisitor Balmorlan," Sedge drawled, "I know every law on the books and that's not one of them." I could hear the smile in his voice. "I believe in government circles, an attempt to sully an opponent's reputation is called politics."

"We're not here for petty arguments," Carnades snapped at Balmorlan. He turned those arctic eyes on me. "You and Nathrach are working together to get more souls to feed the Saghred, building its power until it and you are strong enough to destroy us all. Your lover drives the coach, and conveniently drops the general at your feet. You think this gives you an alibi, but I will prove that the two of you killed General Aratus together, feeding his soul to the Saghred and attempting to blame a ghost for your crimes."

Carnades must have been one of the idiot mages Mychael told me didn't believe in ghosts or specters. I wasn't surprised. "So you don't believe in ghosts?"

"They are but feeble vapors that are of no harm to anyone, except the uneducated and superstitious."

"When you're face-to-face with Sarad Nukpana, you be sure to call him a 'feeble vapor.' I'm sure he'll get a kick out of it, right before he sucks your life out through your face."

"Are you threatening me?"

I actually laughed. It felt surprisingly good. "No, Carnades. Once again, I'm warning you. Perhaps if you didn't have all that education clogging your head, you'd realize that Sarad Nukpana is regenerating himself, and to do a good job of it, he needs powerful victims, the more magical mojo, the better."

"That which no longer exists cannot be regenerated. Such stories are merely fairy tales to frighten children."

"They'd be smart to be frightened. I guess there's a difference between smart and educated," I noted. "I understand you met Sarad Nukpana while you were at the goblin court, so I'm sure you know how he feels about elves. He thinks the only good elf is either enslaved or dead. I think he plans to do both to you, one right after the other. He hates you, doesn't he?"

The elven mage's lips narrowed to a thin, angry line. "I'm sure he hated me when he was alive, but since that's no longer the case, his feelings are irrelevant."

"Did you see General Aratus's body, Carnades?" Mychael had released the body to the elven embassy this morning.

I saw a flicker of revulsion in the elf's eyes—and fear.

"Then you saw that there was nothing left but a dried husk. Nukpana took everything." I jerked my head toward Tam's cell. "You think you're safe. You think you've got your killer. You're wrong. *Your* killer is still out there, and he's starting an elf collection. If your name's not next on his list, it's near the top."

"You describe a monster," Carnades said. "And that monster is in the cell behind you. The two of you murdered our finest general in the most heinous way possible. I don't know how you did it, but I will see you both in elven custody." His voice went deathly quiet. "And soon I will have your secret accomplice there beside you. He mistakenly thinks his high station will save him. Inquisitor Balmorlan is having cells prepared in the elven embassy for you all; this arrangement is merely temporary."

"That is the only way anyone on this island will be truly safe," Balmorlan said. "And a very gifted young man will be free from your poisonous influence."

Piaras. I stifled a growl.

"Yes, Mistress Benares," Balmorlan all but purred. "I refer to Piaras Rivalin. The poor unfortunate whom you have deceived for so long. I attempted to rescue the boy only to have you steal him from the only people able to truly protect him."

"*Guardian Cadet* Rivalin is perfectly safe where he is," came Mychael's clear and sharp voice from the door. "Under Guardian protection. And Tamnais Nathrach is merely accused. Until proven guilty, he is innocent, and is due every consideration and due process of the law."

A litany of curses ran through my mind; I'm sure Mychael heard every last one of them. He was wearing a long, dark gray cloak that covered him from his neck to the heels of his boots.

Mychael slowly walked toward Balmorlan and Carnades. "Though it seems you have forgotten the law—or have chosen to ignore it. *Raine, get next to Tam's cell.* Neither the law nor I will allow you to take Tamnais Nathrach from this building. *Do it, now!*"

Mychael was talking to Carnades, but thinking at me. I slowly backed away in the direction of Tam's cell. Conveniently a few of the watchers had taken a step back, too. No one wanted to be in Mychael and Carnades's immediate vicinity, because even the best spellslingers could miss a shot if things suddenly got nasty.

Carnades was like a snake poised to strike. "Chief Watcher, lower the wards on the goblin's cell." I could hear the undertone of anticipation in his voice. His mage cronies with him shifted uneasily.

"I can't do that, sir," Sedge told him. "Not without the direct order of the archmage. Tamnais Nathrach is considered too dangerous a prisoner to risk it."

"That wasn't a request, Rinker. That was an order."

"My hands are tied by the law, Magus Silvanus. Surely you wouldn't want me to break the law and risk the safety of our people?"

I let out the breath I'd been holding. Like I'd said, Sedge Rinker was good people.

"You yourself declared Tamnais Nathrach a most dangerous prisoner," Mychael noted. "The chief watcher cannot legally do what you ask, nor can I—or you."

Carnades had brought his own rope, and Mychael was letting him hang himself with it. I also realized what else Mychael had done.

Tam was behind the wards; I was next to the wards; Mychael was completely out of the wards' range. Carnades expected our combined magic to ring like a clarion; instead the wards kept Tam's magic inside the cell, distorted mine, and left Mychael standing alone and seemingly not linked to either one of us.

The simplest plans were the most brilliant.

Nachtmagus Vidor Kalta strode into headquarters, took one look at Tam, and laughed, a short bark. Tall, thin, and black-robed—Kalta looked like Death with a newfound sense of humor. Creepy.

"That is your cha'nescu culprit?" he asked Carnades.

"What?"

"A cha'nescu, my dear, deluded Carnades. The ritual that turned General Aratus into the dearly departed and dried General Aratus."

The elf was livid. "You will show respect—"

Kalta dismissed him with a wave of one pale hand. "No disrespect intended or implied; I merely call him what he is. The general is departed; he was probably dear to *someone*; and he is most definitely dried."

A watcher behind me muffled a snicker.

Carnades sneered. "And being a nachtmagus, your *expertise* in such matters told you that General Aratus was murdered by some sort of vampiric—"

Kalta actually made tsking sounds. "Carnades, even a child knows that there is no such thing as a vampire." He paused, a tiny smile flicking at one corner of his mouth. "It is, as you said, a fairy tale." The smile vanished. "But specters are real, or as we refer to them, disenfranchised souls. And a cha'nescu ritual is not only real, but a very real danger. Only a fool would dismiss it."

"I didn't dismiss the danger; I locked it up. Tamnais Nathrach fed General Aratus's soul to the Saghred through the body of this traitor to her people. Now she dares to further her desecration by claiming that Sarad Nukpana threatened the mages of this island by speaking through the general's dead body."

"It's not a claim; it's the truth," I told him, though I knew I was wasting my breath.

"And I suppose you are the only one to have heard the words? Now, if there was someone else who had heard him . . ." The question was for me, but Carnades was staring in challenge at Mychael.

With our bond, if I had heard something, so did Mychael. If Carnades couldn't get the wards lowered on Tam's cell, an admission from Mychael would work just as well.

"Mychael, don't."

Mychael's smile was slow and actually amused. "I heard every word."

"If Sarad Nukpana indeed communicated with this traitor through the general, then how did you hear the words?" Carnades murmured. "The only way Nukpana would have been able to speak to her is through her bond with the Saghred." He paused as if the thought was just now occurring to him. "Unless you share a similar bond with her." The air around him almost vibrated with anticipatory triumph.

Vidor Kalta laughed. "Carnades, stop being an ass and listen to yourself. First vampires, now a *magical bond conspiracy*. I heard Sarad Nukpana's threats as well, and I share no bond with Miss Benares, Paladin Eiliesor, or a rock. Before I met Miss Benares in the examination room containing the general's remains, I'd never met, seen, or spoken with her before. Yet I can quote word for word what Sarad Nukpana said. Would you like for me to tell you? I assure you it was quite memorable."

Carnades stood utterly still. "That is impossible."

Any sign of flippancy vanished. "I'm a nachtmagus, I deal with the impossible every day, and I assure you they aren't fairy tales."

"You heard nothing."

Kalta stepped past Mychael and crossed the squad room

at a stately pace until he was close enough to make Carnades uncomfortable. "The voice I heard through General Aratus was most definitely not that of Tamnais Nathrach. I have met Sarad Nukpana at some of the court functions that you yourself attended. You know his voice, as do I. The voice Paladin Eiliesor, Miss Benares, and I heard was Sarad Nukpana. Without question." Kalta gave his last two words special emphasis, daring Carnades to challenge him.

"I question." The elf mage's voice was flat and ugly.

"Do you question my skill?" Kalta grinned with a slow baring of teeth, and his voice dropped to a precise whisper. "Or are you calling me a liar?"

The glitter in Kalta's black eyes said that he would love for Carnades to openly say that he didn't believe either one. I kind of wanted to see what would happen if he did.

In his own twisted way, Carnades considered himself a champion of all that was right and moral. I didn't know what Kalta considered himself or stood for—but he was lying. He hadn't heard a word Sarad Nukpana said. Though considering that Tam and Mychael's lives were at stake, he could have claimed the world was flat for all I cared. Vidor Kalta was lying to Carnades's face in a room full of Mid's watchers and appeared to be enjoying himself immensely. I was all in favor of personal happiness. Kalta's sharp black eyes bored into Carnades's ice blue ones. He ignored Balmorlan completely. It had the potential to get ugly, but it wouldn't, at least not here, not now. Mages like Carnades preferred a figurative knife in the back rather than a literal punch to the gut. If Carnades answered "yes" to Kalta's accusation, I had no doubt that Kalta would politely ask him to step outside. I actually wanted Carnades to say that word. That was a fight I wanted to see and, better yet, enjoy the results of.

Carnades drew himself up and did his best to look down on Kalta even though they were the same height. "I have never personally heard you speak anything but the truth."

That wasn't good enough for Kalta. "What I have said to

others in the past is not the issue here. What I just said to you is. Am I lying to you now before all these witnesses?"

The silence hung thick and heavy in the air. Everyone was holding his breath for the next volley.

"I cannot prove otherwise." Carnades paused and if looks could kill, Kalta would have been one of his disenfranchised souls. "No, you are not lying."

Kalta graciously inclined his head. "Thank you. Your trust honors me and my house."

"This isn't over," Carnades hissed.

"Of course it's not," Kalta said mildly. "Sarad Nukpana is still at large."

Chapter 9

"*That does nothing to disprove that Tamnais Nathrach kid-napped General Aratus*," Carnades said. "If Sarad Nukpana is regenerating as you say, he would need an accomplice; and who better than a goblin dark mage and an elven traitor? Mistress Benares has been inside the Saghred on two occasions and has spoken with Sarad Nukpana." He looked to me and his eyes narrowed in cold, reptilian fury. "Don't think I have forgotten that he referred to you as a partner."

"Yeah, it still gives me the creeps, too."

Mychael turned away from Carnades, dismissing him entirely. "Sedge, I want to see the statements of all witnesses who said they saw Tamnais Nathrach abduct the general."

"You won't have to go far for two of them; they're right over there," I said, indicating a pair of elves who clearly wished that they were elsewhere right now.

"They just finished giving their statements," Sedge told us. "There were four others who have come over the course of the afternoon."

Six lying witnesses. Carnades had been busy. He wasn't taking any chances that Tam was going to get away.

"I want copies of their statements, and their addresses sent to my office within the hour," Mychael said. "I'll be conducting my own investigation—beginning with interviewing the witnesses."

Carnades sneered. "So you think our chief watcher is incapable of properly—"

"Chief Watcher Rinker is more than capable in every capacity of his job." Mychael's voice was level and professional—and cold enough to give Carnades frostbite. "The continued safety of the Conclave's mages is *my* responsibility. And I will do everything in my power to bring those responsible to justice." He paused meaningfully. "And that includes any false witnesses. If Tamnais Nathach has been falsely accused with malicious intent, I will see those responsible prosecuted to the full extent of the law. Valuable hours have been lost here tonight, hours that may have cost the life of another citizen of this island—a life I was sworn to protect."

Carnades was livid with outrage. "You will not roust our good citizens out of their beds in the middle of the night."

"Watch me. And speaking of the middle of the night, Sarad Nukpana is out there. I can't allow you out in the streets alone."

"I have two bodyguards who—"

"Insufficient," Mychael told him. "You are the senior mage on the Seat of Twelve and it is my duty to see you safely home."

Taltek Balmorlan stepped forward. "It is not Magus Silvanus's intention to go home yet, nor is it mine."

"Then my men will escort the two of you wherever you need to go, and then see you both safely home."

If Carnades or Balmorlan wanted to report back to Markus, Mychael had just thrown a big crimp in their plans. His Guardians would report every stop they made to their commander. Another flash of brilliance on Mychael's part. Best of all, he was just doing his job.

I had a sudden feeling of cold dread. I hadn't heard Talon come up behind me—the kid was too light on his feet for that—but he was there. And Carnades and Balmorlan were still there.

Taltek Balmorlan looked like he'd just been handed a present with his name on it. Carnades looked like he'd just seen one of those ghosts that he didn't believe in.

I sighed. "Talon, you were supposed to stay put."

"You know I only do as told if there's something in it for me." His voice slipped smoothly into a lower register and his magic flowed around us all, warm and silvery. I don't think he was aware that he was doing it.

Balmorlan was aware and delighted.

Damn.

"Young Master Nathrach." The elven inquisitor's lips curved into a jackal's smile. "I have seen you perform at Sirens on more than one occasion. You have a most impressive talent."

"Let me guess," Talon shot back smoothly. "You're the type who enjoyed my dancing *much* more than my singing."

A few watchers did a fine job covering their snorts or guffaws with spontaneous coughing fits. Vegard sounded like he'd swallowed a bug.

Taltek Balmorlan's look was murder.

Talon flashed him a dazzling smile, but his aquamarine eyes were pale fire. He knew exactly who and what he was playing with, and he was doing it anyway, cheerfully even. These were the bastards who had put his father in a cell, and the kid was out here to show them that Nathrach men didn't intimidate and they sure as hell didn't hide in conference rooms.

Vidor Kalta leaned toward the elven inquisitor. "The boy has your number, Taltek," he murmured, laughter running under his words. "I've always said you need to find another hobby."

Carnades hadn't found any words. His stare was fixed on Talon's pale eyes; eyes only a shade darker than Carnades's own. "Abomination," he whispered hoarsely, whether to himself or Talon, I didn't know.

"Your mother was a pure-blooded high elf," Vidor Kalta said gently to Talon. "And was no doubt very beautiful." His black eyes were daggers on Carnades. "And his father is a good, noble, and *innocent* man." He looked back at Talon. "You should be proud of them both."

"Yes, sir. I am." The kid's voice was steady as a rock.

Vidor Kalta might be creepy, but I liked him.

Mychael moved smoothly between Talon and Carnades, forcing the elf to break eye contact with the young goblin. "My men are ready to escort you to your next destination." Mychael's words were polite; his voice said that both Carnades and Balmorlan were leaving. Now.

They left with Carnades's two bodyguards in tow, and through the windows, I saw a whole bunch of mounted Guardians who looked only too glad to escort all of them around town. Carnades's mage cronies dispersed. I guess it was no fun being on the losing side. They'd go home and lick their wounds; Carnades and Balmorlan were no doubt hatching another plan before they were in their coach.

I wanted to run directly to Tam's cell, but knew that wouldn't look good for either of us.

I draped an arm over Talon's shoulders. I knew I'd probably get groped for my trouble, but a show of guts like that shouldn't go unrewarded.

"Phaelan has a saying for what you just did," I told him.

"Yeah?"

"Yeah. He'd tell you not to trip over those things."

"What things?"

"Your balls that are dragging on the ground."

Talon's grin was slow and lascivious. "Not literally, but they are impressive. Would you like to see?"

"I'll pass, kid. It's a thrill I'll have to live without."

"Anytime you want the thrill, just let me know."

Mychael appeared at my side. "Talon, why don't you go see your father." He glanced over my shoulder. "Sedge?"

"I'll lower the sound barrier on the ward so they can talk."

"Thank you," I told him.

The chief watcher sighed. "I really didn't want to do this, Raine."

"I know. We all have our jobs to do."

"And sometimes they suck."

"That they do."

While Talon was reunited with Tam, I stepped up to Vidor Kalta.

"Well played," I murmured. "You didn't hear Nukpana say one word in that examination room."

Kalta's response was a brief upward twitch of his thin lips.

"And you knew exactly what he was going to do," I said to Mychael in mindspeak.

"And approved."

"The paladin and I—how do you say—got our story straight before we came in." Kalta spoke while barely moving his lips, and his words didn't carry past my ears. Nifty trick. "It simplifies so much. My conscience is quite clear. I merely countered one fabrication with another. Carnades cannot prove his claim; and he knows that I cannot prove mine." His eyes were the flat black of a shark's. "I know what is at stake if Sarad Nukpana succeeds. I will do whatever is necessary to prevent that from happening. And to prevent more innocent people from being infested by those who escaped with him."

I glanced over my shoulder. It looked like Tam was giving his son a serious talking-to, and for once it looked like Talon might actually be listening. I wasn't about to interrupt that. Besides, there was a question I wanted an answer to. That answer was probably going to creep me the hell out, but I wanted to know.

"Uh, Nachtmagus Kalta—"

"Vidor, please."

"Okay." I drew that word out. "Vidor. May I ask you a probably tasteless and possibly offensive question?"

His lips curled in a knowing smile. "About my calling?"

"That would be the topic."

"Miss Benares, I have never been offended by sharing knowledge with those who sincerely want to know." He paused meaningfully. "Nor by having the opportunity to dispel an unfortunate misconception."

Just ask it, Raine. "Do you resurrect the dead?"

"No, I do not," he replied simply. "However, there have been instances when I have prevented a soul from leaving its body."

"But they were dead."

"Their bodies, yes. But as long as the soul remains, true death is a technicality." He gave me a quizzical glance. "You seem surprised that I do not resurrect the dead."

"I thought that was what a nachtmagus did."

"Once the soul leaves the body, it may linger for as long as a day, but usually it is only for a few minutes. After that the soul moves on. Attempting to summon a soul back to its original body is dangerous for precisely the same reasons you have experienced during the past few weeks."

I had an unwanted image of Banan Ryce and Alastair Kratos. "Bad souls looking for any body they can get."

"Precisely. There is no guarantee that the soul you summon will be the soul you want. And once that spirit takes possession of the body, what you have is no more than an animated corpse, a tool and nothing more for the spirit infesting it. And make no mistake, it *is* an infestation—and to any moral nachtmagus, it is abhorrent." His black eyes sparkled. "Does that answer your question?"

"And then some." I glanced down at my boots and then up at Vidor. "Thank you for what you did for us."

"I was more than glad to be of assistance, Miss Benares."

"Call me Raine."

He looked genuinely pleased, almost happy at that. "Raine."

I let out a wry chuckle and shook my head. "You made Carnades admit in front of a roomful of people that not only did you not lie, but that he was wrong. He's not going to let either one of those go."

"I would be stunned into insensibility if he did. Unlike Carnades, I trust the word of others. If you and the paladin say you heard it, you did. If Carnades doesn't hear, see, or feel it himself, he believes it simply does not exist. The man has no intellectual curiosity whatsoever. Most unfortunate. I know Tamnais Nathrach from the goblin court, Raine. He was not responsible for this, and I will not stand by and watch while Carnades's pigheadedness imprisons the innocent while the guilty go free and continue to kill. And as to the possibility of you and Paladin Eiliesor sharing some sort of bond, I believe that what is between two consenting adults should stay there."

I said nothing, but inclined my head in gratitude.

His lips twitched again. "And I would never pass up an opportunity to antagonize Carnades, as I have since we were boys."

"You two knew each other as kids?" I whistled. "I hope your parents hid the knives. He hates your guts."

"Then that would make our relationship unchanged since childhood."

Mychael glanced over at the cells. "Vidor, will you stay here overnight with Tam?"

"Of course."

I looked from one of them to the other. "You expect Sarad Nukpana to come after him?"

Mychael shook his head. "That would be too risky. There are Sedge's watchers and wards to contend with, and I will be posting a few Guardians here as well. They're trained to recognize and counteract spirit activity of any kind."

"Won't someone tell Carnades that you have Guardians protecting Tam?"

Mychael held up a finger. "*Guarding* Tam. And if they want to tell Carnades, they are more than welcome to. Carnades claims that Tam is the most dangerous man on the island. My men routinely supplement Sedge's watchers whenever we have a high-risk prisoner."

"Your boys are just doing their job," I said. *"And protecting Tam."* I hesitated. *"Is it safe for me to speak to him?"*

Mychael knew what I meant. Would having lowered the

sound barriers on the ward covering Tam's cell reveal our bond if we got too close? There were still plenty of watchers in the squad room. On an island full of mages, watchers who could sling spells of their own went a long way toward keeping the peace. Some of them probably had enough on the ball to recognize the umi'atsu bond between me, Mychael, and Tam.

"It won't be a problem," Mychael assured me. *"Tam will be able to hear us, and we can hear him—just sound, no magic spillover."*

I took a breath and blew it out. More than enough had gone wrong tonight; a change would be nice.

With the sound barrier down, the wards on Tam's cell glowed orange instead of red. It wasn't a warm, welcoming glow; it was an angry "one step closer and I'll toss you across the room" kind of glow. Mychael and I stopped about two feet from the cell.

"Entertaining exchange," Tam drawled. "That's one thing I can always depend on from Carnades—he's never boring."

I blinked. "How did you—"

"Lipreading. A useful trick I picked up at court. I got most of what was said. By the way, thank Vidor Kalta for me."

"You can thank him yourself," Mychael said. "He'll be staying with you for the rest of the night. If all goes as planned, you'll be out of here by tomorrow morning."

Talon froze. "Do you think he needs protection?"

"No. But I'm not taking any chances. A few of my men are specially trained to deal with specters." He paused. "And Kontar and Garai are on their way here."

I recognized the names. They were goblin dark mages. Tam called them friends and colleagues; our family would have called them high-priced, out-of-town talent. They were powerful, and dirty was the only way they knew how to fight.

Tam snorted, a short of laugh. "Only two?"

"Unfortunately, those are the rules."

Talon's eyes flashed in fury. "What rules? Why can't they all be in here?"

"Two personal guards qualify as protection," Tam explained. "Any more than that is a jailbreak waiting to happen."

"What's wrong with that?"

"A jailbreak means Tam would be a fugitive," Mychael told Talon. "A confession from Sarad Nukpana's accomplice makes Tam a free man."

"You've got him in custody?" I asked.

"I plan to by morning. And if Sarad Nukpana strikes somewhere in the city again tonight—"

Tam indicated the bars of his cell with a rueful smile. "I'll have a literally ironclad alibi." He shrugged a shoulder. "I've certainly spent the night in worse accommodations." All signs of humor vanished. "Mychael, take care of Talon for me."

"I'm staying right here," Talon told us all.

"Talon, I—" Tam began.

"What if they come back?" he shot back vehemently.

I knew who he was talking about. Carnades and Balmorlan.

"They won't," Mychael assured him. "You're staying with Piaras for tonight." He looked out into the courtyard, where five minutes ago Carnades's coach had been. "I'll be having you both stay in the archmagus's apartments."

Talon was incredulous. "I'm spending the night with an old man? Like a babysitter?"

I knew what Mychael was doing and thought it was a damned fine idea. Piaras and Talon had become close friends, and Justinius would obliterate anyone or anything that threatened either one of them.

"He's an old man who'll kick your ass at cards and drink you under the table," I told Talon.

"I'll pass on the ass kicking, but I could use a drink."

"Talon, go over and stand with Vegard," Tam said. "I need to talk to Mychael in private."

The kid looked like he was about to give his dad some lip, but thought better of it and nodded tightly instead. What do you know? He did have some sense.

Tam slowly took a breath and let it out, waiting until Talon was out of earshot.

Then he told Mychael what Talon had done tonight and who had seen him do it. Mychael didn't seem all that shocked. I guess as paladin, he'd seen his share of exotic magical talents.

"And Banan Ryce saw it all. He's gone and gotten himself possessed by Alastair Kratos."

I quickly told him about our encounter with Banan Ryce—the new, improved, and possessed Banan Ryce. Lure a specter, give him a body. In return, all they had to do was help with an assassination or two. Banan's boys had missed Imala Kalis this time; next time they'd get it right. One of the nice things about a bond was that I could supplement my thoughts with images. Within a few seconds, Mychael knew exactly what had happened.

"And if Taltek Balmorlan's paying Banan's fee, he knows all about Talon—like the kid needs that kind of trouble now."

"Mychael, I know we don't always see eye to eye," Tam admitted. "And Talon's almost more than I can handle, but it would ease my mind if you would stand as fal'kasair for him. It's what goblins call a godfather."

"I know what it is." Mychael's jaw clenched. "Tam, you don't need to do this—"

"Hopefully not, but it's a chance I don't want to take. It's a little late to be giving Talon a fal'kasair. They're usually chosen before a child is born, someone with enough political influence and magical power to protect them." Tam paused uncomfortably. "Would you do this for me? In case this doesn't turn out like we want."

I just stood there. A fal'kasair also took over raising a child if the father died—or was executed.

"Nothing's going to happen to you," I told him.

"I don't plan on anything happening to me, either." Tam sighed. "Raine, it's different when you have a child, especially one who would never admit that he depends on you.

Talon's gone through most of his life fending for himself." Tam paused, his voice tight with emotion. "I never want him to go through that again."

"And he won't," Mychael promised him. "I would be honored to be Talon's fal'kasair."

"Thank you."

Mychael tried for a smile that didn't quite make it. "You'd asked me when Talon first came here to try to reform him. Between me, Justinius, and Piaras—who knows? It might stick."

Tam barked a tense laugh. "That'd take a miracle." He looked at the bars crackling with wards. "Like one other thing I can name."

Mychael smiled fully and his eyes gleamed. "Have faith."

Tam snorted. "In what?"

"Greed."

Mychael's hand cupped my elbow and steered me toward the back of the squad room. "Talon, you're with us," Mychael said as we passed him and Vegard. "We're not leaving through the front doors," he told me quietly.

"Too many people?"

"That, too."

"You know a lot of back-door exits in this town."

He flashed a grin, but his eyes were alert. "It keeps me healthy."

The door Mychael exited through put us in the courtyard of the city watch's stables. Kalinpar was in the center of the courtyard, and there were a lot of nervous horses in their stalls. The insides of Mychael's personal sentry dragon's nostrils glowed with an orange uncomfortably similar to the wards on Tam's cell. Except Kalinpar didn't have wards up his nose; he had fire, and was easily twice the size of the largest horse I'd ever seen. I'd sat in the saddle strapped across his scaled back once before with Mychael behind me. That was a flight to the citadel that my stomach was in no hurry to repeat.

A Guardian stood by his side.

"I need you to take Talon Nathrach back to the citadel and escort him to the archmagus's apartments," Mychael told him. "And bring Piaras Rivalin up from the barracks. They're staying with the archmagus tonight."

The Guardian didn't even blink at the request. I guess taking orders was what a soldier did best. That was why I'd never be a soldier.

Mychael stopped and spoke to Talon. "Your father is going to be fine, and I'll personally see to it that he's out of that cell by morning."

"Do you promise?"

"Everything in my power."

Talon considered for a few seconds. "Thank you." His smile was crooked. "So the old man likes to play cards?"

"He likes to cheat even more," I warned him. "And if you try to cheat him, he'll turn you into a slug." I grinned and clapped him on the shoulder. "Good luck, kid."

Talon left the courtyard with a trio of armed Guardians behind him. I looked with trepidation at Kalinpar.

"Can't we take horses back to the citadel?" I asked.

Mychael leaned down, his lips next to my ear. "We're not going back to the citadel."

I couldn't believe my ears. I glanced up at Mychael's eyes. Yep, still blue, no flicker of flame that signaled a specter in residence. "You don't look it, but you haven't gone and gotten yourself possessed, have you?"

His teeth flashed in the dim courtyard light. "I assure you I am quite myself."

"You don't want to lock me in my room in the citadel, so what am I supposed to think?"

He gazed down at me. "I'd like nothing better, but I don't have that luxury tonight. I need your help."

I was stunned. "You *what*?"

In response, Mychael took my hand and hurried into the stables.

What was waiting for us in that stall confused me more than Mychael needing my help. An elf who could have been Mychael's twin brother stood before us, and standing next to him . . . Well, if I'd had a sister, this woman would have been it. The man was wearing a uniform identical to Mychael's and the woman was in midnight blue leathers from head to toe. Just like mine.

What the hell?

Mychael swept off his massive gray cloak and handed it to the uniformed man. I looked over at Mychael and my mouth fell open. I let it hang there; I had better things to do, like determine why the paladin of the Conclave Guardians was dressed like someone you'd meet in a bad bar, dark alley, or darker highway just before he demanded that you "stand and deliver."

Mychael wore dark, rough leather from head to toe: high boots, formfitting trousers—*extremely* formfitting—and a doublet with various slits that I recognized all too well. Hiding places for dozens of small, bladed weapons. Straps from a sword harness hugged his wide shoulders. Mychael out of uniform signaled a heavy frost in Hell; but what raised my eyebrows and left them there was that he looked perfectly comfortable, relaxed even. I closed my mouth, lowered my brows and made a conscious effort to keep them that way, and decided to just let the strangeness play itself out.

The man and woman didn't speak, but the woman noted the way my blades were angled over my shoulders and adjusted her own sword harness to a perfect match.

Vegard shifted uneasily. "I don't like this, sir."

Mychael put on a broad-brimmed hat and pulled it low over his eyes. He handed me a dark cloak and I took it and put it on. "None of us do, but it's necessary. Vegard, it's critical that everyone, especially Carnades and Balmorlan, believes that Raine and I are in the citadel tonight. Escort our doubles to my apartments and post guards to see to it that no one gets in. When Sedge delivers those statements to my office, take them to Justinius, and then stay there. He knows what to do. Raine and I will see you in the morning."

The big Guardian took a deep breath and blew it out in a stubborn puff of steam in the cold night air. I gave him the hug I'd wanted to earlier. To my surprise, he hugged me back. Tightly.

"Be safe, ma'am," he murmured against my hair.

"I always do what I can." *"Though I could do a better job of it if I knew what the hell your boss was up to,"* I thought directly at Mychael.

"In a moment."

"It better be a quick one."

We watched as the fake Mychael and Raine went into the courtyard and mounted Kalinpar. Vegard quickly walked past them and out into the street. A few moments later I heard the clatter of horses' hooves as the remaining Guardians headed back to the citadel with Talon. The sentry dragon unfolded his leathery wings and in three beats was hovering over the courtyard. Then Mychael's double turned the dragon toward the citadel; in a few moments they, Vegard, and the Guardians with him were gone.

And Mychael and I were alone.

"How are you holding up?" he asked me.

"I'm ready for anything." I looked him up and down and took my sweet time doing it. "So, is this what you wear when you're off duty?"

"I'm still on duty, just a different kind of job."

"When someone in my family dresses like that, it means they're up to no good."

"No doubt certain people would see it that way."

"Like Carnades or Balmorlan."

"That's two."

"You knew what was going to happen in there."

"Carnades is many things; fortunately predictable is one of them. When I found out that he'd framed Tam, I knew what he would do to try to make it stick. So I did what Carnades expected and wanted me to do—I came here." He flashed a grin. "Though I don't think he got what he wanted and neither did Taltek Balmorlan."

"Incriminating ourselves as being in an umi'atsu bond," I said silently. Our bond was something that I would *not* discuss out loud. *"Three birds with one stone. Or in our case three birds and one stone."*

"Counteracting Carnades was a simple matter of Vidor and me working out a few details ahead of time." Mychael moved to mindspeak, too.

"The lie about him hearing Nukpana—"

"Was one of them. This was another. Coming here gave me the opportunity to be seen leaving here—with you."

"Where are we going?"

Mychael reached out with both hands and pulled my hood up to hide my face. *"Hunting."*

Chapter 10

Watcher headquarters was on the edge of the city center near the entertainment district. When you're law enforcement in a college town, it makes sense to be close to the most likely source of disturbances. With the dusk-to-dawn curfew, the only people on the streets were either watchers or Guardians. Within a few minutes of leaving headquarters, Mychael pulled me back into the shadows as a pair of watchers turned the corner across the street from where we were.

Okay, it was now officially snowing in Hell. Mychael Eiliesor was hiding from the law.

Once the pair had gone far enough down the street, Mychael took my hand tightly in his and we quickly slipped around the corner of the next side street. It was narrow, not much more than an alley. I didn't speak and Mychael didn't slow down. We passed another four patrols, two of them Guardians. We hid from all four, and Mychael supplemented the shadows concealing us with a veiling spell as the Guardians passed.

My nose told me that we were getting close to the harbor. My instincts told me we were getting close to our destination. I was right.

Mychael stopped at a boarded-up building that looked like its best days had come and gone long ago. He led me from the street and down some narrow stairs to a door without a knob. He laid his hand flat against the wood and murmured a few words. The door opened on silent—and well-oiled and maintained—hinges.

Mychael shut the door behind us and, with a word, wove a lightglobe into existence that floated above his open palm. We were in a basement that looked like some of the more comfortable hideouts Uncle Ryn had in every major port city. It had the basics: table, a couple of chairs, a bed in the far corner.

And weapons. Lots and lots of weapons.

"So this is your secret hideout."

"One of them," Mychael said out loud. "And there's no need for mindspeak; this room is soundproof and spellproof."

I grinned and shook my head. "Damn."

"What?"

"Mychael Eiliesor has a secret lair and is hiding from the law."

He held up a finger. "Not hiding. I just don't want to answer any awkward questions or have anyone know where I am."

"Sounds like Phaelan after he's pulled a job." I gave him a slow smile. "What job are we pulling this evening?"

"Sarad Nukpana has an uncle—" Mychael began.

"Janos Ghalfari, the nachtmagus who's helping him," I interrupted. "Tam told me. He also told me that he found four houses in the city owned by Nukpana's mother's family, and that Nukpana isn't in any of them."

"He's not. What else did Tam tell you?"

I told him about the coach, horses, houses, and how Uncle Janos had nicely come all the way from Regor to help his dear nephew grow his body back.

Mychael nodded in approval. "Good, that saves me a lot of talking. We don't have time. We have a meeting to go to."

"Okay, now I'm completely confused."

"No doubt."

"What kind of meeting?"

"When a goblin needs something done that another goblin can't or won't do, there are a handful of humans on Mid who will get them anything they need for the right price. Janos Ghalfari is helping his nephew regenerate, but he's not the kidnapper. As far as Ghalfari is concerned, that's why you hire servants. A goblin would be too easily traced. I've discovered that he's hired two humans through an intermediary." Mychael paused. "A man and a woman."

Shit. Mychael didn't need to say anything else, or even think it. I knew what he wanted me for.

A glamour. To use my magic to make myself look and sound like someone else. It was something I'd never been able to do before the Saghred had done its enhancement work on my previously meager magical skill set.

"We've got the two of them under lock and key," Mychael was saying. "I can do a glamour to alter my face and ears. The man is close enough to me in build so that won't be a problem. And as a spellsinger, I can change my voice."

"That doesn't do me any good. I've only done a glamour once and it didn't go well." And I didn't want to do one again.

"Raine, you glamoured yourself into a man, an elven embassy captain no less, and talked your way into the embassy when every guard in the place was on battle alert."

"And I lost the glamour."

"Only when Piaras thought you were one of his jailers and punched you in the balls. That'd make any man lose any number of things, least of all his concentration. The embassy was on lockdown, yet you waltzed right in."

I scowled. "Yeah, I had big balls that night."

Mychael grinned. "So I heard. I've never heard of an anatomically correct glamour."

"What can I say? I'm gifted. I was also motivated as hell. That might have been the only reason why the spell worked."

"You don't believe that and neither do I, or I wouldn't have brought you here." Mychael's eyes were intent on mine. "Raine, I need your help. Kester Morrell and Maire Orla are the names of the humans Ghalfari hired through a local procurer by the name of Karl Cradock. We're meeting Cradock in less than an hour at a tavern called the Bare Bones down on the waterfront."

I sighed in resignation. I had to do this and I knew it. "What's supposed to happen at this meeting?"

"Cradock will pay Morrell and Orla and give them the name of their target—and most important, we'll be told where to deliver him."

"What are the chances that it'll be where Sarad Nukpana is hiding?"

"Slim, but if we can follow, we can find."

I grinned slowly. "And lucky you, you've got one of the best seekers there is with you."

"I think I'm the luckiest man in the world," Mychael said softly.

Those words had more than one meaning and from his heated gaze, he meant all of them.

No time to think about Mychael getting lucky, though the visual popped into my head before I could stop it. Mychael knew and the heat in his eyes turned to a challenge.

"Are you in?" he asked, his voice very deep, very male.

I also tried not to think about Mychael's strong hands roaming all over my naked body, touching, healing—heating. My face wasn't the only part of me that flushed with warmth.

Mychael responded with a crooked grin. He knew exactly what I was thinking. "Well, are you?"

A wry smile curled my lips. "All the way."

"Then let's do it."

Sarad Nukpana would want to kidnap either someone I cared about or someone whose death could be pinned squarely on me. I'd either be heartbroken or executed—someone I loved would die or I would. One or the other, and the choice hadn't been mine until now. If I didn't screw this up, and we pulled this off, and I found the son of a bitch, we could stop both from happening.

"One question."

Mychael paused. "Yes?"

"What happened to 'protect Raine at all costs'?"

"The costs have gotten too high. Kester Morrell never goes anywhere without Maire Orla. They're partners. It'd tip Cradock off immediately if Morrell showed up for the payoff without her. What you did in the elven embassy was beyond amazing. You have a gift, and one that right now, quite frankly, I'm glad you have."

"Even if that 'gift' came from the Saghred?" I didn't even try to keep the sarcasm out of my voice.

"Raine, you're only linked to the Saghred—you are not that rock, and you never will be. You're stronger than it is, and you need to start believing that."

I snorted derisively. "Yeah, I'm stronger than a rock that flattens armies."

"Has it flattened any armies lately?"

"No, but—"

"Because you haven't let it. You haven't fed it, and whenever it has tried to control you, you've stopped it. That strength is your gift, Raine."

"I'm not strong. I'm just stubborn."

A corner of his mouth quirked upward. "There's no doubt in my mind that you're stubborn, but you need to get rid of any doubt that you're not strong enough for anything the Saghred, Nukpana, Carnades, Balmorlan, or anyone else throws at you, because they're going to be throwing plenty."

"And if all else fails, I'm a Benares, so I know how to fight dirty."

"Strength, stubbornness, and underhanded tactics—you can't lose." Mychael's expression turned solemn. "Raine, when we were first bonded I saw you, all of you. I know who you are; I saw your strength, your beautiful spirit. I know what you can do if you simply believe and give yourself the chance." His next words were deliberate. "And I know what you would never do. That voice you hear, the Saghred's voice, it's lying when it says you're weak; it says that to make you doubt, to make you afraid. Not of the Saghred, but of yourself. It lies because it is the one afraid of you."

"Mychael, I'm afraid of myself." I closed my eyes. I had to get the words out; I had to say it out loud. The fear had haunted my thoughts; maybe if I said it, admitted it, the fear would go away, or at least I could control it, before it and the Saghred completely controlled me.

To forget how good the Saghred's full power coming awake inside of me had felt.

The power, the strength that had coursed through every part of me, to take, to kill. In the bordello, the urge to take that specter had felt good. Too good. Deep down, some dark core of me wanted to do it, wanted to feel that dark magic heating every part of me, needed to feel that destructive power hammering into my enemies.

I could defy the Saghred; but would I deny myself? And if I could deny myself, how long could I keep doing it?

I knew the answer to that question. That answer, that truth, scared me more than Sarad Nukpana, the Saghred, and every specter loose on the island.

My voice was a bare whisper. "What happened in the bordello, when the specter challenged me . . . I enjoyed it. I wanted to destroy that thing. I wanted to consume it."

"I know."

"I don't want to be like that." I felt my fingers clench into fists. "I *won't* be like that."

"I won't let it happen to you."

My laugh came out bitter. "It already has and you know it."

Mychael closed the distance between us and his long fingers slid under my chin, tilting my face up to his. His eyes were blue fire. "One step does not damn you."

"There's been more than one and you know it. Weeks ago when I crushed that demon in watcher headquarters, I—"

Mychael shook his head. "I don't care how much you enjoyed what you did. It was a demon. It possesses and destroys, or kills and consumes. You killed a *thing* that needed to be killed. Yes, you may have enjoyed it; and yes, that exhilaration you felt undoubtedly came from using the Saghred. Power *is* exhilarating." The fingers that had been holding my chin gently touched my face; his other hand was warm against my cheek as he cradled my face in his hands. "Using that power for good does not condemn you." He paused. "Raine, would you have killed that demon again, even if you knew you would have to use the Saghred to do it?"

"Without hesitating."

"Why?"

I blinked. "Why? Because it was trying to kill people. It might have succeeded. One of those watchers wasn't moving; several weren't moving. I don't even know what happened to them."

"You killed to protect, to defend. Does that sound evil to you?"

"No. But I—"

"Because it's not."

"But I still enjoyed it."

"That doesn't make you evil. The nature of the Saghred is temptation. It can't do anything alone. It wants someone to use it. It *needs* someone to use it."

"It's chosen lucky me. And now it's chosen you because of me. I'm the one who should be apologizing."

"I wouldn't take it, because you have nothing to apologize for. Nothing you have done or will do is your fault. I will see to that."

My throat tightened. "Thank you," I managed. "That means a lot, especially coming from you."

His hands slid down to my shoulders. "You have nothing to thank me for."

"I have *everything* to thank you for. You believe in me, and you believe I can do this—*all* of this."

"I have no doubt."

I looked up at him. "So what happened to Mychael Eil-iesor, protector of the people by the book?"

His smile held many secrets. "Occasionally I have him take the night off." The smile faded. "By the book doesn't always get the job done—and sometimes it can get innocent people killed."

I glanced around the room. "Looks like you give him the night off a lot."

Mychael's eyes gleamed in the dim light. "A few times."

"So who else knows about this place?"

"Just me and the archmage."

"Not Vegard?"

Mychael shook his head. "I trust him with my life, but some things he's safer not knowing."

"Would this place have anything to do with Justinius flushing his enemies out of hiding?"

"Occasionally."

I flashed him a grin. "Secretive and cryptic with a touch of deception. Don't take this the wrong way, but sneaky suits you."

"It's just another side of me."

"You should let him out to play more often."

"The way things are going, that'll be unavoidable."

"Okay, say we go to the bar, get the name, the place, and the money—a nice added bonus, by the way. But what happens when Morrell and Orla don't deliver Sarad Nukpana's next meal? I don't think Nukpana or his uncle will be too pleased with their procurer. Not that I have a problem with that."

"Anyone who arranges kidnappings and murders for a living deserves anything they get," Mychael said. "Though if, when everything plays out, Nukpana's uncle wants to take any revenge on his hireling, he'd better act fast. My plan is for Sarad to cease to be a problem in the next day or two, and his uncle right behind him."

"I like the 'cease to be' part."

"And in addition to meeting with Karl Cradock, and preventing the next kidnapping and murder, we'll be getting proof that Tam has had nothing to do with any of this."

"Did Morrell and Orla confess?"

"They didn't kidnap General Aratus. Karl Cradock did that himself."

I had a bad feeling about this. "Then why is he hiring someone else now?"

"My guess is this next job is more than he could handle— or wanted to risk. Karl Cradock isn't a magic user. Kester Morrell and Maire Orla are."

"What can they do?"

"Conveniently, Morrell is a spellsinger. Orla is a most proficient hypnotist."

"I'm not," I told him.

"The Saghred helped you literally turn yourself into a man; I think a little hypnosis is well within your magical range now."

I froze. "That tells me Nukpana's next victim is a magic user, moderate to high powered. Like Piaras. His bodyguards are sticking to him like glue, right?"

"Raine, when we have the name, we'll take action. Immediately. Worry doesn't do us or Piaras any good right now. Besides, even on their best days, Morrell and Orla couldn't get into the citadel. And they sure as hell couldn't get into Justinius's apartments."

"Do you have proof that Karl Cradock snatched Aratus?"

"I know he did, but I don't have tangible proof; I'll get that at our meeting."

"Uh, Mychael, even if we do get him to spill his guts, Carnades doesn't consider us the most reliable sources of information."

He grinned crookedly and pulled out what looked like a large marble on a silver chain from beneath his shirt. There was a narrow band of silver around the middle of the stone, about the diameter of a man's ring. "Which is why we'll be wearing these."

I leaned forward for a closer look, but wasn't about to touch any kind of pendant on a chain. An amulet was what had gotten me into the whole Saghred mess to begin with. "Which is?"

"It will record everything I see and hear for one hour."

"What's it called?"

"The inventor never named it. He's an old friend of mine, a prolific inventor, not big on naming his gadgets. This little beauty hasn't failed me yet."

"Then why do I need to wear one?"

"Because there's a first time for everything not to work." He held out the second pendant to me. "I'm not about to take any chances."

I put it on and held the tiny globe up by the chain and looked into it. It was a flat blue on the surface; it could have been a trick of the light, but I thought I saw swirling strands of pale blue light beneath the surface. "So if Cradock incriminates himself, this little thing will record it?"

"*When* Cradock incriminates himself," he corrected me. He smiled gently. "I've done this before, many times, and I like to think I'm rather good at it."

"Sorry. I'm just having trouble with the whole 'Mychael Eiliesor as con man' thing."

"Understandable. No offense taken. The gem will play back the entire hour in any common crystal ball."

"So when this guy gets a case of loose lips, we'll have a record of it, and Carnades, or anyone else who wants to keep Tam behind bars, will have no choice but to let him go—with an apology."

"I think an apology from Carnades would be pushing it."

I frowned. "Mychael, we're going to have to do something permanent about him. Phaelan's offered to contact some people, and I'm about to let him."

"I agree that he needs to go, but let's do it my way." There was that secretive smile again. "I've got a few irons in the fire; they'll be getting hot enough to use soon."

"What's your way?"

"Destroy his credibility, take away his influence, and get

him dismissed from the Seat of Twelve." Mychael's voice turned cold and each word was sharp and clipped. "And when he can't buy a vote or bribe an official, and none of his bought-and-paid-for allies will even admit to knowing him, *then* I will personally kick his ass off of my island."

Now, *that* was a plan I could get behind.

"When's this meeting?" I asked.

"Two bells. That gives us a little less than an hour."

"Where do you have Morrell and Orla locked up?"

"A Guardian safe house."

"Mychael, I don't mean to stick pins in your plan, but if I'm going to do a glamour of this woman, I have to see her. I can't do this without details."

"I've got all the details you need." He laid his index finger to his temple. "Right here."

"Use our bond."

Mychael nodded once. "The cell where we're holding Morrell and Orla has a ward across the bars so they can't see out, but I can see in. You'll have to reproduce her clothes yourself as part of the glamour, but I have all of her weapons here."

"*All* of her weapons?"

"I think she carries even more steel than you do, if that's possible. They're over there on the bed."

I went, I looked, and I really liked.

There were assorted daggers of various sizes, and a brace of throwing stars, but what made my hands itch with "gimme" was a Nebian scimitar. I picked it up and pulled the blade from the scabbard and kept pulling, and it kept coming. Long, curved, and utterly lethal. It almost made my pair of goblin blades look puny.

"I think I'm in love." I glanced back at Mychael. "Will I like her taste in clothes?"

Mychael gave me a crooked grin. "I don't think so; but who knows? You may surprise me."

"So how do we do this?"

"The easiest and most direct way is through palm-to-temple contact."

"We're spending a lot of time lately touching each other."

Mychael's grin broadened into a mischievous smile. "Do you have a problem with that?"

I chuckled. "I haven't yet, even when naked. After we're touching, then what?"

"I'll show you what I saw, and you just let me know when you've seen enough of Maire Orla to do a glamour."

Mychael put his palms to my temples, and within moments I had Orla's image.

Maire Orla was beautiful, brunette, and busty—and she was dressed to show as much skin as you could in public and not be arrested. Now I knew why she carried all that steel; there was no way a woman could walk around looking like that and wearing that little and expect to be left alone.

She wore blood-red leather from head to toe. Her boots extended to mid-thigh. Thighs that were otherwise left bare by her short leather skirt layered with overlapping disks of brass armor. The armor was mostly for decoration, but it would also direct any ogling male eyes to the bare thighs between the tops of the tall boots and the bottom of the short skirt. I wondered if she wore anything underneath, and I was sure every man who saw her wondered the same thing. I imagined her throwing stars had discouraged some wandering eyes from becoming wandering hands. Her own hands were covered by red leather gloves that came up to her elbows. Between the gloves and the scimitar, it was obvious that Maire Orla was a woman who knew how to accessorize.

A wide leather belt studded with brass was laced high and tight around a crimson leather bustier, pushing up and out what I had to admit were a very impressive pair of breasts. If she so much as breathed wrong, any ogling eyes would get two more things to gander.

"Jeez, you could set a beer on those things," I said.

Mychael grinned. "Have you seen enough?"

"*Amply* more than enough." I opened my eyes and Mychael lowered his hands from my temples. I didn't step back; neither did he. "You're enjoying this, aren't you?"

"Seeing you turn yourself into another woman? I prefer you just the way you are."

"But you wouldn't mind seeing me in red leather."

His voice turned husky. "There isn't a man breathing who wouldn't enjoy seeing that. I'm breathing, and last time I checked, I was a man. But for the record," he said deliberately, "I enjoy seeing you in whatever you're wearing." A slow, wicked smile spread across his face. "But mostly in what you're not wearing. The vision of you nude in my bed isn't leaving anytime soon."

"That's not a very professional healer attitude," I chided lightly.

"I'm not a healer right now."

I took another glance at his leathers. He could say that again.

"Do you think you can hold your own glamour knowing that it's me under that magic and leather?" I wove a subtle challenge into my voice. "Mixing business with pleasure can be dangerous. We should be careful."

He laughed. "For a living you find things that shouldn't be found, and have apparently taken up chasing specter-possessed naked men through bordellos as a hobby. Since when do you play it safe?"

Chapter 11

The mechanics of doing a glamour are easy. The thoughts of all that could go wrong are hard.

A couple years ago, I'd seen someone get stuck halfway through their transformation. It wasn't pretty. It also tossed a bucket of cold water on any inclination I might have had about trying it myself. I'd done it once to rescue Piaras from the elven embassy, and up until getting punched in the balls made me lose my concentration, my glamour, and nearly my lunch, I thought I'd done a fine job.

Maire Orla didn't have balls, but she had plenty of everything else, and chose to cover her bounty with barely enough red leather to be considered decent. I closed my eyes and gathered my focus, and began recalling her image.

Mychael was giving me the space I needed, both physical and magical. At the moment he was sitting in an armchair in the far corner of the room, the sense of his magic tamped down to a flicker. That by itself was no mean trick.

But he was watching me, and that was a problem. My own eyes were closed, so I couldn't see him, but I sure could feel him. It wasn't his magic; it was Mychael. Intensity controlled until it pulsed in the air. He was watching me from the shadows, and liking what he saw. That, he couldn't control. I knew it as surely as if he'd said it out loud.

"Close your eyes," I told him, without opening my own.

"But you can't see me." I could hear the smile in his voice.

"I can *feel* you watching. This is hard enough without an audience—especially an audience who's looking at me like I was naked. Again."

"Am not." Those blue eyes had to be glittering.

A tiny smile curled my lips. "Con man *and* a liar," I murmured, stubbornly refusing to open my eyes. "What other talents are you hiding from me?"

"You'll just have to wait and find out."

I bit my lip against a full smile. "Close your—"

"As you wish, Miss Benares. Closing my eyes, controlling my thoughts."

And hopefully his impulses.

All sense of him vanished. Utterly gone. It was as if he'd disappeared from the room. I'd only heard of a handful of mages who could negate their presence that quickly and completely. It was impressive as hell.

Concentrate, Raine. Time isn't on your side.

I closed my eyes, took a deep breath, and slowly exhaled. While we didn't have much time, there was no way I was rushing a glamour. Too much could go wrong, and all of it was ugly. I recalled the image Mychael had sent to me through our contact. Beautiful, brunette, busty, and belligerent. Mychael's contact had also included sound, and Maire Orla was definitely belligerent. I couldn't really blame her. If I was locked behind bars and wards, I'd be pissed, too.

Just like Tam.

"Shit," I hissed softly, and lost what concentration I had.

"What is it?" came Mychael's deep voice from the shadows. No sense of him, just a voice. A shiver ran up my back.

I breathed in through my nose and out through my mouth. Once. Twice. "Nothing I can't handle," I murmured, steering my mind back to the work. Focus on the work, Raine. Tam is fine. He's safe and protected. If you get this right, you'll get him out of there.

I focused on the image of Maire Orla, committing it to memory little by little, internalizing the smallest detail.

When I had it firmly in my mind's eye, I released the slightest touch of my power into the image in my mind, projecting it outward.

As I felt the glamour solidify around me, I opened my eyes and looked down. Damn. So this was what looking hot felt like. "Uh, you can open your eyes now." My voice was Maire Orla's, too.

"They're already open."

Of course they were. As soon as her breasts had popped up, Mychael's eyes had probably popped open—one of those involuntary male response things.

Mychael stood and came toward me, the candlelight flickering on his face.

Kester Morrell's face.

I instinctively reached for a dagger that wasn't there. I put out a hand between us. "Stop right there and let me get used to this."

Mychael stopped and I started breathing right again.

"I didn't mean to startle you," he said. At least it was still Mychael's voice.

"It's okay. It's just that closing my eyes to one man and opening them to another is a little unsettling."

Kester Morrell's eyes took in the scenery that was Maire Orla. "I can understand that."

Glamoured as Kester Morrell, Mychael's eyes were hazel and there was a little more brown to his otherwise auburn hair. He sported a short, neatly trimmed beard and mustache; and since Morrell was a human, the tips of Mychael's ears were rounded out. But the glitter in those hazel eyes was all Mychael, and all for me.

I couldn't really blame him. I thought I looked hot, too.

I ignored the heat in his gaze and strode over to the bed and started strapping Orla's weapons on. I'd used throwing stars before, but I'd never carried more than half a dozen. Maire Orla carried a ridiculous amount. I slung the baldric holding the stars across my now-ample chest, and a couple of the steel tips rested uncomfortably close to some bare skin.

"Well, that's one way to get men to stop looking," I muttered. Then something occurred to me, something that could give an awkward angle to our evening's masquerade. "What kind of relationship do Morrell and Orla have? They work together." I paused to ask what I thought I already knew the answer to. "What else do they do together?"

"When they travel, they only request one room or cabin," Mychael replied smoothly.

"And if they're good at what they do, they're not lacking for money, unless they're just being cheap."

"They're not being cheap."

"I kind of thought that'd be the case. So how publicly demonstrative are these two?"

"Do you *want* to be publicly demonstrative?" he teased.

"I want to get this right."

"When Morrell is working, he's all business."

"How about Orla?"

"Constantly looking for an excuse to use her steel."

And she and Morrell would be meeting with a scumbag who was hiring them to possibly kidnap someone I loved. The scimitar made a gratifyingly steely hiss as I resheathed it. "I might just enjoy being Maire Orla after all."

I had to admit that if I saw us coming down the street, I'd give serious thought to crossing to the other side. Maire Orla wasn't the shrinking violet type, and with all the steel I was carrying, and magic I was packing, my stride turned into a bit of a strut. I just couldn't seem to help myself, and to tell you the truth, I didn't want to.

Mychael was walking next to me, but we were giving each other enough room to move should the need arise, though Maire Orla would have thought of being ambushed as more of an opportunity for entertainment.

"We're being watched," Mychael said in mindspeak. *"Though with the way your hips are moving, I don't think they've noticed me."*

"Who?"

"Karl Cradock is the paranoid type. We're two blocks from the Bare Bones. He'll have guards posted outside, but it appears he's posted lookouts here." His gaze, shadowed by his hat, was on me, and a crooked grin curled his lips. *"I imagine they'll try to take our weapons before we go inside."*

I added an evil smile to my sashay. *"They're welcome to try."*

We got to the Bare Bones without bloodshed, but the place looked suspiciously like a trap from the get-go. Either that or Karl Cradock really was one seriously paranoid son of a bitch. Though considering who he was working for, both scenarios were possible.

It had been my experience that that many men didn't casually loiter outside of a bar unless they were looking for company of the curvy kind, or waiting to instigate an encounter of the violent kind. Since there wasn't a working girl in sight, I thought they were here for us. I'd had worse welcoming committees, but I was in no mood to play whatever games they had planned.

"Take it easy," came Mychael's voice in my mind. *"Cradock is just being careful."*

"I don't think he told his bully boys that."

"Let me do the talking."

That was fine with me; what I wanted to do didn't involve words. I dropped my hand to one of Orla's daggers.

Mychael was getting violent looks; I was getting looks usually reserved for dessert.

There were six that I could see; there were probably more. There always were. The burly ones stayed put; two lean men standing more or less on either side of the bar's door started out into the street toward us. I knew the drill. The big muscle stays put and the quick muscle comes out to say hello. I knew exactly what they were going to do; I'd been on the receiving end before. The two coming toward us would ask us in their own charming way to give up our weapons. Naturally we would refuse, and while our attention was on the duo, at least two of the big bruisers would try to sneak up behind us. If they caught you, you had a choice: give up your weapons or the big boys would shake you silly until you dropped them.

I'd found that the trick to getting past all of them while remaining armed and unshaken was to make the first move and make it count.

Mychael wanted to handle it. I was curious to see what he was going to do.

Mychael stopped in the middle of the street. I stopped about three feet on his right side, leaving him plenty of room to draw the blade strapped across his back. Conveniently, I was right-handed and Mychael was a lefty. It worked out nicely; we could fight and stay out of each other's way at the same time.

My weapons were all out in plain view, though it wasn't like I had anywhere to hide anything. As Kester Morrell, Mychael had plenty of hidden weapons. I also knew that getting frisked wasn't a part of his plan.

One of the men slowed but kept coming, holding his hands up, cocky grin spreading across his face at the sight of me. "We don't want any trouble, gorgeous."

I casually drew a dagger. The blade was in my left hand; a painful surprise was about to be in my right. "Then act like a gentleman and go open the door for me." Orla's voice was rich and sultry as hell with a razor's edge. I absently wondered if I could glamour just the voice for future use. It could come in handy.

"No can do," said the man walking toward me. "We've got our orders not to let you inside with all that steel. The boss can't be too careful."

The other guard was coming up on my right side. "We've been ordered to search you." I heard the leer in his voice. "And we always obey orders."

Both men had their hands empty, the better to grope me with. Another two steps and one of them would be close enough to slice in half. I had no doubt Orla's scimitar was up to the task, but we'd come here to get information, not kill the bodyguards of the source of that information. I didn't think Karl Cradock would like us killing his men, though he'd probably understand why we had to hurt them a little. Heck, for all I knew this was some kind of twisted test.

I waited until my quarry was within reach and his eyes were hungrily locked on Orla's breasts. Dang, but these things were coming in handy. He reached out for me, and I reached out for him. With his eyes fixated on my breasts and his peripheral vision watching my dagger, he never saw my other hand dive in low for the grab.

I was really glad Maire Orla wore gloves. Some things a woman just didn't want to latch onto bare-handed.

Thug number one squealed and sucked in air through clenched teeth. Thug number two started to come to his friend's rescue. I say "started" because he never got there. Mychael took one step forward, grabbed the wrist of thug number two, and, with a move so fast it was a blur, put the man on his knees with his arm twisted at an impossible angle up and behind his back.

The big muscle moved in. Mychael twisted his man's arm and got a scream; I twisted the handful of what I had and got a squeak.

Mychael's voice was cold, mocking, and not his own. I didn't know what Kester Morrell sounded like, but I imagine Mychael's tone and inflection were an exact match. "Gentlemen, come any closer and I will break this man's arm, and my partner will . . ." He glanced over at the now-ashen-faced man who stood frozen at attention next to me, and I saw his shoulders shake with silent laughter. "My partner will finish what she started. We are here to see Karl Cradock. He invited us; that makes us his guests. Now, is this any way to welcome your employer's guests?"

"Put your weapons away," came a raspy voice from the now-open bar door. The light from inside cast a shadow of a tall form out into the street, but I couldn't see any details. "The gentleman is right. They are my guests, and hopefully my new business associates."

The four big men backed off. Mychael and I made no move to release our captives.

"Now, Morrell," Cradock chided from the doorway. "Surely my men's actions didn't warrant such abuse."

"No, it didn't," I shot back. "It warranted more."

"Jack, Enger, apologize to the lady immediately."

Words weren't coming easily to either one of them, but they managed to make some contrite noises.

"Release my men," Cradock told us. "You can keep your weapons for the duration of our talk."

Mychael laughed, a short bark. "And for the duration of our exit and trip back to our rooms."

Cradock smiled with a slow baring of teeth. "Never miss a loophole, do you?"

"It's healthier that way."

"Agreed. Now, if you please, release my men."

I gladly complied. There was only so long I wanted to twist the nuts of a complete stranger, wearing gloves or not.

My man groaned and dropped to his knees. Mychael's man decided to stay on his knees and cradle his arm. Our path to the front door of the tavern was now gratifyingly clear, and Mychael and I, glamoured as a pair of human kidnappers, strolled right on in.

The place was empty. Almost.

The only other person in the room was a man standing behind the bar who obviously was not a bartender. I'd trust him to mix ingredients for explosives or whip up a tasty poison—but not to serve me anything in a glass. I also noticed that one of his hands stayed suspiciously under the counter. He was smiling at me. I really hoped his hand was playing with a crossbow trigger.

"Privacy," Mychael noted. "I like it."

"I thought you'd approve," Cradock said.

Mychael pulled out a chair and made himself at home; his back to the wall and facing anything that remotely looked like it was, or could be, a door. I took up a post at his right shoulder. I didn't even want to try sitting down in that skirt.

"Did you forget to tell your men that we're all on the same side?" Mychael asked.

Cradock laughed. "You're on the same side you're always on—whatever side pays you the most."

"That was supposed to be you. But your welcoming committee out there makes me think that you'd rather get someone else for your smash and grab."

Cradock's hand went over his heart. "Your lack of trust wounds me."

"Not half as much as you'll hurt if you try to screw us over."

"Would I do that?"

"In a beat of your black heart," Mychael said.

"You understand that sometimes it's safer to talk business without unsightly weapons around."

"You mean without *us* having unsightly weapons." I negligently toyed with a throwing star near my cleavage. "And I don't find them unsightly in the least."

Cradock laughed, an ugly, hollow sound. "Vincent, get our guests some drinks. What will you have?" he asked Mychael.

"I'm not thirsty."

"What about the lady?" He said "lady" with a suggestive leer. "We can be most accommodating."

"The lady's blade would like something hot and red." I felt my lips slip naturally into a chilling smile. Orla must have used that one a lot. "Still willing to accommodate me?"

Mychael glanced around. "All this peace and quiet must have cost you. Beckett doesn't like losing business."

Cradock shrugged. "I'm not footing the bill."

"That would be the same person and the same money who

is footing *our* bill," Mychael reminded him. "I do hope you left enough to cover our expenses."

"I wouldn't insult you by offering you any less than we agreed. Five hundred kugarats of imperial goblin gold, fresh off a ship from Regor."

I had to stifle an impressed whistle. Not only was imperial goblin gold the purest there was and worth twice the same amount of any other gold; it was attainable only by a member of the goblin court. Tam wasn't a member, at least not anymore. Janos Ghalfari was. Though no doubt Balmorlan could claim that Tam could get his hands on anything he wanted to from court.

"Five hundred kugarats up front." Mychael paused. "Plus expenses."

Cradock slowly sat up in his chair. "Expenses?"

"Horses, lookouts, distractions, bribes."

"Bribes? You're kidnappers, not politicians."

"You should have paid a few people around town to keep their mouths shut; it would have been a good investment. You and your boys snatched that elf general. It was easy enough to find out. You passed on this job; I want to know why."

Cradock held up his hands. "An elf general turned up dead in the whore district; I had nothing to do with that. I'm only the middleman between the talent and a client who knows how to pay for what he wants."

"Your man outside—the one my partner tried to geld—was seen leaving the White Street stables after hiring four horses for a certain black carriage night before last. The horses were brought to a town house off Park Street. You and two of your men arrived soon after. They hitched up the horses, one man played coachman, the other got in the carriage with you. You went to the house where the general was having drinks with the Count of Rina." Mychael leisurely leaned back in his chair, the wood creaking in the sudden silence. "Is your memory sufficiently refreshed, or shall I continue?"

Anger flickered across Cradock's face. "No need."

The man behind the bar shifted. My fingers flicked a pair of throwing stars out of their leather slots.

"Hands on the bar," I told him. *"Now!"* Maire Orla was no spellsinger, but her voice cracked like a whip.

Bar boy's hands stayed right where they were. Oh yeah, he definitely had a crossbow under there. One big enough to splinter the front of the bar before it splintered me. Karl Cradock didn't want either one of us dead, at least not until we'd finished the job. But that didn't mean he wasn't going to let his bar boy have his fun. Cradock was finished playing games, and he wanted to be sure we knew it.

I had news for him. I wasn't in a playful mood, either. Maire Orla was a hypnotist, so I let her voice and eyes do their thing.

"Let's see your hands, bar boy," I whispered.

After a moment, the man's mouth went slack and his hands came out of hiding.

"Good," I purred. "Now put them on the bar and keep them there."

The man slowly put his hands on the bar, fingers spread.

That was entirely too easy. I kept my eyes on bar boy, while Mychael continued the negotiations.

Mychael's voice was as cold as bare steel. "You didn't want to touch this job. I want to know why and I want to know who I'm working for."

"Neither have anything to do with you."

"*If* I still accept it. Maire and I have the next job, so it has everything to do with us. If we're dead, we can't spend all that goblin gold you're about to pay us—plus a hundred extra to keep some mouths shut, or the deal's off."

"We had an agreement."

"An agreement that didn't involve us taking a stroll to the executioner's block because you were cheap."

Cradock shrugged. "The goblin wouldn't give me his name, not even a fake one, but his gold is the real thing, imperial pure. He came in on the same ship as that gold."

"What's he look like?"

"Why do you need to know?"

In my peripheral vision, Mychael stopped just short of rolling his eyes. "We're doing a job for him; chances are we'll see each other at the exchange. I want to be sure I'm handing over the merchandise to the man who paid for it."

"He's a goblin," Cradock said. "Gray-skins all look alike; you can't tell the bastards' ages."

"Guess for me."

"I don't know; fifty, maybe sixty. He had streaks of white in his hair."

That sure as hell wasn't Tam. It had to be Uncle Janos.

"Why does he want us?" Mychael asked.

"You're not elves. No one suspects humans in this town. Besides, you two have a reputation for good, clean work. My client needs the same attention to detail with this job."

"Our target is an elf?" I kept my voice level and business-like. Piaras was an elf; so was Mychael; so was my whole family.

"Yeah, he's an elf."

Dammit.

"Who's the job?" Mychael asked.

"Duke Markus Sevelien."

Chapter 12

"*And my client wants him delivered to the old Ta'karid temple* at sundown tomorrow," Cradock said, with a smug smile that held no hint of apology for any death and dismemberment we might incur from trying to pull off a major kidnapping in less than a day.

Mychael didn't move. "No deal."

"You agreed to the terms."

"Terms that gave us at least three days' planning and prep time." Mychael stood. "The deal's off."

"Are you saying you can't do it?"

Mychael didn't bite. "I'm saying we won't. If your client wants the duke, he'll have to pay more and wait longer. One day to get inside the elven embassy, get Sevelien, and get out isn't kidnapping; it's suicide."

Cradock smiled like a man with a secret. "The duke isn't staying in the embassy. Two days ago he moved into the house at the end of Ambassador Row."

That was more than a little disconcerting. Why the hell did Markus move out of the embassy?

"Ambassador Row, which is conveniently around the corner from the elven embassy," Mychael noted dryly. "Still no go."

Judging from the sweat beading on Cradock's upper lip, if the deal didn't go down, and Markus didn't get taken to the Ta'karid temple, Cradock wasn't going to live much longer than sundown tomorrow himself.

I knew exactly what he'd done. "The goblin has already paid you, hasn't he? Though perhaps a better question would be what is he going to do to you when he doesn't get what he's already paid you for? I think he'll take his gold back with interest out of your hide." I leaned forward and crossed my arms on the back of Mychael's chair and lowered my voice. "Unless he said he'd take you—just like he did the general."

A twitch took up residence in the corner of Karl Cradock's left eye. Yep, I'd hit a nerve.

I pushed on. "You heard what happened to him, didn't you? Or did you get to watch while it happened?"

Cradock's continued silence was all the answer I needed.

"Sounds like you did the job, then stayed to help with the cleanup," Mychael noted. "While your client no doubt found your attention to detail commendable, I wouldn't exactly call pushing the general's body out of a coach tidy."

"You're not paying us enough to clean up that kind of mess," I told Cradock. "We're in acquisitions—and I don't do housework."

In a blink of his twitching eye, Cradock's bravado was back, though he still looked a tad pasty. I didn't blame him; riding in a dark coach with a dried corpse would turn me pasty, too.

"My client made it worth my while," Cradock told us. "For that much money, I'd toss my mother into the street."

I snorted. "You have one?"

He flashed a grin. "Not anymore. And he'll probably offer you the same deal."

"I wouldn't call being allowed to live only if I help dispose of a body a deal." Mychael adjusted his cloak, and I saw the flicker of light reflected in the gem on the chain around his neck. My own hung just below Orla's ample breasts.

"We'll take the job," Mychael said. "On the original terms *plus* an extra hundred in expenses—but we'll pass on the client's bonus. We're not undertakers." He leveled his gaze on Cradock. "And we want it all now."

"Half now, half when the job is done."

"Karl, I don't think you're going to be here when the job is done. There are two freighters in port, both of Caesolian registry. You're from Caesolia; you know the captain of the *Reliant*, and you've already booked passage."

Karl Cradock tried to look cool and calm, but his eye twitch was back. "The client hasn't paid me my bonus, and I'm sure as hell not leaving Mid without it."

"Yes, you will, because you value your life more than a few goblin coins; I don't care how much they're worth. We want our money now." Mychael put both hands flat on the table in front of Cradock and leaned forward. "Every. Last. Coin."

Karl Cradock told us we wouldn't find Markus Sevelien in the elven embassy, which was good because I'd been in there once, almost got caught, nearly died, and was in no hurry to repeat either experience.

Where we were going was worse, if that was possible. It only confirmed my opinion about the wee hours of the morning—nothing good ever happened after two bells.

Generally, if you've just been paid an obscene amount of money to kidnap someone, you stash your gold and then you snatch your target. Not that I've had personal experience, but my last name was Benares.

We were carrying our payment, all of it. Goblin gold is lighter than normal gold, so one man could carry what it'd normally take a pack mule to haul. Mychael was doing the carrying. He had a satchel and pockets; all I had was an absurd amount of cleavage.

We were doing our walking-and-hiding thing again. Walk until we spotted another living soul, then hide in the shadows. And when we talked, we kept our voices low.

Markus was staying in one of the lavish homes on Ambassador Row, which was conveniently around the corner from—and within screaming distance of—Embassy Row with all the guards and weapons and death and destruction. A great place to visit in the middle of the night, if you had a death wish. A fly couldn't sneeze on Ambassador Row without attracting attention of the fatal kind. Not exactly the ideal scenario for a kidnapping that Mychael said wasn't going to be a kidnapping.

Not that I thought knocking Markus over the head and hauling him off was necessarily a bad plan. And it definitely wouldn't take much right now to get me to knock Markus over the head. In my family, kidnapping was often the first step to productive negotiations with a rival or enemy. Any decent strategist knew that negotiations were better conducted from a position of power. For a Benares, that often meant a small room, a chair, and your rival blindfolded and tied to it.

I suspected Mychael's plan involved warning Markus in some way that he was next on Sarad Nukpana's menu, but if the two of us as Mychael Eiliesor and Raine Benares couldn't be seen anywhere but the citadel, I didn't know how we could do whatever Mychael wanted to do and still remain among the living, or at least the un-jailed.

I didn't know because Mychael hadn't told me.

"So are you going to tie a note to a rock and throw it through his bedroom window? Or toss a carrier pigeon over the wall and hope a trigger-happy guard doesn't shoot it?"

"What?"

"How are you going to tell Markus that Nukpana's uncle put a price on his head—and the rest of him?"

Mychael gripped my upper arm and pulled me into an alley.

"I think a personal visit would be best." He gave me a look that spoke volumes, and then he sighed. "Though this would be much easier if you weren't with me."

I knew exactly what he was getting at. "So suddenly I'm not so indispensable?"

"Suddenly you're a woman with a vindictive glint in those pretty gray eyes."

I pursed my lips against a smile I felt coming on. "Compliments will get you nowhere."

"Which one? Vindictive or pretty?"

I shrugged. "Either one works for me. But if you're worried that I'll choke the life out of Markus, I promise I'll be perfect."

Mychael chortled. "A perfect what?"

"Whatever Markus deserves."

"No punching or choking."

"I would never dream of it."

"Raine." That one word held a world of warning.

"Okay, I'd dream of it, but I wouldn't do it."

"Because you'd rather stab him."

I just smiled. Mychael was getting to know me way too well.

"That's not what we're here for," he told me.

"That's not what *you're* here for. If Markus had anything to do with Balmorlan kidnapping Piaras or getting Tam charged with murder, there are some impulses that I won't even try to control."

"Can you control yourself long enough for us to get into the house?"

My smile was tiny and perfect, maybe even demure. "Oh, you can count on it. I *want* to get in the same room with Markus. The question is how you propose to do that. We can't exactly stroll up to the front door looking like this, knock, and hope we get invited in for drinks."

"I thought we'd start by dropping our glamours." Mychael dropped his.

I followed suit. I have to admit, it was a relief. My back was starting to hurt from carrying around what was no doubt Maire Orla's pair of pride and joys. "Though what about the guards? If everyone's supposed to believe we're in the citadel and then Markus's men see us, guess what? Cover blown."

"We won't be seeing the guards and they won't see us."

"Then what—"

"If you can't control a situation, you have to know every detail, don't you?"

"What's wrong with that?"

Mychael's eyes twinkled from under the brim of his hat. "I'll bet you don't like surprises for your birthday, either."

"No, I don't. And what the hell does that have to do with anything?"

He leaned in close with a conspiratorial whisper. "Not all surprises are bad."

Mychael took my face in his hands and those blue eyes gazed down into mine. There was no question reflected there, no uncertainty, and he sure as hell wasn't asking my permission. Those eyes told me what he wanted.

He kissed me.

His lips didn't demand; they simply took. With delicious slowness. His fingers of one hand ran lightly up the curve of my ear, lingering for a breath-catching caress at the tip before sliding down to my throat, leaving a trail of tingle-inducing heat in their wake. By the time his hand slipped around the back of my neck and pressed me to him, my hands were on him, sliding up to his chest and around his neck. My hands didn't ask my permission, either. Traitorous hands.

Mychael's kiss turned into a tantalizing nibble, gently pulling my bottom lip between his teeth, sucking, teasing.

I opened my eyes and was met with twin pools of deep ocean blue, gleaming with mischief as he released my lips and planted light kisses on my nose and forehead. His lips lingered there, the warmth of his breath and body doing a fine job of banishing the night cold—or at least giving me something better to think about. His lips had released mine, but his arms were wrapped firmly around my waist and didn't seem to be in a rush to let me go.

"What was that for?" I found myself short of breath.

"Hopefully, a pleasant surprise."

I looked up at him, a slow smile spreading across my face. "Eh, I've had worse."

Mychael grinned and his fingers found that ticklish place on my ribs and I squealed before I could stop myself. His lips instantly covered my mouth, muffling the sound. He took his sweet time muffling.

"See, not all surprises are bad," his lips murmured against mine. "And some are more enjoyable than you'll admit."

"Was that a distraction to keep me from stabbing Markus?"

"That depends. Did it work?"

"As a distraction, it was first-rate."

"My lips humbly thank you."

"As a deterrent . . . sorry, no dice."

Mychael pressed his lips together. I actually think he was trying not to laugh—at me. I narrowed my eyes and glared at him.

"That sounds like a challenge to me," he said. "I'll have to make every effort to do better next time."

"So what's your plan?" I asked. "For Markus," I quickly added.

Mychael ran his hands down my ribs to my hips and back again before releasing me. "Very well. After we're in the house and have informed Markus of the situation, I plan to find out the truth of his involvement in all this."

I bared my teeth in a fierce grin. "Now, *that's* a plan I can—"

"My way," he told me firmly.

"Your way what?"

"We're going to find out *my* way. No fists, no daggers."

"And which way is that?"

"I'll ask him."

"You expect him to be honest?"

"I'll know if he's lying, and so will you."

True. Part of me didn't want to know that Markus was lying—or that he would lie to me. It was the same part of me that didn't want to know that I had been a part-time agent and a full-time patsy. I thought I meant more to Markus than that, and if I didn't . . . well, dammit, it hurt. It hurt like hell. Not to mention it made me feel naïve and downright stupid. I didn't like either one. During my life, I'd been screwed over by professionals, people who'd done it before and would gleefully do it again. I really didn't want to add Markus's name to that list.

"What if he is lying?" I asked quietly. "Or what if he tells us the truth and admits he did it?"

Mychael's expression was cheerfully grim. "*Then* we'll do it your way."

"Best idea I've heard all night," I muttered. "So, how do we get in the house?"

"I thought I'd give my usual signal and Markus's butler would let us in through the back door. A quick veiling spell and the guards don't see us. Markus has plenty of clandestine meetings in the middle of the night."

I just stood there, and then I think I blinked. I wasn't sure if I had or not; I was too stunned by what I'd just heard.

"Your *usual* signal?"

"I've been there before."

"Apparently. What about the not so little fact that Markus is Taltek Balmorlan's boss?" I asked. "The sadistic son of a bitch who kidnaps people for his personal armory. Carnades's new best friend. Minion to the late and leathery General Aratus."

"You have suspicions but no proof that Sevelien condoned any of Balmorlan's activities," Mychael said.

"When his people are attacking my friends, suspicions are all I need. Just because Markus's name isn't on Balmorlan's orders doesn't mean he's innocent."

"Nor does it condemn him as guilty." His look softened. "You've worked with him for how long?"

"Nine years."

"That's a long time, Raine."

"Yeah, it is," I admitted reluctantly. I didn't want to let go of a perfectly good vindictive anger.

"During that time did Markus Sevelien ever do anything to earn your distrust?"

"No, but—"

"What do your instincts tell you?"

"The same thing they always tell me. Be careful."

"Good advice in any situation. Do they tell you anything else?"

"Markus is Balmorlan's boss; he gives the orders."

"That's not an instinct; that's an assumption." His hands slid up my arms to just above my elbows. "Raine, many things are not as they seem, and people aren't always who you think they are. But that doesn't mean you can't trust them just as much as you always have. And that includes their plans."

"Are we still talking about Markus?"

"What I said applies to both me and Markus Sevelien."

I paused. "Do *you* trust Markus?"

"I do."

I sighed. "And I trust you."

"Why, thank you."

"Don't take this the wrong way, but I'm going to reserve judgment on Markus."

One side of Mychael's lips curled in a crooked smile. "I wouldn't expect anything else."

Mychael decided to hide the gold. Made sense to me. If we needed to run away from anything, Mychael's clanking would be a sure giveaway. He found a neat little hidey-hole in the alley he'd yanked me into. He hid the satchel in the hole and kicked some alley garbage over it. When we finished with Markus, we'd stop back by and collect our ill-gotten booty.

We got within fifty yards of Markus's house without incident. I was nothing short of stunned. But what didn't stun, surprise, or shock me in the least was a stone wall around the property that had to be at least eight feet tall. The only way I caught a glimpse of the house was through a pair of massive iron gates wide enough to admit a carriage and outriders. The iron glowed blue with protective wards that snapped and sparked whenever a moth flew too close. That was one hell of a bug zapper—or elf-kidnapper zapper. The top of the wall sported the same blue glow. Cozy.

"Other than this one, the only other occupied house on the street is at the far end," Mychael said in mindspeak.

That would explain the quiet—that and it was past two bells in the morning. Just because we didn't see Markus's guards didn't mean they weren't there. Markus hired only the best. Our dark leathers helped us blend into the stonework of the building at our backs.

We'd been standing in the shadows for nearly ten minutes, motionless, letting our eyes adjust to the darkness surrounding the house, to discern what was a shadow and what might be guards standing as still as we were.

There were no guards.

There should have been.

Something was very wrong.

I knew Markus well enough to find him using my seeking skills. If he was in that house, I'd know it. No need to step in something deep—or worse, a trap—if the man we needed to see wasn't even there. But if he was there, and he was in danger, or hurt, or . . . or he was the man who ordered the people I cared about kidnapped and arrested and threatened with execution. If he'd done that, whatever danger was in his house with him right now was welcome to him. But if he hadn't signed those orders and Balmorlan had acted alone . . .

Dammit. Why did this have to be so complicated?

Mychael's hand was a comforting pressure on my shoulder as I took a deep breath, letting it out slowly and silently.

"Is he in there?" Mychael asked.

"I don't know."

"Can you find out without anyone—"

"Yes."

"Do it."

I closed my eyes and tried to relax, breathing deeply. Breathing I could do; relaxing wasn't going to happen, so I stopped trying and just went to work. I focused my will on an image of Markus in my mind until it was almost real enough to touch. Then I reached out across the street, over the wall, and froze.

I started shaking, but not from cold. Death was on the other side of that wall, inside that house. A chilled, spidery-light touch, a manipulator of death.

Mychael's fingers tightened on my shoulder. *"Reapers?"*

I kept my will focused on not moving, not giving myself away. It wasn't a Reaper; what was in Markus's house didn't harvest the dead. It was alive and took a perverse pleasure in bringing back the dead. And he was powerful. Oh yes, he had power in spades, bone deep and cold as the grave.

It was a nachtmagus—and Evil with a capital *E*.

A pair of tall figures stood on either side of the front doors. A breeze shifted the branches of the tree shielding the house from the moonlight and I saw the face of the figure standing closest to me.

Gray skin, black armor, red serpent insignia over whatever heart the bastard had.

Khrynsani temple guards.

There was only one nachtmagus in town who could command a Khrynsani escort.

Janos Ghalfari. Sarad Nukpana's uncle.

Ghalfari had hired two human kidnappers to take Markus, but now he was here himself. Why? And if Ghalfari was here, was Nukpana with him?

Through our bond, Mychael saw everything I did; and from the dangerous narrowing of his eyes, I wasn't the only one who smelled a rat.

"Who knew that you had Morrell and Orla locked up?" I asked.

"Five of my men."

I didn't say someone squealed. Mychael knew it as well as I did.

The little voice that'd kept me alive for most of my adult life screamed for me to run. I thought the little voice's idea was brilliant, but I wasn't running. I wasn't even leaving. Even if Markus had signed Balmorlan's orders with his own hand, I couldn't leave him for Sarad Nukpana to feed on for hours, slowly draining every drop of life.

If Markus was guilty, I had to know. If he was innocent, I had to save him.

Sometimes having a conscience was a bitch.

Though this wasn't just about Markus. If Sarad Nukpana took Markus's knowledge and memories, he would know the names of double agents, undercover operatives, plans, plots, defenses—in one stroke he could cripple elven intelligence, and a lot of good people would suffer and die. As far as agency knowledge, power, and influence, no one was Markus's equal. Sarad Nukpana was fueling himself up to be an elf-annihilating juggernaut.

"You're leaving and going for help," came Mychael's words in my mind.

That told me he was staying while I went. And while I was gone, he'd go in. No way. *"I'm not going anywhere."* The elven embassy was a block away, but if I showed up at their gates, they'd just arrest me and jerk me inside. Or they'd try. None of which would get help here in time to save Markus. *"You just want me away from here."*

"Raine, I can't risk you being captured."

I knew what he meant. If Sarad Nukpana was in there, the Saghred was going to try to make me take him.

"I'm strong and stubborn, remember? Or have you changed your mind about that, and think the Saghred and I will find Sarad Nukpana so scrumptious that I'll lose control?"

"If Sarad Nukpana is in there, he's not alone. If you were going to kidnap Markus Sevelien, how many people would you bring?"

"More than two, that's for damned sure." I glanced toward the house again. Lights were on and entirely too many people

were home, the wrong people. *"I think I can control myself,"* I said dryly. *"I'm not going to get caught—and neither are you."* No one, whether living, dead, or anywhere in between, was going to lay a hand on Mychael.

We both knew what I meant. Yes, the Saghred and I were one. And yes, I was Sarad Nukpana's planned dessert, but I would use the full force of that rock against that murdering goblin if I had to. Actually, this was the chance I needed. End this now, here, tonight, before anyone else died, before Sarad Nukpana was strong enough to make his own rules and break all the others.

Mychael's silence told me he knew he was wasting his breath, and that he didn't have time to argue with me. His hand went from my shoulder to clasp my hand.

"Then we need to veil," he said, and I felt his magic run up my arm and into every part of me. Instantly, it felt like I was still there, but not quite. I looked down at myself and up at Mychael. We were both still there. But from past experience, I knew no one else could see us.

"If Janos Ghalfari is inside, those two Khrynsani might be keeping watch because he and his men are still trying to find Markus—or Sarad Nukpana might be with them."

And Markus might be slowly dying right now.

Mychael tightened his grip on my hand, making sure I stayed put. *"There's a street at the back of the property that runs the length of Ambassador Row,"* he told me. *"There has to be a coach waiting. Can you sense if Sarad Nukpana has been in it without getting too close?"*

I'd been up close and personal with Sarad Nukpana before, and each time had been one time too many. I knew his scent and sense.

"Yes."

"Let's go."

There was a coach and horses, and guards for both. I'd gotten a good look at the coach Nukpana had transported General Aratus in; this wasn't it. That meant Tam's dark mage associates and Mychael's Guardians were at this moment at an abandoned carriage house watching a coach that wasn't going anywhere, at least not tonight. If it had been the same coach, they would have followed it and ended up here. We'd have backup.

A different coach meant no reinforcements. No help.

Just us.

The guards around the coach were Khrynsani temple guards, not mages. That was good. While all Khrynsani were magically skilled, temple guards spent more time with blades than spells. I could seek past the four guards that I could see. There were probably more close by, but as long as they weren't high-level Khrynsani mages, I should be able to find out what I needed to know without giving myself away.

I reached out across the thirty yards or so between me and the coach. There were no shields or wards on the coach. Uncle Janos was depending on his Khrynsani to keep his means of escape safe. I didn't want to steal it; I just wanted a look inside.

I felt myself grin. Or maybe I did want to steal it.

Spook the horses, they'd bolt, then Nephew Nukpana and Uncle Janos would have to walk home. Now, that image was a keeper. Take away their transportation and get the added bonus of a distraction that might just get us into the house, or at least on the grounds.

"Raine, just see if Sarad Nukpana has been in that coach in the past hour and leave the horses to me."

I was incredulous. *"You like my plan?"*

"I like this plan."

I really didn't want to look inside that coach and find Sarad Nukpana sitting there while his uncle was inside catching his dinner, so I got close enough to sense anything inside and took a big, psychic sniff.

My skin did a full head-to-toe crawl. Sarad Nukpana had definitely been in that coach; that meant he was here, inside the house. A black, oily sensation crawled along my skin, accompanied by the smell of musty air and mold. Death. Ancient and eternal. I didn't know if it was from Nukpana or from the lives he'd taken. It didn't matter. He was inside, so was his death-dealing uncle, and so was Markus.

Musty air and mold.

The same things I'd sensed when I touched General Aratus's corpse.

Sarad Nukpana's lair.

I needed more than confirmation; I needed a location.

I stopped, forced down some damned near overwhelming revulsion, and inhaled with all my senses. I got an image instantly. Smooth, hard stone, darkness, flickering firelight at the end of a long corridor or tunnel. The walls were smooth and cool, definitely man-made, a corridor or hallway, then. Shafts of cool blue light shone down from a light source embedded in the ceiling, possibly lightglobes. Rats scuttled and squeaked in the darkness next to the walls, running away from the light.

Away from what was in that room.

I'd been on enough ships to trust the instincts of rodents. In packs they could be downright brazen, so if a pack of rats ran from something, they had a good reason.

I had to see what that reason was, and I couldn't do that without going into that room.

The coach lurched and my link snapped. Dammit. The guards couldn't sense me, but the horses could, and they jerked in their harnesses to get away.

I usually ended up on the ground when a seeking link broke that quickly. I wasn't on the ground now. Mychael was holding me up, one arm tightly around my waist, the other on the back of my head, pressing my face into his chest. I guess he didn't want to chance that I'd make any noise.

With our link, he knew what I'd seen.

"Recognize it?" I asked.

"No." He didn't sound happy about that.

I wasn't, either. It seemed like Mychael knew every bordello, alley, and abandoned building on the island, but he had no idea where the spooky room with the running rats was.

The image and memory wasn't going anywhere. That was something about seeking. What you saw, you got to keep whether you wanted it or not. We'd find out where it was later. Now we had to get into Markus's house. We had a family reunion to break up.

"*Well, if you were planning on spooking the horses, I got them started for you. What's the plan after that?*"

"*The back gate is just beyond where the coach is,*" Mychael told me. "*Just inside is a gardener's shed. It stays unlocked. There's a trapdoor with a short tunnel leading into the house's basement. The basement door is warded, but I can get around it.*"

"*You* have *been here before. Okay, we get in the basement, then what?*"

"*We'll evaluate the situation and act accordingly.*"

Which meant Mychael's plan was changing with our situation. He was flexible; I liked that. What I didn't like was that we didn't know what was waiting for us inside that basement.

I was right. Nothing good ever happened after two bells.

Chapter 13

Mychael began humming at a level so low it barely registered in my ears, but I was close enough to him to feel the rumbling deep in his chest. There were four horses harnessed to that coach. A split second later, every last one had its ears flat to its head. Then they started neighing nervously and pawing the cobblestones. When two Khrynsani guards came up on either side to calm them, the horses screamed and reared as if those goblins had stepped straight out of their worst nightmare.

Then they bolted. The coach went up on two wheels as the terrified horses tore around the corner, the friction of their horseshoes raising sparks against the cobbles. They rounded the next corner and were gone. Two of the guards took off in pursuit. Two remained.

We went from outnumbered to piece of cake in under ten seconds.

"Can you hold the veil on your own?" Mychael asked.

"Oh, yeah."

"Get to the gate. I'll take care of the guards."

Mychael glided swiftly and in complete silence to the pair of goblin guards and snatched them up by the scruffs of their necks like a pair of kittens. They didn't even have time to reach for their weapons. I felt Mychael's surge of magic as the goblins' eyes rolled back in their heads and they went down. It helped that they were standing close together, no doubt trying to come up with an excuse for their bosses as to why they had no way to get back home to the family lair. Mychael altered his grip from their necks to the backs of their uniform collars and quickly dragged them down the street and tossed them behind a pile of garbage.

The garden gate had probably been warded, but the goblins had deactivated it for a quick getaway. I appreciated their consideration almost as much as I appreciated that someone had kept the gate's hinges oiled. There was a bit of a breeze, so a slowly opening garden gate could be blamed on a loose latch and the wind. I slipped through and left it open for Mychael. I didn't see any goblins in the garden. If they were there, and I was sure they were, they were probably sticking close to the house, making sure Nukpana and Ghalfari weren't disturbed.

The door to the garden shed was conveniently located on the side of the small building and the only thing it faced was an ancient oak in the garden's corner. True to Mychael's word, it was unlocked. A few seconds later, Mychael joined me inside.

"How long will those two be out?" I asked.

"At least an hour."

Within minutes, we were through the trapdoor, down the ladder, and, with the help of a lightglobe that Mychael conjured, quickly covered the distance to the house under cover and underground. I'd never liked tunnels, and events during the past few weeks hadn't given me any reason to change my opinion, but I was grateful for this one. When we reached the basement door, Mychael disabled the ward with a single word. But before turning the knob, he carefully reached out with a searching spell.

Mychael didn't have to say anything, out loud or otherwise. I felt it myself. No one was on the other side of that door, or even anywhere near. I didn't have to say I didn't like it; from Mychael's expression, he liked it even less than I did.

I knew what it meant. There was no one down here because everyone was upstairs. And if we were going to save Markus, that was where we had to go.

Mychael turned the knob and slowly opened the door.

Nothing. No Khrynsani welcoming committee, but I could feel them and hear sibilant goblin voices coming from the floor above us.

I hadn't seen any horses other than the ones harnessed to the coach. That told me there couldn't be that many goblins upstairs. Probably. Hopefully. Though considering that there were only two of us, anything more than that was too many.

An acrid smell tickled my nose, familiar and potentially helpful. I took another whiff to be sure. I felt myself smile. Oh yeah. It was dark in the far corner, but my Benares nose had never lied to me when it came to these little beauties. I tapped Mychael twice on the shoulder and jerked my head toward something that just might even the odds—or eliminate the odds entirely.

Markus Sevelien was a connoisseur of the finer things in life, most notably wines and exotic liqueurs. Even though Markus was only living here temporarily, he probably had a nicely stocked wine cellar down here somewhere, but this wasn't it.

This was an ammunition cache that would have made Phaelan green with envy.

There were eight plain wooden crates stacked in the corner. The lids on the top two were open. Mychael increased the glow from his lightglobe and I took a peek inside. Carefully nestled in three rows were a dozen of what looked like metal kegs so small I could have easily wrapped my hands around one. Nebian grenades. Someone who didn't know what was inside might have called them cute. Just one of those little kegs contained enough Nebian black powder to turn the ceiling above our heads into the floor beneath our feet. Regular black powder didn't have anywhere near the punch that the Nebian variety did. It was literally powder fine, highly unstable, and obscenely expensive. The Nebians were a wealthy people, and the contents of these little kegs was one of the reasons.

The simple beauty of a Nebian grenade was that no fuses were necessary—just throw and run; the metal was thin and the impact would take care of the rest. Once the powder inside was exposed to the air, you had ten seconds to run like hell or become a permanent part of whatever was left of what you were blowing up.

Very nice.

Markus favored less obvious and more elegant means of dealing with his enemies. And until two days ago, he'd been staying at the elven embassy, which made me wonder if he even knew these were down here. Maybe, maybe not. It depended on if the Markus upstairs was the Markus I knew or the son of a bitch I suspected. If all of those crates were full of Nebian grenades, there was enough "kaboom" to turn this end of Ambassador Row into Ambassador Crater. It wasn't that I wanted to use a grenade, but if the situation went to hell in a handbasket, I wasn't going to turn up my nose at any viable solution.

I found myself grinning. *"Are you thinking what I'm thinking?"*

Mychael took a look in the crate and shook his head. *"You're thinking extreme property damage; I'm thinking quick and messy death—for us."*

I emptied the leather pouch clipped to my belt of anything that a girl in a house full of evil goblins didn't need and reached for the closest grenade.

Instantly Mychael's hand locked around my wrist. *"Raine."*

The look I gave him was calm and cool—and if he thought he saw an explosives-crazed Benares glint in my eyes, he was mistaken. *"For use only if necessary."*

"Define 'necessary.'"

"If Nukpana and his uncle give us Markus and let us leave, then it won't be necessary."

Mychael just looked at me. *"When and where have you used these before?"*

"If I told you, you might have to arrest me. Besides, since my arms and legs are still attached to the rest of me, it means I know what I'm doing."

He sighed and released my wrist. *"If you jostle that thing around, I'll be picking what's left of you out of the rafters."*

"You mean there'll be rafters left?" I asked innocently. *"How disappointing."* I tucked a grenade inside my pouch, followed by a second one. If our situation went down the crapper to the point where I needed to cause one explosion, chances were I'd need two. *"Now, what's your plan?"*

He told me. I think my jaw dropped.

And he thought *I* was nuts.

The first part of Mychael's plan involved getting upstairs, getting the lay of the land, and not getting caught. I thought that was an excellent start. From there, it sailed into uncharted territory, at least as far as I was concerned. Mychael's plan was twofold: he would take care of every goblin between us and Markus, and I would stay out of sight. While I was all for Mychael eliminating goblins and I liked how he was going to do it, I wasn't a big fan of being a wallflower.

According to Mychael, the first floor was the public reception area: sitting rooms, a small ballroom, and offices. The second floor was mainly personal quarters, and the third was servants' quarters. The goblins were on the first floor. At least that was where Sarad Nukpana was. I was getting the same black, oily sensation crawling along my skin that I did outside with the coach. Nukpana was here and he was close. That oily trail went to where Mychael said were the front reception rooms, probably the sitting room, which was one flight up, down one corridor and take a right, cross the entry hall and we'd be there. It was right next to the front door and freedom.

Except we weren't going there, at least not until Mychael had done his work.

He had the reputation of being the best spellsinger in the

seven kingdoms. If everything went according to plan, no one would hear a single note until it was too late. Mychael would be singing a concert for one set of goblin ears at a time, taking out every guard between us and that sitting room. Once we got there, the plan was to hit Nukpana, Ghalfari, and anyone in that room with the same song. It'd have to be a lightning-quick strike. If they sensed or heard one note beforehand, the plan was shot to hell and probably us along with it. Sarad Nukpana and his uncle were that powerful; they were also within killing distance of the man we needed to rescue. It was a classic hostage situation with a sick twist: Nukpana wanted Markus's knowledge, memories, and life force for himself, but if push came to shove, he'd slit Markus's throat out of sheer spite. If he couldn't have him, he'd kill him.

Mychael would be using a sound shield for his voice that extended about twenty feet in every direction. Anyone outside the shield wouldn't hear a thing, but any goblin within twenty feet of Mychael's pipes would be taking an hour-long nap that a cannon blast wouldn't disturb.

Mychael and I were at the top of the stairs, still veiled, and about to go into the main house.

"I wish you'd reconsider staying here," Mychael said.

"We don't know what's waiting for us up there, and you're not walking into that alone. In case you've forgotten, you're near the top of Nukpana's lunch list. I don't want to use the big gun, but I will if I have to."

We both knew I meant the Saghred, and Mychael knew: where he was going I was going. This was the time to act, not argue. I didn't think Sarad Nukpana was going to kill Markus here. According to Vidor Kalta, it took more than an hour to do a cha'nescu ritual. Nukpana would want somewhere safe where he wouldn't be interrupted. That meant as soon as they had Markus tied up and ready to go, they'd leave. We were running out of time, if we hadn't already.

"You need to shield your thoughts," Mychael told me. *"And once we're through this door, no talking, not even mindspeak."*

"Won't your sound shield cover us?"

"It will cover my sound—my voice, our footsteps—but not strong emotions. Strong emotions or thoughts will cause my shield to ripple, buckle, and possibly fail. We have to keep our minds as clear as possible."

"You mean the Saghred, too."

"I mean the Saghred and your temper. There can't be a flicker of either one. If you feel the Saghred stirring, push it down and do it fast, with no emotion, no fear, no panic."

I about said he had to be kidding, but I knew he wasn't.

"I'm in the same house with a goblin who wants to kill me and an elf who may have sold me and mine down the river, and I'm supposed to keep me and the rock on an even keel?"

"Raine, you don't have a choice. Anger or fear will give us away and so will the Saghred. We'll be invisible in every sense—"

"Unless I lose control."

"You lose control; I lose the shield."

"We lose our lives."

"Good reason to keep your temper under control, isn't it?"

I nodded. "I'm motivated."

"I hoped you would be. Let's go."

There weren't any goblins in the kitchen. However, there were lots of knives. I silently helped myself to a pair of long carving knives, tucked one in my belt, and kept the other in my right hand in case it needed to make itself useful in the next few minutes. I walked two paces behind Mychael on his right side and out of his way.

We encountered the first Khrynsani temple guard leaning against a doorway. His bosses were on the other side of the house, and he was left to stand watch over a lot of empty space that, with the arrival of me and Mychael, suddenly wasn't so empty anymore. He was confident and complacent right up until the instant Mychael's whispered voice sent him sliding down that doorway onto the floor. He never knew what hit him.

Mychael's spellsinging voice was softer and more soothing than a whisper, gently nestling into the place between sleep and wake. It was low, it was velvety, and if he'd been aiming at me, I'd be in a happy little puddle on the floor. Damn, he was good. I'd known that for some time; the Khrynsani guards got to find out the hard way.

Mychael flowed smoothly through the house. We had no time to lose, and Mychael wasn't wasting a second. Nukpana and Ghalfari hadn't brought as many Khrynsani guards with them as I would have expected. Normally this would be good news, but normally there would be someone for them to guard or kill.

There weren't any elves, dead or otherwise.

Markus Sevelien was the newly appointed head of elven intelligence and Mychael said that he'd brought his own security with him from Mermeia. So where were they? All we saw as we worked our way through the house were Khrynsani. I didn't see or sense a single elf. There were a lot of things wrong with that, and every last one of them smelled like a setup. Mychael took out the next four goblins we encountered in the exact same way and just as easily.

We'd reached the entry hall. There were doors leading to several rooms, but only two interested me: the one that led outside and the one directly across from us. The massive front door was guarded from the outside by a pair of Khrynsani. Mychael's voice did its thing and I dimly heard a pair of thumps as the goblins hit the ground.

Mychael inclined his head, indicating the door directly across from us. It was stately, beautifully carved, and behind it was evil incarnate. Sarad Nukpana had gone through that door; I knew it as surely as if I'd seen him do it myself. The front door was tantalizingly close. Instant escape. All I'd have to do was not trip over the unconscious Khrynsani when I ran out.

I heard a voice. Cultured and velvety.

Sarad Nukpana.

He was talking to someone. I couldn't hear his words and I didn't need to. Markus Sevelien was in there with him, probably restrained, definitely conscious. Oh yes, Nukpana would want his next victim conscious. The better for him to torment and terrify and for his victim to realize his helplessness, his impending and agonizing death. Hell, Sarad Nukpana probably fed on their fear before he even laid hands on them. Perverted son of a bitch.

Mychael lightly touched my arm, and I slowly stilled my thoughts.

Just thinking about Sarad Nukpana set me off.

Shit.

"Are you going to keep us waiting all night, little seeker?" came a chilling voice from the other side of the door.

I froze, swore, and fought the urge to run—all in the same split second. Anyone watching would have probably thought I'd had some sort of spasm. It was exactly what Nukpana wanted. I was terrified, but I forced it down—actually I had to shove it down and hold it there until it stopped squirming. Then I scraped up some rage. Rage and I had always worked well together.

"I'm so sorry." Me and my temper had just signed our death warrant.

Mychael's lips were a grim and determined line. *"Not your fault. He already knew we were here."*

No use tiptoeing now. They knew we wanted Markus, so they knew we were coming in. Mychael and I glanced at each other. Might as well do it in style.

I dropped my veil and reached down deep for every bit of power I could scrape up without kicking the Saghred into action. Focus, not fear. Nukpana wanted me terrified.

He wanted *me*. He could have taken Markus and been long gone, but he hadn't. He had waited.

For us.

For me.

I didn't kick the Saghred into action, but I did relax the hold I had over it.

Mychael's power blazed like a burning sun as he calmly placed his outstretched hand against the wood and the door vanished, incinerated in a white-hot flash of power. And his glow didn't diminish one bit; in fact, he grew even brighter.

Mychael and I stepped through the door together.

Duke Markus Sevelien was sitting in a chair, his feet bound, his wrists tied to the chair's gilded arms.

And lashed firmly to his right wrist was a Nebian grenade.

My heart skipped a few much-needed beats.

There had been two open crates in the basement; I'd only looked in one of them. That one had been full. What did you want to bet a keg was missing from the other crate?

Or more.

Standing immediately behind Markus was a goblin who looked like an older version of Sarad Nukpana.

He was only slightly taller than me, slender and compact beneath his rich, silk robes, robes so black it was like he absorbed the light from the fireplace. Streaks of silver ran the length of his long hair.

Nachtmagus Janos Ghalfari.

The goblin held a sickle-like dagger to Markus's throat; its blade flickering with light down its curved length, light not from the fireplace, but from a ward that fed the blade and shielded Ghalfari from attack and Markus from rescue. That blade could slit Markus's throat or just as easily puncture that grenade. Ten seconds wasn't a lot of time for Ghalfari to put much distance between him and that grenade before it blew, but I was betting he knew something I didn't, like a quicker way out of here than the front door.

Standing near them both were two Khrynsani. I couldn't see Sarad Nukpana, but he was here, watching me. I could feel him, sense his hunger.

So much for Plan A. I wondered if Mychael had a Plan B.

"Bravo, Paladin Eiliesor." Janos Ghalfari's voice was cool and urbane, just like his psycho nephew. "An impressive performance." He took in Mychael's shady street leathers and smiled until his fangs showed. "Though your performance for Karl Cradock was even more impressive. What would the Seat of Twelve say if they knew their noble paladin was a mercenary for hire by common criminals?"

A sick feeling rolled through me. We'd been betrayed bigtime. Ghalfari had picked Markus as his nephew's next victim as bait for us. Sarad Nukpana didn't just want dinner; he wanted a feast.

"I've felt your delectable presence for the past hour, little seeker," came Sarad Nukpana's whisper from the shadows just beyond the firelight's reach. I could barely make out a shape that seemed to float in the corner, darker than the shadows concealing him. His words came with an effort, but since they were for me, apparently it was an effort he was willing to make.

I wondered if he'd fed since General Aratus. That would explain why he was hiding in the corner, why his uncle and the Khrynsani were doing the dirty work. If Sarad Nukpana hadn't fed, he'd be weakened; now was the time to end this. Markus was dead if Mychael and I so much as breathed wrong; we were all dead if Janos Ghalfari punctured that grenade. Though if Markus knew what Sarad Nukpana was going to do to him, he'd want us to act.

At least the Markus I used to know would want that.

"You can hide yourself from me, but you can't hide my former prison," Sarad Nukpana was saying. "The Saghred calls to those who have escaped it." His laugh was hollow, soulless. "And now the loyal agent has come to rescue her handler." His tone turned gleefully mocking. "I believe that is the correct term, is it not? It sounds like an animal that belongs in a kennel. But having met many elven agents over the years, I find the term to be all too accurate."

I pretended to ignore him. Truth was, I didn't trust myself to look at that dark shape floating in the shadows and not scream my head off. I kept my eyes on Markus and tried to keep my voice steady. "Markus, you've looked better."

The elven duke's lips twisted in a brief smile. "You, my dear, are the most beautiful sight I've ever seen."

"Only because I've come to save your ass."

"That, too."

Markus Sevelien was as lean as whipcord and just as tough, with dark hair swept back from a high and pale forehead. Dressed entirely in his customary black, the wiry elf sat utterly still, though it wasn't like he had a choice with Ghalfari's blade at his throat. Markus's only movement was the tapping of one long, tapered finger against the arm of the chair to which he was tied—wisely the one without the grenade. Markus knew a lot of codes, but this was one I knew as well. His finger repeatedly tapped out a two-word message to me.

Kill them.

Markus was a realist; he knew he'd be dead right along with them. He didn't care.

Kill them.

I could wipe the floor with every goblin in the room, but if I let the Saghred off its leash, I didn't know if I could get it back under control—and considering who I'd be wiping out, I didn't think I'd want to stop. The Saghred's full power was terrifying, overwhelming, but it was also intoxicating. And deep down, some dark part of me wanted to do it again. It'd kill every goblin in the room, but it could just as easily do the same to me and Mychael.

I was in the same room with a pair of monsters and the scent of death was so thick in the air that it was all I could do not to gag. I was scared. More than scared, I was literally shaking in my boots. Though I didn't know who scared me more: Sarad Nukpana, his death-loving uncle . . .

. . . or myself.

The goblin drifted out of the shadows.

My breath stopped and my heart tried to do the same thing.

Sarad Nukpana wasn't solid, nor was he a formless specter. His feet were on the floor, but I don't think he was using them to move. He'd retained every bit of his dark beauty. His angular face was flawlessly beautiful without sacrificing one bit of masculinity. His ethereal body drifted ever so slightly. Back and forth, back and forth, hypnotic, mesmerizing as a cobra, silent and beautiful—and just as deadly.

Nukpana smiled slowly. "Yes, my body remains the same. I have no interest in possessing others. Why would I want another body? I have always been most satisfied with my own." He glanced at Markus. "Though it might be amusing to possess the duke's body and pretend to be him for a day. Any longer and I'd be an elf permanently. Such a fate would almost be worse than being trapped inside the Saghred." His eyes glittered like the black of a bottomless pool in a haunted forest. "But the feeling of my soul violating the body of another, pushing their soul aside, taking them completely." He exhaled on a sigh that could only be described as pure bliss. "I have heard it said that the victim remains aware through all of it— the taking, the possession—and is helpless to stop anything I want their body to do."

He wasn't talking about Markus anymore.

My throat threatened to close up. "Then you'd be an elf *and* a woman," I managed. "You couldn't handle the pressure."

"You're right. The alternative would be so much more pleasurable." Sarad Nukpana's voice dropped to a sibilant whisper. "The cha'nescu—the soul kiss. Feeling your soul fighting me will be so much sweeter. Once I've taken you, I will control the Saghred as well." He flashed a smile revealing fangs that looked all too solid. "It is as you would say, a win-win situation."

I felt rather than saw Mychael move to step in front of me. I held out a hand to stop him, never taking my eyes from Sarad Nukpana.

"He fears for you and for good reason," Nukpana purred. "The Saghred is even hungrier than I am. You can feel it, can't you? I'll take your silence as a yes. I fed earlier this evening; why shouldn't you?"

"Who?" Mychael growled.

Nukpana dismissively waved a pale hand. "No one you knew. Don't worry; there will be no corpses turning up in inconvenient places. My remaining two allies from inside the Saghred have finally served their purpose. I chose them specifically for their age and power." The goblin's smile was like the cat that ate the canary. "You might say that they gave their all for my cause."

"You ate them." Mychael was holding his power in check, but just barely.

"'Ate' would be an overstatement." He laughed softly. "Considering there really wasn't much to them to begin with. More like a refreshing drink complete with memories, skills, and power." He stretched luxuriously and appeared to become more solid. "Yes, I'm feeling most refreshed."

Those were the last two sorcerers, the ones we hadn't found yet. Now we didn't need to; they were here inside of Sarad Nukpana. Two of the most brutal and insane sorcerers in recorded history, and the goblin floating not ten feet in front of me had all that brute strength at his beck and call—at least, he would when he'd fully digested them.

And I had the Saghred at mine. My chest warmed, the power pulsing beneath the surface in time with my heart, the combined beat throbbing, a nearly deafening drum in my ears.

Sarad Nukpana knew. Whether he heard it or sensed it, he knew. "The Saghred grows tired of you."

I forced myself to breathe around the urges the Saghred sent through my mind, images of sacrifice and blood, torture, and death. And feeding, always starving, never satisfied.

"The feeling's mutual." My voice was tight. It was all I could do to hold the rock back. "I'm sick and tired of it."

"It desires someone of a like mind, someone who will use it. It desires a partner. You fear me, but most of all you fear yourself." Sarad Nukpana's voice was the barest whisper, coaxing, seductive. "You want to give in to me, to the Saghred's hunger. But what you fear most is the certain knowledge that you will enjoy it. You've tasted its power before and your deepest desire is to taste that power again."

Raw need swept over me, the need to take, to possess, to exult in the magic, the power. Sarad Nukpana was right, and I hated him even more for it. The rock was starving.

And so was I.

"Come to me, little seeker. Let us feed on each other."

Sarad Nukpana was mine for the taking.

Mine. I could take him first, end this now, here in this room. Destroy the evil before it killed again.

And I would destroy myself if I killed. Once I started using the Saghred to take souls into myself, once I started killing, I would become the evil I had struggled against.

Once I crossed that line there would be no turning back.

My breath shook as I let it out, pushed down the hunger, the desire to possess. I stood there trembling with the effort.

"You can continue to defy us," Janos Ghalfari told me. "But you cannot deny what you are—and what you are becoming." He glanced at Mychael. "Why leave with only one meal when we could take two?" Something dark and ugly glittered in the goblin's black eyes, and I felt the air tighten with the beginnings of black magic. "Or perhaps three."

Mychael stalked slowly to the right, away from me, and toward Ghalfari. I agreed with him moving away from me. Hell, I wanted to get away from me, too.

"Step away from the duke," Mychael said smoothly. "And we can discuss it."

The goblin nachtmagus smiled. "Why should I open myself to attack when you will surrender rather than see his lifeblood spilled out? Come with us now and you will preserve the duke's life for a while longer. I'm certain you will find another opportunity to attempt to escape. Which is it, Paladin Eiliesor? Surrender and attempt a rescue and escape later, or don't surrender and ensure the duke's death?"

The flames in the fireplace popped and snapped at a sudden shift in the air. Cold air moved the heavy drapes on the window. I knew that paralyzing cold didn't come from outside. A wave of goose bumps ran up my arms and down my body. Janos Ghalfari stiffened, his magic probing the air around him, then his lips pulled back from his fangs in an enraged snarl.

Oh hell.

Reapers.

Sarad Nukpana was nearly dead. His uncle played with the dead. I was linked to a rock that was filled with thousands of unclaimed souls.

Guess who the Reapers came after first?

Chapter 14

"Run!" Mychael screamed at me.

I wanted nothing more, but running was easier screamed than done.

I dodged one filmy appendage and almost ran smack-dab into another one. The damned things had floated in through the walls. Right now I didn't care if the Reapers had followed me or Nukpana. I just wanted to survive the next few seconds.

There were enough Reapers to go around, so while I was the odds-on favorite, Nukpana and his uncle still had their hands full. Reapers were flowing around the Khrynsani mages, ignoring them completely. The mages started hissing some sort of spell that had absolutely no effect on them.

I'd seen fear in Sarad Nukpana's black eyes once before—right before the Saghred took him. He knew he was screwed then, and he knew the same thing now. He's wasn't wholly spirit, but he wasn't solid enough to put up any kind of physical fight, either.

And I couldn't reach the bastard. He'd never be more vulnerable than he was right now, and I couldn't get anywhere near him.

Janos Ghalfari put himself between the Reapers and his nephew; the black magic he'd been gathering to use against me and Mychael was now turned to repelling Reapers. The fireplace was the room's only source of light and it dimmed more with every poisonous word that came from between the goblin's lips. The air tightened and a stench like brimstone came from the corner of the room that Ghalfari was defending. He jerked back the heavy drapes, revealing barred windows. He screamed in rage and frustration.

The Reapers had no interest in Markus, and at the moment, neither did the goblins. Markus didn't have a blade to his throat but was still tied to a chair with a grenade lashed to his arm.

I had to reach him.

The space separating us wasn't the problem; the Reaper floating between us was. All of its attention was on me. Markus wasn't the one linked to thousands of imprisoned souls.

I had a worthless kitchen knife in my hand, and my eyes on the Reaper who was floating just out of reach. I didn't know if the thing was being cautious, prudent, or freaking polite—it was a feeding machine; it didn't think. I was in the same room with the goblin who'd framed me, threatened me, and promised to kill me. Then there was Markus. I had no proof of what he'd done, but if he died, I'd never know anything. I wanted to get my hands on both of them, but standing in my way was a nightmare that'd nearly killed me.

I'd barely lived through my last Reaper encounter. Now I had to get past one to reach my former boss, who was going to go "kablowie" if one of those Khrynsani knocked his chair over. I just wanted to cut the grenade off of Markus, cut my losses, and get the hell out of here. I knew I'd get another shot at Sarad Nukpana because he wanted another shot at me.

I drew on my power, not the Saghred's. It wanted no part of this fight. It had coiled down tight, protecting itself, and to hell with me. I gathered my power into a white-hot ball of rage and sent it into the palm of my hand, curling my fingers around it in a glowing fist. It seethed and quivered in anticipation of getting to do something, anything, just as long as it was violent. I didn't think what would be the wisest use of what I'd summoned. I just punched the Reaper where its face should have been, slamming my fist and my power into that gelatinous body. The impact was so satisfying that I hit it again, adding an enraged scream for good measure.

The Reaper glowed incandescently—and got bigger. A lot bigger.

Oh crap.

And it vanished in a wink of light.

What the hell?

No time to ponder what I'd done, what had happened, or why. The hand that had punched the Reaper hung limply by my side, numb and tingling, and I was panting like I'd run a mile uphill. I didn't think about the why or how of that, either. There was nothing but open space between me and Markus, and I closed that distance. I had a kitchen knife in my good hand, and no doubt I looked like a woman with a purpose. A murderous purpose.

Markus's only reaction was a slight raising of one dark and perfectly arched eyebrow. I guess it took more than one exhausted and pissed-off elf to scare Markus Sevelien. Later, when I got my wind back, I could always punch him, if either of us lived that long.

A tendril from another Reaper lashed between us and I instinctively slashed it with my knife. The blade went straight through, the tendril instantly retracting back into the Reaper's body, emerging to try again.

Suddenly Mychael was there, shielding me and Markus, his entire body blazing with white light, driving that Reaper and all the others back from us, herding them toward the goblins. I knelt to cut the cord that tied the keg to Markus, but I could barely feel my left hand. That meant I had one hand to cut the cord holding the keg *and* catch it. I wasn't that good on my best day, and if I tried it, today would be my last.

"Dammit!" I snarled.

I glared up into Markus's dark eyes and sliced through the ropes binding his left wrist to the chair. When his hand was free, I gave him the knife.

"I'll hold the grenade; you cut the cord. If you try *anything* else, you're a dead man."

Markus's brows knit together in a puzzled frown. "We need to talk about that."

"Count on it," I snarled.

I could easily wrap my hands around a grenade, but one hand would only clutch the thing. And I wasn't about to trust my clutching skills right now. I took the grenade in my good hand and clutched it against my chest, tight but not too tight. If it got stabbed, sprung a leak, or just decided to break in half, I'd be covered in Nebian black powder and in ten seconds *I'd* blow up.

That would really piss me off.

Markus had the knife under the cord. "Ready?"

"Do it," I growled.

He cut the cord, I held the grenade, and no one went boom—at least not yet.

I shot a glance at the knife in his hand. "Finish yourself." As far as I was concerned, Markus could take that any way he wanted to.

"Bravo, Raine." Markus quickly bent and sliced through the ropes binding his ankles.

A couple of days ago, Sarad Nukpana had said much the same thing. I'd rather hear it from Markus.

I think.

Mychael's charged glow was keeping the Reapers at bay, though now they actually seemed to find the goblins more interesting. At this point, I'd take any speck of good luck I could get.

Even though the Reapers had found someone more fun to play with didn't mean they couldn't change their minds, or whatever it was they had. I risked a glance over my shoulder. Nothing between us and the front door and freedom but blessedly empty space.

When we got there, the door was locked, bolted, and for all I knew nailed shut.

Mychael's hands glowed blindingly white. "I'll get this." He saw my left hand hanging limp. "Your hand?"

"Being lazy." I carefully pulled the grenade away from my chest. I had it in a firm grip, perfect for throwing. "But this hand's still good."

Mychael put his hands to the door and nothing happened. "Level Twelve wards?" He didn't bother to hide his anger and disbelief.

"I had them put there," Markus said. "Damned things only activated *after* the goblins broke in."

Mychael glared at the elven duke and I swear I saw murder flash in those blue eyes, or at least extreme violence. Nice to know I wasn't the only one fighting those urges.

I didn't take my eyes off of the Reapers. "Can you get through?"

"Yes," he snarled.

Janos Ghalfari's chants reached a crescendo, and my skin tried to crawl somewhere and hide. With his words came the smell of death, bloated and decaying. My stomach threatened to heave. I had no idea what his spell would do, but I knew we didn't want to be here when he released it.

I tried breathing through my mouth. "Can you get through faster?"

"No!"

Ghalfari was facing the Reapers, keeping them at bay, his features a contorted mask of pain and effort. Nukpana was protectively surrounded by Khrynsani mages, and the door to the left of the fireplace glowed red hot with their efforts. They were going to get away. Dammit. I couldn't get to them, but if they escaped, we'd just be doing this again at a new place and time.

"Are any of your people still in here?" I asked Markus. "Alive?"

"Any elves in this house aren't mine."

I jerked my head toward the door the goblins were burning their way through. "Where does that go?"

"Servants' quarters." Markus's smile was chilling. "It's a maze back there."

Just what I wanted to hear.

I felt a whoosh of outside air behind us and Mychael kicked a Level Twelve ward's ass and blew through the door in one fell swoop.

Janos Ghalfari gave a shout as their escape door disintegrated in a cloud of charred wood and ash. The Reapers turned and rushed toward us.

I hurled the grenade into the room and into the Reapers.

Mychael grabbed my arm and all but threw me through the door.

I didn't know if Reapers could be blown up, but when you're scared shitless, desperate, and fresh out of nonsuicidal ideas, you'd try anything. If I couldn't take out the goblins, I'd take out the house they were running through.

We ran like hell and then some.

Until I saw the eight-foot-high stone wall and massive iron gate, both crackling with protective wards. They were meant to keep intruders out, now they were keeping escaping elves in.

Mychael kept running and held his hand back to me. "Grenade!"

I gave it to him.

We had to be at least thirty yards from the gate when Mychael growled a spell and with a dead-on throw sent the grenade smashing into the gate's massive latch. He jerked me and Markus behind the trunk of what had to be the biggest oak I'd ever seen. We were about to have chunks of a house blown at us from one direction and an iron gate from the other, and Mychael wanted us to hide behind a tree. I didn't care how big it was; the house was bigger.

Time slowed to that speed that meant you were about to die and the powers that be were giving your mind one last chance to figure out how to survive. My body just told me to run faster. Mychael's iron grip ordered me to stay put. He got an arm around me, and his shields formed around all three of us.

I heard odd popping sounds coming from the house and Mychael pulled us to the ground. There were four explosions, each bigger and louder than the one before. The house and everything in it exploded in what I could only compare to broadsides from an entire fleet of ships. A smoke-filled breath later, a fifth blast came from our other side as the gate blew.

Bricks and flaming debris slammed into the wall around the house. The wards on top of the wall did what they were made to do and vaporized anything that touched them, sending blue sparks drizzling down to pop and sizzle against Mychael's shields.

His shields buckled with each blast, but they held. Call it a miracle or preternatural strength and skill. Whatever it was, we'd thumbed our noses at Death again. If the Reapers didn't get blown up, at least they got blown back to where they came from.

Mychael released his shields and us. "Move!" he screamed. "Through the gate, now!"

I was hacking and coughing smoke and soot. It had cleared enough to let me see the gate, or rather where the gate used to be. That little grenade had more than done its job. The gate's metal bars looked like a massive fist had just punched its way through. Best of all, no more elf-frying blue wards.

Markus pulled me to the right. "Down the street is an alley that empties on Hawkins Court. It should be deserted."

"That's away from the elven embassy," I said.

"The embassy is the last place I want to go."

Now I wasn't just pissed at Markus; I was confused.

I had to consider the possibility that Markus wasn't the power behind everything bad that had happened to me or any future plots against me, but I'd always felt a deep and abiding satisfaction with anything that went boom. Pretty flames were an added bonus.

Markus glanced back. "You blew up my house."

"Consider us even."

Markus flashed a quick smile. "Consider yourself thanked."

I blinked. "What?"

"If all goes well, everyone will think I'm dead."

Maybe a flying chunk of brick had hit him in the head.

The street was still empty, but it wouldn't be for long. After those explosions, we were about to have a lot of company. Embassy guards, goblins, take your pick. I didn't want to stay around to run into any of them.

"We go the way he wants?" I asked Mychael in mindspeak.

"It's the best way out."

I didn't want to do anything that Markus suggested, but Mychael knew what he was doing.

We were a couple of houses away from the alley when I heard the hooves.

Crap it.

A squad of elven embassy guards on horseback came around the corner of Ambassador Row headed straight for us. The smoke was thick, hiding the three of us as we dived behind a thick hedge growing at the base of the wall surrounding another house. Fortunately this one wasn't crackling with wards. The horses galloped by on the street just beyond where we were hiding. The lead horseman was Taltek Balmorlan. For a few seconds, I didn't move or breathe. With all the smoke, if I took a decent breath, I'd probably start coughing. As the shouting and galloping passed us, I let out my breath and slowly took in another, muffling a cough.

"Did you see Balmorlan?" I asked Mychael in mindspeak.

"I saw."

"Where do you propose we take Markus?"

"My safe house is too far, and the quicker we get him off the streets, the better."

"And I'm an accused accomplice to murder in possession of Nukpana's next victim."

But this accused accomplice wanted to have a long talk with the almost victim. And the safest place would also be the last place anyone on the island would think to look for Duke Markus Sevelien.

"I know just the place."

"Nebian grenades," I told my cousin.

Phaelan whistled.

"Eight crates of them."

"Damn. *Full* crates?"

I nodded. "That's my guess. Took out the entire house, most of the wall, and punched a hole the size of a mountain troll through an iron gate."

"Eight crates would do that. I hate that I missed it." Phaelan flashed a grin. "Got to hear it, though. Hell, the whole damned island did. Beautiful work, cousin."

Not unless it took out Sarad Nukpana and Janos Ghalfari. Though I wasn't holding my breath.

Phaelan had come with me to Mid to protect me; Uncle Ryn followed the two of us to Mid to eliminate the need for protection. My uncle, who was Phaelan's father, had dropped anchor in the harbor to motivate the Conclave's mages to find a way to separate me from the Saghred. He said his anchors were going to stay right where they were and grow barnacles until that happened.

We were on the *Red Hawk*, Uncle Ryn's flagship. Mychael and Markus were with Uncle Ryn in his cabin. I'd join them in a few minutes, but there was something I needed to do first.

Calm down.

The trip from the hole in the ground that used to be Markus's house to the *Red Hawk* had been quiet, not only because we didn't want anyone out and about at four bells to see or hear us, but because I didn't trust myself within choking distance of Markus Sevelien quite yet. After a slight detour to collect the goblin gold, we headed straight for the harbor.

Mychael was a wise man; he'd kept himself between me and Markus the entire way here. I was exhausted, I was scared, and I was pissed at more people than I had names for. But most of all, I was confused. Too much had happened and I hadn't had enough time to sort through any of it. That was bad enough, but I knew it was going to get worse before it got any better. That was if I lived long enough to see it get better. Anything Markus Sevelien was involved in was guaranteed to be intricate, not like a seaman's knot, but brilliantly intricate, like a finely woven web—and just as dangerous. I'd played chess with Markus on occasion. I'd always lost. Though I'd never stood a chance of beating a man who could think at least ten moves in advance.

If I was in the middle of whatever game Markus was playing now, losing would cost me more than my life. It could cost the lives of my family and friends, and probably anyone who just had the piss-poor luck of knowing me.

I gave Phaelan the condensed version of my evening.

"So let me get this straight," he said once I'd finished. "Carnades and Balmorlan framed Tam for that elf general's murder and got him locked up. Two weeks ago he had Piaras kidnapped, and he's been trying to get his hands on you since the day you got here. And you and Mychael just saved this bastard's *boss*? I'm not sure which is worse, saving him or bringing him here."

"I want answers from him, Phaelan. What better place to bring him?"

Phaelan pursed his lips as he considered the implications. "Some of Dad's crew are rather gifted when it comes to convincing people they want to talk. And if Markus's people think he's dead anyway . . ."

"That's not what I want."

"But that's what might be necessary. If he's the one that's been pulling Balmorlan's strings, the only way he's leaving this ship is over the side hugging a rock."

"It would hardly be the first time an underling didn't tell his boss what he was up to," I heard myself say. I couldn't believe I was defending him. I guess doubt would do that to you.

"You said Markus knows what all of his people are up to."

"Yes."

"Considering how high the stakes are here, I hardly think Markus picked now to stick his head in the sand."

I blew out my breath. "And even if he was acting under orders from his superiors, he still acted."

Phaelan nodded. "He takes orders and obeys them, just the same as every man who has to answer to another man. And if they're using him, maybe it's because he's letting them. How well do you really know him?"

"I thought well enough."

Phaelan was silent as he looked out through the porthole. The water in the harbor was that glassy calm that came only with the predawn. Phaelan keeping his mouth shut meant he was about to open it and say something he knew I didn't want to hear.

"Raine, you might have thought wrong," my cousin said quietly.

He knew I didn't like being wrong, but I despised being used, taken advantage of, or duped. All of the above made me feel stupid, and right now being stupid would get me and the people I loved a couple of steps closer to being dead. And one of those people was standing next to me. Any mess I'd found myself in, Phaelan had been right there with me in the muck. He claimed he didn't want me having all the fun; truth was he was determined to protect me every step of the way even though one of those steps might be his last.

Markus had never told anyone in the agency that I worked for him. I was always paid under the table. But he could have been ordered to reveal his connection—or he could have volunteered it himself. Hell, Taltek Balmorlan knew; who else was running around with that information?

"A better question is how much do you trust him?" Phaelan asked in that same subdued tone.

I didn't answer, because I didn't know the answer.

"The number of people you can trust, believe in, and stake your life on, you can count on these." Phaelan held up his hand with five spread fingers. "And if Lady Luck is really smiling down on you, maybe one or two more. But beyond that, *everyone* has a price for selling you out. And it doesn't have to be money. It's not always what you're paid, but what you're not willing to pay. You have to consider the possibility that the bastards in the agency's big offices found Markus Sevelien's price."

That was what I was afraid of.

Chapter 15

I smelled the food before Phaelan and I got to Uncle Ryn's cabin, and my stomach rumbled in appreciative anticipation. Uncle Ryn knew me well. I was pissed and he knew I needed to be levelheaded and reasonable. Get me fed and I could be reasoned with. I guess Uncle Ryn didn't want to risk having to clean Markus Sevelien's blood out of his carpets.

I knocked.

"Come," Uncle Ryn boomed.

I opened the door and the scent of a heavenly dinner was nearly overwhelming.

The captain's quarters on the *Red Hawk* were spacious, but contained only the things Uncle Ryn needed: bed, table with six chairs, fold-down sideboard, desk, and a cabinet where he kept his liquor. He didn't want anything fancy or needless cluttering up his cabin. He liked his space. And Uncle Ryn didn't take kindly to invasions of his personal space. He had a favorite response to someone stepping in on him. He'd reach out, grab you by the throat, lift you off your feet, and replace those feet at a respectful distance. This response was a warning; if you tried it again, it would be your last time stepping in on anybody. Uncle Ryn didn't tolerate rudeness.

Most elves were tall and leanly muscled. Uncle Ryn was just big. He wore his dark hair short, his beard trimmed, and had a booming voice that'd carry clear up to a crow's nest. He had a booming laugh to go with it and a sense of humor to match. He was somewhere around fifty, but he didn't look it or act it.

I was a firm believer in being happy doing your chosen work. If you were going to make a living at something, you should enjoy doing it. Ryn Benares was still in his prime and basking in the benefits of his chosen calling—the most feared pirate in any body of water larger than a bathtub.

Judging from the three used dishes on the sideboard, Uncle Ryn, Mychael, and Markus had already eaten.

"I hear you've had yourself a rough evening, Spitfire," Uncle Ryn rumbled softly. "Come get yourself something to eat."

Mychael arched a brow in amusement. "Spitfire?"

"His pet name for me," I told him.

"Also an ill-tempered breed of small dragon."

"She knows I've always meant it as a compliment," Uncle Ryn said. "But like Raine, those little buggers get even more ill-tempered when they're hungry." He nodded toward the sideboard. "Fix yourself a plate before it gets cold."

For once I did as told, no objections.

Uncle Ryn got out of his chair with his empty glass and went over to the liquor cabinet. "You want a drink?" he asked me.

I snorted past a mouthful of food. "You have to ask?"

Uncle Ryn poured me a glass of something the color of fine rubies. A Caesolian red, a good one. Aside from the one look I'd given Markus when I came through the door, I was ignoring him until I'd gotten some food in my stomach. I occasionally felt his eyes on me as he, Mychael, and Uncle Ryn made polite small talk waiting for me to finish. I didn't rush my meal, but I didn't take my time, either. I'd waited long enough.

When I'd finished, I pushed my plate back and gave Markus my full and undivided attention.

"No doubt you want to know why I'm here," he said.

"What I want is your honesty." I put down my wineglass. I didn't trust myself with anything that could be thrown or broken over someone's head. Besides, it was an expensive glass.

"Raine, you don't know what you're asking for—or how much danger you're in."

I laughed. I had to. That had to be one of the most ridiculously obvious statements I'd ever heard. "Markus, I know exactly how much danger I'm in. I'm up to my eyeballs in it, and if it gets deeper, I'll have to start swimming." I leaned forward; it was more civilized than diving across the cabin for the elf duke's throat. "What I want to know is how much of it is your doing. I can't begin to tell you how much I've looked forward to getting you in the same room with me. I know exactly what I'm asking for. Entertain me."

Markus Sevelien told me.

I wasn't entertained in the least.

Officially, Taltek Balmorlan was an inquisitor working for elven intelligence. In reality, Taltek Balmorlan was an arms dealer working for Taltek Balmorlan. And in a world of magic where mages qualified as weapons, he was dealing in living, breathing people, collecting supernaturally powerful elven mages. I knew that much. Piaras hadn't been the first. I'd suspected that. The bastard preferred them young and vulnerable, easily influenced or intimidated. And being an agent of the elven government, Balmorlan could concoct a legal claim to them, like drafting them into the army. And that was precisely how he planned to use them—as weapons in a war against the goblins.

Markus steepled his fingers in front of his face. "When you came here, Taltek followed you—and put his plan into motion. You being able to wield the Saghred without any adverse effect was his dream come true. His greatest fear was that you would go over to the goblins first."

"Is that your greatest fear, Markus? That I'll go to the goblins? Or that I'll sell my services to the highest bidder because I'm a Benares?" I was getting mad and I let myself. This boilover had been a long time coming. "Because any elf worth their pureblood knows that we're filthy criminals. We can't be trusted and only care about filling our pockets with as much gold as we can carry. Is that your fear?"

"You know that's not what I think."

"No, Markus, I don't know that. It's your job to root out traitors. Balmorlan's here, and now so are you. You're Balmorlan's boss. I think you're here on business, and that business is me."

"Yes, it is part of my job to find traitors." His voice was carefully modulated. "You are not a traitor, Raine. You never have been—and you never will be."

"Because you're not going to allow it? I won't work for the elves, the goblins, or anyone else," I snapped. "I want to be rid of the damned rock and I want my life back. If you call that a traitor, then that's what I am. No amount of gold can hire me, and I won't allow myself or anyone I love to be used or threatened. And thanks to the rock, I can enforce my wishes." My voice dropped to one step above a growl. "Don't think for one moment that I won't use it."

I expected anger; what I got was calm acceptance, maybe even a trace of amusement.

"I know that, Raine. And I told the queen that's what you would say." He smiled. "She asked that I give you a message."

That took me by surprise. I didn't know the queen and I wasn't sure I wanted her to know of me.

"She's never met you but she already likes you, and she would like very much to tell you that in person one day."

"Huh?" Way to use the rapier wit, Raine.

Markus leaned forward. "I no longer work for elven intelligence."

"But you just got promoted to the head of the whole agency."

"In a manner of speaking. I work for the queen. I report to her and only to her. There are some good people in elven intelligence. Unfortunately, their influence isn't what it once was. People like Taltek Balmorlan have bribed or blackmailed their way into positions of power. When the Saghred surfaced, Her Majesty and I knew we had to act quickly. Yes, she appointed me head of the agency, and that appointment upset more than a few people, Taltek among them." He took a sip of his wine. "The queen wants him and his allies exposed and stopped. When Taltek kidnapped Piaras Rivalin and attempted to remove him from this island, that act exposed Taltek's network of mage procurers. The queen finds the practice abhorrent and she wants it stopped, as do I. Lisara Ambrosiel is a good and honorable woman. As are you, Raine." He smiled. "And as to you being a Benares and my being a duke, you may be gratified to know that I am the chief of elven intelligence in name only; what I'm actually doing is more along the lines of a janitorial service. Her Majesty wants to clean house, and I've volunteered to be the broom."

I looked over at Mychael, an eyebrow raised in question.

"It's the truth," he told me.

I was incredulous. "You knew?"

"I had some idea of what was going on, but not to this extent. Markus filled me in while you were up on deck getting that temper of yours under control."

Markus laughed once. "This is under control?"

"If she'd been feeling really feisty, she'd have stabbed you," Uncle Ryn said. "Don't worry; it would have only hurt the first time or two."

I knew an apology would be the right thing to do, but truth be told I wasn't feeling particularly apologetic. "You could have told me sooner," I said to Markus.

"Actually, Raine, I couldn't. I have my reasons, and for now they have to remain mine."

"Still keeping secrets."

"It's what I do."

"You're worse than a goblin."

Markus inclined his head graciously. "Thank you. When it comes to intrigue, the goblin mind is without peer. I take that as the highest compliment."

"I didn't mean it as one. Right now, goblins piss me off just as much as elves, if not more." I took a breath and exhaled slowly, my eyes never leaving Markus's. "I will, however, apologize for entertaining thoughts of killing you."

"No doubt you found them highly entertaining."

"I did."

"I sincerely wish it had been possible for me to be forthright with you from the beginning. As we were both being watched, it was quite impossible."

"So why can't you pull the plug on Balmorlan now?"

"It's imperative that I know how far the conspiracy extends, and the name of every man and woman involved—from men like Taltek Balmorlan down to the messengers they use to communicate."

"And a damned lot of good that does Piaras or anyone else Balmorlan goes after in the meantime. You're their boss; you don't need to know how far it goes. Just make the bastards stop."

"And what about the generals and intelligence agents who secretly report to them? And the bureaucrats under them? Raine, you know as well as I do that if I pull down a vine, but leave the roots in the ground, that vine is coming back, and it will grow back stronger."

"Shit."

"An accurate assessment," he noted dryly. "The only way to make sure that it doesn't come back is to get it all the first time." His expression turned solemn. "Raine, I won't let Taltek Balmorlan have Piaras. You have my word. Though from what I understand, that young man is more than capable of defending himself."

I barked a laugh. "Your word."

His black eyes locked on mine. "I have never lied to you. I may not have told you everything, but I have never lied."

He sounded like Tam. While I'd felt the urge to throttle Tam on more than one occasion, he'd never been secretive without good reason. I was sure Markus also had a good reason, but that didn't mean I had to like it.

Mychael knew what I was thinking even without our link.

"Raine, I'd like nothing better than to lock Taltek Balmorlan away in the smallest, dampest cell I have, but Markus is right. If we take him now, someone else will step up to take his place, possibly someone even worse."

"Better the enemy you know," Phaelan muttered.

Uncle Ryn grunted in agreement. "Spitfire, it's like a bloody hydra. Slice the head off and it'll just grow two more. You need to blow all of it out of the water the first time." He looked at Markus. "I have a question of my own. Why are you sharing all this with a pair of criminals? You say my niece isn't one, but my son and I sure as hell are, and we've never tried to hide it."

Phaelan plopped down in a chair next to his father and tossed a leg over the arm. "I'm kind of curious about that myself."

Markus's thin lips quirked upward in a brief grin. "Because the true criminals aren't always the ones on wanted posters. Besides, you're Raine's family, she trusts you, and I trust Raine. To keep a war from happening in the not-too-distant future, I may need your help." He paused. "That is if you would be willing to give it."

Uncle Ryn scowled. "You're talking about privateering."

"I am. And more."

"I'd be willing to hear any proposal you might have," Uncle Ryn said. "I've been through wars before, Markus. There's no profit in it, unless you consider death profitable."

"More than a few of our nobles want a war with the goblins. Their sons would be officers, if they even participated at all."

Uncle Ryn scowled. "Nice and safe on the rear lines sending good men to their deaths."

Markus nodded. "While the sons of working elves and goblins die by the thousands for a war of pride, a war that will gain nothing, and potentially lose the best of a generation."

"You say that you can't tell my niece everything," Uncle Ryn rumbled quietly, his face set like stone.

"That's correct."

"Do you understand that I've raised the girl as one of my own daughters—and that I love her like one of my own?"

"I understand."

"If some of this information you're hording would keep my little girl safe, I expect you to stop hording it."

"The information that I have would not affect Raine's safety and that is the truth."

"I accept you on your word. But be sure that your 'truth' doesn't change." My uncle paused meaningfully. "Do you understand me?"

Markus's face was carefully expressionless. "Perfectly."

"Excellent. Would you like a glass of port? You look like you could use it. I took it off a royal frigate on its way to Regor. No doubt King Sathrik missed it. A fine year and vintage."

As Uncle Ryn opened a bottle of royal port in celebration of his and Markus's newfound understanding, some of what happened tonight actually started to make sense.

"Taltek Balmorlan has been running his own show and now you step in and he has to report to you," I said to Markus. "Until two days ago you were staying in the elven embassy. Did he try to kill you and you decided it was healthier to stay elsewhere?"

"He's made no overt attempt against me; however, I thought it prudent to leave the embassy," Markus said, savoring a sip of port. "My compliments, Commodore Benares, on a fine acquisition. I've rarely tasted its equal."

Uncle Ryn raised his glass in salute. "We only steal the best."

He wasn't going to weasel out of this answer. "What happened to your guards, Markus?"

"Two contracted a fatal case of food poisoning, one 'slipped' and fell from the embassy roof, and the other three simply vanished." His words were matter-of-fact, though his eyes were smoldering with carefully controlled anger. "At that point I thought it best that I occupy the house I've used before on Ambassador Row."

"Markus, you should have contacted me," Mychael said. "I would have provided protection and a safe house."

"I'm the chief of elven intelligence, Mychael. To get to the bottom of this, it's critical that I continue to act the part. If I came to the Guardians rather than to my own people, what little cover I had left would have been blown."

"I'd say it's blown now," I said. "Along with your house. Did you know that you had eight cases of Nebian grenades in your basement?"

"I knew I had one tied to me. I thought Janos Ghalfari had brought it with him."

"He did, from your basement. I can't imagine that many explosives sitting in a previously unoccupied house. Looks like Taltek Balmorlan left you a housewarming present."

"Once he'd eliminated your men, did Balmorlan replace them with his own?" Mychael asked.

Markus nodded. "He 'graciously' provided embassy guards for my protection, who conveniently vanished minutes before Nukpana and Ghalfari arrived with their Khrynsani."

"The prick set you up," Phaelan said. Not a man to mince words, my cousin.

Mychael and I exchanged a glance. Or the person feeding information to Taltek Balmorlan could have been doing the same for Janos Ghalfari.

Mychael glowered. "The goblins take you and the blame, and Balmorlan publicly laments that he couldn't save you. You're dead, giving him the excuse he wants to avenge you against the goblins."

Uncle Ryn nodded. "He gets rid of you and gets a clear shot at everything he wants."

"Thanks to Raine and Mychael, I'm not at the tender mercies of Sarad Nukpana right now," Markus noted. "And for that I cannot thank them enough."

"For the possibility of having blown up that monster, it was our pleasure."

"Do you think he's dead?" Phaelan asked me.

"If he's not, I'll know soon enough."

Sarad Nukpana had ingested two of history's most nefarious and notorious mages, and after tonight, wanting me had probably turned into more of an obsession than it already was. If Nukpana got me, he'd become the Saghred's new bond servant by default, or in my case, by digestion. Nukpana's own prodigious skills, combined with the power of the Saghred and the two mages he'd absorbed, would give him the magical muscle to do anything he damn well pleased. Add to that General Aratus's knowledge of elven strategy and troop levels, and Sarad Nukpana could depose King Sathrik Mal'Salin, install himself as king, and with the Saghred's power he'd be an evil demigod.

Annihilating the elves would be just the beginning.

I pushed my thoughts away from that. Nukpana hadn't gone on a world-domination rampage, and I wasn't dead yet, though Markus had come close tonight. I glanced at him. "Balmorlan probably thinks you're dead."

Markus smiled slowly. "A death I intend to put to full use. Being the living chief of intelligence, I couldn't move and act as freely as I would have liked. As a blown-to-bits intelligence chief, I intend to turn myself into Taltek Balmorlan's worst nightmare." He lifted his glass in salute. "Who says being dead can't be fun?"

Chapter 16

So Taltek Balmorlan wanted to be a hero. As a general rule,
people were more likely to follow a hero than a sadistic nutcase. I didn't think Balmorlan harbored any illusions that
kidnapping and murder made him heroic, but he didn't see
himself as a nutcase, either. Like Carnades Silvanus, he had
a single goal and he thought it was a good one—destroy the
goblin race. And he wasn't going to lose any sleep over anything he had to do or anyone he had to kidnap or kill to achieve
that goal.

"Those embassy guards arrived entirely too fast after the
explosion," Markus was saying. "Taltek has always had a sense
of the dramatic. No doubt he waited an appropriate amount of
time to ensure that I was either dead or taken, then he coura-
geously leads his men to the rescue and kills any remaining
Khrynsani. In the eyes of the elven people, Taltek would be a
hero, and his actions could help justify going to war with the
goblins, even though it's a war the vast majority of the elven
people don't want."

Mychael spoke. "If Balmorlan comes up with a way to prove
that goblins are killing off high-ranking elven officials, elven
public opinion could shift in favor of a military response."

"I can't allow that to happen," Markus said. He looked at
me. "I know you have no intention of working for anyone,
but the elven people know what the Saghred is capable of
from our history. If you or the Saghred were to fall into goblin
hands, Taltek would claim that the goblins wouldn't stop this

time until they destroyed every last elf—and he could very well be right. Queen Lisara would be forced to mobilize the elven military, and the generals would pressure her for a pre-emptive strike."

I glowered. "And the goblins would strike back."

"Either way it would be war."

"Or if the elves got their hands on me, they'd destroy every last goblin," I reminded him pointedly. "Neither one's going to happen as long as I'm still breathing. I will not be used."

Lamplight gleamed off of the gem attached to Mychael's cloak. I reached down and pulled my own from beneath my shirt by its chain. I'd completely forgotten about them.

"Do you think they worked?"

"Only one way to find out." Mychael pulled the chain over his neck. "Ryn, you wouldn't happen to have a crystal ball, would you?"

My uncle snorted. "I make my own future, Mychael. No ball gazing needed." He thought for a moment. "Though I've got a deck prism, clear as fine glass. Would that do?"

"Perfectly."

Phaelan swung his legs over the chair arm and onto the floor. "I'll get it."

Markus looked intently at the marble-sized gem dangling from my hand as Phaelan shut the cabin door behind him. "A recording gem?"

"You know what they are?" Though I shouldn't be surprised. If it was a spy gadget, chances were Markus had one of his own.

His thin lips quirked upward in a brief grin. "It's a night for firsts. Mychael's out of uniform and you're out of the citadel, and it's doubtful the two of you were taking a stroll past my house in the middle of the night."

"We weren't," I told him with a secretive smile. Two could play at that game.

Mychael's blue eyes twinkled. "Would you like to tell Markus what we were paid to come to his house to do?"

I beamed back at him. "Love to. Some secrets are too fun not to share. Markus, we were paid an obscene amount of goblin gold to kidnap and deliver you to Sarad Nukpana."

I got the unprecedented treat of seeing Markus Sevelien stunned. If I'd have blinked, I'd have missed it. Fortunately I didn't blink, because it was an expression I knew I'd never see on him again. The next instant, Markus was once again in perfect control.

Mychael reached around behind him where the satchel lay on the floor, and put it on the table with a thump.

Uncle Ryn whistled. "Pure goblin imperial, six hundred kugarats."

Mychael was clearly impressed. "Has he always—"

"It's a family gift," I said.

Mychael sat back in his chair and looked at Markus. "We were coming to tell you that a pair of human operatives by the names of Kester Morrell and Maire Orla had been hired to kidnap you."

Markus traded stunned for merely confused. "But Raine said that—"

"A glamour," I told him. "Thanks to a boost from the Saghred, I'm discovering a couple of talents I didn't know I had. Apparently an incredibly thorough glamour is one of them. Mychael and I went in as Morrell and Orla, got a scumbag to admit that he'd kidnapped General Aratus." I held up my gem by its chain. "Plus we got his confession on these little beauties. Then we accepted the job to snatch you, took the gold, and came over to warn you that we'd done both."

"And ended up saving my life."

I shrugged. "An added bonus."

Markus's expression gave absolutely no indication what was going on beneath that calm and polished surface. "Do you truly think it was a bonus, Raine?"

I didn't respond immediately. I knew my answer to that question, but I wanted Markus to wait for it, like I had to think about it first. I know; it was petty. But after tiptoeing through a house full of Khrynsani and being in the same room with a half-regenerated Sarad Nukpana and his uber-evil uncle, petty was the least of what I was feeling right now.

"Yes, it was a bonus," I finally told him. "You being Balmorlan's boss . . . Damn, Markus, what the hell was I supposed to think?"

"Exactly what you needed to think. If one of Balmorlan's snitches witnessed one of your outbursts . . ." He stopped and smiled. "And I'm certain that you had at least one—it helped me maintain my masquerade for a little longer. You were most helpful. And now that you've blown up my house, with any luck Taltek thinks I was blown up with it."

"You're not the only government official on this island to squeak past Death tonight," I said. "And the goblins don't have the market cornered on trying to start a war, either. Imala Kalis and her men were ambushed by Nightshades outside of Sirens. They took a couple of shots at me and some Guardians, but Banan Ryce was there and had been hired to assassinate Imala Kalis."

Markus sat up straighter. "Imala is unharmed?"

First-name basis. Interesting. "Not a scratch. From what I saw, she and her boys have dealt with this sort of thing before. All it did was make her mad. The lady's got one heck of a vocabulary and the lungs to use it."

Markus's face bore signs of concern. "Mychael, have you offered Imala Guardian protection? I seriously doubt that she will accept it, but have you asked?"

"I was going to do so in the morning. You're right. She'll turn me down. But I think she'll permit Guardians on the embassy's outer perimeter. That way she wouldn't lose face."

Markus paused. "Imala Kalis is the woman Queen Lisara wants in charge of the goblin secret service. The elves who want war with the goblins want her dead. Imala's concern is what's best for the goblin people and she knows that a war isn't it. Two of her own agents have attempted to kill her in the past month alone. One of the assassins belonged to King Sathrik's inner circle. The king has never hidden his desire to finish the extermination of our people that his ancestor started. Imala is one of the obstacles in his way."

"You say the assassin *belonged* to Sathrik. Past tense."

"Imala killed him herself."

A killer with dimples.

"We have proof that Banan Ryce and his men were contracted to come to Mid by a high-ranking elf," Mychael said. "Before tonight we didn't have a name. Balmorlan's now at the top of a very short list."

"Carnades Silvanus is number two," I said.

"The trick is bridging the proof gap between Ryce and either one of them."

"That would let you arrest Balmorlan?" I asked.

Mychael smiled with a baring of teeth. "For hiring Nightshades to assassinate Imala Kalis, I could put him *under* the citadel."

"Sounds like a good, wholesome family project," Phaelan said from the open doorway. "Set him up and take him down, then we'll let Mychael take him out. What do you think, Dad?"

Uncle Ryn's teeth flashed white against his black beard. "I think I can carve out time in my schedule for such a noble cause."

Phaelan came in the cabin, shut the door, and handed the deck prism to Mychael. Then he rubbed his hands together, a devilish gleam in his eyes. "So, where does Balmorlan get his funding?" he asked Markus.

"Some from the elven treasury; most he raises privately."

"Just what I wanted to hear. Treasury money has to be accounted for. With private fund-raising there doesn't have to be a paper trail." My cousin's grin turned gleefully malicious. "Unless someone creates one."

I knew where he was going and I liked the destination.

Phaelan froze, stood ramrod straight, and sniffed the air

twice. "Gold. Goblin imperial." His hands were virtually twitching with unfulfilled avarice.

"In the bag, Phaelan."

My cousin's eyes locked on that leather satchel like it was his own little slice of heaven. "A couple hundred, at least."

"Six, to be exact," Uncle Ryn said.

One of Phaelan's hands reached out to touch. I smacked that hand.

"Ow."

"Not yours."

Phaelan's grin was seven times wicked. "Could it be?"

I told him where it'd come from.

My cousin nodded in approval. "You got to keep the gold and the mark. You do the family proud, cousin. But you didn't answer my question. Can we keep it?"

"I have an idea or two that will earn us the best return on our investment," Mychael said, his smile sly.

"Frame Balmorlan?" I asked.

Mychael nodded once. "I think it may prove fruitful. Un-explained goblin gold being found in Balmorlan's possession would raise all kinds of uncomfortable questions."

Phaelan's expression was pained. "But we can take it back, right?"

I just looked at him. "Do you want to take out the evil son of a bitch or line your pockets?"

My cousin had to think about that one. "Can't I do both?"

"No."

Phaelan plopped down in his chair in disgust. Unrequited greed wasn't a good look on my cousin. "Evil son of a bitch first."

"That's better."

"Where do Balmorlan and his cronies keep their money?" Uncle Ryn asked Markus. "Not the small stuff they let the government accountants see. Where do they keep the real money they don't want anyone to find?"

"Brenir."

"Which bank?"

"First Bank of D'Mai."

Phaelan smiled like the sun had come out. "Adequate security, but not adequate enough."

"Mago?" I asked.

"None other."

Markus looked from me to Phaelan, perplexed. Another expression I didn't see on him often.

"How much does Balmorlan have?" I asked Markus.

"If he has access to Carnades's sources of income, Taltek can lay his hands on more than is in Queen Lisara's treasury."

Phaelan whistled, then he slowly shook his head in disapproval. "No one needs that much money. It's obscene."

"Unless it's in one of your accounts," I noted.

"True."

"Son, remind Mago to siphon slowly," Uncle Ryn cautioned. "We wouldn't want to make anyone suspicious."

Mago didn't need reminding. He was a Brenirian banker, respectable even as far as Brenirian bankers went. He'd elevated embezzlement to an art form. Professionally he was known as Mago Peronne. His real name wouldn't exactly be welcome in banking circles.

Mago Benares. Uncle Ryn's eldest. Phaelan's brother. And one crafty and cunning weasel.

I could virtually see the nefarious little wheels turning in Phaelan's head. "Though . . . if we're going to set the bastard up, let's do it right. Mago could set up an account in Sarad Nukpana's name and siphon Balmorlan's money into it," Phaelan said. "That way no one except Mago would have access to the money. He even knows a forger who could put Nukpana's signature on the documents authorizing the transfer, and predate it to before he got sucked into the Saghred."

I smiled and leaned back in my chair. "And the next time Balmorlan went to bribe or buy off anyone . . ." I spread my hands. "No cash, no cohorts."

"The notion does have appeal," Uncle Ryn agreed. "Markus, since you're supposed to be dead, it might be best if you stay with us for a while. You'll be safe, comfortable, and have all the goblin port you care to drink."

"And while we drink, we can plot," Phaelan added. "We know people."

Mychael had set his recording gem next to the deck prism. With a few murmured words, we all watched as Mychael and I, glamoured as Morrell and Orla, struck a deal with Karl Cradock, and best of all, we got to see and hear him admit to the crime that Tam was sitting in a cell for committing.

Phaelan whistled. "Damn, cousin, is that you?"

"Yeah, it's me. Roll your tongue back up in your head."

"Who is she?"

"Maire Orla. Kidnapper and assassin."

"I think I'm in love."

"I think you're a sick man."

Phaelan shrugged, never taking his eyes off of Maire Orla's bounty. "I never claimed to be anything else."

I squeezed my eyes shut and pinched the bridge of my nose. Exhaustion had caught up with me and was pounding on my head with a vengeance. "So Sarad Nukpana is regenerating himself and turning powerful and influential elves into beef jerky. Any chance we can sic him on Taltek Balmorlan?"

"I'm sure Balmorlan is aware he's on Nukpana's list," Mychael said.

Markus solemnly studied my face for a moment and then Mychael's. "There is something else of which Taltek Balmorlan is aware. It concerns the two of you and Tamnais Nathrach."

My heart pounded in my chest, but I kept my expression neutral—at least, I tried.

Our umi'atsu bond. The fact that Tam could now tap the power of the Saghred, and Mychael and I could tap each other. Extreme caution was called for here. "What about it?"

Markus's eyes darted briefly to Phaelan and Uncle Ryn.

My silence told him that no, they didn't know; and no, I didn't want them to. I couldn't protect my family from much, but I would protect them from this.

Do you only want to protect them, Raine? Or do you just not want them to know?

"Commodore and Captain Benares," Markus said, never taking his dark eyes from mine. "I wouldn't want to ask you to leave your own cabin, but is there a place where I may speak privately with Raine and Mychael?"

Uncle Ryn made no move to leave. "Is that what you want, Spitfire?"

What I wanted was to wrap my family around me like a blanket, but that'd just get them killed or worse right along with me.

"Raine, we're in this." Phaelan knew me too well; he knew exactly what I was thinking. "We're with you. We're not backing down, and we sure as hell aren't running."

"If you're in more danger than we've already heard about, I want to know," Uncle Ryn rumbled. "Any enemy of yours is prey of mine."

"Thank you," I said softly, my throat tight. There wasn't much more a woman could ask for than a family she could count on to kill the people who wanted to kill her.

I glanced at Mychael. He nodded once.

"I want my family with me, Markus."

"Very well. I know about the umi'atsu bond between the three of you." Markus wasn't one to mince words. "Carnades told me when I arrived on the island, and Balmorlan not only knows, but he also plans to use it—and the three of you."

"We know they want to expose us, but to get us out of the way."

"It goes further than that."

I remembered Balmorlan saying he was building prison cells, and suddenly my dinner wasn't sitting too well.

Phaelan stood motionless. "Wait a minute—what's this umi'atsu bond?"

I forced the contents of my stomach to stay put, and quickly filled them in on all the details.

"And only death can separate the three of you now?" Uncle Ryn asked when I'd finished.

Mychael answered him before I could. "It is the only way we know at this time. If there is another way, we will find it."

"And Balmorlan has a reason for not wanting you to find a cure."

I looked at Markus. "Apparently."

"The three of you in an umi'atsu bond proves that the Saghred's power can be distributed between more than one person at a time," Markus said. "Mychael, I have to ask: have you experienced any side effects from being linked even tenuously to the Saghred?"

"None whatsoever."

"Which is precisely what Balmorlan is hoping for. He believes that the more people the Saghred's power is divided among, the less chance for mental instability."

My voice came out thin. "Power without paying the price."

Markus nodded. "Balmorlan has recruited some of his favorite agency mages. They have been arriving on Mid for the past week. He appealed to their racial pride to make the sacrifice. Balmorlan plans to keep presenting mages to the Saghred until it selects those he deems suitable for his purpose."

"What do you mean 'presenting mages to the Saghred'? The thing's locked up in the citadel."

Phaelan stiffened. "What purpose?"

"The Saghred wants to be wielded," Markus said. "Balmorlan wants to use that power against the goblins."

Horror and panic choked my words. "There's no way in hell anyone else is joining our bond."

"Did the Saghred ask you when it bonded you with Tamnais Nathrach?" Markus asked. "Or Mychael?"

I felt sick. "No."

The Saghred had bonded Tam and me when we'd joined

forces to save kidnapped spellsinging students. The rock had taken Mychael when he'd linked with me to attempt to slow the progression of my bond with Tam.

"Proximity and magic are all that's needed," came Mychael's voice inside my head.

"There's no way we're getting anywhere near Balmorlan's pet mages."

"You've heard about the cells Balmorlan is constructing in the elven embassy," Markus said quietly.

"I've heard."

"Level Twelve wards, detainment spells layered for strength, and magic-depleting manacles bolted to the walls."

I knew what that meant. Suddenly there wasn't enough air in the cabin.

If Taltek Balmorlan got me in that cell, he could throw anyone he wanted in with me. Mychael's touch had been enough for the Saghred to bond him to me. I wasn't letting any of Balmorlan's mages touch me. Suddenly I wanted to run and keep running. Chained to a wall with magic-depleting manacles, I wouldn't have a choice. I'd been locked in those kinds of manacles before; they were used to keep mages from using their powers. The Saghred would still be free to act.

I would be helpless to stop either it or Balmorlan's pet mages.

I didn't know which would be worse: to be slowly drained of life by Sarad Nukpana or helpless to stop the Saghred from bonding mages to me that would wield it.

And when they used the Saghred, they'd be using me.

I felt Mychael's strong hands on my shoulders.

"Raine, it won't happen. I won't allow it."

My breath was coming quick and ragged. Slow down, Raine. You're going to pass out. Balmorlan wants you terrified. You will *not* give him what he wants. I took a deep breath and let it out. It only trembled a little. "Markus, is Taltek Balmorlan reporting to anyone right now?"

"No."

"Is he working with anyone?"

"Yes."

"Are they vital to his operation?"

"At this point, very much so."

"I want names."

"Raine, I—"

"I want names," I snapped. It took every bit of self-control I had not to scream those words.

I think Markus knew that. He listed three names. One had a title; two had military ranks.

All three had just become a Benares family project—along with their boss.

"Raine, I can help," Mychael said.

I stood. "This isn't within the law, Mychael. Your Guardians can't help me."

"I wasn't referring to my Guardians." His blue eyes were glacier cold.

"You know people?" Phaelan asked him.

"I do. Me."

Chapter 17

The sun was coming up, birds were singing, and the breeze from the harbor didn't stink yet. Most people would consider this to be the start of a good day.

I wasn't most people, but I was determined to make today go my way for a change. I'd crammed my terror of elven prison cells into a dark corner of my mind. We were about to free Tam, and Markus was still on my side. Those two things, plus the vision of a financially and professionally ruined Taltek Balmorlan, were enough to put a smile on my face. It was probably a smile that most people would run from, but for a Benares, it meant we were happy.

"Thinking violently vindictive thoughts?" Mychael asked from beside me.

"I am." I inhaled the harbor air as if it were a bouquet of flowers. "And enjoying myself while doing it."

Mychael smiled slowly, a dangerous sparkle in his eyes. "You're a bad girl, Raine Benares."

"I do what I can."

We gave any patrols and early risers the slip, and arrived unseen at Mychael's basement hideaway. He didn't mind his men seeing him, at least not once he was back in uniform and not wearing something a highwayman would be apprehended in. I was beginning to wonder if the real Mychael Eiliesor was someone in between.

Mychael closed the door behind us. I waited until he'd locked it.

"The only thing better than a ruined Taltek Balmorlan would be you telling me how you can help make him that way and be the paladin at the same time. I don't see you tossing the law aside, even if it means getting Balmorlan."

"I won't be tossing the law aside; it has always dictated my actions."

"Like your actions last night? The man I was with wasn't the upright, law-abiding, and proper paladin. You handled Karl Cradock like a pro, and I don't mean a Guardian." I tossed my cloak on the bed. "Listen, your life is your own, so you don't owe me an explanation, but I'd—"

"I want to give you one." Mychael hesitated, his eyes focused on the closed door. "I protect those who need it by arresting or taking down those who deserve it. That is the *intent* of the law."

"But not the letter of the law."

"Sometimes the two aren't the same," he agreed.

"Don't get me wrong—I approve completely of what you did last night. Hell, even *I* was impressed and I've seen some slick con men at work." I took a deep breath and pushed on. "I'm going to need all the help I can get—legal and otherwise. But I'd never thought that someone who went to the Conclave college, became a Guardian cadet, then raced up through the ranks to paladin could be an 'otherwise' kind of man."

"I didn't go to school here; I've never been a cadet, so I didn't race up through the ranks."

I just stood there in stupefied silence. "What?" I finally managed.

"I didn't—"

"I heard what you said. I just—"

"Assumed."

"Apparently a hell of a lot."

"Raine, I've *never* lied to you. You never asked."

"How long have you been paladin?"

"Almost four years."

"And you weren't a Guardian before then?"

"No."

The consummate Guardian, the proper paladin, had never even *been* one before. My thoughts ran around in confused circles, bumping into each other and getting nowhere fast.

"Doesn't the paladin have to at least have *been* a Guardian at some point?"

"It's the way it's always been done—but not in my case."

"But you said you were a student of Ronan Cayle."

"Ronan sees a lot of already trained spellsingers. It helps our voices stay in shape."

"Then who taught you?"

Mychael watched me in silence. "Is that what you really want to know?" he asked quietly.

I stood there, looking up into those sea blue eyes. Eyes that met mine unwaveringly. They were the eyes of an honest man, or so I thought.

"I want to know who you are."

"Mychael Eiliesor."

"A name doesn't tell me who you are." I stood there, looking up at him, trying to see beneath the surface. I was *bonded* to the man and I still didn't know who he was. I had seen the avenging angel that he was inside. But the armor hadn't gleamed and his robes hadn't been white—maybe they had been that way at one time, but they weren't anymore. They were singed, dirty, and bloodstained. Mychael Eiliesor had fought a lot of battles against others—maybe even against himself.

And in every last one of them, he'd done what he had to do.

An hour ago on the *Red Hawk*, he'd promised to do the same thing.

For me.

"Mychael, you've said that I can trust you with my life. I can do that—and I have done that." I paused. "But I need you to be willing to trust me with yours."

He crossed the small room to an armoire in the corner,

opened it, and pulled out an exact copy of his paladin uniform. He began unbuttoning his leather doublet. "Justinius contacted me about four years ago and said he needed me as paladin."

"'Contacted'? Sounds like one of Markus's agency terms."

"I've never worked for the agency."

"Who, then?"

Mychael took off the doublet and tossed it on the bed next to my cloak, quickly followed by his shirt. He half turned toward me. His arms and chest were sculpted with muscle, his shoulders broad. I knew this; I had seen the man virtually naked just a few days ago. Hell, I'd been in bed with him. But I still looked and couldn't look away, and the urge to close the distance between us and let my fingers explore that smoothly muscled expanse was almost too much to resist.

Almost.

I needed answers, not a distraction. Focus, Raine.

"Who did you take your orders from?" I asked.

"I reported only to Queen Lisara's father."

"Do you report to the queen now?"

"No."

Retired, then. Or at least on inactive status. And he couldn't exactly be paladin of a politically neutral military order and take orders from the elven queen. Well, he could, but one thing I did know for certain was that Mychael Eiliesor would never split his loyalties.

"You were in the army?"

"For a while."

I started doing the math. "You're a highly skilled warrior who can use your voice to make almost anyone do anything; you can heal yourself; you can veil and glamour like nobody's business, pretending to be anyone and conning your way into and out of sticky situations—then there's the talents I haven't even seen yet. No doubt the old king found your services invaluable."

"I was adequately compensated."

I'd heard of them, the men and women who reported only to the old king. Officially, they had no name, though they were called Black Cats by certain criminal elements who had the misfortune to come into contact with them. And since my last name was Benares, I'd heard the term more than once. Like a black cat in a dark alley, you might catch a glimpse of one, but before you could blink, it was gone. Black Cat operatives were trained to do what was needed, where it was needed, and to whom it needed to be done. They operated where the law couldn't go or reach. They were never seen, never heard.

Never known.

Until now.

"A Black Cat," I said simply.

Mychael arched a quizzical brow at me. He didn't deny it. That was as close to a direct admission as I was likely to get.

"Yeah, I've heard the name," I continued. "And I know the reputation. Legendary. So by being paladin, you're just playing another role, albeit for a different boss."

Mychael sat on the side of the bed and began removing his boots. "I am the paladin in every way that the law and my duties dictate. With the deteriorating political state of affairs on Mid during the past few years and the Saghred resurfacing, Justinius needed someone who could work within the law, but also knew how to work the system." He pulled one boot off and tossed it aside. "Unfortunately, the law can't solve all problems, and people like Carnades and Taltek Balmorlan are quite adept at circumventing it. Justinius asked me to serve as paladin because he needed someone he could trust to work cleanly outside of the system." His second boot joined the first.

"Cleanly meaning not getting caught."

Mychael stood, unhooked his belt, and began unbuttoning his trousers. He grinned at me. "At least not getting caught with my trousers down. Would you prefer to turn around while I finish changing?"

I shook my head. "I can safely say that I've seen everything you've got. So I'll stay right where I am and keep getting answers."

He dropped his trousers and I tried to keep my jaw from doing the same thing.

"I . . . uh . . . Dammit, I forgot my question."

Mychael's eyes sparkled. "I'm also an expert in avoiding interrogation."

Black Cats were experts at vanishing into the night. I didn't want Mychael doing the same to me.

But I also didn't want Mychael getting killed because of me.

"How much longer will you stay here as paladin?" I tried to make the question sound matter-of-fact, but my voice sounded kind of small even to me.

"Raine, I'm not going anywhere. My job here is far from finished."

"But let's say you did need to leave. I mean, if you had to . . . I want you to know that . . . well, that I would understand." I forced out a little laugh. "I know some kick-ass mages, and I could always call in more of my family. Some of them are crazy enough to take on anything."

Mychael had pulled on his gray uniform trousers. His feet and chest were still bare. He padded over to me and put his arms around me, pulling me close. Words couldn't describe how good that felt.

"You don't need to call anyone," he murmured against my hair. "We're going to take care of this together."

I took a slow breath and let it out against his chest. Just say it, Raine. "Mychael, you're in enough danger without feeling obligated to me."

He loosened his hold so he could see my face. "Obligated?"

"You feel responsible for getting me into this and now you feel obligated to get me out."

"Raine, I don't—"

"Please, let me finish. I'm poison to you. If Nukpana or

Balmorlan . . . or hell, even if Carnades manages to bring me down, I won't take you with me. I don't know how I'll stop them, but I'll do what I have to." I put my hands on his chest, keeping the distance between us. "Please . . . please, don't take any more chances with your life because of me." My vision blurred and there was no smoky fireplace to blame it on. "I care too much about you." I tried to force down the emotions that thickened my voice. "I couldn't stand it if you—"

Mychael looked down at me for a long moment, then he slowly put one of his hands over both of mine. "Raine, some chances are worth taking; they're so rare and precious that it's worth risking everything." He said it with conviction. He said it like a man who had made up his mind and Death itself wasn't going to budge him.

I was talking about him surviving the next few days. Mychael wasn't.

He was talking about me. About us.

I felt a surge of panic. "And sometimes they're not worth taking." My mind raced. If I left the island, I'd take my trouble with me and Mychael would be safe . . . at least safer. My dad had left Mid nine hundred years ago. He'd had no choice—

Mychael curled his fingers around my hands, holding them tight. "Then I will come after you." He paused, the smooth muscles working in his jaw. "And if someone takes you, be they man or mage, I will find you."

I didn't need our bond to tell me what he was thinking, what he felt. I could see it in his eyes.

Mychael Eiliesor loved me.

"I don't regret anything I've done—or anything I'll have to do in the next few days." He pulled my hands to his lips one after the other, kissing the center of each palm. "I regret nothing," he whispered, "especially you."

Mychael bent his head, his lips hesitating over my mouth. When his lips lightly touched mine, I expected him to pull away after a brief kiss as he'd done before, his passion denied, our propriety maintained.

Not this time. He didn't deny himself—or me.

Mychael's lips gently explored mine as if tasting them for the first time, or memorizing them if this was the last time. One of his hands cradled my neck and throat, his thumb lightly stroking my face. The other was more insistent, wrapping around my waist and gathering me to him.

He opened his eyes and gazed down at me. The question was there in those sea blue eyes, unspoken, lingering between us. Did I want him to stop?

I didn't need words to answer him.

My hands reached up to either side of his face and pulled him down to me, the stubble on his face a delicious roughness beneath my fingers. Mychael's lips had been gentle explorers; mine were conquerors, taking what I'd wanted from almost the first moment I'd seen him. Mychael wasn't the only one who had denied himself. Death had knocked on my door one time too many; I wasn't going to deny myself anymore. I'd take what I could, while I could. Plunder, pillage, leave no treasure behind.

Mychael responded, his passion, his need matching my own. Any fear of the present and uncertain future faded to nothing. All that was left was him and me, taste and sensation, both delicious—both dangerous. His hands slid down my arms and around my waist and back, crushing me against him. A fire flickered and caught between us, familiar to me, new to him. Mychael's breath caught when he felt it, but he didn't stop. Instead he pulled me closer, as if he would wrap himself around me, shielding and protecting me. The fire was the Saghred, but it wasn't alone. Overshadowing it, forcing it aside, was another fire, white-hot, pure, and unrelenting, burning bright and searing the darkness away from me.

His magic. Mychael.

I saw a light through my closed eyelids, and felt a glow, a warmth down the length of me, of both of us, wrapping and entwining, joining us together. I slowly parted my lips from his and looked up at him, my pulse absurdly loud in my own ears. We stood there, our bodies touching, our breathing the only sound. Mychael's breathing was ragged as he gazed down at me in wonder—and in expectant hope.

"I'm a Benares, remember?" My voice was low and husky. "If we see something we want, we take it."

"Do you see something you want?"

"I'm looking right at him." My mouth was suddenly dry, and I tried to swallow. "Do you want me?" I told myself it was a stupid question, but I had to ask. I needed to hear him say it.

His hands were on my shoulders and he slid them down to just above my breasts. "I've wanted you—and loved you— since the moment I woke up in that bedroom in Mermeia and saw you standing in the corner."

I think my heart stopped for a few beats. "Loved me," I heard myself say.

His hands slid down farther. "Loved you."

He was wearing only his uniform trousers. I was wearing way too much. I reached up to unbutton something, anything, but I was suddenly at a loss as to where to start.

Mychael caught my hands in his. "May I undress you?"

"Okay." I suddenly felt shy, awkward.

"Are you sure?" His deep voice rubbed against me like hands in velvet gloves, sending a delicious shiver down through my belly and lower.

"No one's ever undressed me before."

Mychael grinned. "I have, but you weren't awake for it."

I was awake for it now and then some. I wrestled my way out of my sword harness, then I let Mychael take it from there. Truth be told, my hands were probably shaking too badly to undo my doublet's buttons. Mychael made short work of them, and shorter work of the buttons on my shirt. Then he slowly pulled my shirt and doublet aside and stopped, staring down at me. The room wasn't cold, so I didn't have any excuse for my breasts tightening and nipples hardening except for the truth. They wanted to be touched and they wanted it badly.

Mychael bent and wrapped his arms around my hips and lifted me off my feet. When his lips closed around my nipple, the shock of sensations made me gasp.

He raised his head and my mouth took his, tasting, delving, devouring, and he backed to the bed, one arm holding me tightly against him, the other exploring, kneading. The backs of his knees bumped against the edge of the bed and he sat down, pulling me with him. I opened my eyes and looked at him. I'd seen his eyes darken before, but nothing like this; his pupils were dilated so much that they were dark pools that I could fall into, wanted to dive into.

Mychael's fingers were spread wide under my shirt and against my bare back to touch as much skin as possible. I unwrapped my arms from around his shoulders and dropped them to my sides. Mychael didn't need me to say what I wanted him to do. He reached up with his other hand, grabbed a handful of my doublet and shirt at the back of my neck, and pulled them down. They came halfway off, then stopped, snagged on something just below my elbows.

What the— "Dammit . . . hold on."

Mychael's lips were busy on my throat. "Daggers," he murmured, his mouth working its way down to nip at my breast and lower still to pull on my nipple.

A sweet shiver ran through my body, ending with an unbearable ache between my legs, and I suddenly forgot how to breathe or what the hell daggers were.

Mychael's mouth and tongue and hands paused from doing those wonderful things they were doing. "Daggers," he said again, and went back to sucking and rubbing and kneading and teasing.

A tiny part of my mind that wasn't dazed from sensation shouted at me what the rest of me couldn't remember. *Daggers. In forearm sheaths. Doublet can't come off until they come off, stupid.*

"Oh . . . wait." I wiggled my doublet back up on my shoulders and with shaky hands unfastened the cuffs and reached inside. I pulled off one sheath, then the other. Only then did I look at Mychael. "There," I almost panted. "Try again."

He did. He grabbed my doublet's leather in both fists at my shoulders and, in one smooth move, pulled it and my shirt off and threw both across the room. *Nice.*

I pushed him back on the bed, kissing him again, deep enough to taste the tannins of the Caesolian red he'd had. I tried to shift my hips to get closer to him, to satisfy that ache. I still had my trousers and boots on. This was a problem. A big one. I swore silently, but the only thing that made it out of my mouth was a whimper.

Mychael heard, and better yet, he did something about it. He looked up at me and grinned. "Hold on."

I did.

He slid his hands down to pull me tight against him, and flipped me over onto my back.

I yelped in surprise, and then laughed and wrapped my legs around him.

Mychael's grin broadened, then he leaned down and trapped my bottom lip between his teeth, nipping. "You like?"

"Oh yeah." My heart was only about to pound its way out of my chest, I liked it so much.

"Uh . . . if you want me to do anything else, you're going to have to unwrap your legs."

"What? Oh . . ."

I slid my legs down from his hips and Mychael got off of the bed and went to work on my boots. They were tall boots, over my knees, and weren't easy for me to take off under the best of circumstances, but Mychael made short work of them, and they joined my doublet and shirt on the floor.

I reached up and tugged him down on top of me. Mychael's eyes were gleaming as he put his hands on either side of me and dipped his head to my belly, the tip of his tongue running a quick, warm swirl around the edge of my belly button. My hips arched up in a shock of sensation. Mychael slid one of his hands under me, the other quickly unbuttoning my trousers.

I swallowed and tried to pull in some air. "Nimble fingers," I noted.

He smiled up at me. "Just wait."

I couldn't.

Mychael slipped his fingers into the top of my trousers and after a few squirms from me, they joined the pile of my clothes on the floor. Then he stood and I watched. Pulling his uniform trousers on was a lot easier than taking them off now, but a few minutes ago, he didn't have nearly as much to pull them over.

I'd seen him naked before, but then just a peek briefly visible above a sheet, and the room had been almost dark. I could see everything now, and my power of speech abandoned me completely.

Mychael slid onto the bed and I hooked my leg around his hip, pulling him down to me. The hard length of him slid against my thigh until it touched the source of my ache, and my breath caught in my throat. Mychael's eyes met mine, dark pools of midnight blue, steady, certain of what he wanted . . . and hungry.

My eyes flicked toward the door. "Is it locked?"

He blinked. "What?"

"The door, is it locked?"

"Yes."

"Are you sure?"

"Positive."

"I mean, well . . . it doesn't have a latch."

"It doesn't have a latch on the outside, either."

"But what if—"

"It's sealed. The door and this room are spellproof." His grin was slow and wicked. "*And* soundproof." He grabbed me around the hips, rolled, and swung me up on top. "There. You want control? You got it." His eyes glittered up at me in challenge.

I opened my mouth and Mychael laid his fingers across my lips. "This is bodywork, Raine."

I smiled beneath his fingers and reached down to touch

him. Smooth and velvety at the same time. I ran my fingers across the tip and he gasped and jerked beneath me.

I reached for him again, but he caught my hand in his.

"You don't like it?"

Mychael took a ragged breath. "I like it too much." His voice was hoarse, raw. "I've wanted you for too long to let it end like that."

I grinned. "Say no more."

"If you do that again, I won't be able to."

Neither one of us said another word as I lowered myself onto him, settling with a trembling sigh. Oh . . . *yes.* Oh yeah, that was good. That was so nice. That was so far beyond good and nice that a word hadn't been invented yet to describe it. I stayed like that, panting, unmoving, then Mychael shifted beneath me with a gentle thrust and someone moaned softly. It was me.

I braced my hands on his chest as we moved together, his hands on my hips, his fingers spread wide, gripping me. A warmth spread through me that had nothing to do with our mysterious bond and everything to do with us, what we were doing, together, here and now. I leaned down and Mychael rose up to meet me, our lips meeting, our quickened breath mingling. The heat swirled faster, and lower, building in my belly and beyond, tightening, gripping. Molten. Our bodies moved faster to match the liquid fire spiraling through us, and I heard Mychael's long drawn-out growl from beneath me as he thrust once more, hard enough to send us both over the edge.

In the next instant, for both of our sakes, I really hoped that room was soundproof.

I sprawled on top of Mychael, my breathing harsh and ragged against his shoulder. His hands slid lazily up my spine and down along the curve of my waist and hips and back again, the heat sparking beneath his fingers, sending little shivers through me. I stretched, slow and languid, and I swear I purred.

"Sleep would be great," I murmured against his lips.

"Too bad we can't have any." His eyes sparkled. "Though we had something even better."

"Yes, we did." I ran my fingernails lightly down his chest. "Thank you, very much."

"My pleasure, Miss Benares."

"Oh, I can assure you that the pleasure was all mine."

Mychael laughed. "So I heard."

I playfully smacked him on the ass and he just laughed harder.

I rolled off of him, snuggling in the crook of his arm, my head on his chest. "I hope no one else did. I can do without an applauding crowd when we step outside."

We lay there in the silence, arms and legs entwined, warm and safe. The only sound I could hear was Mychael's heartbeat against my ear. I closed my eyes and drifted. This felt good. Better than good, this felt right. We were still in as much danger as before; that hadn't changed. But everything else had. Though it wasn't a change, not really. It was more like a confirmation. Yes, a confirmation. My heart had known how I felt even if my head wouldn't admit it, even if I was afraid to admit it. And it was past time for me to say it. I had to. I didn't plan on dying in the next few days, and anyone who was determined to try to make me was in for one hell of a fight. They were in for a lot worse if they laid one hand on Mychael. I didn't want to think about losing him, but the image came in my mind's eye before I could stop it. If something did happen to him . . . or to me . . . I wanted him to know that I—

I tilted my head and looked up at Mychael. His eyes were closed, but he was awake. He sensed me looking and opened his eyes. I'd just made love to the man and was naked in bed with him. Shy should be the last thing I felt. Then why was I nervous? Just say it, Raine.

"I . . . I love you, too."

Mychael tightened his arms around me and pulled me up close enough to kiss. Then he did just that, slow, delicious, and maddening. And I started having naughty ideas that we didn't have time for me to have.

Mychael's lips released mine and he just looked at me, as if memorizing my face, storing away this moment. Like he was trying to get a picture in his mind of something he was about to lose, something that would be taken from him.

He wasn't going to lose me.

And no one was taking Mychael Eiliesor away from me.

"We're going to get out of this." I didn't ask it as a question. I stated it as an irrefutable fact. "So are our friends and so are my family." I smiled and I knew it was fierce. Hell, I felt fierce. I was also determined, and I was happy. Yes, dammit, for the first time in a long time, I was happy. And no one was going to take that away from me. "And today is the beginning of the end for anyone who thinks otherwise."

Mychael and I got back to watcher headquarters just before sunrise. We walked through headquarters' front doors this time, like we'd come from the citadel after a night of questioning false witnesses, not an evening of kidnapping an elven duke, blowing up a house, and making mind-blowing love in a secret hideout. Mychael pulled me into a side street twice for quick, heated kisses. But by the time we got to headquarters, the proper paladin was back.

I smiled. I wasn't going to be fooled by that act ever again.

Sedge met us at the front door, a big grin on his broad and honest face. "You don't need those witnesses to recant," he informed Mychael. "Director Imala Kalis brought evidence of her own."

Tam's cell was empty and all eyes were on the closed door to Sedge's conference room. And half of those eyes belonged to enough goblin secret service agents to no doubt make Imala feel comfortable and Sedge's boys more than a trifle edgy.

"The two of them are in there," he responded to our unspoken question, and my obvious concern.

Mychael inclined his head toward the conference room. "Was that Imala Kalis's idea?"

"Nope, the second he was out of that cell, Nathrach damned near dragged her in there." Sedge's grin broadened. "The lady landed a solid kick to Nathrach's shin, but she told her men not to interfere."

"What's with the goblin spy convention?" I asked, bothered by any room that was wall-to-wall fangs.

"The lady showed up about an hour ago with the paperwork she needed and the law on her side," Sedge told us. "As a keeper of the law, I had to agree that she was well within her rights to demand Nathrach's release."

Mychael's expression darkened. "What papers?"

"Papers proving that Nathrach was still a member of the goblin royal family and as such he has diplomatic immunity from prosecution of any crime except in a goblin court of law. And while the lady was at it, she claimed that Nathrach had been taken as a political prisoner and Magus Silvanus's and Inquisitor Balmorlan's accusations and groundless arrest were an act of war."

I snorted a laugh. "Sorry, but that's priceless. Did Carnades get to hear any of this?"

"He wasn't here, just Balmorlan. And when the lady told him, she was in his face, about as close as she could get and not be standing on his boots. Balmorlan had turned up not ten minutes after she arrived. It's like he was lurking outside."

"He probably was," I muttered.

"The lady said she'd drop the charges if Nathrach was released and Balmorlan apologized to him in front of her and her staff. And from the lady's own lips: 'If I deem your words to be contrite and sincere, I won't sue the hell out of you and Carnades Silvanus.' Unquote."

Mychael smiled. "And what did Balmorlan say to that?"

"He told her that the only person on Mid who could make

and enforce such a claim was the goblin ambassador, and since she was his underling, her charges carried no weight."

I winced and grinned at the same time. "Underling. I'm betting he shouldn't have said that."

"He didn't get very far," Sedge Rinker said. "Director Kalis said that the goblin ambassador had mysteriously gone missing, she was in charge, and Balmorlan would be dealing with her." He chuckled. "The top of her head barely came to the middle of Balmorlan's chest, and Hell was going to freeze over before that little lady backed down."

If Rudra Muralin was missing, it sounded like Imala Kalis had won their game of tit for tat. I wondered if Rudra was "missing" in the embassy latrine with his lackeys and staff, Imala Kalis having bolted and warded the door shut. That image was a keeper.

Vidor Kalta leisurely strolled out of Sedge's office, a steaming mug of coffee in his hand.

"That's far from the best part," the nachtmagus told us. "Then Imala Kalis informed him with that adorable dimple of hers that goblin law stated when an ambassador was dead, missing, or incapacitated, the senior official present had the duty and right to assume all diplomatic duties and authority. But unless elven law had changed in the past five minutes, one of Balmorlan's superiors being dead and the other presumed dead just made him a man without a job."

Mychael wasn't laughing, but his eyes sure were. "I hate I missed that."

Sedge added a nod to his grin. "A thing of beauty, it was."

Kalta took a satisfied sip. "Imala Kalis appeared to be having the time of her life." His black eyes glittered with malicious glee. "Taltek was apoplectic."

Mychael's humor vanished. "One of Balmorlan's superiors is presumed dead?"

"There was an explosion at a house on Ambassador Row," Sedge explained. "By the time my men got there, the place was surrounded by elven embassy guards. Since the house is a part of the embassy, it's elven soil. My men couldn't go in without permission, and the commander in charge wasn't inclined to give it, though it sounded more like they didn't want anyone interfering. Since there wasn't anything left but a pile of smoking debris, I had my men back off to a suitable distance." He paused uncomfortably. "Supposedly Duke Markus Sevelien was staying there. That was one bit of information the elf commander was willing to part with."

"I'll bet he couldn't wait to 'leak' that one," I said to Mychael in mindspeak.

Mychael's lips narrowed in an angry line. "When did you get this information?"

"Just before Director Kalis got here. I sent a runner to the citadel with a report for you."

"We must have just missed each other." Mychael said it with the perfect mix of concern, frustration, and professional poise. The man was a veritable master of misinformation, though in my family we called it being a good liar. Though sometimes lying wasn't just the best thing you could do; it was the only thing you could do.

"If he couldn't find you, his orders were to deliver it to the archmagus."

"Good enough," Mychael told him. "Sedge, I need to hear what Tam and Imala Kalis are saying."

"Not a problem. I've got just the spot in my office. It shares a wall with the conference room, and in one place a piece of wood is missing. There's a cabinet in the conference room that covers up the hole. If you're quiet about it, you should be able to hear anything you need to." He did his best to look contrite. "I've been meaning to get that hole fixed, but just never got around to it."

Mychael gave the recording gem to Sedge Rinker. We were keeping mine. When you have incriminating evidence, it's always good business to have a copy.

"Karl Cradock," Mychael said. "One of the men who needs to be in that cell. He's staying above the Bare Bones tavern."

"He killed General Aratus?"

Mychael shook his head. "Sarad Nukpana killed General Aratus. Karl Cradock did the kidnapping and stayed around to throw the general's corpse out of the coach."

Sedge tossed the gem in his hand. "And it's all here."

"And a couple of other interesting things," Mychael told him. "I have the kidnappers in custody that he was hiring to take the next victim. Interestingly enough, Markus Sevelien was to be that victim. You'll want to get some men to the Bare Bones quickly. No doubt Cradock will be trying to leave the island on the morning tide. I don't believe he feels safe here anymore. If you don't find him at the Bare Bones, try the west docks, a Caesolian freighter named *Reliant*."

Sedge shook his head and laughed. "You make me look good, Mychael."

Mychael flashed a crooked smile. "You help me, and I help you."

We made ourselves at home in Sedge's office. A sergeant quietly brought us some much-needed coffee, and we settled back to be both informed and entertained.

Interestingly enough, Tam wasn't happy with the lady who'd sprung him from jail.

Mychael and I had used Sedge Rinker's conference room before when we'd needed to have some privacy for a conversation that turned into an argument. Tam and Imala Kalis were putting it to similar use. With typical goblin gentility, they were managing to sound civilized and verbally slice each other to shreds at the same time. It was an impressive display.

"No one has paid me anything," Imala Kalis all but spat. "I work for the goblin people." She paused meaningfully. "For the *good* of the goblin people."

Tam's laugh was more like a short bark. "Meaning you work for Prince Chigaru Mal'Salin."

"I never spoke his name."

"So your new career goal is to be the featured entertainment in Execution Square for treason? And you've come all this way to get me into more trouble than I already am just so I can keep you company while you walk to the block."

"I won't be going anywhere near Execution Square, and if you would hear me out, neither will you."

"I have been listening and you have yet to say anything that isn't suicidal for you and fatal to me."

"Just because King Sathrik wants it doesn't mean he's going to get it. Sathrik does what's best for Sathrik. I'm trying to do what's best for the goblin people." She was silent for a moment. "You could at least thank me."

"For what? For getting me released by telling everyone that I'm a royal retainer who still works for the Mal'Salins?"

"The queen," Imala corrected him.

"Who. Is. Dead." Tam sounded like he'd said that more than once in the past hour or so.

"Ah, but who never accepted your resignation."

"Who cannot because she is now *dead*."

"Never accepted, never terminated. Diplomatic immunity is such a beautiful thing, is it not? It gets one out of all sorts of unfortunate situations."

"What an appropriate word choice."

"I beg your pardon?"

"Terminated. Get me out, then get me killed, which is precisely what Sathrik sent you here to do."

"I don't work for Sathrik." Imala hissed the name like something she found sticking to the bottom of her boot.

"You're not working both sides of the family? Come, now, Imala. That would be a first for the secret service. Though wait—let me guess. You've gone into business for yourself. So how much are you thinking you can collect for my head? Anything less than three thousand in imperial gold and you've been robbed, and we wouldn't want that. Wasn't that the price on my head? Or has it increased?"

"No one has paid or will pay me anything for any part of you, least of all your apparently empty head. The person who I represent is interested in all of you. Intact. Alive and breathing—and thinking."

"And on behalf of all of me, I refuse."

"Without hearing his offer? For the last time, I am trying to keep you alive, you pigheaded ass!"

"The farther away I am from anyone with the last name Mal'Salin, or from anyone who works for a Mal'Salin, the longer my life expectancy will be—*without* your assistance."

"Don't be so sure about that."

"Is that a threat?"

"That's me telling you that the lines are being drawn in Regor, and when sides have been chosen, you and your son should be certain that you're on the right one."

Tam's voice was lined with steel. "Leave Talon out of this."

"You're the one who hasn't left him out of this," Imala retorted. "Instead of hiding him for his own safety, you've publicly acknowledged him, given him your name, made him your heir, and put him in more danger than even *you* can protect him from. I heard and saw what he did last night, and so did a few of those Nightshades."

"And a few of your men."

"My men are trustworthy."

"So you're certain that every last one of them is unwaveringly loyal to you? Would never betray your vaunted trust? Never slit that pretty little throat of yours if given half the chance?"

"Pretty little throat?" That caught her off guard.

"I have working eyes, Imala. But more important, I have working ears. Never mention my son's name again."

"After last night's little display, I won't need to because everyone else will. *And* you have an umi'atsu bond with Raine Benares and are linked in some way to Mychael Eiliesor. You have become a very desirable commodity among our elite—people you don't want desiring any part of you or your son."

"Khrynsani," Tam hissed.

Her words were fire voice. "I have never, nor will I *ever*, refer to those jackals as elite anything. Complete extermination cannot come too soon." She paused and then laughed. "Though that explosion a few hours ago certainly diminished their numbers. I shall have to discover who was responsible for that delightful display of pyrotechnics and thank them. Unfortunately, it seems that the ultimate prize escaped. A coach was seen racing from the scene. A coach driven by a Khrynsani. I imagine Sarad and Janos were inside."

Tam hissed a single obscenity in Goblin.

"For once I share your opinion, and sincerely wish our clever arsonist better luck in the future."

"Have you found Sevelien?" Tam asked.

"Not a trace. What's left of the house is still too hot to search, and the elves have it cordoned off, ostensibly waiting until they can get in to look for him." Imala actually snorted. "He's not there and they know it. They're going through the motions, nothing more. My bet is that he was in that coach, taken by Sarad Nukpana, or somehow the crafty fox managed to escape."

"And blew up his own house?"

"Entirely possible. Markus always had an exquisite sense of irony." Her voice turned grim. "And I hope he still does. He is a brilliant tactician and a charming opponent. I've enjoyed sparring with him in the past. Only now we find ourselves with a similar goal." She paused. "Odd, isn't it? Me, a goblin, wanting to keep an elven duke alive, and his own people wanting nothing more than to find him dead. These are indeed strange times."

"And Imala Kalis wanting to protect me is even more strange."

"Someone has to, because you seem to have little interest in protecting yourself. From the reports I've received, you've done everything in the past few months short of putting your own neck in a noose."

"I've done what I've had to do."

"I'm doing the same thing now—if you will rein in your innate stubbornness long enough to consider my offer."

"Imala, I can't do what you ask."

Her next words came out on the barest breath. "Even if Sathrik were no longer king."

"The changing of a king won't change the court—or the way the court is run."

"But it can." The silence was thick and tense. "Your people need you, Tam."

"And what about my dear extended family who say they need my head?"

"Leave them to me."

"What are you going to do, poison the entire municipal water supply?"

"If I have to."

"Why are you trusting me with this?"

"If you hadn't left the court, Sathrik would have killed you."

Tam laughed, a contemptuous sound. "Sathrik would have *tried*."

"Success or failure wouldn't change the fact that he never liked you; he certainly never trusted you."

"He murdered his own mother, who was also my queen, a queen I was sworn to serve."

"Then serve her *now*, Tam. Yes, she is dead, but what she stood for and believed in is not—at least not yet."

I didn't know if Sedge's office was dusty or I still had smoke up my nose from blowing up Markus's house, but I did something very bad.

I sneezed. Loudly.

Then just to make sure everyone in headquarters heard, my nose decided to do it again. Even louder.

"Crap," I muttered.

The wall vibrated as the cabinet was shoved away from the

hole in the wall. Tam's face appeared at eye level with me. He was not amused; actually, he looked rather pissed.

"And how long have you been here?"

I hoisted my mug. "About half a cup's worth."

"I'm here, too, Tam," Mychael said.

"Dammit." Tam blew out his breath to keep from saying something worse.

"Tam, I'd like to speak with Director Kalis," Mychael told him. "May we come over?"

The lady's face appeared next to Tam's. She'd probably been up all night like the rest of us and she was still cute. "We'd be delighted, Paladin Eiliesor."

Tam rolled his eyes and muttered something not so nice under his breath.

"Do ignore him," she said. "He gets this way whenever he spends the night in jail."

Mychael passed his hand over the opening in the wall, murmured a few words, and the hole in the wall turned into a wall with no hole.

Sedge Rinker just lost his peephole.

Mychael didn't want anyone listening in on the four of us.

A few minutes later Mychael and I came into the conference room with a watcher right behind us bearing gifts—a tray laden with coffee and pastries. Leave it to watchers to know where to get great coffee and pastries. That should take Tam from pissed to pacified.

Mychael poured a cup and passed it to Imala Kalis.

"Thank you, Paladin."

"Mychael."

She flashed a smile, complete with that increasingly famous dimple. "Imala."

Tam muttered something else.

"Oh here," I said, pushing a coffee and pastry at him. "Eat this and put us out of your misery."

He glared, but he ate.

"You okay?" I asked.

He growled around a bite of pastry.

I took that as a yes. Note to self: Tam is not a morning person.

Imala was looking at Mychael and me with a quizzical look on her face; a moment later quizzical turned to slyly knowing.

"Pardon my bluntness, Mychael and Miss Benares. But the two of you smell of smoke—and Nebian black powder."

We'd cleaned up while on the *Red Hawk*, but apparently not enough to fool a goblin's heightened sense of smell.

Mychael didn't say anything. I certainly wasn't going to admit to bombing and arson.

Imala Kalis's lips turned up in a secretive little smile as if the two of us stinking of smoke had made her day.

"Markus is alive," she whispered.

Mychael's expression didn't change one iota. Heck, he didn't even bat an eye.

She waved her tiny hand that was holding a pastry. "But of course, you can't tell me that. Quite all right, I understand completely. Though about the black powder . . . What you did—excuse me, *may have* done . . . The evidence is merely circumstantial, of course." She actually winked at us. "Well-done. I wish I could have been there to see it, better yet to have helped. Bravo."

I was getting told that a lot lately.

Mychael frowned. "While we are being blunt, Director Kalis—"

"Imala," the tiny goblin corrected him.

"Imala. You spoke of Prince Chigaru Mal'Salin."

"His name was mentioned, but not by me."

"My question concerns his chief counselor. I recently sent a message to A'Zahra Nuru asking that she come to Mid. She sent word back that she would come. She has not arrived, nor have I received communication from her explaining—"

"Considering the present situation with Sarad Nukpana,

I told Grandmother I didn't feel it was safe for her or the prince—"

I blurted, "A'Zahra Nuru is your *grandmother*?"

"She is."

I looked from Mychael to Tam. "Why didn't either one of you tell me this?"

Imala shot Tam an arch look. "Tam prefers not to speak of me at all."

"It is a relationship that not many are aware of," Mychael explained.

My look spoke volumes and all of them loud. "Since when have I been one of the many?"

"Raine, you just met Imala last night, and I'm seeing her this morning for the first time in at least a year."

"Almost two," Imala said.

"And it's been a busy evening," Mychael reminded me. Like I needed reminding.

Imala took a delighted sniff of our collective smokiness. "And satisfying, I would say."

In more ways than one. I felt myself blush.

Tam looked at me and his eyes widened slightly. I suddenly found the coffee in my cup simply fascinating. When I glanced back up at him, his eyes were still on mine, but they weren't accusing or angry as I'd thought they might be. Tam's gentle gaze told me that he understood. A moment later, I felt his lips brush my forehead in a warm kiss. He still stood three feet in front of me. He hadn't moved, but had reached out with our umi'atsu bond. I gave him a small smile and sent a kiss to his cheek. Tam looked at Mychael and raised his cup in salute, as if to acknowledge the victory of a noble and worthy opponent. Mychael inclined his head in response.

Imala gave us all a quick, knowing look but didn't say a word.

I realized that I'd been holding my breath.

"That doesn't explain what's going on with you two," I said, changing the subject with no attempt at subtlety. I waved my finger back and forth between Tam and Imala. "I'm a little confused by something; actually I'm *a lot* confused. Tam, A'Zahra Nuru was your teacher; you trust her. You've said it yourself." I didn't mention that she was also the one who helped pull him back from the brink of the black magic abyss. Imala might not know that and if she didn't, she wasn't going to hear it from me. "And Mychael, you wouldn't have asked A'Zahra Nuru here unless you trusted her. Am I correct in both instances, gentlemen?"

"You are," Mychael said.

Tam nodded once.

"So what's your problem with her?" I jerked my thumb at Imala Kalis and aimed my question directly at Tam.

"Imala is not her grandmother," Tam said stiffly.

"Well, I wouldn't expect that she is. From what I overheard, she wants Sathrik out; and from what I assume, she wants Chigaru in. While I'm not the prince's biggest fan, getting rid of Sathrik sounds like one hell of a good idea. So what's with the animosity?"

"It's complicated," Tam said.

"You're a goblin, Tam," I said flatly. "Everything's complicated. You were the queen's magical enforcer, and Imala is the head of the secret service. You were both serving in the court at the same time."

"We were."

"Considering your jobs, you'd think you'd have common ground."

Imala blew out her breath through her nose. "You would think that, wouldn't you?"

"So all you two did was piss each other off on a daily basis?"

"I wouldn't go that far," Imala conceded. "Weekly would be more accurate."

"How pissed?"

Tam scowled. "She stabbed me."

Imala snorted. "A mere flesh wound. He had driven me quite beyond rational thought."

"Yeah, he's done the same to me. In other words, he deserved it."

"I thought so."

"She tried to kill me," Tam protested.

Imala turned on Tam in exasperation. "If I had truly tried, you would not be here."

Tam glared at her. "And if I had truly desired retaliation, you would no longer exist."

I clapped my hands together. "So, as far as goblin behavior is concerned, you two sound downright cozy."

"Cozy is not in Imala's vocabulary, and apparently neither is loyalty."

"Tam is referring to the fact that I remained in the Mal'Salin family service after he left. He sees this as a betrayal of the late Queen Glicara."

"You serve Sathrik; enough said."

"I believe we have been sufficiently over this ground—I serve the goblin people."

"By carrying out Sathrik's orders?"

"I do my job and I remain in power; but most important, I continue to gain influence with the people we will need."

"*We.* You persist in using that word. Leave me out of this."

"You're in it whether you like it or not, and I had nothing to do with it. The fault is yours. Your relationship with Miss Benares has hardly gone unnoticed. Not ten minutes go by in the court without me hearing her name."

"I'm famous in the goblin court," I muttered. "Great. Just great."

"Notorious would be a more apt description," Imala told me. "Tam has thwarted Sathrik's attempts to capture you, and he has spat in the face of the king's commands." She turned to Tam. "Your reasons are your own, but Sathrik has labeled your actions treason. Over the past few months, you have defied him at every turn." Imala stopped and positively beamed. "Grandmother and I couldn't be more proud."

Since we'd set foot in the room, I'd had my eye on the

biggest, most decadent-looking pastry on the tray. I handed it to Tam instead; he looked like he needed it. "Well, it looks like you can take the boy out of the court, but you can't take the court out of the boy," I said softly. "Tam, you should have walked away from me. Cancel that—you should have run."

"You know I wouldn't do that."

"I know. Imala said you're going to have to choose sides. I'd say you've already chosen. And when Sathrik made Rudra Muralin goblin ambassador, that wasn't just to help him get the Saghred or me—it was to give him the authority he needed to legally take you out, wasn't it?"

Tam's silence answered for him.

"You needn't concern yourself about Rudra any longer, Miss Benares." Imala Kalis sank her dainty fangs into a pastry. "He isn't missing. He's quite dead."

Chapter 18

"*I made sure of it myself,*" Imala *continued without missing* a beat. "I wouldn't want to be mistaken about a thing like that."

"How did he die?" Mychael's voice was terse. The paladin was back.

"I assure you, I had nothing to do with Rudra's demise. He was found behind the embassy at five bells this morning, propped against a garbage bin. I was all for leaving him precisely where he was. The garbage is due to be picked up later this morning, but propriety demanded I do otherwise. Propriety and precaution."

"Precaution?" I asked. "That doesn't sound good."

"Rudra Muralin returned from the dead before. I wanted to make certain that it did not happen again. One mad goblin regenerating himself on this island is quite enough."

"You didn't answer my question, Imala," Mychael pressed.

"Merely saving the best part for last. He was dried and shriveled and delightfully dead. Sarad Nukpana must have been very annoyed at not having Markus for dinner. When my people called me out into the alley to see, I maintained my professional decorum, but my staff was cheering and applauding." She gave us a quick smile. "I do like to see my people happy; it's good for morale."

Goblin humor. What other race would applaud a dead body? On second thought, elves would, especially if their last name was Benares.

Mychael's face was grim. "Where did you put his body?"

"His husk is lying in state in the embassy."

Oh no. "Uh, Imala, last time Rudra Muralin died, the power buildup he had from using the Saghred all those years brought him back to life."

One corner of Imala's lips curled ever so slightly. To a casual observer, it almost looked demure. "That scenario is unlikely to repeat itself. I cut off his head."

Tam's lips twitched against a smile. "You what?"

"I cut off his head," she repeated matter-of-factly. "I tried my dagger, but the dried skin was too tough, so I ended up using an axe. It was quite heavy, but once I got past the upswing it worked beautifully."

I burst out laughing. The visual of that tiny woman dragging an axe across the floor and lopping off Rudra Muralin's head was too much.

"Well-done, Imala," Tam grudgingly congratulated her.

"Thank you. I derived immense satisfaction from it."

"I imagine the Khrynsani in the embassy feel otherwise," Mychael pointed out.

Imala shrugged. "What they feel is immaterial since they are no longer there. Eight Khrynsani came with Nachtmagus Janos Ghalfari. They have been out with him all night, and should they have the poor judgment to return, they will be taken into custody as accessories to kidnapping and murder. As acting ambassador, I can hardly be seen harboring criminals. Janos and his Khrynsani are connected to who knows how many murders in the past week. The two that we know of are enough for me to have their heads, if I can get proof. Killing an elven general is an act of war, and to slaughter our very own ambassador—while very much needed and long overdue—is treason in the eyes of our government."

"Shit," Tam hissed. "Where is Rudra's head? Please tell me you didn't leave it close to the body."

Imala finished off the rest of her coffee. "Give me a little more credit than that, Tam. It's on the other side of the room in a locked strongbox and only I have the key. The box is warded and my most trusted agents are standing guard. No one will get in that room without my permission."

"You left him there?"

She arched one flawless brow. "To come and get you out of jail."

"Rudra Muralin's death solves one problem," Mychael said, "but makes another one worse. Since it's almost a certainty that Sarad Nukpana was responsible, he now has all of Muralin's memories, power, and knowledge. Centuries' worth."

Damn. If he got his hands on me or the Saghred, he'd know exactly how to use both of us. Double damn.

"So in a way, Muralin's not really dead." Dread churned through me. "He's just joined forces with Sarad Nukpana."

"I seriously doubt that it was his idea," Mychael noted, "but essentially, yes."

"How much power would that give him?" I knew the answer, but I really wanted someone to tell me I was wrong.

"Enough to take any mage on this island," Tam replied. "I know I'm stating the obvious here, but we need to find him. Now."

The tunnels I'd seen when I touched Sarad Nukpana's coach seat had smooth stone walls, a long corridor, and shafts of blue light from the ceiling. And rats. Mychael had only been here for four years. The archmagus had been here a lot longer.

My dad had been here for hundreds of years longer than that.

One of them had to recognize the place I'd seen.

We got to the citadel as fast as we could only to find that Talon had flown the coop.

Last night, he'd gone as far as the citadel courtyard with his Guardian escort, then he'd bolted. Not just bolted; he'd used that voice of his to freeze nearly thirty Guardians in their tracks to make his getaway. Vegard had been one of them.

Mychael, Tam, and I were now standing in that same courtyard and I'd never seen Vegard that pissed. The big Guardian was a barely contained, seething mass of fury. If I hadn't been on the verge of dropping from exhaustion, I'd have been seething right along with him.

Talon wasn't the only teenager missing from the citadel.

Piaras was nowhere to be found.

Mychael had his men patrolling the city looking for Sarad Nukpana add Talon and Piaras to their "people to be apprehended" list. Apprehended without undue force, but apprehended and brought directly back to the citadel.

"Talon asked me where Balmorlan and Carnades were going after they left headquarters." Vegard was responding to Mychael's rapid-fire questioning.

"And Piaras was here in the courtyard when you arrived?"

"No, sir. He was on the stairs there leading up to the parapet."

"His guards?"

"With him, sir. Likewise zapped by that little . . ." He clenched his jaw against what he really wanted to say. "Sorry, sir," he said to Tam, "but your son caused a major security breach. Thirty Guardians, frozen like bloody statues. Anyone could have strolled through those gates and slaughtered the lot of us. How Piaras managed to avoid being—"

Tam spoke, his voice a marvel of forced calm. "Apparently Talon can now pick and choose who he wants the spell to affect." Until now, Tam had been entirely too quiet. Scary, deadly quiet.

"He has enough focus for selective targeting?" Mychael was fighting to maintain what calm he had left. "That's a dangerous combination under the best of circumstances. Tam, why didn't you tell me?"

"I didn't know it had gone that far," Tam snapped and so did his control.

That was probably the honest truth. Most mages came into

their full power in their late teens to early twenties. Unfortunately, that wasn't an age known for rational, responsible thought—or any kind of thinking before acting. And when their power came, it came fast. Last night, Talon had held one Nightshade. In the predawn of this morning, the kid had put thirty Guardians into suspended animation. I guess the Nightshade was just a warm-up.

Piaras had inadvertently put half of the Guardians in the citadel to sleep during one of our first days on the island. Talon had just stopped time for thirty Guardians in the citadel's courtyard. He probably could have done more, but the men in the courtyard were all he needed to take out.

Two inexperienced, unbelievably powerful teenagers loose in the city, in all likelihood hunting Taltek Balmorlan. Talon knew what Balmorlan wanted with his father—and with him. And he knew that Balmorlan was likely responsible for the Nightshades who tried to kill us all. While I approved of their target, their methods and inexperience were going to get them killed.

Or worse.

I should have known Talon was going to do something like this the moment he agreed to go to the citadel. There was no way the kid was going to stay in the citadel while his father was imprisoned and charged with murder by elves. He probably considered being in the citadel a prison, too. And in a way Mychael had intended it to be just that. A full Guardian escort to get Talon here, the archmagus to keep him in. Next time, gagged and hog-tied would be the way to go.

Talon had believed that Mychael would free his father. Now he wanted to get his hands on one of the elves responsible for locking him up.

I turned to Vegard. "How long were you—"

"Best we figure, nearly half an hour."

Damn. All this had happened nearly four hours ago, with Talon and Piaras having a half-hour head start. What the hell was Piaras thinking? I didn't ask it out loud because I knew. He had wanted to do something, anything, to help. He'd told me himself.

"I don't think Piaras would go along with Talon's half-brained scheme," Vegard was saying. "The boy's got too much sense."

"But he would go *after* him," I said. "He knows how dangerous it is out there, but he's got a good head on his shoulders. Let's hope he uses it." Unless teenage impetuousness had erased that good sense. Just following Talon through those gates had been bad enough.

Piaras hadn't brought Talon back yet. I didn't have to say all the things that could mean; we all knew.

At least the kids didn't just go running off into the dark armed with nothing but their voices and wits—though I was starting to have serious doubts about Talon's wits. At least he'd pilfered a couple of Guardians before he left. Best we could figure, the kid had a crossbow, a full quiver of armor-piercing bolts, a brace of throwing knives, and a sword.

And for good measure, he'd swiped the purses of two Guardians.

Phaelan always said, if you're gonna steal, be thorough about it.

Those two Guardians had just been paid. Those were two very angry men. I bet if we turned them loose, they'd hunt down Talon real quick.

According to Piaras's bodyguards, he had his cadet's daggers, but there was a pair of sleek elven swords missing from a Guardian who'd been on duty at the main gate when Talon did his thing.

I forced myself to take a couple of good, deep breaths on the off chance that it might delay the screaming rant I felt coming on. And to make matters worse, standing in the middle of the courtyard didn't give me anything to hit.

Right now, Tam wasn't a badass dark mage. He looked like

what he was—a tired, worried father. "Raine, can you find them?"

"I can and will find Piaras," I promised him. "And if he went after Talon to talk some sense into him, hopefully they'll be in the same place." And hopefully that place wouldn't have bars, wards, and magic-sapping manacles—or a life-sapping regenerating goblin. I didn't say that out loud; I didn't need to. Tam knew.

I tried to still my thoughts enough to work, but it wasn't going to happen. The sun had been up for a good two hours and every Guardian still in the citadel was awake and going about their duties.

Hundreds of magic-wielding warriors didn't exactly make for peaceful surroundings. The air was seething with macho magic. Trying to get a fix on Piaras was like trying to catch; a gnat with a fishnet.

I had to find one obscenely powerful goblin psycho in a city where magic was running rampant. I didn't need a clue; I needed a location and I needed it now.

I had to get above the Guardians.

The parapet could work, but ideally I needed to see the whole city. The few times I'd done a seeking on Mid, it had been at night, meaning that most people had been in bed. Mid was an island full of magic users, and right now students, professors, and Conclave mage bureaucrats were awake and so was all of their magic. I needed to get above it—way above it.

I turned around and kept turning, looking for something that would work.

The seawall watchtower on the south side of the citadel.

It might not be the perfect solution, but it was as good as I was going to get as quickly as I needed it.

"Vegard, how do I get up there?"

True to his determination to stay by my side, Vegard didn't tell me; he took me there.

My dad and Vidor Kalta were already in the tower looking out over the city. I could feel Dad's magic scanning the city below. Apparently I wasn't the first to think of the idea.

"No doubt you're wondering what we're doing here," Dad said.

"Find Piaras."

"Find Sarad Nukpana." Dad gazed out over the city. "Balmorlan is good, but he is a child compared to Sarad's new strength level. If those boys were captured, it would be by Sarad."

"Nukpana ate Rudra Muralin," I told them. "As well as two of the other specters that escaped the Saghred."

Dad didn't say anything, but he thought some choice words. "That kind of power can't be concealed. Even on an island of mages, it'll shine like a beacon."

"Sarad could still infest a host body," Kalta said, "but after another victim or two he will be too solid to leave his own body. Then he can be killed like any other man."

After another victim or two. Like Piaras and Talon.

"Sarad Nukpana contains the souls of those who are now dead, murdered by his own hand," Kalta continued. "This will make him easier to locate. He will attract attention he does not want."

I snorted. "Yeah, me."

"Reapers, Miss Benares. Reapers."

I swallowed hard. Not easy to do when your mouth suddenly stopped making spit.

"I had a run-in with one last night," I said.

Kalta's black eyes were on me like a shark. "You what?"

I mentally smacked myself in the forehead. Way to tell everyone what you did last night, Raine. And that you weren't in the citadel like everyone was supposed to believe.

"At Sirens," I lied. Everyone knew I was at Sirens; no one could know I was at Markus's house. Vegard was at Sirens; he knew I was lying, but I'd deal with that later. "I didn't think about what I was doing. I dug up as much magic as I could without tapping the Saghred, and let him have it."

Kalta arched a dark brow. "Let him have it?"

"I punched him right where his face should have been. I felt a little winded afterward, but at least the thing went away."

Kalta went a shade or two paler, if that was possible. "Miss Benares, I wouldn't do that again if I were you."

"Why not?"

"You didn't defeat it; you overfed it."

"But I didn't feed it anything."

"You felt fatigued afterward?"

"Yes, but—"

"You fed it rage—Saghred-powered rage, whether you realized it or not."

"I didn't use the Saghred."

"The power the Saghred has already given you was more than sufficient. You fed it your life force. Reapers take souls; it's all that remains of life. It 'went away' as you phrased it, because it was full of Saghred-fueled magic. The Saghred is also fueled by souls. What you fed it was extremely powerful. If Reapers become stronger, they can take the living. You just made one stronger. It will be back for more."

"Oh shit."

"Quite."

As if there weren't enough monsters loose in the city this morning, now I'd created a Super Reaper. I pushed the thought aside. If it came after me, I'd deal with it then. With the souls he'd ingested, Sarad Nukpana was probably almost as tempting a target as I was. Though it'd be just my luck that evil souls tasted bad.

"Sarad may have the power," my dad said. "But it takes more strength than he can spare to hide it. He grows confident and even more arrogant."

I quickly stepped up beside him. "You've seen him?"

"We've sensed him."

"Where?"

"The north side of the city."

I looked where Dad's attention was riveted. I saw the smoke from an unknown number of chimneys and a thin layer of morning fog from the harbor. The buildings were hidden; apparently Sarad Nukpana wasn't.

"The Conclave's section of the city, mainly office buildings," he told me.

I couldn't believe it. The bastard was hiding in plain sight. "He's in there?"

"That is my belief, yes."

It made sense, brilliant sense. Uncle Ryn had always taught us that the best hiding place was smack-dab in the middle of those you were trying to hide from.

"Are the buildings old?" I asked.

Dad gave me a quizzical glance. "Yes, some of them are quite old."

"As old as you?"

"A few of them. Why do you ask?"

I described what I'd seen last night when I'd touched the coach seat where Sarad Nukpana had been.

"Does that sound familiar?" I asked.

Dad gave a small, harsh laugh minus the humor. "Mid's known for its winters. What you just described are the transit tunnels."

"You don't make it sound good."

Dad nodded. "You saw only a small section of nearly a hundred miles of tunnels connecting every building in the Conclave complex."

"*Every* building?"

Kalta spoke. "Conclave mages don't spend all that money on elaborate robes to drag them through the mud and snow. We're fastidious creatures."

I certainly couldn't see Carnades Silvanus getting his silk hems dirty.

I exhaled. I did not need this. "Are they still in use?"

"Not as much as they once were," Kalta said. "The buildings are now connected aboveground."

I stepped in front of my dad and Kalta to get an unobstructed view of the city. The buildings looked like children's toys from this height and distance. I let the morning breeze—and the magical residue it carried—pass over me. "Gentlemen, would you stand on the other side of the room? Better yet, if you could step out into the stairway and close the door, it'd really help my concentration." The less magical interference I had to sort through, the better my chances for locating Piaras and hopefully Talon.

I stood staring out over the city until I heard the door close quietly behind me. Then I closed my eyes, forcing the noise from the courtyard far below into the background until it was no more audible than a fly buzzing. Then I separated the magical residue from the breeze until all I felt was ocean breeze, no harbor stench, just clean, clear air.

I opened my eyes.

The city was spread below me, and I not only sensed what my dad had; I could see it. A black, oily trail spread over the north side of the city, concentrated in a small cluster of white buildings in the far distance. I knew they weren't small; Conclave buildings probably covered acres.

And Sarad Nukpana was beneath one of those buildings, somewhere in a hundred miles of tunnels. Once I was closer I could narrow the search. But Nukpana was second on my search list.

Piaras had left the citadel over four hours ago, through the main gate. I'd known him since he was a child, long before he'd come into his magic. I was living in the apartment above his grandmother's apothecary shop when adolescence had set in and Piaras's voice had changed. Magically speaking all hell had broken loose when that'd happened.

My throat tightened at the thought of him out there alone. I forced my emotions down. Find him, Raine. He's alive; you'd know if he wasn't. He's fine and he'll stay that way if you just do your job.

I knew Piaras's magical scent. I closed my eyes halfway and gazed down at the citadel's gate, filtering out everything but what I knew as Piaras. A lot of magically gifted men had gone through those gates over the past four hours, but only one of them had been Piaras. I methodically sorted through each layer, pushing sensations of others aside until I found it. I don't know how long I had been standing there, but a trace of magic, silvery and faintly glowing, rose to the surface of my awareness.

Piaras.

It wasn't just a trace.

It was a trail.

Piaras had left me a trail to follow. It led out the front gates and down a side street. He'd followed Talon and he'd left a trail. Relief washed over me in a wave and I started breathing again. I closed my eyes to the barest squint and became a part of that glowing path, following it, gaining speed as I went. I'd never been able to track that fast before. The power the Saghred had been gradually giving me sent me at dizzying speed through Mid's streets, people and buildings a nauseating blur. I slowed and then stopped. White granite buildings loomed over me, blurry around the edges in my mind's eye.

I knew what those buildings were.

I knew where Piaras and Talon were.

Conclave complex, north side of the city.

Same place as Sarad Nukpana.

I snapped out of my trance and sagged down to the floor, breathing hard. Speeding through the streets had made me dizzy; coming back to my standing-still body made me sick. I kept my eyes open, focusing on the floor, breathing in and out until the floor stopped moving and my mind accepted that I had as well. The seeking-induced whirlies stopped.

A familiar presence brushed my mind, knew my thoughts.

Knew what I had seen.

Oh no. Don't.

"No!" I screamed. I scrambled to the window and pulled myself up. Wind blew my hair back. Wind from Kalinpar's powerful wings.

Tam was mounted on his back.

"Dammit, Tam! No!"

He heard me, but was way beyond listening. Talon was in the same place as Sarad Nukpana.

Tam was going to save his son, even if he had to face a sadistic demigod to do it.

Chapter 19

The Conclave complex was the epicenter of all that was magical in the seven kingdoms. Magic—new, old, and ancient—virtually oozed from the granite walls. And then there were the mages, some of the most powerful and pompous, displaying their magic like peacocks with a full fan of tail feathers. The distortion was unbelievable. And unless we could clear hundreds of mages from a maze of buildings, that distortion was staying right where it was.

Piaras's trail was defused, diluted, buried.

Gone.

Shit, *shit, shit*!

I didn't spit the words, or scream them like I wanted to, but with our link, Mychael heard them loud and clear—as well as all the others I'd been using since we landed. At least something in this place was loud and clear.

"Raine, anger isn't going to help us find anyone."

"Neither is much of anything else," I said. "Why do you think I'm cussing like one of Phaelan's gunners with wet powder?"

There were fancy-robed mages freaking everywhere, though I noted with satisfaction that they were giving me a wide berth. I didn't know if they sensed the Saghred on me or were just steering clear of a heavily armed—and clearly pissed to the point of killing someone—elven woman. I didn't know if it was a man thing or a me thing, and right now I didn't give a damn.

We'd found Kalinpar in a courtyard in the west end of the complex. No Tam.

We were presently standing in the middle of said courtyard, our own sentry dragons landed and secured where they were supposed to be—away from people and horses. Apparently under the right circumstances, both could be considered tasty. I thought about turning Kalinpar loose in the crowd. That'd clear the place of mages real quick.

Even with our umi'atsu bond, I couldn't locate Tam. Hell, I couldn't even tell which way he went. I'd probably have better luck asking the damned dragon. And the Saghred wasn't helping matters at all. Kalinpar wasn't the only thing that considered powerful mages potentially tasty. I could literally feel the rock's hungry anticipation. I had no intention of feeding it anything, but either the rock was delusional with starvation or it knew something that I didn't. Probably the latter, but I wasn't going to think about it or the rock. I had enough problems to deal with right now other than having to worry about the Saghred looking forward to a future meal.

In the buildings around us were offices, conference rooms, commissaries, libraries, dormitories, apartments, auditoriums, and more courtyards—and underneath it all ran the transit tunnels.

Mychael had brought his best trackers; Sedge Rinker had sent his.

A roar split the air above our heads. I jumped and swore, then looked up with a fierce grin. A sleek, black sentry dragon was hovering above the courtyard, its massive claws extended for landing. Its rider had told the dragon where to land, and if there were any mages in its way, getting squashed was their problem, not his.

Archmagus Justinius Valerian could get away with that.

In about half a minute, we had the courtyard all to ourselves. While gratifying, it did nothing to get rid of the magical distortion. If anything, Justinius's arrival had kicked it up a notch. But I was still glad to see the old man. As Guardian paladin, Mychael's job was to coordinate and lead the search. Justinius was here to keep any of the aforementioned pompous mages from impeding that search.

The old man smoothly dismounted and strode over to where we were, his robes whipping out behind him as his dragon settled his wings. He was armed for ogre, with a massive sword on his hip and long daggers tucked in his belt. Though with Sarad Nukpana somewhere under the ground we were standing on, Justinius would have to make good use of his magical arsenal. I'd only seen the old man cut loose once, and dozens of demons had died ugly deaths. I'd love to be treated to that show one more time, this time with Sarad Nukpana as the star attraction.

"Anything?" Justinius's blue eyes were as hard as agates. The old man was just as pissed as I was, and for much the same reasons.

"Nothing, sir," Mychael told him. "Plenty of mages saw Tam land; no one knows where he went."

Justinius scowled. "I recall he's got himself a damned good veil."

"One of the best."

"Shit."

I snorted. "Yeah, that's my take on the situation, too."

"What about Nukpana?" he asked me. "Is the Saghred telling you anything?"

"Just that it's hungry."

Mychael adjusted his sword on his hip. The blade was glowing through the scabbard. "Let's go."

Mychael had laid down the law for his men before they'd gone into the tunnels. Four men per search party, no one was to go anywhere alone, and each party was to check in every quarter hour with the Guardian contact wizards Mychael had stationed at five of the main tunnel intersections. Either the distortion was less in the tunnels, or Guardian contact wizards could work around it. Both would be fine by me. They were to alert Mychael the moment Tam, Piaras, Talon, or Sarad Nukpana were found. If they found Nukpana, they were not to attempt to kill, only contain. Mychael didn't want to lose any of his men. Since Sarad Nukpana had eaten the souls of two mages over two thousand years old, plus Rudra Muralin, none of Mychael's men could take down Nukpana if the goblin got the upper hand.

And if he'd fully assimilated the strength and skill Rudra Muralin had absorbed from years of wielding the Saghred, there was only one person who could kill him now.

Me.

And I would have to use the Saghred to do it.

I wasn't only here as a seeker; I was here as a weapon.

Yeah, "shit" definitely described how I felt.

The transit tunnels were well lit—for the most part. As with all ways to get from one place to another, whether be it alley, street, or tunnel, some were used more than others and kept in better repair. And when you were talking about a man-made tunnel, better repair often meant lighting that actually worked. There were long patches of dark down here, way too long, and way too dark. To make matters worse, it turned out that the magical distortion was just as bad down here as it was on the surface. Mages had been using these tunnels and working magic in the buildings above for centuries—and all that magical residue had seeped into the ground and the tunnel walls.

Mychael drew his sword, barked a word I didn't recognize, and the glow from his blade cut through the dark for twenty yards in every direction. A few seconds later, it kept me from turning my dad or Vidor Kalta into pincushions when they came around the next corner.

I lowered my throwing daggers. "Why the hell aren't you using a lightglobe?" My hands were shaking, so I gripped the knives harder.

Dad continued toward us like he and Kalta were just out for

a stroll. "You're more likely to find things that prefer the dark when you're sharing the dark with them."

"Logical, yet suicidal," Vegard muttered from beside me.

"Can you work down here?" Dad asked me quietly.

"I'm getting nothing," I spat.

"Mychael, we need to get out of the main tunnels," Dad told him. "Sarad isn't in any tunnel that a mage has walked recently."

"My men are covering them all."

"And they won't find Sarad. Hopefully they will find the boys or Tam Nathrach—but they won't find Sarad."

I tried to see into the darkness behind him. "If you know where he is—"

"I know the only place he can be. What you saw when you touched the seat in that coach confirms it. You saw an open doorway with light coming from inside. The bunkers."

Mychael frowned. "What?"

"In case the island ever came under attack, there were twenty bunkers built behind these tunnel walls. Each bunker could accommodate fifty men, not comfortably, but there'd be room."

As if a hundred miles of tunnels weren't enough. "Where are they?"

"Mid was never attacked, so they were never used," Dad told me. "And for security purposes, only the Seat of Twelve knew where they were."

I felt sick. "So Carnades knows, and we have to ask—"

"No, Raine. The Seat of Twelve from the time when the bunkers were built back in my cadet days."

Over nine hundred years ago.

Mychael picked up my thoughts and scowled. "They're not on the maps."

Mychael and Justinius had looked at a map of the tunnels just before we'd come down here. An intersecting mess of granite walls.

"Nothing was written down," Dad confirmed. "Only committed to memory. Since there was never an attack, the bunkers were never used, and the mages died and took the location to their graves with them."

"And this helps us how?"

"Raine, no man down here can find Sarad's bunker."

I knew what he was saying and I didn't like it. Not only did I not like it; it scared the crap out of me.

"I can find it, but only if I let the Saghred loose."

"You can still feel the Saghred's hunger, can't you?"

Oh yeah, I could feel it, like I was being gnawed from the inside out. I didn't have to say it; my dad knew. He'd been the Saghred's bond servant for centuries; he knew the hunger.

The temptations.

"The Saghred wants what it has lost," he said quietly. "Sarad has consumed two of the other mages who were imprisoned in the stone with him. The Saghred exists beyond magic; the distortions won't affect it." He hesitated. "If you let it go, it will lead you to Sarad."

I didn't want to let the rock go or run into Sarad Nukpana in the dark. If I let the Saghred go in tunnels full of Guardians seething with magic, the rock might try to take a pre-Nukpana snack, and it would start with the men around me: Mychael, Dad, Vegard, Vidor. And I might not get control over it again.

I might not get control over myself again.

The only sound was my ragged breathing echoing against the granite walls. I did not want to do this. I so did not want to do this.

"And you're not going to." Mychael's voice said no argument. His mind knew there was no other way—and he still wasn't going to let me risk myself.

Piaras and Talon were down here somewhere, maybe captive in that bunker with Sarad Nukpana and Janos Ghalfari.

Tam was down here.

I had no choice. Time to let the monster off its leash.

• • •

Dad said Sarad Nukpana would keep to the dark, but that didn't mean we had to. Mychael and Vegard lit any dark stretch of tunnel bright as day. Their light came from behind me.

Way behind me.

Following the Saghred's lead was one thing; ignoring the sheer collective power of the men behind me was quite another. And quite impossible. In addition to his power, I felt Mychael's need to protect me just as strongly as his magic. Both were interfering with what I needed to do through the Saghred.

Touch, hear, see, smell, and taste evil.

My senses were running wide-open. The Saghred was telling me which way to go, when to turn, when to pause and let the air flow over me, and then change direction. The rock was like a tiger by my side, stalking its prey in complete silence, quietly confident that it would soon feed. It didn't try to take over and make me go on a killing spree. It wanted a killing spree of one goblin.

For now.

I walked on the very edge of the light, close enough that Mychael could still see me, far enough that in front of me was nothing but dark emptiness with an occasional dim blue glow of a lightglobe set into the ceiling. Twice, a quartet of Guardians saw me and started to approach, then quickly changed direction. I didn't need to be told why. I wasn't the only one who could sense the Saghred on the prowl. No doubt to them, *I* was the Saghred and I was hunting. They didn't want to cross my path. I didn't blame them.

I was scared of me, too.

I kept moving toward the next intersection, tempted to walk faster to get there quicker. This intersection was well lit, the lightglobes actually working like they were supposed to. Well, at least the tunnel to the left was lit, flooding its light in the other three directions. I already knew I hated tunnels. But I really liked light; I never realized how much I liked light. The

Saghred told me to turn left. About damned time the rock told me to do something I wanted to do.

Except I didn't do it, not yet. I stopped in the middle of the intersection, facing left, just standing there looking down the tunnel. It was long, straight, well lit, and completely clear. Inviting even. No evil goblins down here, it seemed to say. I wasn't buying it. I held up a hand, telling Mychael and the others to stop. Yes, that was where the Saghred wanted me to go, and yes, it was so well lit it was downright cheerful. But "listen before you leap" had never been a bad rule for me. Paranoia was even better. You might even say they were words to live by—or stay alive by.

I wanted to find Sarad Nukpana.

I didn't want Sarad Nukpana to find me first.

I didn't smell or sense the goblin, and the Saghred wasn't all aquiver.

"Ma'am, stop," Vegard said.

I jumped and my sword was halfway out of its scabbard.

"Ma'am, it's okay," he quickly added. "The boss is getting reports from the contact wizards. He needs for you to wait."

I relaxed. A little. At least enough to let my goblin blade slide back into its scabbard across my back.

It wouldn't hurt to wait. The happy tunnel would still be there, and if one of Mychael's patrols had found something, my search might be over, or at least focused in another direction.

Dad walked toward me and stopped about twenty feet away. "Is it okay if I talk to you?"

I nodded once. My breath trembled a little when I let it out. I tried a smile; I didn't think it quite made it. "My nerves are shot. A little small talk might keep me from crawling out of my own skin. Or is this one of those father/daughter talks where you tell me not to play in dark corners with goblin boys?"

He came to stand by my side. "I wish you didn't have to."

"It's not my idea of a fun date."

"Raine, your job is to locate Sarad Nukpana. Please promise me that you'll only confront him directly as a last resort."

"Isn't that what I'm down here for?" I snapped. "Confront and kill?" I glanced up at the stone ceiling and tried to force myself to relax. "Sorry. That came out sharp, didn't it?"

A hint of a smile curled his lips. "It did, but you're entitled." What little smile there was vanished. "Sarad Nukpana has the souls of Rudra Muralin and two other goblin black mages inside of him now." He paused and swallowed. "Raine, inside the Saghred's like the inside of a prison; you hear things about other inmates. Sarad cultivated those two as allies because of their skill and strength, and their sadistic eagerness to use both. If you and the Saghred had been working together for years—"

"Like it did with Rudra Muralin," I said, my tone flat.

"Yes, like Rudra. If you were that close to the stone, bonded so tightly that your will was instantly its command—then you might stand a chance of surviving an encounter with Sarad Nukpana as he is now."

"Dad, if this is your idea of a pep talk, you need to work on your delivery."

"Just promise me that you will not take him on alone. Mychael and I are down here, so are his best Guardians, and Justinius Valerian contacted Mychael not long ago." He flashed a boyish smile. A boy's body with a nine-hundred-year-old soul. I just couldn't get used to it. "Apparently the archmagus thinks he'll be more useful down here. He's on his way."

I breathed a small, harsh laugh. "The old man just wants to get his bony hands around Nukpana's neck."

"He doesn't want to sit this one out. Said it's his duty to be down here with his men."

I reached out and put my hand on his shoulder. Lean and wiry. My centuries-old father in a teenage body still had some growing and filling out to do. "It's my duty, too, Dad," I said quietly. "The Saghred tricked me into taking it. It did it for survival. I sure as hell can't imagine why it'd want a second-rate seeker as its bond servant; the thing was clearly desperate. Regardless of its reasons, it did choose me. I don't like it, I want to get rid of it, but for right now I'm stuck with it—and the responsibility that goes with it. Sarad Nukpana has to be stopped, and thanks to the Saghred, I've got the biggest fist."

Mychael approached us.

"What's the word?" I asked.

He scowled. "No Tam, Piaras, or Talon."

"And no Nukpana."

"That, too."

I readjusted my grip on my daggers, and looked down the tunnel. "Let's see if we can change that." I swallowed. "Wait here. I'll wave when there's enough distance between us for the rock to track him."

I walked into the tunnel, lightglobes working at full capacity humming steadily around me like bees in a hive. The walls were smooth with no sign of a seam or crack that would indicate a bunker behind the wall. Great. I reminded myself that these tunnels were mage-made. All they would have needed to hide the entrances would have been a decent veil or illusion spell, a damned long-lasting one to keep working for nearly a millennium. Normally I could sense that sort of thing, but with all the magical distortion, normal didn't exist down here.

The air shifted above me.

"Raine!" Dad screamed.

I whirled to see him running toward me, Mychael right behind him—and a massive metal door slicing through the air like a guillotine between us. Everything went into slow motion, the door, me running toward it before it closed. The only thing not moving slowly was Dad. He dived and rolled as the door slammed into the granite floor, cracking the stone with its force and weight. The metal erupted with glowing green wards, like a net woven with living snakes, hissing and spitting sparks.

Dad landed in a groaning heap by the wall, close to the wards. Too close.

"Dad! Move—"

I frantically tried to reach him. Light exploded in my eyes as the ward flung me like a doll, sending me flying ass over elbows through the air. I slammed into the floor, flat on my back, mouth gaping like a beached fish. I dimly heard my dad scrabbling away from the wards.

Taking even the tiniest breath made the muscles in my back seize up in agony. Just my luck I'd probably broken some ribs. I blinked and breathed, waiting for my eyes to focus. I slowly turned my head. Dad was sitting up against the wall, his eyes blazing with fury at the ward that'd just kicked my ass. I dragged air in and out of my lungs and pulled myself up against the opposite wall. I'd never seen a ward like that in my life. The Saghred constricted inside me; even the rock didn't want anything to do with it.

"You . . . all right?" I rasped.

Dad breathed and nodded.

"What the hell was th—"

He swallowed and breathed some more. "Safety gates."

I blinked. *"Safety?"*

"For the mages."

"Why didn't . . . you tell us abo—"

Dad actually looked sheepish. "I forgot."

I couldn't believe my ears. "You forgot about *that*?"

"It's been nine hundred years."

I couldn't remember what I had for lunch yesterday, so I couldn't throw much blame at him.

It took a lot of wincing and gasping, but I pulled myself to my feet. I didn't think anything was broken, but plenty was bruised. "So how do we open it?"

"We don't."

I froze. "We what?"

"They're meant to protect mages from invading mages. They can't be opened, at least not by any way that I know of."

"Would Mychael or Justinius know a way?"

Dad shook his head. "The more power they throw at those wards, the stronger they'd get."

I looked down the hall and asked an unpleasant question. "Why did the door pick now to close?"

"These doors don't fall unless triggered."

"Someone told it to."

"Yes."

I didn't need any extra time or three guesses to know who was playing with the switches. And to Sarad Nukpana it was exactly that—play.

The lightglobes in the ceiling above us flickered, dimmed, and died.

I hated tunnels.

Chapter 20

"Sarad knows we're here."

I didn't need Dad to tell me that. The skin between my shoulder blades was doing a fine job. It was itching like crazy. It only did that when something sharp and steely was aimed at my back—or when a crazy goblin was stalking me. It was pitch damn dark, so it could have been either one or both.

Though my little pessimistic voice informed me it wasn't both. Sarad Nukpana wanted me alive, very much alive. That meant no steel, which left stalking.

I summoned a lightglobe, the kind Vegard had taught me how to do, with the blue lightning inside that would fry anything it came in contact with—or anyone I threw it at. It bobbed eagerly by my shoulder.

Sarad Nukpana had to know the tunnels were full of Guardians hunting him. His lair was about to become his prison. He had no time to waste getting the Saghred under his control. To get the Saghred, he had to get me first. But with that iron door and wards crackling behind us, and a dark, one-way tunnel in front of us, I suddenly wasn't all that sure who was the prisoner and who was the jailer.

My breathing was absurdly loud in my own ears. "Dad?" I whispered.

"Yes?"

"We're going to find Nukpana or he'll find us."

"Either's a safe assumption."

"You were the Saghred's keeper for a long time."

"Too long. What are you getting at, Spitfire?"

I shot him a surprised look, and smiled. Leave it to a dad to know just what to say to his scared-witless daughter.

A grin lit his boyish face. "What? I can't call you what Ryn does? I think it suits you."

"When we find Nukpana or he finds us, do you have any suggestions other than let the bastard have it?" It took me a few seconds, but I managed to swallow. "Something sneaky that doesn't involve the Saghred having its way with me?" I tried a smile that no doubt looked sickly. "Because I'm not that kind of girl, know what I mean?"

Dad slipped his arm around my shoulders and pulled me close. "I know exactly what you mean. You're not like that nor will you ever be."

"Mychael said pretty much the same thing."

Dad gave my shoulders a gentle squeeze. "Mychael's a wise man; he knows what he's talking about."

And I knew what I had to do. Find Sarad Nukpana and try not to get my body possessed by the goblin—or my soul taken by the Saghred.

Two against one, the goblin and the rock against me. I didn't factor Dad into the equation, because when push came to shove, there was only so much help he could give me. This was my battle; no one could fight it for me.

Come and try to get me, goblin.

I took a deep breath and tried in vain to see through the dark. "Let's go."

The formerly well-lit and welcoming tunnel went on for entirely too long. Dad and I weren't running, but we were moving at a good clip and I'd traded daggers for one of my goblin swords. If anything came at me, I wanted to slice a vital chunk out of it before it got close enough to do the same to me. Dad had an elven sword. We stayed close enough to each other for protection, but far enough away to keep an accident from happening if one of us got too jumpy.

Then I heard it, the soft scraping of steel on stone, then silence. We stopped, listening. It came from a side tunnel up ahead. A breath later, something was being dragged, something heavy, like a body. Then silence again. I shot a glance at Dad, his lips narrowed into a grim line. He nodded once.

They knew we were here; we knew they were here. No use trying for quiet. That body being dragged could be Piaras, Talon, or even Tam. My jaw clenched. If it was, that body dragger was mine.

Dad's hand locked around my arm like a vise, his other hand making an arcing motion in front of us. He wanted to shield us first. I was all for that.

Within seconds, we had the best shield I'd ever sensed protecting us. We ran toward the dragging sounds and the shield kept pace about five feet in front of us. I couldn't see it, but I could feel it. Just as long as the murderous son of a bitch in the dark ahead of us could feel my blade through it.

A body appeared on the edge of our light, and a few feet beyond lay another. The attack had been quick and obviously deadly. It was who the victims were that surprised me.

Goblins. Khrynsani temple guards, to be exact.

What the hell?

I whirled around, my lightglobe keeping pace with me. Anyone who would kill a pair of Khrynsani might not be my friend, but at least we shared some of the same goals. No one was there. Just two dead goblins lying on the stone floor, their blood pooling around them.

And drops of blood leading away from them. I caught Dad's eye, then glanced down at the bloody trail. He saw and swiftly moved to cover my flank. I tracked the drops a few yards down the tunnel. They ended, just stopped, as if our Khrynsani killer had either stopped bleeding, which was highly unlikely, or had vanished into thin air.

That was entirely too likely. I knew from unpleasant experience that not all air was thin.

With Dad covering me, I bent to get a closer look at those drops. Goblin blood was slightly darker than the elven or human variety. Though in this light, I probably wouldn't be able to tell the difference.

A body slammed into me from behind, knocking me to the floor, and putting us all in the dark. Keeping a lightglobe going took concentration, and right now all my effort was on skewering the man I was rolling around with while staying unskewered myself. My attacker was wiry and strong. A hand grabbed my wrist and slammed my knuckles hard into the floor, once, twice, three times. My fingers surrendered without asking me, and my sword clattered out of reach. Dad swore. He couldn't stab anything without risking injury to me, so he spat a quick conjuring spell, and a flash of light flickered and quickly spun itself into a lightglobe. I twisted, catching my attacker with a sharp knee to the ribs. He grunted in pain and surprise, mostly pain.

I knew that grunt.

"Piaras?" I blurted.

The kid froze with his forearm against my throat. His expression was nothing short of stunned amazement.

"Nice attack," I managed past his arm.

Piaras scrambled off of me until his back hit the far wall, dagger still clenched in his fist, amazement turned to fear. The kid looked scared to death.

"Don't worry," I quickly assured him. "No harm done."

Scared turned to extreme caution. "I felt . . . I thought you were . . ." Piaras's chest rose and fell with quick, shallow breaths.

The Saghred.

Dammit.

I sat up and straightened my doublet. "I stink like a soul-sucking rock, don't I?" Battle-hardened Guardians didn't want to be anywhere near me. What did I expect from a cadet, even if that cadet had known and trusted me for years?

Or used to trust me.

I got to my feet. "The Saghred's the only way I can find Sarad Nukpana," I explained. "It's not controlling me; I've just loosened my hold a little so it can track him."

Piaras was holding his dagger arm tightly to his chest. His tunic sleeve was slashed and bloody.

"You're hurt."

"It's just a cut." ·

"You're bleeding." I started toward him. "Let me—"

"Raine, no!" Instantly, Dad was between us.

Keeping me from touching Piaras.

A retort died on my lips. I knew why he'd done it. With sick realization, I knew.

I'd almost killed Piaras. I could have done worse than kill Piaras.

The Saghred had been quietly waiting. Knowing that to take care of that wound, I would have to touch Piaras, and if I touched even one drop of Piaras's blood . . .

The Saghred would have taken him.

I was the walking Saghred. Piaras's bleeding made him a sacrifice waiting to happen.

I backed against the far tunnel wall, into the dark where monsters belonged, my breathing ragged.

Piaras used his legs to push himself up, his back sliding against the wall while cradling his arm against his chest. "It's only a cut," I dimly heard him tell Dad.

Dad cut a strip of cloth from his own undertunic and used it to bandage Piaras's arm. Mychael could have healed it, closed the wound, stopped the bleeding. But Mychael wasn't here. Dad was. He'd been the Saghred's Guardian and bond servant for centuries. He knew the danger. If he hadn't dived under that door, I would have found Piaras and I would have . . .

"Thank you." Horror at what nearly happened choked my words. "I'm so sorry, Piaras."

His fear turned to confusion. "I don't understand."

He knew he didn't want the Saghred touching him, but aside from a natural revulsion of the Saghred's evil, he didn't know why.

I told him.

When I'd finished, I wiped my eyes with the back of my hand. "Good instincts, kid. You knew you were dealing with a killer."

"You're not a killer," he said vehemently.

"But the rock is. And right now, we're one and the same." My throat constricted as I spoke. "You need to stay away from me." I stared at my dad for a long hard moment. When I spoke, my words were clipped and hard. "Once Sarad Nukpana is dead, contained, confined, or whatever the hell it is I have to do to him—we're going to find a way to separate me from this damned rock."

Dad smiled with a baring of teeth. "Know it, Daughter."

Piaras's mouth fell open. *"Daughter?"*

Oh crap. That was the problem with secrets—remembering who not to tell.

With a pair of dead Khrynsani at our feet and probably more on the way here, there wasn't time for the extended version. "It's long and complicated, but yes, he's my father. I'll explain later. Have you seen Sarad Nukpana?"

Piaras managed to drag his eyes away from my dad. "Only a glimpse."

"Was he solid?"

"Hard to tell; he was wearing a cloak." Piaras glanced down at the dead goblins and looked a little pasty.

Dad shone his lightglobe on the bodies. One across the throat, the other through the heart.

"You killed them." I didn't ask it as a question. Piaras had every bit of Sarad Nukpana's sword skills, and had obviously put them to lethal use.

"I had to; I had to get Talon out of there."

Oh hell, Talon. "Where is he?"

Piaras pointed at the wall at my back. "In there. These two were guarding him."

Dad laid his hand on the smooth granite. "Has to be a bunker."

"Nukpana's?" I asked.

Piaras shook his head. "He's using it as a holding cell. They caught Talon before I could get to him. I followed them down here."

"Why didn't you go for help?"

"If I left, I'd never find it again. When the guards stepped away for a few moments, I tried using my dagger to mark the stone. It didn't even make a scratch." He looked at the flat stone in frustrated anger. "I couldn't leave him—and I had to do something before Sarad Nukpana came for him. I was trying to come up with a plan when I . . . uh, sneezed."

I winced. "That'll get you noticed real quick."

"I had to kill them." Piaras's words came out in a rush. "If I only knocked them out, they'd come to and go for help. I had to stop—"

"You did what you had to do," I calmly finished for him.

"And you did a clean job of it," Dad reassured him. "You did what a Guardian would have done. I know you don't think it's fine work, but it is."

"Would throwing up also be fine work?"

"Not right now," I told him. "See if you can't hold off until we're out of here, and I just might join you." Goblins could see like cats in the dark. But there the goblins lay, unliving proof that Piaras had gotten the drop on them and made it count. "How did you hide?"

"Negating spell and a full-body veil," Dad surmised without turning from his inspection of the stone wall.

Piaras blinked in surprise. "Yes, sir. How did you—"

"I've been a Guardian for a long time, Piaras. It's the first thing they teach cadets. Don't confront when you can hide."

"Was Talon conscious when they locked him in?" I asked.

"Yes, and mad as hell."

"How did the guards open the bunker?"

"I wasn't close enough to see. I'm sorry."

"Don't be. If you'd been any closer, you'd probably be in there with Talon." I quickly moved next to Dad. "See a way in?" The longer we stood here, the more likely we'd have company we didn't want.

"I don't sense a spell or ward, so it would have to be a talisman, keyed to this bunker."

"Piaras, help Dad search the bodies," I told him. "Since they're dead, they probably don't have anything the Saghred wants, but with all that blood, I can't risk touching them."

I hadn't even finished speaking before Dad was kneeling next to one of the dead goblins and doing a highly professional job of pilfering the body: going through pouches, pockets, then taking his dagger and cutting the ties off the goblin's leather armor to search through the layers.

Piaras searched the other one, doing what needed to be done, but trying not to think about what he was doing—stripping the body of a goblin he'd just killed. The first time Piaras had killed had been less than a month ago; it'd been self-defense. This had been the same thing. Almost. Piaras had kept himself concealed, plans running through his head because every option led to him doing exactly what he'd just done: kill two Khrynsani guards. He hadn't wanted to do it, but it wouldn't be the first time that an ill-timed sneeze had forced a man's hand.

Piaras stood, a palm-sized metal square gleaming dully in his hand. "Could this be it?"

Dad took it from him, studying one side, then the other. "It looks old enough." He shone his lightglobe slowly up the length of the wall.

"Wait," I told him.

Dad stopped the globe.

"A few inches to the left."

The globe moved and the shadowed dint in the stone revealed itself to be a shallow square, about a foot from the ceiling, easily reachable by a tall man. With the disk in his hand, Dad reached as high as he could go, then he stood on tiptoe.

"Dammit, my old body wasn't this short."

Piaras stepped forward. "Let me, sir." He slipped the disk into the hollow, no tiptoeing needed. There was a click and the stone panel slid back.

I expected one big room. By no stretch of the imagination could this room be large enough to house fifty mages. If Mid had been under attack, I'd have taken my chances out in the tunnels. There were two doors on either side of the room, probably for storage. Though the first one on the left was storing one goblin teenager. A big clue was a hole cut into the door and set with iron bars. But the red cloud of a ward drifting restlessly in front of the door was the clincher. I guess the mages who'd built these bunkers had made provisions should they catch one of their attackers.

Dad swore quietly but extensively.

"What?" I asked.

"Those wards are wicked bitches."

"Can you take them out?"

"Eventually."

"Eventually isn't now."

"I know," Dad all but growled.

I felt the wards, and under that a gag spell. Sarad Nukpana was being careful. He knew what Talon was capable of, especially after the kid's performance last night. But most important, Talon was his prized catch. He wasn't taking any chances.

The wards shifted and I saw it—a hinged door a little over a foot high and that much again wide. I'd seen similar in modern jail cells. Guards could pass food to a prisoner without the risk of unlocking the door. The wards shifted again, covering the hinged door. I counted all the way to ten before the wards moved away again. The little door stayed untouched by the ward for another count of ten. Nice and regular.

I grinned. This could work.

"No, Raine." Dad's voice said his word was final. He'd looked where I'd been looking. I wasn't the only one who could count to ten.

"It's the only chance we have," I told him. "You said it yourself—those wards are wicked bitches. So I'll go under them."

Dad scowled. "In ten seconds."

"So I'll go fast." I kept my eyes on the wards. Ten seconds on, ten seconds off. I loved predictability.

"No, *I'll* go fast," he told me.

"Your shoulders are too broad."

"I'll fit," Piaras said.

I looked at him and his shoulders. "No, you won't. Plus you're too tall; you'd never make it through before those wards touched you."

"What would happen?"

Dad's eyes had gone back to tracking the wards. "Well, you'd be a lot shorter for one thing."

I realized something distinctly unpleasant. "Dad, if Talon has any wounds, I can't touch him."

Dad handed me his gloves. I didn't know if they'd work, but I tried them on. They were a little large, but manageable. "I'll just try not to touch the kid." I slid out of my sword harness and started stripping off my doublet.

Dad stared at me. "What the hell are you doing?"

"Making myself as narrow as possible." I would fit, but most of my clothes wouldn't. After I'd stripped off everything extraneous, I was left wearing high boots, trousers, a small pouch with some necessities, and an awfully thin shirt. I suddenly noticed it was really, really cold down here. Dad noticed the parts of me that didn't like the cold and quickly looked away. Piaras noticed and then tried not to notice.

I shoved a dagger into my belt at the small of my back and pulled the gloves back on.

Piaras nervously glanced back at the bunker opening. "If there's nothing I can do in here, I'll stand watch outside."

Dad nodded once. "Thank you, Piaras."

The kid looked at me, his dark eyes solemn and afraid—for me. "Be careful, Raine."

"Whenever I can."

I started to kneel, and Dad laid a firm hand on my arm.

"If for some reason you can't get out the way you went in, I'm taking that door off its hinges. Wards or not."

I smiled. "That's what I'm counting on."

I knelt and waited for the ward to move. I opened the flap and quickly looked inside. It wouldn't do me any good to risk life and limb wiggling through that flap if Talon wasn't in there.

Or if a goblin guard was. It'd suck to avoid having my legs cut off by a ward only to have my head lopped off by an ax. I looked. Talon was in there and he was alone. He seemed to be asleep—or unconscious. I was hoping for asleep.

"Dad, the room's big enough. When I start through, get your hands on the bottom of my boots and shove me through."

He knelt beside me. "You got it."

I waited for the next ward cycle to start, dropped to my stomach, started squirming through, and Dad gave me a shove that damned near drove my head into the far wall of the cell. It felt like I left parts of me around the edges of that door.

I scrambled to my feet. Talon was awake and giving me a lascivious look that I'd gotten on numerous occasions from his father. The similarities made me uncomfortable in ways I'd never imagined.

Talon was chained to the wall. There were enough links to allow limited movement, but that was about it. I thought it was a little overdone. No doubt the kid was nimble, and he was a knockout spellsinger, but wards, a gag spell, *and* chained to the wall? Apparently I could add paranoid to my list of Sarad Nukpana descriptors.

Talon rattled his chains and grinned, slow and wicked. "I've had this dream before."

Yep, like father, like son.

I just looked at him. "Kid, I can go right back out the way I came in—without you."

"I'll shut up."

"Smart choice."

His grin turned sheepish. "It appears I didn't make the smartest choice last night."

"Let's see . . . you froze a courtyard full of Guardians, ran away, got yourself snatched and brought here when Mychael and your dad told you to go to the citadel and stay there—so I can see where you might think that."

"Would 'sorry' cover it?"

"Doesn't even come close."

"How did you find me?" Talon asked, nimbly changing the subject.

"Piaras led us to you."

"Piaras?"

"He followed you from the citadel, saw Nukpana grab you, and risked his own life to follow you down here—then he had to kill two Khrynsani to try to save you."

Talon gave a low whistle. "He's so going to kick my ass for that."

"Safe assumption."

I wasn't just making small talk. I was trying to figure out the best way to get those shackles off Talon. Naturally, they couldn't be just any shackles. They were the magic-sapping kind. And I'd have to touch them to get them off. Another nasty surprise was that if the magic user shackled with them tried to use magic, the jolt they'd get would make them think twice about ever trying again.

I noticed burns on Talon's wrists. Looked like he'd tried, more than once. I didn't see any blood, but burns definitely qualified as a wound. I didn't know where the Saghred drew the line as far as what wounds qualified as a sacrifice, and I wasn't about to use Talon to find out.

I nodded down at the manacles. "Tried to sing your way out of those?"

"It didn't go well."

"I imagine not. I think I'll go with the old-fashioned way."

Among the tools of the trade that I'd brought with me was my favorite set of picklocks. A good seeker never went anywhere without them. I pulled them out of the pouch at my back, knelt, and examined the lock on one of the ankle shackles, careful not to touch it. The construction looked simple enough, but I knew better. I'd start with his ankles. As long as I was within groping distance, I wanted Talon's hands secured.

I leaned over the left ankle shackle.

"I think I'm in love," Talon told me.

I looked where Talon was looking—right down the front of my shirt. I sat back on my heels.

"Kid, do you think you can control yourself long enough for me to free you from this hellhole, or would you like to stay here and wait for Sarad Nukpana to come back?"

"I'll be good."

"I'll believe it when I see it. By the way, once I start working on these, you might need all the breath you can get. You might want to take a few good ones now."

"You're not using magic, so there shouldn't be any pain. Right?"

"Possibly, but probably not. I've got the Saghred partially powered up to find Nukpana, and I'm going to have to touch these shackles to pick the locks. I'll work fast, but you might get the same jolt you did when you tried to get out of them."

That tossed a bucket of cold water on his lust.

"And by the way," I continued, "the Saghred's hungry and your wrists are raw. Touch me and you could be lunch."

Talon raised his hands defensively, chains clanking. "Keeping my hands to myself."

Maybe being the Saghred with feet wasn't all bad.

"Sarad Nukpana told me some of the things that he was going to do with me." Talon's aqua eyes were angry and terrified at the same time, mostly terrified. "Do whatever you have to. I can take it."

I hoped he could, because there was no other way around this. And nothing disturbed the peace—and would bring more Khrynsani guards running—like a screaming goblin teenager.

"I'll work fast."

"I won't scream." Talon took a deep breath and then nodded.

I went to work.

And the shackles didn't like me.

They expressed their displeasure straight to Talon. He was made of tough stuff; Tam would be proud. There was a lot of hissing, and when the last manacle dropped to the stone floor, all the kid had to show for it was a trickle of blood where the he'd bitten his lip.

"Dammit, you're bleeding. Do *not* touch me."

"No touching." Talon was panting and his voice quavered a little, but that was it.

I was impressed. That had to have hurt like hell, but the kid hadn't so much as whimpered.

"We're going out the same way I came in. There are wards out there that cover the door on a ten-second interval. You have to be out in ten seconds."

"I can do that."

I certainly hoped so. I knelt next to the door. "Ready?" I asked Dad.

"Ready." There was a whole world of relief in that one word.

"Let me know when and Talon will stretch his arms out. His wrists are burned, so grab his forearms if you can. Pull hard. I don't want to touch him, not even his boots. Talon, get down on your belly and get ready."

Dad counted from the other side. "Five, four, three, two, one."

Talon pushed his arms through the opening and Dad pulled. Fortunately, Talon's shoulders weren't too wide to fit.

"Got him," came Dad's voice from the other side.

I stretched out on the floor. "You're not bleeding, are you?"

"No."

I exhaled sharply. "Then grab my arms, too. But make sure you grab cloth and not skin."

"Got it."

"Tell me when."

"Three, two, one."

Dad pulled and I swear I left skin on the stone floor. It hurt, but I was out and so was Talon.

The kid made a break for the open door. Dad jerked him back.

"Not so fast," Dad snapped.

Talon yanked his arm back—at least he tried.

"There is only one way out of here." Dad's voice was clipped and hard. "So we have to take you with us. Chances are we're going to run into Sarad Nukpana or at the very least more Khrynsani. You will do exactly as told, precisely when told."

Talon turned and went toe-to-toe with my dad. I kept any and all expression off my face. Oh, this was going to be good.

"And what junior knight wannabe is going to give me orders?"

Dad didn't say a word; he just let Talon see him, truly see him. The real him with his old soul, not the twenty-year-old, baby-faced Guardian whose body he inhabited. I knew why he did it. Talon was the type that you had to scare the shit out of to get his attention. And for once we had to have Talon's complete attention and unquestioned cooperation. All of our lives depended on it.

Talon knew what he was seeing and his eyes went as wide as saucers. I thought he was going to faint. The last time he'd done that was after seeing Phaelan slice the ear off of an undead minion of the demon queen. I had to admit that ear plopping on the floor followed by oozing black blood was kind of gruesome.

The kid's mouth opened and words finally made it out. "Who . . . *What* are you?"

"Talon, meet *my* dad."

"How can you be—"

Dad didn't bat an eye. "I'm 934 years old."

"Damn, you're old," Talon blurted.

And who said teenagers aren't tactful?

Dad released Talon's arm, but his hard eyes kept the kid anchored to the spot. "If you do anything to endanger my daughter, Sarad Nukpana will no longer be your worst problem. Do I make myself clear?"

"Completely."

"That's what I want to hear."

"Can you find your way back to Sarad Nukpana's bunker?" I asked Talon.

"I was blindfolded."

Crap.

"Any noises, lights, anything you can tell us?"

"No noise and a really tight blindfold."

Double crap.

"We're going to have to get past Nukpana to get out of here," I told him. "I have some business with him; you don't. Your job is to survive. So be ready to run."

"Born that way."

Dad was by the door, listening. Then in one fluid and silent move, both of his swords were out of their scabbards and clenched in his hands.

Oh no.

Piaras.

I armed myself and quickly took up position beside Dad.

His lips were next to my ear. "Piaras was there. Now he's not."

Damn.

Chapter 21

I was relieved to see that not only were the dead goblins right where we'd left them, but they were also still dead. Lately "dead" had become an entirely too relative term.

Talon's breath came in a startled hiss when he tripped over one of the bodies. Oh yeah, he was only half-goblin. Elven blue eyes, not goblin black—no preternatural night vision for Talon.

Talon quickly stepped back into the shadows with me on one side of the bunker door. Dad slipped silently into the dark on the other side. Talon didn't need anyone to tell him to stay quiet.

The bunker's dim light spilled out into the tunnel, just enough for us to see that we were out here all alone. From the tunnel in either direction there were no sounds, no light, no life. At least not any that I could sense.

And definitely no Piaras.

The Saghred's presence inside of me was perfectly still, waiting. Waiting for something that it didn't see fit to share with me—at least not yet.

Life with a soul-sucking rock. Never a dull moment.

If Piaras had been veiling next to the wall, he would have stepped out by now. I didn't need intuition, seeker magic, or the Saghred to tell me that he wasn't here. Perhaps he thought he could guard us better from farther down the tunnel, where he could intercept any goblins before they knew we were in Talon's cell and trap us there. If he'd scouted ahead, we'd find him.

Unless he'd been captured. In which case, we'd be joining him shortly. By activating that iron door and its ward, Sarad Nukpana had given us no choice but to go forward. That was the direction Talon's guards had come from, so I thought it safe to assume that a certain regenerating goblin psychopath would be happily awaiting our arrival at the other end.

I had a feeling there wouldn't be any ambush or attack—nothing to prevent us from reaching Sarad Nukpana's bunker. The goblin would do everything short of putting out a welcome mat. He needed to kill me. He wanted to kill Dad. And he would enjoy killing Piaras and Talon.

Every goblin down here would be able to see us coming. It didn't matter if we were stumbling around in the dark or had a hundred lightglobes lighting our way. Light or dark—either one would give us away.

But most of all, Sarad Nukpana knew I was here. The Saghred knew he was here. So anything I did would just postpone the inevitable showdown. But that didn't mean we couldn't sneak up on his guards and even the odds a little in our favor. I didn't want Sarad Nukpana in front of me and who knew how many of his minions creeping up behind me.

I spoke on the barest breath. "Dad, tell me how to do a negating spell."

He arched a brow at me. "Raine, it takes more than few seconds to teach—"

"Just tell me," I said flatly. "The rock and I learn fast."

He glanced at Talon. "It's an individual spell, so it won't cover him. We'll have to—"

"I think the rock will cover all of us. It wants Sarad Nukpana. Badly."

I wanted the same thing, but for a different reason. The rock wanted to eat him; I just wanted him dead, preferably the old-fashioned way—just steel, no soul sucking. The longer we took getting to the goblin, the longer he'd have to prepare for us.

A prepared demigod would be very bad.

Dad told me the spell. I understood, but most important, the rock knew what to do and how to do it.

A few minutes later, we were sporting a solid negating spell courtesy of my magic and the rock's knowledge. Dad and I wove a quartet of lightglobes and sent them down the hall in pairs at intervals of about twenty feet. We stayed behind the second pair close enough to the light to be able to see what or who was in front of us, but far enough away to have a hope of not being glaring targets. And if the negating spell was doing its job, any goblins would see four lightglobes coming down the tunnel by themselves with no one behind them. Goblins liked the dark, so you had to wonder what, if anything, they considered spooky. I knew that four disembodied lightglobes floating down a dark, deserted tunnel would do it for me.

The spell just negated our presence. Blades would still work, Talon's voice could still do its thing—and now the Saghred was itching to get a piece of the action.

We hadn't gone fifty yards before the rock started stirring. We were getting close. The Saghred could smell Sarad Nukpana, and through our bond, so could I. Gleefully sadistic, relishing the torment he'd caused, the death he'd brought, and eager to do it all again. The Saghred was experiencing much the same emotions. It had absorbed Nukpana and held him captive for nearly three months. It knew its own. And now, so did I.

I also knew something else. I had never been this scared in my whole life.

Facing Sarad Nukpana in Markus's parlor had paled in comparison to this. This was raw terror of the whimpering kind. I tried to steel myself against the fear, at least the whimpering part. I could deal with Nukpana's goons finding me if I got stupid and tripped over something in the dark, but I'd die of embarrassment before they could kill me if a whimper actually made it out of my mouth. Though that didn't stop my nearly overwhelming need to do it. I bit my lip to stop any wayward, cowardly noises.

The only way I could defeat Sarad Nukpana was to use the Saghred. And the only thing the rock was interested in doing was eating Nukpana's soul and anyone he'd consumed. That included one elven general, two ancient psychotic mages, and Rudra Muralin. The thought of their souls being forcibly pulled through me and into the Saghred was enough to make me want to scream my throat raw. I was going into this confrontation monumentally ignorant of what else to do and fatally unprepared for any of it. I'd tricked Sarad Nukpana once; that kind of luck wasn't going to happen to me again. Phaelan would say that a Benares makes her own luck.

Phaelan wasn't here. I was, and I didn't want to be.

The farther we went, the worse the air got. Then my brain registered what my nose had caught wind of and my skin tried to crawl somewhere and hide.

Musty air and mold.

I'd smelled it before. In Sarad Nukpana's coach behind Markus's house. The smell was here, right here. The actual smell, not Nukpana's memory of it.

We were within spitting distance of Sarad Nukpana's lair.

Step into my parlor, said the spider to the fly.

I stopped and so did Dad and Talon. Dad didn't question why. Talon just settled for keeping his mouth shut. I was grateful for both.

I slowly dimmed our lightglobes, then let them flicker out of existence. We didn't need them anymore. We could see just fine.

I'd seen it through Sarad Nukpana's memories. Now I could see it with my own eyes.

The tunnel curved, and flickering firelight came from beyond an opening at the far end. A bunker. Nukpana's bunker. Though with that crazy goblin in there, it was more like a crypt. Between us and the opening, cold blue light shone dimly from globes embedded in the ceiling, forming pools of light on the floor at regular intervals all the way from us to the door. Circles of pale light with plenty of shadows for hiding evil minions along the wall. Rats scuttled and squeaked in the dark next to the walls, running away from the light.

Away from what was in that room. The rats had the right idea.

I was shaking. Terror would do that to you.

So would a soul-sucking rock thinking it was going to get its biggest meal in centuries.

That thought just made me shake harder.

A rat brushed past my foot. I sucked in air through my teeth. I didn't get this far to squeal like a girl now. Then I remembered a little fact about rats.

They knew the way out—and the way in.

Rats didn't live where there wasn't a food source. And when they ran, it was to safety. I'd seen nothing but bare tunnels, no food here. Nukpana and his Khrynsani didn't just choose this bunker for privacy; they would have chosen it because it gave them a quick and hidden way to get out into the city. I saw two of the rats run into the darkness of a side tunnel and heard squeaks from farther into the darkness.

Down there, somewhere in the dark with the rats, was a way out.

Before I could stop him, Dad slipped into the shadows and moved quickly along the wall to the bunker opening. I started to call out to him, but that would just get us killed faster. Though I hadn't seen or sensed even one Khrynsani guard.

Dad reached the end of the tunnel and with his back against the wall to the right side of the opening, cautiously peered into the room. I'd expected him to look, see what was in there, and then run like hell. I didn't get what I expected, and apparently neither did Dad. He looked at me, confusion and disbelief on his face.

What the hell?

I went, I looked, and I didn't believe my eyes for one second.

Sarad Nukpana was laid out on a stone bier in all of his dark beauty, his long black hair flowing over the side in an ebony wave. His eyes were closed, hands folded serenely on his chest. He wasn't moving and I didn't need the Saghred to tell me he wasn't breathing, either.

The bastard was dead.

I froze. That meant his soul was no longer in his body. The damned thing could be anywhere.

A flash of panic gripped me and my breath came shallow and fast. Nukpana had told me that he wanted my body, to push my soul aside, to possess me completely. My shields went up, the strongest I had.

The Saghred suddenly felt like a tiger in a crouch. Its prey was in that room, waiting.

For me.

The Saghred had no interest in the empty corpse on the bier. All its attention was on someone standing in the shadows. There was someone in that bunker, a living, breathing someone. There were no guards, none at all. I didn't trust it, but I couldn't think about it, not now.

I had a job and I was going to do it, through the terror and with knees shaking so badly I had to concentrate to get one foot in front of the other.

I stepped into that bunker, brushing aside Dad's attempt to stop me. Fear it and face it. I wasn't going to run like the rats, so there was no going back. That left forward and fighting. I'd do whatever I had to, be it steel—or soul sucking. This had to end. Now.

My mouth was bone-dry and open; I was panting. "Come out, you son of a bitch."

Black magic, thick and vile, hung in the air like an oily stain. This was evil, fetid and dripping. I felt it through my clothes, crawling on my skin, slick and cloying.

The shadows in the far corner literally parted like curtains, revealing who they had hidden.

I stopped breathing, paralyzed with a fear so sharp that it staked me to the ground where I stood. I whimpered. I didn't have the breath to scream.

"A final gift for you, little seeker." The words were from Sarad Nukpana.

The voice and body belonged to Tam.

Talon screamed, a full-throated roar of denial, anguish, and rage. He lunged at his father, and it took all Dad could do to hold him back.

"For shame," Nukpana chided from inside Tam's body. "And Tamnais risked everything to find him. Let the boy embrace his father. It may be the last chance he will ever have."

Terror tried to sucker punch me, but I grabbed it and shoved it down. Terror had no place here, only cold logic, and even colder action. That didn't stop my stomach from twisting into a tight knot and another whimper from escaping my lips.

It was my worst nightmare and it was standing right in front of me. The combined magical power of the mages' souls that Sarad Nukpana had ingested made the air around Tam's body ripple with the sheer magnitude of it. I'd never seen or heard of shields that strong.

Weapons couldn't reach him; neither could magic.

The Saghred was squirming inside of me, desperate to try. I kept my breathing even, and held as tightly as I could on to the stone's power. Sarad Nukpana was too strong now. When I made my move, it had to count. I'd only get one chance, and that chance hung on those shields coming down.

"I want to speak to Tam." I had to force the words out past the pressure building in my chest.

"What if he doesn't want to speak to you?" Nukpana taunted lightly. "Though even if he wanted to, he's powerless to do anything about it." Nukpana twisted Tam's lips into a smirk. "He's quite helpless to do anything."

My hands clenched into fists as a white-hot rage took control of me. I didn't fight it; I let it in, embraced it, and aimed it squarely at the goblin standing not ten feet away. Had he moved toward me? Or had I stepped closer to him? The Saghred wanted to be much closer. I remembered training with Tam: lose control, lose life. Though now my life wasn't the only one at stake.

Neither was my soul.

I forced myself to see Tam not as Tam, but as Sarad Nukpana. He was holding Tam hostage, the only difference being that it was from the inside. Big difference, but the same problem.

I'd freed hostages and prisoners before. Find and free them. It was my job, and I was good at it.

I would free Tam.

"You're welcome to try, little seeker."

The bastard was reading my mi—

"There is no need to read that which I am bonded to."

Oh no.

Nukpana sighed in unabashed pleasure. "It saves so much time and trouble to know precisely what my future partner is thinking even as she thinks it. Your umi'atsu bond with Tamnais is most convenient." Tam's voice dropped to a familiar seductive purr. "And the intimacy is absolutely delicious. When I took Tamnais, I took your umi'atsu bond. It links you with his magic and his mind. I am in possession of Tamnais's mind, so I can easily see inside of yours. Soon I'll be able to control the Saghred—and you just as easily. Rudra Muralin's knowledge of the stone is extensive, though I am still absorbing his memories. He was detestable as a goblin, but he will prove useful in the coming hours and days."

I lunged for the body on the bier and drove the point of my dagger against the big artery in Sarad Nukpana's throat. It just broke the skin and cool blood welled up around it. Nukpana hadn't been in Tam's body for long; the corpse on the bier was still warm. "Release Tam now or you're not going to have a body to come home to," I snarled. "No blood, no life." I drew my long goblin sword from the harness on my back. "Or better yet, no head, no Nukpana."

"My previous body and its identity have become more of a burden than an asset," Nukpana/Tam replied mildly. "Being notorious has been fun, but it is hardly productive for the work I have planned. So by all means, little seeker, decapitate my corpse. I have no further need of it. It is my intention to remain precisely where I am." His smile was full of fang. "Would you enjoy that, Raine? Unlimited power in the body of your lover."

"He's not my lover."

Nukpana/Tam took a slow, deliberate step toward me. "Then we shall have to change that very soon. I know Tamnais has desired you for years. Pity he will be a helpless bystander, only able to watch what I will use his body to do to you."

"Hey," said a quiet voice. "Remember me?"

Dad had slowly circled and was now within ten feet of Nukpana/Tam. "Looks like we both found bodies." The steely glint in his eyes promised payback, and his smile said he was going to enjoy every second of it. "Too bad you won't be keeping yours."

Nukpana/Tam laughed in a perverse mixture of voices. "Eamaliel Anguis, still a noble Guardian, only now your host is barely old enough to shave. Coward, you took the first body you could find."

"You took a body you're going to regret."

"The seeker will not kill her soon-to-be lover—and neither will her father."

Tam rolled his eyes.

I didn't move a muscle; I didn't even dare to breathe.

That eye roll was all Tam. Nukpana didn't have a thing to do with it.

And the goblin knew it. That eye roll was followed by a flash of panic. The panic was all Nukpana. Tam may not have been in control, but Sarad Nukpana didn't have a firm hold on the reins. At least not yet.

The Saghred smelled Nukpana's fear and relished it. The tiger was licking its chops. The goblin knew that, too.

Dad chuckled. "Problems, Sarad? Is your control slipping? Apparently even your host body finds your antics ridiculous."

"Then the time for play has passed," came Janos Ghalfari's

smooth voice from the doorway behind us. The nachtmagus had five Khrynsani temple guards with him. They were completely blocking the opening.

Dad casually glanced past them down the tunnel. "That's it? No Khrynsani welcoming committee?" The air around him virtually crackled as he powered up his magic. The guards shifted uneasily. Dad flashed them a smile that was more a baring of teeth that told them to bring it on.

"These men are merely an escort," Ghalfari said quietly. "Many more are here with me, brought from Regor. And you are . . . ?"

"Uncle, allow me to present the infamous Eamaliel Anguis," Nukpana/Tam said. "New body, old nemesis."

Ghalfari's black eyes glittered with something ugly. "The Guardian who stole the Saghred from Rudra Muralin and our king a thousand years ago."

"I prefer to call it a retrieval," Dad replied dryly. "From a boy with far too much power and not enough sense or sanity to use it. And I'm only 934. Why does everyone insist on making me older than I already am?"

Ghalfari turned his head slightly to speak to the Khrynsani guard waiting just behind him to the right. "Go and get your brothers in arms. We will have need of them all." He turned to his nephew. "We must move quickly, Sarad. The paladin knows where Mistress Benares has gone. The map in his possession shows this tunnel. We must prepare."

Which meant Mychael knew the way in, or someone with him did. That knot in my stomach loosened a little. When it came to backup, you couldn't have too many, especially when that backup was Justinius Valerian and half a citadel's worth of Guardians. Ghalfari's other Khrynsani must be waiting in a nearby bunker.

The Saghred burned in my chest. It didn't want backup. It wanted the souls in Tam's body—including Tam's. I took a deep breath and pushed the urges down, nearly overpowering urges.

"Hungry, Raine?" Nukpana murmured.

"The rock's on a diet until I say it's not," I said through clenched teeth.

"You being here will keep us from going to the trouble of finding Mychael," Nukpana/Tam said. "Tamnais is trusted by a surprising number of people on this island. Tamnais and the paladin are friends of a sort, are they not?"

"Good enough that Tam told Mychael to kill him if the Saghred ever took control of him," I said deliberately. "The same would apply to a certain goblin psycho. That is, unless I let the Saghred take a bite out of you first."

One side of Tam's lips briefly jerked into a lopsided smile. Tam may have lost control of his body, but he'd kept his sense of humor.

An instant later, Nukpana forced that smile down.

"That's the beauty of it, little seeker. Mychael won't realize the truth until it is too late. I did promise you prolonged torment, did I not? I don't want you to die; I want you to watch. I fully intend to return to Tamnais's body, but for a few hours, I will require the body of a certain paladin who knows where the Saghred is being kept—and who can take it and walk away unchallenged."

Hellfire and damnation.

"Yes," Nukpana/Tam replied smoothly. "No doubt to Mychael Eiliesor, it will be hell. It will also confirm everything Carnades Silvanus has accused him of—that he's been contaminated by contact with you and the Saghred. His stealing the stone will prove it. When I have finished with Mychael's body, no doubt Silvanus will have plans for it—or at least his severed head."

And we were the bait. Talon for Tam. Me for Mychael.

Like hell. I felt a growl building in my throat, and the Saghred's hungry fire flared in my chest.

"Speaking of watching," Nukpana/Tam continued. "Tamnais's memory of when I took him is still quite fresh." His smile was smooth, horrible, and all Nukpana. "Would you like to see?" he whispered. "With our bond, I'm certain that I can share it with you. He put up an impressive fight—but as you can see, obviously not impressive enough."

Talon broke free of Dad's grip and threw himself at Nukpana/Tam. The kid never made it past the bastard's shields. The impact slammed him back against the bunker wall, not hard enough to kill. No, Nukpana was still playing, and to him Talon was a toy to be enjoyed. Dad was instantly by his side, helping him to sit up. Talon's aqua eyes narrowed in raw hatred and he sang a single, discordant word—the same word he'd used to freeze the elven Nightshade on Sirens' roof.

Nukpana/Tam dismissively waved his hand and the note froze in Talon's throat. The kid tried again but no sound came out, and his eyes went wide with panic.

The Saghred's fire roiled in my chest and I let it. "If you have taken—"

Dad helped Talon to his feet. "I've seen it done before, Raine. The loss is temporary, an hour at the most."

Nukpana/Tam never took his eyes from Talon. "Though I could have ripped his voice from his throat and never left a mark. Children should be seen and not heard."

"And this one should have been killed at birth." Janos Ghalfari's words were calm and precise.

Dad pushed Talon behind him.

The Khrynsani guard came running back into the bunker, his gray skin a couple of shades paler than it should have been. "Sir, the men . . . I can't wake them."

"Wake? What do you mean 'wake'? What are you—"

My growl turned into a chuckle. Nukpana/Tam knew. He didn't have to read my mind to know what had happened to every last one of his uncle's Khrynsani guards.

Piaras had been a very busy young man. Brilliantly busy. Sleepsongs were what he did best.

"You're looking for an elf, Uncle Janos," Nukpana/Tam snarled. "A Guardian cadet named Piaras Rivalin. He is a spellsinger and obscenely gifted. I want him brought to me. Alive. The account I need to settle with him is long overdue."

I had to get Sarad Nukpana out of my head. I needed to think and think fast, and having my target know my plans as I thought them would be counterproductive to say the least. I knew how to block someone from my thoughts. This was different; this was a bond, forged by the Saghred.

And sustained by the Saghred.

My lips twisted into a smug grin. If the rock wanted a meal, it'd better start cooperating with me.

Hear that, rock?

Instantly a wall of white noise went up between my mind and Nukpana/Tam's. It didn't block thoughts, but it distorted the hell out of them. If Nukpana tried to read my mind, he was going to get dizzy.

Nukpana/Tam's head turned sharply toward me. He knew what I'd just done.

"Hasn't anyone ever told you that eavesdropping is rude?" I told him.

Nukpana/Tam's eyes darkened and expanded to solid black orbs with no white visible. The air chilled and tightened, and the black magic pressed on me like a giant hand, constricting, crushing—and caressing. My breath came in shallow, rapid gasps. He had no intention of killing me; this was just a show of force, of control.

I let the Saghred push back.

My eyes were locked with Nukpana/Tam's in a silent battle of wills. The power of centuries of dark mages versus the power of the Saghred. Rudra Muralin knew how to control the Saghred, but Nukpana hadn't digested all of that knowledge. The pressure lifted enough for me to speak.

"Looks like the rock . . . doesn't want you in my head, either."

Fire burned in my chest, throat, and behind my eyes. I sucked in a breath and bit my lip until I tasted blood to keep from crying out. Blood. A Saghred sacrifice. I dimly wondered if I could absorb myself.

At full power, the Saghred could probably blast through Nukpana/Tam's shields. Though the force of it would kill Tam and bring the ceiling and any building above that down on all of us. And even if I could get past those shields, the Saghred would take every soul in Tam's body—including Tam's. I didn't know of any other way to get Sarad Nukpana's soul out of Tam's body.

I couldn't risk it. I wouldn't risk Tam. There had to be another way. I just couldn't think. Hell, I couldn't think at all. Focus, Raine. Think. What stomped flat any idea I came up with was one simple fact: if Sarad Nukpana escaped with Tam's body and was in it from one sunrise to the next, the possession was permanent, and there would be nothing even the best exorcist could do to change it.

Sarad Nukpana wouldn't be tricked, not this time. I clenched my hands around my weapon grips until my nails dug into my palms.

My gloved palms.

I didn't know if a layer of leather would stop the Saghred from satisfying centuries of starvation, but I didn't have a choice. If Sarad Nukpana took me, he could use the Saghred, and he'd have the power to do anything to anyone at any time. He would be unstoppable. I had to warn Mychael. That meant leaving Tam. We were bonded. Once we were out of here there'd be no more magical distortion and I would follow Tam to Hell and back if I had to—by myself, with my own seeking skills.

I had to escape.

But escape meant first being captured.

I trusted Dad to know what to do. I slowly let my shields dissolve and loosened my grip on my weapons. My hands went slack, my fingers limp, then my blades clattered to the floor.

"That's it, little seeker."

Nukpana/Tam's voice had dropped into a seductive lower register. I closed my eyes and took one deep breath and slowly let it out, then again.

I dimly heard Dad swear and scream at me, trying to break my trance, to make me hear him, heed him.

Nukpana/Tam laughed, low and confident. "Come to me, Raine."

I did.

I put one foot in front of the other, hesitant, allowing myself to be drawn in. Closer. Exactly where Sarad Nukpana wanted me to be.

Exactly where I had to be.

With a will of its own, my right hand reached out toward him, and he took it, imprisoning my hand in his, drawing me to him, inside his shields. It was Tam's body I was held against, but it was Nukpana's hands that ran all over my body.

"You are already mine, Raine," he whispered, his lips against my throat. "Your magic, my strength, the Saghred's power." His words rumbled deep and soft in his chest. "The acts we will commit, the kingdoms we will conquer." His fangs nibbled the soft, vulnerable skin covering the artery in my throat, my blood pulsing frantically, in fear.

In anticipation.

"You will be by my side, the instrument of my will." I felt his lips curl into a smile against my skin. "I will use the Saghred by using you."

I ran my trembling hands up his chest to his shoulders and around the back of his neck, intertwining my fingers, stroking the skin there. I raised my face to his, my eyes wide, my lips parted, entreating.

Surrendering.

Nukpana/Tam lowered his head to mine.

I clenched the back of his neck and jerked his head and upper body down as my knee came up, slamming into Tam's ribs—the second rib on his left side. The one that had never healed.

I heard it break. Hard.

Nukpana/Tam's shields buckled along with his knees. He landed in a groaning heap on the floor.

I ran like hell.

Dad had cleared the five Khrynsani out of the way, the force of his magic slamming and pinning them to the wall like armored bugs. That left Janos Ghalfari and he stood squarely in my way, disbelief on his face giving way to determination. The Saghred's power still coursed through my veins. I hissed a single word and Ghalfari folded and collapsed like he'd taken a giant fist to the gut.

There was no time to retrieve my blades. The three of us cleared the doorway and ran for the rats' tunnel.

Tam's weak laughter floated on the air behind us.

Tam, not Sarad Nukpana.

I brushed tears out of my eyes and kept running. And hated myself for it.

Chapter 22

Most people run from rats. We ran after them.

While trying not to stumble and fall on my face, it occurred to me that rats didn't need a door to escape; a hole or a crack would work just fine. I hoped there was a door at the end of that tunnel, but if there wasn't, I was fully prepared to make my own.

A tall figure ran toward us out of the shadows and Dad damned near skewered him with his sword.

Piaras neatly parried the blade. "Glad to see you, too. I found a way out. This way."

I didn't ask him how he knew and we sure as hell didn't need any urging to follow. Dad summoned a lightglobe and rats squealed as they ran for their tiny lives. We were doing the same thing, minus the squealing, at least for now.

"We're coming back for him," I told Talon. "We need help."

"You've got the Saghred!" he managed in a hissing whisper.

"Which would have eaten his soul," I shot back.

So much for filling in Piaras. He swore, a word I'd heard Guardians throwing around the citadel. "He got Tam."

"Not for long," I growled.

I wanted to scream, I wanted to kill Sarad Nukpana, I wanted to cry, but most of all I wanted to use what I had. I mean *really* use it. For the first time, and possibly the last, I wanted to cut loose with the Saghred. Take down anyone who had hurt me or had hurt anyone I cared about. But through the red haze of my rage and pain, I knew that once I did that, there might not be any going back. Cancel that—there definitely wouldn't be any going back.

As of this moment, I did not care.

Everybody said that Saghred had unlimited power. I had a big damn surprise for them. It wasn't unlimited. All it could do was kill, suck souls, and destroy—none of which would get Sarad Nukpana out of Tam's body without taking Tam with him.

Killing everyone in that bunker except for Tam would have been smart. Leave no live enemy behind, receive no dagger in the back was a Benares family mantra. But that would have taken time. Even with steel and magic, it would have taken time we didn't have.

Get out, get clear, *then* get even.

The bad thing about any kind of defensive spell, even one with a touch of Saghred power, was that unless you broke their legs, the bad guys would get up and come after you. It might take them a few minutes, but you could count on a group of very pissed-off, armed people on your ass pronto. So you escaped and you did it fast. I had to get out, warn Mychael, and when the goblins followed us, they'd have plenty of trouble and we'd have plenty of backup.

And Nukpana/Tam would be out in the open where either I or Mychael or Justinius—or hell, it might take all of us—might be able to get him immobilized long enough to get a team of exorcists to work on Tam.

The success of that plan depended on Mychael and Justinius not being on the other side of the Conclave complex. I was counting on Janos Ghalfari being right. Mychael was close by.

The tunnel was longer than it had any right to be. Piaras was ahead of us with Dad's lightglobe, his sword held deceptively relaxed in his hand, his eyes alert. Piaras wasn't relaxed; he was ready for anything. The kid who I loved like a little brother wasn't little anymore. His shoulders were back and the responsibility he carried now just made him stand all the straighter, his quick strides sure and determined. It couldn't have been a trick of the light—there was just one lightglobe—Piaras shimmered with a luminescence that I'd only seen once before when he'd fought at Justinius Valerian's side, his back against a wall, killing every demon that came against him.

A faint green glow the size of a fist shimmered unmoving in the dark ahead of us.

My gut knew what it was before the Saghred told me.

A ward.

I didn't care about the ward, either.

"That's the door leading outside," Piaras told us. "That glow is a ward; I don't know what kind."

The door was huge, metal, and looked like it'd been forged from the same mold as the one Nukpana had closed on us. The rats ran out of a hole under the base of the door. A breeze stirred the dust and dirt on the floor. Fresh air, outside, and so close.

Shouts and booted feet ran toward us down the pitch-dark tunnel.

Khrynsani.

"It's a goblin ward," Dad said, getting as close as he dared. "I don't know how to—"

"Fuck the ward," I snarled. "Dad, get behind me and shield them." He did and I aimed all of my rage and my will and my pain at that lock and ward and hit both of them with everything I had. Metal screamed as the door was ripped off its hinges, sending it flying up and out into the blinding sunlight. Panicked shouts and screams erupted from all around us as we shielded our eyes and scrambled out onto the grass of a massive quad, surrounded by buildings—and full of mages and young apprentices.

Crap in a bucket.

My eyes were blinking and tearing with the light, but there was no mistaking mages running at the sight of us—or probably at the sight of me. I glowed with the remnants of the power I'd just used, and a few feet away was the door I'd turned into a twisted, smoking metal ruin. No doubt we made quite a picture.

Damn, but that had felt good.

My vision cleared and I saw two goblins, walking quickly away from the chaos I'd caused.

Nukpana/Tam and Janos Ghalfari.

There'd been another way out of that bunker, and they were getting away.

Oh, hell no, they weren't.

I ran after them and black-robed mages scattered like startled crows to get away from me. I couldn't let Nukpana and Ghalfari out of my sight.

"Mychael!" I screamed in mindspeak. The leftovers from the power that'd blown that door sky-high amplified my voice into a massive mind bellow. The mages closest to me fell to the ground, clutching their heads. Just what I needed: sensitives.

Nukpana/Tam and Janos Ghalfari quickened their pace toward a group of young student apprentices. Ghalfari glanced back at me and smiled. Those young mages were hostages for the taking. He expected me to stop or at least slow my pursuit.

I was finished doing the expected, the noble, and the sane. Rational thought had no place in my mind anymore; it'd been drop-kicked by revenge.

"Damn, girl, think you made enough noise?" barked a familiar voice coming up behind me. Someone who liked revenge just as much as I did.

Justinius Valerian.

I turned to see that the mages who had scrambled out of my way scuttled even farther away from the old man and his phalanx of armed Guardian escorts.

"Not nearly as much as I wanted to," I told him. Tam being possessed by Sarad Nukpana didn't need to be public knowledge, even to Guardians. I got next to the old man and whispered in his ear, my words succinct and clipped with rage. "Nukpana's possessed Tam; they're getting away. Where's Mychael?"

Justinius calmly nodded toward an archway that appeared to be the only way out of this side of the quad. Nukpana/Tam and Ghalfari were about to pass under it. "Taking on those two goblins."

I looked up. Mychael was on the roof.

Oh hell. He didn't know.

"Nukpana's possessed Tam." I tried for quiet this time.

Mychael's head snapped up and so did the crossbow he had trained on Janos Ghalfari. He'd thought Tam was a hostage. He was, just not in the normal way. Apparently Saghred-amplified mindspeak cut through all of the mage distortion. At least the rock was doing something useful.

We couldn't confront Nukpana/Tam and Ghalfari, at least not here. There were too many chances for too many people to die, and Tam was one of them. If Ghalfari took an apprentice hostage, a trigger-happy Guardian or hero-wannabe mage might just think that Tam was his partner, not his prisoner.

When I looked back at Mychael, the roof was empty.

Oh crap. "What's through that arch?" I asked Justinius.

"The stables. And this time of day, it's full of horses and coaches."

The goblins would have their pick of transportation.

I started forward. "He's not getting away with Tam."

Justinius's wiry and surprisingly strong grip on my arm jerked me back. "He can't get away with you, either."

The Saghred's power surged like liquid fire through my veins. The old man slowly removed his hand from my arm, though I know the rock had burned him. Badly. I'd felt it strike. Most men would have screamed and been on the ground. Justinius definitely wasn't most men. We had enough terrified mages looking at us—looking at me; he didn't want to add to the show. He just stood there, regarding me with cool, blue eyes, assessing, not judging. At least not yet.

The Archmagus of the Conclave wanted to know right here and now if I was a danger to his people. If he decided that I was, he would act.

Right here and right now.

I slowly let out my breath and met his eyes; hopefully they weren't glowing, too. "Sorry, sir. The rock's pissed. I wouldn't let it eat Tam."

"Understandable." Justinius's face was expressionless; his question for my ears alone. "Do you have it under control?"

His real question was, or was it controlling me.

My lips narrowed into a thin line. "As much control as I'm willing to get until after I save Tam."

His hard eyes never wavered. "Then let's go get him."

The stable area was busy bordering on chaotic, but not because of Nukpana/Tam or Janos Ghalfari. Mages were coming to work, meetings, or classes, and the grooms more than had their hands full stabling horses. Just beyond the stables themselves was an area for coaches and their drivers to wait for their employers to return.

It was noisy, busy, and damned near impossible to spot two dark-garbed goblins in the sea of dark-garbed stable hands.

Damned near, but not quite.

There were more horses and grooms than mages and the magical distortion lifted just enough for me to sense Tam through our bond, muffled though his presence was—and for Sarad Nukpana to sense me. That was fine; it wasn't like I was trying to hide. He knew I was following him.

Mychael's presence suddenly flared strong and clear. Then I spotted him. He and Vegard were quickly coming down the stairs leading from the building's second story down into the stable yard. Nachtmagus Vidor Kalta was close behind them.

Uniformed Guardians were covering doorways and exits, as were some men in plain clothes who didn't look any less military or deadly. Any spell let loose in here could ricochet and kill who knew how many. Mychael said something to one of his men as he strode past, and the man sprinted to where a uniformed Guardian stood. The Guardian nodded to a man in a window across the courtyard, and the signal was passed on from there. I didn't know what the signal was or what Mychael had told them to do.

He was keeping it from me.

I knew why, but that didn't mean I had to like it. I didn't, not one bit. Mychael had to have seen or heard what I did in the quad, and like Justinius, he couldn't take the chance that I wasn't in complete control of myself.

Or because of Nukpana's possession of Tam, had the goblin managed to tap the Saghred—and me?

Laughter welled up in my mind, mocking, derisive. *"No one trusts you anymore, little seeker. Like Tamnais, your hours are numbered."*

Then Nukpana's presence vanished, suddenly and completely.

The bastard was making his move.

I had to tell Mychael. Nukpana might still be able to hear every word, which was fine with me. The goblin certainly knew his own plans. *"Nukpana's going to leave Tam's body, infest yours, go to the citadel, and steal the Saghred."* Short, sweet, and supremely scary.

Precious seconds ticked by in silence. Dammit. Come on, Mychael. Answer me.

"How long?" Mychael asked.

Huh? *"How long, what?"*

"How long has Nukpana been in Tam's body?"

"An hour at the most."

"Good." Then all presence of him vanished from my mind, too. Mychael had plans of his own and didn't want the goblin listening in.

Or maybe me, either.

I scowled. "Is Mychael talking to you?" I asked Justinius. The question came out more like a snap, definitely sharper than was wise considering the man might be toying with the idea of my annihilation.

The old man grinned impishly. "The boy likes to keep his thoughts to himself when he's about to ruin some asshole's good time. Don't take it personally."

"So you're not planning to exterminate me?"

"And miss watching you rip Sarad Nukpana a new one once we get him out of Tam's body? No, girl. I'm long overdue for some fun."

Then a lot of things happened.

Shouts, the screams of panicked horses, and the hollow thumps and whistles of crossbow bolts.

Shooting. I couldn't believe it; the Guardians were shooting at them. Surely Mychael had told them not to hurt Tam. My eyes tried to look everywhere at once. Mychael was nowhere to be seen. I swore and ran for the main gate. I heard the whistle of the bolt a split second before I flattened myself against the gatehouse to avoid being tacked there like a bug to a board.

Khrynsani.

So much for where the ones chasing us down the tunnel had gone. But there were definitely more than four keeping the Guardians at bay. Looked like Ghalfari had arranged some manpower to cover his escape.

They were firing on the Guardians, and Mychael's boys were letting them have it with the same and more.

Fire was the Guardians' weapon of choice and magic was its fuel. A Khrynsani timed his shot wrong and the next instant a thin shaft of blue fire punched a hole through him as clean as a lance. The fire didn't go out but continued to spread and consume until the goblin was a dark stain on the cobblestone street.

Two other Khrynsani went up in flames exactly the same way, but the others kept firing crossbows and throwing red flaming spheres. The goblins were outnumbered and outmagicked, but they didn't retreat one step.

It was a suicide attack. The crazed bastards were dying as a distraction so Nukpana and Ghalfari could escape.

"Step aside," Justinius told me calmly.

I did. I had no problem with that. The old man was aiming for Khrynsani guards.

I wanted their bosses.

Justinius chose a target, pointed at it, and a fiery needle of molten silver shot from the tip of his finger, passing completely through a goblin in the act of summoning a red ball of flame. He raised his other hand, palm out, and with a shaft of white fire, vaporized two Khrynsani who had the poor judgment to shoot at him. I didn't stick around to watch the old man have his fun; I had my own pair of goblin targets.

The coachmen with the bad luck to have high-strung horses had all they could handle just keeping their teams from bolting. If you asked me, the horses had the right idea. I darted among the coaches, following Nukpana's trail while trying to keep myself from being trampled by terrified horses.

A surprised shout turned into a pained scream as a coachman went flying over the top of the coach parked next to his.

I bared my teeth in a savage grin. Found them.

Janos Ghalfari quickly climbed into the now-empty coachman's seat, then stared directly at me.

Oh crap.

With a wave of his hand, the horses around me erupted into terrified screams. Diving under the coach next to me was all that kept me from being pounded into cobblestone paste by rearing and thrashing hooves. I saw the door of Ghalfari's coach open and Tam's boots step up and inside. Two more pair of boots, probably worn by Khrynsani guards, jumped in after him.

Dammit.

"Raine!"

It was Mychael. A real shout, not mindspeak. I rolled out from between the wheels of the coach I was under and scrambled to my feet.

Mychael leapt onto the driver's bench of a coach near the

one Ghalfari had taken, his crossbow slung across his back. I threw together some shields and ran toward Mychael, ducking, weaving, and dodging, but mostly trusting my magic to deflect anything a terrified horse could hit me with.

I was nothing short of stunned when I reached the coach with all my pieces and parts intact. Then I saw the thin metal step to the driver's bench and stopped cold. The freaking thing was chest-high on me. Who the hell drove these things? Giants? Mychael held the team's reins easily in one hand and leaned over the side—way over the side—and grabbed my arm right above the elbow.

I just looked up at him. "You're kidding."

Mychael's reply was a grin and a pull that lifted me off my feet and landed me on the seat beside him. Impressive.

Ghalfari's coach had just turned onto the street. Hope surged through me. We could catch them; I knew we could. We had to. I had no idea in hell what we were going to do when we did, but I'd figure it out on the way or deal with it when it happened.

The axle springs creaked and our coach lurched to one side. I turned to see Vegard getting inside on the heels of Vidor Kalta's black robes.

"You need ballast, sir," Vegard called from inside. "Just tell us which side you need us on."

I felt the blood drain from my face. Ballast?

Below the bench, four sleekly muscled black horses pulled hard at the reins, eager to go. The coach was covered in ebony enamel that virtually gleamed. Dustless. Pristine.

I gripped the bar on the side of the bench and held on. "Nice ride," I managed. "Whose—"

Mychael flashed a fierce smile and snapped the reins. "Carnades."

I hung on for dear life.

There was a tilted metal footrest for the driver to brace his boots on, and I was definitely bracing mine. Before now, I thought my experience with coaches had been pretty extensive: I'd fought inside a coach, clung to the back of a coach, damn near been thrown under a coach, but I'd never been on the driver's bench going at a speed that was so far beyond insane it was ridiculous.

That was Janos Ghalfari's fault, not Mychael's. The goblin set the speed; Mychael was simply hell-bent on catching him.

We reached a smoother patch of street and my teeth stopped knocking together long enough to speak. "You stole Carnades's coach."

Mychael gave me a crooked smile. "Appropriated. In pursuit of wanted felons."

"There were other coaches."

His smile broadened into a grin. "Yes, there were. But Carnades has some of the fastest horses on the island."

"Plus you taking them would piss him off."

"That, too."

When Ghalfari and Mychael took the first corner, both coaches' wheels stayed on the street where they belonged. But when Ghalfari took the next corner sharp—and on two wheels—the need for movable ballast became all too apparent.

Oh crap.

"Vegard!" I shouted. "Right side!"

He and Vidor moved and our coach's wheels stayed on the street. Disaster averted. At least until the next time Ghalfari turned.

The good thing about coaches and horses was that pedestrians could hear the hooves and wheels coming and get the hell out of the way. It was late morning; the streets should have been filled with people going about their business. A few people were on the sidewalks; most watched the coaches thunder past from the safety of shop and office windows. I figured that the streetlamps flashing with bright blue lights had everything to do with it.

"The lights warn citizens to take cover," Mychael told me. "Justinius would have had them activated." Now that we were away from the Conclave complex, Mychael could scoop up my thoughts like dice off a table.

That meant he picked up the word I thought loud and clear when one of the Khrynsani threw open a small door on the back of Ghalfari's coach and hurled a red fireball at us.

I didn't think; I just reacted.

I threw up a shield in front of me and Mychael, and neatly deflected the fireball. My next deflection wasn't so neat and a signpost on the street corner burst into flames. Oops. Any people left on the street promptly dived for cover.

The Khrynsani grinned in a flash of fangs as red flame spun over his hand. His eyes were fixed on somewhere out in front of us, down low. The fireball became a solid sphere and he aimed.

At our horses. The bastard was going to torch our horses.

I gritted my teeth pushed my shield out in front of the lead team, one hand still gripping the handrail, the other extended palm out, struggling to hold the shield in place. Keeping a shield steady while I ran was one thing; doing the same in front of four racing horses was virtually impossible. If the shield touched them, they'd spook. If they saw that fire coming at their faces, they'd definitely spook.

I felt Mychael's will combine with mine and the shield darkened. The horses could still see to run, but any fireballs coming at them would just look like a ball, not horse-terrifying fire.

"Vegard!" Mychael called.

"I'm on it, sir."

I felt a surge of power from behind me. I glanced over my shoulder and Vegard was half out of the window, his eyes intent, silently mouthing something I hoped the fireball-throwing goblin wasn't going to like, or better still, wouldn't survive. I felt a tug and a sharp yank from Vegard as the goblin came flying out of the back window of that coach like he'd been jerked out by a giant hand. The goblin slammed into a metal lamppost with a hollow clang.

Beautiful.

"Wagon ahead!" Vegard shouted.

Oh no.

One man, one horse, and a cart loaded with what looked like firewood.

And Janos Ghalfari was going to run right over them.

The man saw the coach bearing down on him and desperately pulled the horse's lead, trying to get him to move. The horse reared, dumping the logs into the street. The man and horse got clear just in time. Ghalfari's horses jumped or dodged the logs.

The coach wasn't nearly as nimble.

The right front wheel hit one of the smaller logs and the coach lurched sharply to the side, enough to knock around anyone inside, but not enough to turn the coach over.

The next log was much bigger.

Everything seemed to go into slow motion. Ghalfari's coach flipped over on its side, sliding along the street in a spray of sparks. Janos Ghalfari was thrown to the curb and lay there unmoving. Mychael pulled back on the reins as hard as he could to stop our horses from slamming into the overturned coach.

And Tam.

The panicked horses were still trying to pull the wrecked coach. A moment later there was a sharp crack of breaking wood and the horses were running loose down the street, dragging their rigging behind them.

"Carnades's driver keeps a crossbow under the seat," Mychael told me. He pulled back the coach's break handle and leapt down.

I quickly groped around under the bench and found it, along with a small quarrel of bolts. It wasn't big; it didn't need to be. I was familiar with the model. Medium range, maximum damage. It was built for persuading bandits that robbing you would be a truly bad idea.

Or for convincing Sarad Nukpana to get the hell out of Tam's body.

I jumped down from the bench, crossbow trained on the open coach door. Vegard and Vidor Kalta were already out. Vegard's axe was in his hands and glowing. Vidor was just glowing.

Shields, right. Way to get yourself killed, Raine. Why don't you walk around naked, too, while you're at it? I got my shields up and around me where they belonged.

"The guard's dead," Mychael called.

"Nukpana?" I moved closer, bow loaded and held ready.

"Not here."

"I saw Tam get in," I insisted.

My skin prickled on the back of my neck. Mychael's expression said he felt the same thing.

The bastard was using a negating spell and full veil. I moved protectively in front of Mychael.

Nukpana/Tam materialized on the other side of the coach. Full shields, full power. Incredible power. There wasn't a scratch on him. Our bows were worthless and so was our magic.

Nukpana/Tam's smile was bright and beautiful. "Now that we're all here, may I propose a trade?"

Chapter 23

Mychael smoothly sidestepped me, leaving nothing between him and Nukpana/Tam but about twenty feet of open space.

A lot of damage could be done in twenty feet. I didn't know how fast Nukpana could lunge out of Tam and into Mychael— or if he could even do it at all through Mychael's shields— but I wasn't about to let anybody find out. Vidor Kalta might know, but his attention was on examining Janos Ghalfari's crumpled body.

Nukpana/Tam didn't even spare a glance for his own family. "I take it my dear uncle did not survive his folly."

Vidor stood from his examination. "Broken neck," he declared with cool, clinical detachment. "There appear to be other injuries, but it was the neck that killed him."

I risked a look over to where Ghalfari lay, his head twisted at an impossible angle, his lifeless black eyes staring up at the sky. So much for him having ultimate power over the dead. Good to know that Nachtmagus Janos Ghalfari could do something stupid and get himself killed and stay that way just like the rest of us.

Though lately dead didn't mean gone.

"Where's his soul?" I quickly asked Vidor.

"Dissipated," he assured me. "And to answer your next question, I have no sense of him anywhere in the immediate vicinity."

"Bring him back, Nachtmagus," Nukpana/Tam snapped.

"As I just explained, his soul has fled his body." From the

annoyed clip of his words, it was obvious that Vidor didn't like repeating himself, even to an almost demigod. "Janos Ghalfari was notorious for abusing his gift." The slightest of smiles creased Vidor's thin lips. "Perhaps he feared repercussions."

Nukpana/Tam's lips twisted in a sneer. "From whom?"

"From *what*. Reapers collect the dead, and they do not tolerate mortals who abuse souls—particularly if that mortal is a nachtmagus who should know better." Vidor's tone held a hint of satisfaction. "I don't believe your uncle was anxious to, as they say, pay the piper."

Nukpana/Tam's turned his fury on Mychael. "My uncle lies dead in the gutter like an animal because of your interference. I hope you enjoyed enforcing the law—it will be your last time carrying the burden of morality for us all."

"If you're through with the melodrama, you're wasting our time." Mychael's hands were glowing with a white light, quickly becoming brighter until I couldn't look directly at them.

Nukpana/Tam took two steps forward, his boots tapping sharply on the cobbles. "I agree. Time is of the essence."

The air around Mychael crackled with magic, lethal yet perfectly controlled. "Release Tam. Now."

"I have every intention of doing so." Nukpana/Tam flashed a crooked grin, and the sight of it twisted like a knife in my gut. How many times had Tam given me that same grin, mischievous and playful? Sarad Nukpana's perverse use of it now was sickening.

"Releasing Tamnais is half of the trade that I propose," Nukpana/Tam continued. "Surrender yourself to me and I shall leave Tamnais's body unharmed."

"So you can stroll into the citadel and steal the Saghred," I said.

Mychael's hands grew even brighter and he never took his eyes off of Nukpana/Tam. "The archmagus and my officers know not to let me into the citadel until they're certain I'm not infected by you."

"Infected?" Nukpana/Tam laughed, a short bark. "You make it sound like a disease."

"Parasite is more like it," I hissed.

The goblin chuckled darkly. "Poor Tamnais isn't having a good week, and thanks to the paladin, I'm afraid it's only going to get worse. Mychael's arrangements have left me with no choice but to remain where I am. Tamnais's imprisonment will become permanent—and the fault for his fate rests solely on the two of you."

I'd heard enough, more than enough. I raised my crossbow.

"Yes, kill Tamnais. If you don't kill him now, little seeker, Carnades Silvanus will have enough evidence to execute him tomorrow. The elf mage has been giving the two of you credit for my handiwork. Before this day is over, Tamnais will prove his suspicions correct. Carnades is most eager to see an umi'atsu bond at work, and I'm going to show it to him." His tone became softer, almost compassionate. "However, I do not have to tell Carnades Silvanus your secret. You do not have to take his petty insults, tolerate his feeble attempts to ensnare and imprison you. And make no mistake, compared to your power, his attempts are feeble. You know this—and yet you still fear it." Nukpana's voice became Tam's voice, his words soothing reassurance. "You need not fear your power. You can eliminate the Carnades Silvanuses of the world, the Taltek Balmorlans. No one like them can or will ever harm you or those you love again. Is that not what you desire above all else?"

I wanted it to be true. I wanted it to be Tam. But it wasn't. It was all lies and illusions, trickery of the mind, temptation with the one thing I desperately wanted. The Saghred had been tempting me from day one. It knew what I wanted and had given me the power to do it. To protect myself, my family, my friends. The Saghred would give me everything I needed to keep them safe and more. Much more. All I had to do was take the power, use it—and then feed the stone to replenish it.

Feed the Saghred. Sacrifice lives, imprison souls.

I didn't want to die or watch the people I cared for die. But I would not take the lives of others, the lives of innocents, to keep them safe. I would rather die first.

Mychael and Tam would rather die first.

No deal, goblin.

"Let me guess," I said. "All this and more is mine if I agree to be your puppet."

"Not a puppet; a partner. With the power we will wield, we could defeat Death itself."

"Your partner in death and destruction."

I heard the smile in his voice. "Only if certain governments are willful and do not wish to negotiate."

"You mean unless they submit to you."

"To us." He turned the words into a caress.

"Partners have to want the same thing." I'd made my decision; now all I had to do was live through the consequences. I knew they weren't going to be pretty. "The only thing I want you to do is go to hell."

"You reject my offer," Nukpana said quietly. "You cannot say that I did not give you a compassionate way out. Carnades Silvanus is in the citadel now, is he not, Mychael?"

"Carnades hates Tam's guts," I said. "What makes you think he'll let you within a hundred yards of him?"

"I thought I would invite you to assist me."

"When Hell grows icicles."

His voice mimicked the same words at the same instant that I said them. I had no idea what that implied, but it couldn't be good.

"No, Raine. I don't believe you will like assisting me at all; in fact, it may be rather painful for someone very close to you. My apologies in advance."

Vegard screamed.

Sarad Nukpana extended his hand in the air before him, his fingers slowly tightening and twisting, never taking his black eyes from my face.

Vegard clutched his chest and fell to his knees in the street, his screams catching in his throat, each rattling breath an agony.

I heard another scream, raw-throated with rage. It was me. I snapped the crossbow up to my shoulder to fire.

"I have your guard dog's life in my hands," Nukpana said softly. "I could kill him now; crush his heart as easily as ripe fruit." Softness twisted into a snarl. "Mychael, take one more step and I will squeeze his heart to a pulp and toss his body into the gutter beside my uncle. Tell your men to stay back." His fist tightened and Vegard screamed again. "If they move, my hand moves—and your man dies." There was a hesitation and the sound of retreating men from behind me. "Very good, Mychael," Nukpana murmured. "You're learning. I was beginning to believe it wasn't possible. Now have them move back even farther. This is between the three of us; no one else needs to be involved."

"Raine?"

Tam?

I kept my eyes on Nukpana, and tried to keep my breathing steady. I didn't know how Tam could talk to me in my mind when Nukpana couldn't, but now wasn't the time to ask questions.

Tam's contact was a featherlight touch on the edge of my consciousness, so quiet it barely registered. "Raine. Listen to me . . . I need your help."

"How can—"

Tam didn't answer me with words, but with a sensation—the smooth wooden stock of the crossbow in my hands.

Loaded, aimed, and ready to shoot. All I had to do was pull the trigger.

Tam was telling me to kill him.

No. No way in hell or anywhere else.

Sarad Nukpana's phantom hand still held Vegard's heart, and I dimly heard the goblin talking to Mychael. "Five levels down, third containment room on the left, buried in a spellbound lead casket in the right corner of the room. Is that not correct?"

Mychael didn't answer him; he didn't need to. Nukpana was right and he knew it.

"The spellbound iron casket is to keep anyone from finding it and a feeble attempt to contain it," Nukpana continued. "Cold iron to contain magic. Primitive. Your spellweavers truly are desperate."

Mychael's body was glowing almost as brightly as his hands. "You're not getting anywhere near the citadel."

"Oh, but I am. Raine won't stand by and watch me kill her guard dog. She's become attached to it. Put down the bow, Raine. Come to me and he lives. Refuse me, and well . . ." Nukpana viciously twisted his hand, and Vegard collapsed onto the street, his boots moving weakly against the cobblestones.

"Stop it!" I screamed.

"Lower the crossbow, Raine."

I hesitated and then did what he said. Nukpana unclenched his fist, and Vegard groaned, his breathing ragged, dragging air into his tortured lungs.

"I kept my end of the bargain, little seeker."

"Raine, no!" Mychael's voice rolled over me in a wave of sound; the intensity almost pulling me under. It was his spellsinger voice. He'd force me to stay put if he had to.

"I don't need to dig up the Saghred or open the box," Nukpana said. "I can simply wipe the citadel from the face of the earth with the Saghred's strength and my will." His black eyes glittered. "The stone wants out; it will do everything I ask if I promise to set it free."

But he'd have to kill me first.

Tam spoke, low and urgent. *"Raine, lower Nukpana's shields . . . The three of us . . . you, me, and Mychael . . . together we can do it."*

And a crossbow bolt through Tam's heart would force Sarad Nukpana to flee Tam's body or die along with him.

The rest of Tam's plan came to me in a flash of thought.

It was a plan with a lot of ifs with entirely too much at stake and no guarantee that any of it would work or even be possible. But if Sarad Nukpana controlled the Saghred, Tam would be a prisoner inside his own body with Nukpana in complete control—and to the thousands or even millions that Sarad Nukpana would go on to conquer, enslave, kill, or sacrifice to the Saghred, it would be Tamnais Nathrach who would be held responsible, reviled, and hunted.

And Tam would be helpless to stop any of it.

This wasn't my decision to make; it was Tam's. He'd made it and I owed it to him to do everything in my power to help him.

I tightened my grip on the crossbow until the wood creaked under my white-knuckled hands.

One chance, one shot, no mistakes.

Suddenly Mychael was standing next to me, his body touching mine. Our magic quickly flowed back and forth between us, merging, strengthening, communicating—lightning quick, whisper quiet.

I wasn't the only one Tam had been talking to.

Nukpana/Tam laughed and extended his hand to me. "The fair lady is no longer yours, Mychael. I released her guard dog; now she will surrender to me or I will finish what I started."

To Sarad Nukpana, we were little things to be toyed with, tormented, and crushed at his leisure.

I had news for the son of a bitch—little things mattered.

And when you were working yourself up to destroy a fortress and thought you were an indestructible demigod, shields became a little thing.

Mychael's hand in mine connected him directly to me, and our umi'atsu bond with Tam completed our circle. Sarad Nukpana might have been inside of Tam, but it was Tam's body, Tam's muscles.

And Tam's will. Combined with Mychael's strength and my connection to the two of them, we had access to Sarad Nukpana's shields from the inside and out.

I wanted to yank the bastard's shields down around his ankles, but Mychael and Tam had a better method that was just as quick as mine. When those shields failed, I would have a split second, probably less, to put that slender bolt through Tam's heart. I couldn't hesitate; I sure as hell couldn't miss.

I didn't want to pull that trigger; I didn't want to kill Tam. His words from a few days ago came to me and my vision blurred with tears: *If you hesitate, you're worse than dead and you know it*—finish him. *No hesitation, no mercy.*

Mychael held his own crossbow low but at the ready. He knew what I was thinking, what I felt.

"Raine, I'll do it."

I clenched my jaw against any more tears. My eyes had to be clear for this.

"Mine," I told Mychael.

Mychael didn't take his eyes off of his target, but his quiet response came in my mind. *"Do it."*

"Am I to believe you would shoot down your precious Tamnais in cold blood?" Nukpana/Tam spoke in a perverse mixture of voices: Nukpana, Muralin, and some others that I didn't recognize.

Tam wasn't one of them.

"No, I'm going to kill you and what's left of Rudra Muralin."

As quick as thought, the bottom dropped out of Mychael's magic and it felt like the street was being sucked downward into a vortex of power and dragging us with it. Mychael's hand tightened around my waist and I let him draw on my magic. We weren't at the center of the vortex; our shields weren't being drained from beneath our feet.

Sarad Nukpana's were.

His shields buckled and failed, and Nukpana/Tam's face blanched in sudden realization and panic. Sarad Nukpana couldn't move at all. A smile—Tam's smile—slowly curled his lips at the corners.

"You didn't mean for that to happen, did you?" Mychael asked Nukpana. "Who's the prisoner now?"

In a single blink, the solid black orbs became Tam's eyes, not Sarad Nukpana's.

His eyes were on mine, beseeching. "Now, Raine. Kill me. *Please.*"

I snapped the crossbow up to my shoulder. *"Forgive me."* My thought carried to Tam—and to Sarad Nukpana.

"Now!" came Tam's shout in my mind.

I squeezed the trigger and the bolt flew. And so did Sarad Nukpana, abandoning Tam's body the instant after impact. He knew Tam would be dead before he hit the street.

I felt Tam die.

My breath froze in my throat. Our umi'atsu bond pulled at me, stretching the distance between us, between life and death, becoming thinner and thinner until it snapped. The psychic recoil was like a monstrous whiplash across my entire body.

"Shields up!" Mychael shouted to his men, and pulled me to him, surrounding me with a protective, white nimbus.

A scream like a hundred banshees, a roar of fury and disbelief, shook the very air around us. A dark mist circled us, a bodiless specter. Then it suddenly vanished.

It wasn't gone. Sarad Nukpana definitely wasn't gone. The bastard wasn't going to give up his prize that easily. He was a specter; he knew how to hide.

Mychael clutched my hand in his, keeping his shields around us both, and ran for Tam's body now lying motionless in the street, my bolt protruding from his chest.

"Vidor!" Mychael shouted.

The nachtmagus was there a moment later, one hand on Tam's chest, the other on his forehead.

One of Mychael's officers took command, shouting orders, and we were surrounded by fully shielded Guardians, their backs turned toward us, standing shoulder-to-shoulder, their weapons glowing with battle magic, ready and waiting to be unleashed.

No one could see between or around them. No one could see what we were doing.

Tam was dead.

If the plan worked, he wouldn't be that way for long.

Mychael was keeping the blood in Tam's body, using his healer's magic to stop the bleeding, begin to repair the damage. He couldn't do it instantly, far from it. It would take hours, days—if it could even be done at all. Mychael was the best, but he could only do so much. He snapped rapid-fire orders: a cloak or blanket, a stretcher, a room nearby with a bed, and most of all, more healers. And all of it now.

Vidor Kalta was keeping Tam's soul in his body while Mychael worked.

I had another soul to attend to.

Sarad Nukpana was still here. He had to find another host body or he would lose everything he'd tortured and murdered for. If he found another body, we would be going through this all over again.

"Raine!" came a bellow from outside the wall of armored bodies.

It was Vegard. Dear God, the man was on his feet. The Guardians wisely made a hole for my bodyguard.

I ran to him. "Vegard, you shouldn't be—"

"Up? Walking? Alive?"

"Yes."

I ducked my head under Vegard's left arm, grabbed his wrist, and pulled his arm around my shoulders, my right arm tight around his waist. I knew I was nothing more than a crutch; if the big Guardian fell, we were both going down. I pushed our way through the protective circle of Guardians. I didn't want Mychael to hear or know what I was about to do. Yes, we were bonded, but hopefully he was too busy to notice me right now.

Vegard's breath hissed in and out through his teeth. "Damn, it hurts. Ever been hit in the chest . . . with a war hammer?"

"Can't say I have."

He groaned and sucked in a halfway decent breath. "This is . . . what it feels like."

"Vegard, more healers are on the way. You should—"

"Find that goblin son of a bitch," he rasped.

My eyes stung with tears of gratitude. If I'd been tall enough, I'd have kissed him.

"Nukpana's still here. I can't see or sense him, but the bastard's here." I felt Vegard sway, and tightened my grip. "I can do this by my—"

"No!" Vegard's eyes were blazing. "His ass is mine."

I tried to swallow, but my mouth was bone-dry. "If he runs, he loses everything. He needs another host body." I looked back toward Tam's motionless body and bit back a sob. "We're not going through this shit again," I snarled.

Vegard smiled, fierce and wolfish. "Damn straight we're not."

"I promised that you'd be at my side when the big trouble finally caught up to me."

"Yes, ma'am, you did." I knew that whatever I asked, he would do without hesitation.

"I know a way to find Nukpana and take the bastard out once and for all—"

Vegard knew what I meant. "Reapers."

I nodded. "But they might want me worse than they want him. I don't know if there's anything I can do to stop them if they do—"

"And you made me a promise that I'd be with you."

"Yes, I did. You still want it?"

His expression was resolute. "I'm not leaving."

"Thank you, Vegard."

I was taking the chance that a black mage who had tortured and sucked the life out of who knew how many people, who had stolen, abused, and manipulated the souls of the living and the dead, would be more hated than me. I'd just had the piss-poor luck to be in the wrong place at the wrong time and have the Saghred bond to me. Yes, it was full of imprisoned souls, but I wasn't the one who'd done the imprisoning. In a way, I was the rock's prisoner, too.

I was going to make Death an offer that he hopefully wouldn't refuse.

The Reapers were here, nearby. I could feel them. The death of a nachtmagus of Ghalfari's power had probably drawn them in like a lodestone to true north.

So would the Saghred.

I let the power of the stone flare through me. I knew I was probably ringing a dinner bell, but I had no choice.

I felt them coming and did nothing to stop them. Not that I could, or wanted to. Sometimes Death's minions were downright welcome.

The Reaper rose straight through the cobblestones at my side as from the depths of Hell itself. I could see it, and so could everyone else. It was high noon, bright as a day got, and the damned thing was solid.

There wasn't a swarm of Reapers. There was only one. A really big one. Taller than Vegard.

The one I'd punched at Markus's house.

I looked up at the towering mass of tendrils.

I was so going to die.

It was the one Vidor Kalta said was strong enough now to take the living, thanks to my life force I'd fed it when I hit it. And I'd punched it as hard as I could. I didn't know if Reapers held grudges, but I couldn't imagine it being happy about something like that—then again, maybe it was.

It just floated there. I'd say it was watching me, but Reapers didn't have eyes, so I had no idea what it was waiting on, but at least it was keeping its tendrils to itself.

The Reaper didn't move, but Sarad Nukpana's specter sure did. The bastard had been using a veiling spell floating above where Mychael and Vidor worked frantically to save Tam, waiting for his chance.

I had one imploring word for the Reaper. "Please."

The thing just floated there.

Sweeten the pot, Raine. "Help me and I'll help you."

"Ma'am, no!"

I tightened my grip on Vegard's wrist, asking him not to interfere.

All of my attention had to be on the Reaper floating not three feet in front of me. It knew what I was offering. Souls from the Saghred. Souls who wanted to leave, to move on. The Reaper could have taken me there, taken all the souls it wanted and me along with it.

Instead I swear it inclined its head—or where its head should have been—in gratitude. Maybe even respect.

I saw a flash of movement out of the corner of my eye. It wasn't Sarad Nukpana.

It was worse, the kind of worse that made you want to scream yourself hoarse.

Janos Ghalfari was standing across the street, smiling at me, his head twisted at an impossible angle. He raised his hands and turned his head so it faced the right way.

It didn't stay put. His head fell bonelessly to the side, lolling against his shoulder. I thought I was going to throw up.

Sarad Nukpana had decided to keep his soul in the family.

Janos Ghalfari's reanimated corpse turned and ran, faster than something dead and broken should have been able to. The Reaper snapped around, tendrils writhing like a nest of snakes, and took off in pursuit. Ghalfari's body glowed with blood-red light, so bright I had to close my eyes against it. A flash shone through my eyelids. I opened my eyes. Ghalfari had vanished, and all sense of the Reaper was gone.

Vegard sank to his knees in the street, taking me with him. I didn't try to keep us on our feet. I wanted Sarad Nukpana, but I wasn't stupid enough to go after a Reaper chasing a corpse.

Death would send his collector back for me soon enough.

Chapter 24

I sat next to Tam's bed and watched him sleep, watched the movement of his chest as it rose and fell with a deep, steady rhythm, listened to his quiet breathing.

Against all odds, Tam was alive. And unless I shot him again, he was going to stay that way.

Mychael was the best healer in the seven kingdoms, but he had worked on Tam to the point that he had needed a healer himself. No doubt during his career, he'd healed some horrific injuries.

Tam had been dead. You couldn't be any more horrifically injured than that.

Vidor Kalta had his hands full forcing Tam's soul to stay in his body. Apparently when you died your soul wanted to leave. Immediately. Tam's intention had been to live, but his soul had other ideas. Vidor had done the nachtmagus version of a wrestling match.

All while Mychael had been using every bit of healing skill he possessed to close the hole in Tam's heart and then get it beating again. Justinius Valerian told me later that it was nothing short of a miracle that Mychael didn't die in that street, too.

Mychael and Vidor Kalta had brought Tam back from the dead. If they weren't legends in their fields already, they were now.

Justinius's healer had taken care of Vegard. Last month, the old man had had a spellsong-induced heart attack courtesy of

Rudra Muralin. Vegard had pretty much the same thing from Sarad Nukpana. After nearly a week, today was his first day out of bed.

We were in the citadel, in rooms that were well warded and even better guarded. Justinius wasn't taking any chances. Though he didn't have to worry about Sarad Nukpana, Janos Ghalfari, or what or whoever the hell he was now.

The bastard had actually managed to get away from that Reaper. I had no clue how he'd done it. Maybe having consumed the souls of some of the blackest black mages in history taught Sarad Nukpana a nifty trick or two for dodging Death. Regardless, he'd left the island before an hour had passed, and just before Justinius Valerian could seal the harbor. We knew this because Phaelan and Uncle Ryn could find out things that the harbormaster, city watch, and Guardians would never get wind of. A goblin matching Janos Ghalfari's description had bought his way onto a Brenirian frigate headed for Mipor. He'd had a thick scarf tied tightly around his neck. The weather didn't warrant it, but a broken neck would have. It must have helped hold his head up. Though he would heal. With that much magic surging through his body, he'd heal and he'd do it fast. Normally Brenirians would be reluctant to take on a goblin passenger, but this one had paid in gold—pure goblin imperial. Mipor was in Rheskilia. Goblin territory. A safe haven for an undead goblin son of a bitch who had a ton of payback coming to him.

Though on the upside, maybe since the Reaper didn't fulfill its end of the bargain, it didn't expect me to keep mine.

Yeah, I wasn't holding my breath on that one, either. I kept expecting to have a chill that had nothing to do with cold and everything to do with Death's super-sized minion doing some heavy breathing down the back of my neck.

I wanted nothing more than to get rid of the Saghred and send the souls inside on their merry way, but there had to be a way to do that other than a Reaper using me for a soul straw.

Mychael was asleep on a couch against the far wall. He'd refused to leave Tam's room, even to sleep. But sleep would only be denied for so long.

Mychael's coppery hair gleamed in the faint light of the two table lamps burning on either side of Tam's bed. He was on his back; his hands lay relaxed and open on his flat stomach. Hands that had healed me from the brink of death, and brought Tam back from what lay beyond. I continued to watch him, careful not to move or make a sound. Mychael needed all of the sleep he could get. And like most healers—and warriors— the slightest noise would jolt them from a sound sleep, ready to take care of a patient, or take down an enemy.

A few strands of hair had fallen across Mychael's eyes and I had a nearly overwhelming urge to brush his hair back. Being Mychael, but also being a warrior, one of two things would happen: a kiss or an armlock. One would be welcome; the other wouldn't—though both would probably end up with me flat on my back on the floor with him on top of me. I smiled. That wouldn't be bad; in fact, that would be very good.

I looked at Tam, his long hair spilling over his pillows and down his bandaged chest. His loose-fitting shirt was open down the front for access to the bandages.

When I'd first met Tam, all I'd known was that he was a goblin with secrets piled on top of plots, and that he liked elven women—a lot.

None of that had changed, but everything else had.

He was still a dark mage and he always would be. And as long as I was linked to the Saghred, I was still a dark mage magnet, a temptation he could not surrender to. I knew that—and so did he. Though now he was one big step closer to being out of the Saghred's reach forever. When I'd shot him, at the moment of his death, our umi'atsu bond had been broken.

The Saghred couldn't get its hooks into him now.

I leaned back in the chair at his bedside, sighed, and ran my hand over my face.

"Nice shot," Tam murmured. His eyes were open, watching me. He actually looked rested and relaxed. My eyes felt bloodshot and I probably looked like hell.

I leaned forward and took one of his hands in mine.

It was warm, just like it should be. Tears welled up in my eyes, and I didn't try to stop them. "Hey, you stood still for me," I managed. "How could I possibly miss?" I paused, my throat tight. "I didn't want to kill you."

"You've been mad enough at me before to do it." A crooked grin played across his lips. "I thought I'd finally give you a chance. Imala stabbed me once. Why shouldn't you get to shoot me?"

I sniffed and tried a smile.

"Though that was one hell of a way to get a divorce," he said.

"A divorce?"

"The umi'atsu."

Mychael shifted on the couch, but surprisingly didn't wake up.

"He's been here almost the entire time," I told him.

"He's worried that I'll try to get out of bed and ruin his work."

"Good reason to stand guard, then."

Tam looked at Mychael for a long moment, his expression unreadable. "He's a good man."

I gazed at my sleeping paladin. "Yes, he is," I said softly.

"And an even better friend," Tam murmured. He pulled himself up on his pillows and hissed in pain.

That woke Mychael up.

His hair was tousled with sleep and his face was darkened with his morning beard. He took one look at me, grinned, and just shook his head. "Tam was a perfect patient until you showed up."

My smile was almost demure. "You know I never claimed to be a good influence."

Tam winced as he gingerly settled himself on the pillows. "Has Carnades gathered his lynch mob yet?" he asked Mychael.

I froze. "Lynch mob?"

Tam started to explain and Mychael held up his hand. "Save your strength. Carnades is claiming that Tam invited Sarad Nukpana's soul in."

Some things were just too freaking unbelievable for words, but I managed. "You have *got* to be kidding me."

"The middle of the street at high noon isn't exactly circumspect," Tam said. "There were a lot of people watching and I did put on quite the evil show."

"But you were possessed!"

"Carnades has always believed me to be as bad as Sarad Nukpana, if not worse. My actions in that street just confirmed what he's been trying to prove to everyone since I got here."

I turned to Mychael. "And let me guess, Carnades is claiming that you and Vidor Kalta are Tam's evil minions because you saved his life."

"Essentially."

"So how did he manage to twist the fact that I killed Tam?"

"You took the law into your own hands and deprived the Seat of Twelve their due process."

"Let me get this straight: he's pissed at *me* because *he* didn't get to kill Tam."

"Exactly."

"Mychael, tell me those guards outside are to protect Tam, and not because he's been arrested again."

"He hasn't been arrested," Mychael assured me. "Nor will he be."

"And just who is going to pull off that feat?"

"I am," Tam said. "By pulling the legal rug right out from underneath Carnades or anyone else who cares to challenge me." He paused uncomfortably. "Sarad Nukpana possessed my body for nearly three hours. That included every soul Sarad absorbed trying to regenerate himself."

"General Daman Aratus, two ancient goblin black mages, and Rudra Muralin."

Tam nodded. "There were others as well, poor bastards who Sarad managed to snatch off the streets to sustain himself until he was strong enough to go after bigger game. He absorbed all of their memories, knowledge, and skills. Sarad used my mind to function, my body to act."

I didn't need a reminder. I also didn't need to think about how close he came to getting away with everything, most of all what he'd done to Tam.

"He was in my mind—and I was in his," Tam said quietly. "Raine, I know Sarad Nukpana's plans and precisely how he intends to carry them out. Every step of the way."

"And now he's running home to share his plans and all of his newfound knowledge and power with his evil cohort, Sathrik Mal'Salin."

"Sarad will use the king only as long as it is convenient. Sathrik's crown and throne will be irrelevant once Nukpana puts his plans in motion. Sathrik will be a figurehead king, or he'll be dead. Once he realizes that his former partner in crime has turned against him, Sathrik will go along, waiting for an opportunity to have Nukpana killed."

I snorted. "Like that's going to happen."

"You're right. It won't. Sathrik will be a puppet or he'll be dead, and the choice won't be his to make. When Sarad no longer needs him, he'll kill him. He can't afford to let him live."

"King Sarad Nukpana does have a certain ring to it," I said, "and not a good one. But he doesn't have the Saghred. And he sure as hell isn't getting his hands on me. I'm not going anywhere near Rheskilia."

"You won't need to," Mychael said quietly.

"I don't like the sound of that."

"You shouldn't. Nukpana was only in direct contact with the Saghred through Tam and your umi'atsu bond for a short period of time."

"An hour, maybe a little more," Tam said. "But it was enough."

I knew I didn't want to hear this. "Enough for what?"

"You have only had direct contact with the Saghred on a few occasions," Mychael said, "and only for a few seconds each time. And each one of those times you fought that contact."

"Sarad didn't fight," Tam said. "He was absorbing power like a sponge. And with Rudra's knowledge, and the power of those two ancient mages, you can bet Sarad is going to make the most of everything he got."

"You retained the power that the Saghred gave you," Mychael said. "So will Sarad Nukpana."

The implication of what Nukpana was now capable of was staggering. "Even though he doesn't have the rock itself, he picked up plenty of new evil tricks, tricks he can't wait to take home and use."

Mychael nodded. "So destroying the Saghred has never been more important. If Nukpana wants to increase his power—and he will—he needs the Saghred itself. He's not on the island any longer to do it himself, but Tam tells me that there are some individuals in the goblin secret service who are more than up to the task."

I looked at him sharply. "Imala?"

"Imala is on our side," Tam assured me. "She's been here and we've talked." His lips became a thin line and his brow furrowed. I knew that expression only too well. It was the one that said he'd been wrong and he didn't want to admit it. "I don't approve of some of the choices Imala has made. Being stuck here in bed gave me a lot of time to think, and I've realized that I'm the last person who can stand in judgment of her."

"That still doesn't explain how you plan to pull the legal rug out from underneath Carnades."

Tam frowned. "It explains it all. What Imala said is true; I resigned my position at court, but Queen Glicara didn't accept my resignation. She was murdered before she could do so.

Imala knew who was responsible and why, so she immediately went through Glicara's royal papers and took anything that she felt might be advantageous to have in the future."

"Your resignation was one of them."

"Correct. With the document in her possession, it is as if it were never written."

"And you never resigned."

Tam nodded. "It's not unusual for a goblin noble to leave court for a time to avoid having a dagger planted between his or her shoulder blades."

"And Sathrik never officially stripped Tam of his rank and position," Mychael said. "Since Tam left the court voluntarily, he didn't deem it necessary."

"Too busy plotting evil." I looked at Tam for a long moment. "So you *are* still a duke and the chief mage for the House of Mal'Salin."

Tam inclined his head. It was the same way he'd always done it, but I noticed for the first time how regal it was.

"Diplomatic immunity," I said. "Carnades really can't touch you."

"No, he can't."

"Not unless he and Balmorlan want to start that war of theirs now," Mychael said. "And they're not ready. Neither are their allies. Unfortunately, neither is our queen or army."

I froze in place. "What do you mean 'unfortunately'? We don't want a war."

"No, we don't. However, Sarad Nukpana has the magical skill and force he needs now to start one. Plus he has all of the memories and knowledge of General Aratus. The elven forces would be crippled before first blood was spilt."

"And Sathrik doesn't give a damn about what our people want," Tam said. "He'll want to strike before the elves are ready. So we have to stop him before it goes any further."

"Stop him?" I asked quietly.

"Preemptive strike. The most successful battles are fought from the inside."

I couldn't believe my ears. "You're going back."

"Returning to Regor now would be suicide." Tam flashed a grin. "I've been dead once; it's not an experience I plan to repeat anytime soon."

"But you just said 'from the inside.'"

"With like-minded goblins and allies here on Mid. The island's neutrality makes it perfect for clandestine meetings."

I glanced at Mychael.

"Sathrik has openly threatened the Isle of Mid and our people unless we return Sarad Nukpana's body."

I had an unwanted flashback to Janos Ghalfari's reanimated corpse grinning at me. "We definitely don't want to gift wrap that thing and send it to Sathrik."

"No, we don't," Mychael agreed. "The Guardians are a peace-keeping force, and we *will* keep the peace whatever the means. We are also the keepers and protectors of the Saghred. Anyone who attempts to remove the stone from this island is fair game."

"I like the sound of that."

"Markus Sevelien likes it even better. And since it is in the best interests of both the elven and goblin peoples that the Saghred not fall into Sarad Nukpana's or King Sathrik's hands, Markus has requested a meeting with Imala Kalis to negotiate and reach certain agreements."

I looked at Tam. "And you're going to be smack-dab in the middle."

"I have a responsibility to my people—and to my son. A reign under Sathrik and Sarad would mean death, not only for the goblin people, but for elves and humans alike. Talon and others like him would be slaughtered or worse. It has to stop. Now. I will not stand by while others fight my battle. I not only know Sarad's plans; I know how he thinks. That makes me the best qualified to stop him."

I blew out my breath. "Okay, then. Besides me, Mychael, and Imala, who else has got your back?"

Tam went as still as a statue.

"Don't give me that look," I told him. "If this is anyone's battle, it's mine. I'm in it with you." I flashed a fierce grin. "You're not the only one who wants a piece of Sarad Nukpana."

"As to my allies, not everyone at the goblin court wants my head on a platter," Tam told me. "Many of them are from the old families, powerful and influential. Imala has been cultivating even more allies. And as Sathrik's behavior has grown increasingly erratic, even those publicly allied with him would change their allegiance if a better and stronger candidate presented himself."

I knew exactly where this was going. "Prince Chigaru Mal'Salin."

I didn't like the prince. It wasn't easy to forgive someone who had used Piaras as bait to kidnap me and then threatened him with torture to get me to find the Saghred for him. Somehow I didn't think his manners had improved any since then. The prince was cunning, manipulative, and ruthless, and conspiracies and plots were recreational activities. In other words, a Mal'Salin. But he could be reasoned with and he wasn't nuts. Those were two distinctions that his brother couldn't claim.

"What would Sathrik have to say about you impersonating his right-hand mage?" I asked Tam.

"Sathrik is presently without a right-hand mage."

I arched a brow. "He never gave Nukpana the job?"

"Sarad being the high priest of the Khrynsani would have been a conflict of interest—and too many powerful nobles would have objected. Sathrik couldn't risk it."

"And if Sathrik knew that legally you were still his chief mage?"

Tam smiled. "His Majesty would have a royal apoplexy."

"That'd be fun to watch."

"Yes, it would. Then he'd send every assassin he could hire, bribe, or blackmail after me."

I frowned. "How loyal are your dark mage friends?"

"What do you mean?"

"If Sathrik sends hired blades after you, any goblin who defends you is committing treason. Are they loyal to you or their own necks?"

Tam gave a short laugh. "They won't see why they can't do both."

"How about Talon?"

Mychael and Tam exchanged amused glances.

"What have you done to the kid?" Though if Talon hadn't gone running off, he wouldn't have gotten himself captured by Sarad Nukpana, Tam wouldn't have gone looking for his son, and Nukpana wouldn't have caught and possessed Tam.

And I wouldn't have had to kill Tam.

My fingers started curling into fists. "Let me rephrase that—what can *I* do to the kid?"

Tam's black eyes glittered mischievously. "At this very moment, Talon is being instructed that his actions, no matter how well intentioned, can have fatal consequences, and not only to him. He is also being encouraged to recognize the difference between right and wrong, or at least grow something that faintly resembles a conscience."

I grinned. "He's here in the citadel, isn't he?"

"With Piaras," Mychael confirmed. "Piaras's tutors are now Talon's tutors. Justinius and Ronan are helping."

I whistled. "I'll bet Talon doesn't consider any of it helpful."

"No, he doesn't," Tam said. "But it's needed. I've been teaching him how to fight, but he needs to learn more—and he needs more discipline than I can provide." He sighed, then drew in a slow breath. "When I look at Talon, I see myself at his age. He's coming into his full power entirely too fast, just like I did. I will not have him go down the dark path that I did. I thought I could handle it all myself, but I was wrong."

"Reining in and properly focusing impulsive young talent is what Guardians do best," Mychael said with a slight smile.

And it had taken more than reining in to keep Talon from following us the day we'd chased Tam/Nukpana in that coach.

Dad had more than had his hands full. From what I heard, it'd taken three good-sized Guardians, plus Piaras, to hold the kid down. Dad suspected something bad was going to happen to Tam, and knew that his son most definitely did not need to see it. Me shooting his father down in the street certainly qualified. Grateful didn't even begin to describe what I felt for those Guardians who'd essentially sat on Talon.

"Anyone that comes after me will also consider Talon a target." Tam's jaw clenched and his tone turned cold with anger. "And as a half-breed, Talon has no rights under goblin law. If he was caught, Sathrik could legally do anything with him that he wanted. I've asked Mychael and he has agreed to accept Talon as a provisional cadet. After three months of training, he'll be evaluated, and if he is deemed worthy, he'll be accepted as a full cadet."

I nodded in approval. "And he would be under Guardian protection and law."

"As a provisional cadet, he is now," Mychael said.

"Elves don't recognize his existence," Tam said. "Goblins despise him. This was the only legal step I could take to protect my son."

I leaned back in my chair. "Now that Talon's as safe as he can be, what exactly is it that you're going to do?"

Tam's smile was a baring of fangs. "It'll be like just another day on my old job: destroy an archenemy, depose a king, and put an exiled prince on the throne."

Chapter 25

Sarad Nukpana's body was in a crystal coffin woven with spells to keep it from being opened from the outside—or the inside.

Mychael wasn't taking any chances.

One of the spells inside the coffin was to preserve his corpse. The mortician who prepared the body and worked the spell called it "perpetual repose."

I called it creepy as hell.

Sarad Nukpana was still perfect, still darkly beautiful. He had a shadow of a smile on his face, like he knew something we didn't, something that was about to bite us all on our collective ass.

I had no doubt that he did.

The coffin was in a tower in the highest point of the citadel and at the farthest point from the Saghred. The stairs to the top could be revealed by a spell that only Mychael and Justinius knew. The circular room had one door, no windows, and was lit bright as day.

That had been my request.

Goblins didn't like bright light. I did. And for some irrational reason, I also liked knowing that Sarad Nukpana wasn't lying in the dark. Bad things happened in dark places. Sarad Nukpana was most definitely a bad thing.

I'd wanted the body destroyed and the ashes scattered to the winds in the far reaches of all seven kingdoms. That would get rid of Sarad Nukpana's body, but it wouldn't destroy him. His rotten soul was safe and secure in the body of his dearly departed uncle Janos. Janos Ghalfari's soul was long gone, so Nukpana had the house all to himself, so to speak. Just him and the souls of his closest allies—his own frat house of evil.

Two days ago, King Sathrik had sent Justinius Valerian a letter demanding that unless Nukpana's body was returned undamaged to Regor within the month, he would declare war against the Guardians, the Conclave, and the Isle of Mid, and come and get the body himself. Mychael and Justinius had no intention of returning Nukpana's body, but it never hurt to have an ace in the hole just in case. Hence the mortician's creepy reposing spell.

I'd gone to the tower room this morning. I had wanted . . . No, I had needed to see Sarad Nukpana's body for myself. Vegard had come with me. He'd become my most welcome shadow. He kept expecting that Reaper to come back to collect.

So did I.

But Reapers were eternal; I wasn't. With any luck, I'd be old and gray before it remembered my offer and came back. No, I didn't believe that, either. You knew you had too much bad crap in your life when Death's minion had become the least of your worries.

It was now early afternoon and I was back on the *Fortune*. Four more days had passed since Mychael had pronounced Tam fully healed—and Tam had announced that he was personally declaring war on Sathrik Mal'Salin and Sarad Nukpana.

"Hell, I'd be glad to haul the stiff back to Regor," Phaelan was saying, as he handed me the drink I'd desperately needed after viewing Sarad Nukpana's perpetually reposing corpse. "Things fall overboard at sea all the time." He flashed a grin. "Especially dead goblin psychos."

I remembered Nukpana's still lips with their all-knowing smile. "Define dead," I muttered.

Phaelan poured himself a whiskey. "By the way, Mago's on his way here."

I was in mid-swallow and almost choked. "Here? Is that good? For anybody?"

My cousin chuckled. "This island is teeming with weasel mages and politicians; how much more trouble can a weasel banker be?"

We both knew the answer to that one. But at least this weasel was related to us.

"Besides," Phaelan continued, "Mago is the hands-on type. He's set our plan in motion and has a person he can trust pulling the strings at the bank in D'Mai. Mago prefers to be as close to his mark as possible when an operation goes down." Phaelan raised his glass and drained it in one toss. "My brother takes great pride in his work."

I groaned. God help us all, and not just from conscientious weasel bankers.

The *Fortune* had been deemed to be the safest place to meet—or at least the most neutral and agreeable territory.

Markus Sevelien wanted to talk to Imala Kalis.

Markus had come over from the *Red Hawk* under cover of both darkness and tarp. There was a time and a place for Markus to let the world know that he was alive, but here and now wasn't it. My sometime employer would wait until his return from the dead would have the maximum benefit for him and the elf queen, and do the most damage to Taltek Balmorlan and his allies. I really wanted to see Balmorlan's face when that happened.

I could hear Markus and Mychael speaking in low voices from the next cabin. Eavesdropping wasn't necessary; I could hear every word, though not in the conventional sense. My mysterious bond with Mychael had become even stronger once my umi'atsu bond with Tam had been broken by that crossbow bolt.

Markus's clothes had been blown up along with his house. He and Phaelan were the same size, so my cousin had opened his considerable wardrobe to the chief of elven intelligence. Markus had arrived on board in an incredibly elegant black doublet and trouser ensemble. I would never have guessed that Phaelan had owned anything other than what a peacock would feel at home in.

Duke Markus Sevelien was dressing for the occasion.

Peace talks between the elven government and the hopefully soon-to-be goblin government.

Since Markus had been declared dead, he wasn't exactly the official representative of the elf queen, but that was fine since Imala was the representative of the goblin prince in exile.

But if everyone's plans came to fruition, these would be the first true and earnest peace talks between the elves and goblins in a couple of hundred years.

Markus and Imala had already agreed on one thing: the Guardians should continue to be the keepers and protectors of the Saghred. They had sworn to each other that they would leave the Saghred in peace.

If my plans came to fruition, the Saghred would be in pieces.

Imala Kalis arrived a few minutes later with only two guards. Trust is a beautiful thing; keeping a low profile is even better. Three goblins could be snuck on board without much trouble. Imala's regular entourage would have looked like a boarding party. Phaelan welcomed the head of the goblin secret service with a hand kiss that lingered a little too long and a gleam in his dark eyes that said he'd like nothing more than further exploration. I had to virtually kick my cousin out of his own cabin.

I wanted to talk to Imala alone.

"Could they wait outside the door?" I asked her, indicating her two bodyguards.

Imala kept her dark eyes on me, but spoke to the two heavily armed goblins. "Wait outside, please."

They went, the door closed, and it was just me and the lady who wanted Tam to help her overthrow a government. I knew

Tam had already made up his mind, but I still had a problem with that. A big one. Call me protective of my friends.

"Can I get you a drink?" I asked her. "Uncle Ryn sent over some port that he took off a royal frigate headed for Regor—and probably Sathrik's wine cellars. He and Markus didn't manage to drink it all."

Imala smiled faintly. "I would love a glass." She accepted it and took a sip. Then she sat quietly, her delicate fingers holding the even more delicate crystal. "Even if I'd wanted to, I couldn't force Tam to help," she said quietly. "I could only ask. The decision was his."

I had taken the chair across from Imala, my own posture a virtual mirror of hers. "Am I that obvious?"

"Yes."

"Good. Saves wasting time on small talk. I don't like what Tam wants to do; I don't like it at all . . . but it was his decision and he's made it, hasn't he?" I didn't bother to hide my sarcasm.

"Our people need him, Raine." She paused. "I need him."

"You don't like him, but you need him."

"Actually, I do like him. Even though he's stubborn, infuriating, and a few other things I don't care to mention." She took another sip. "Tam is also the best man for this job."

"A job that's going to use black magic to overthrow Sathrik and Sarad—"

Imala's dark eyes flashed. "No, Raine. I don't want Tam using black magic ever again. When I found out he was leaving court, I convinced him to go to my grandmother for help. Naturally, he didn't think he needed help or that he was in any danger, but I persisted and he eventually admitted that I was right."

"*You* convinced—"

Imala laughed. "So he made it sound like it was all his idea?"

"Pretty much."

She shrugged. "Regardless, he went, and once again the final decision was his. No one forces Tam to do anything he doesn't want to."

"You can say that again," I muttered.

"Now that Sarad Nukpana is no longer here, my grandmother and Prince Chigaru will be arriving within the week."

I blew out my breath through my nose.

"You don't trust any of us, do you?" Imala asked mildly.

"I trust Tam. As for the rest of you . . . well, I haven't exactly been given much reason to trust."

She sat in silence, watching me. "What if I trust you with something?"

I felt a release of magic, a small magic, a tiny glamour that had hidden a pair of dark goblin eyes.

Eyes now glittering with flecks of golden amber.

I just sat and stared. Imala Kalis was part elf.

"Who knows?" I asked.

"Aside from my grandmother, only Tam and one other."

Those were three people who Imala trusted with her life, four now counting me. If she were to be exposed, she would not only lose her position and standing at court; she would lose any and all rights, period. To many pure-blooded goblins, she would be no better than an animal—and she would be treated like one.

"Your trust honors me," I told her in formal Goblin.

A flicker of surprise lit her eyes, and Imala smiled warmly and inclined her head. "Thank you. There are many things I want to change in the goblin court—the perception of those like me is one of them."

"Like Talon."

Imala nodded. "There are more mixed breeds among my people than most will admit. There are many small glamours worn at court."

One corner of my lips curled in a conspiratorial grin. "And you're the head of the secret service. How did you survive long enough to get there?"

"I kept my eyes glamoured and my ears open." Her smile spread until her fangs were visible, fangs she'd probably used many times. "And it helps to know where the bodies are buried."

I bet she had helped put some of them there.

"So you've hidden your eyes, then plotted and schemed your way to the top of the ladder, and now you plan to overthrow your king."

Imala kept the smile and added a shrug. "It's a start."

"Ambitious, aren't you?"

"Protective of my people," she corrected me. "Sathrik wants war. Such a war is not in the best interests of my people, so Sathrik must go."

"And you're willing to risk your life to do this."

"I am."

"And now Tam is willing to risk his."

"That is what he tells me."

I took another sip of port, a big one. "I kill him, Mychael saves him, only to have Sathrik or Sarad Nukpana kill him again."

Imala leaned forward. "Tam survived for five years at Glicara's side, and contrary to what you may have heard, he did it mostly by using his considerable cunning and wits. Tam Nathrach is a brilliant tactician. Sathrik and Sarad wanted him out of the court for that very reason. They feared him then, and they fear him now. He is a very real danger to them and they know it."

"Only now Sarad Nukpana has turned himself into a demigod."

"You killed Tam and Sarad's soul was forced to flee. Sarad has made Janos Ghalfari's body his permanent home. So when he is killed inside Janos's body, his death will be permanent."

I smiled. "You said 'when,' not 'if,' he is killed."

Imala's smile was almost demure, but those gold-flecked eyes glittered in anticipation. "I am confident in my, and my people's, skills—and my own determination."

Like the prince she was determined to put on the goblin throne, Imala Kalis was shrewd, manipulative, ruthless, and plotting a coup was probably her idea of a fun night out, but damned if I wasn't starting to like her.

Imala drained the rest of her glass. "And as to what you were forced to do to Tam, you must set your guilt aside. If Tam had died in that street, you still would have saved him—from a fate far worse than any death. And for that you have my gratitude. I could not bear the thought of him—"

"You're thanking her for killing me," Tam drawled from the now-open door. "How very like you."

Imala arched a brow. "I believe in commending good work," she shot back. Then she half turned and winked at me.

I muffled a grin with my glass.

Tam stepped into the cabin, Mychael and Markus behind him. All I can say is that it was a good thing I had a firm grip on that glass, or it'd have been shattered on the floor.

Tam was wearing his formal court robes.

I guess if you're going to claim diplomatic immunity, you'd better dress the part. Tam's robes were a combination of velvet and raw black silk. They swept the floor but were slit up the sides to reveal Tam's trademark fitted leather trousers and boots. A demonologist friend of mine had once said that if you study demons for a living, it's healthy to be able to haul ass when you have to. I imagine the same was true for serving in the goblin court. Tam's long black hair fell in a wave down his back and was held back from his face by a silver circlet set with a single ruby. A silver chain of office was draped over his broad shoulders. Tam looked every inch a goblin duke and a chief mage to a king. I could imagine him standing next to a throne.

He belonged there.

My throat was suddenly tight. "Tam, the robes really suit you." It was all I could manage to say.

"I made sure Carnades got a good look at me this afternoon." Tam smiled, very slightly. "I think my wardrobe choices made the proper impression."

Mychael laughed. "I think I saw tiny flecks of foam at the corners of his mouth."

Imala and Markus were greeting each other not like adversaries, but as allies in the making. There was even that double-cheek-kissing thing—and not one fang was bared or dagger drawn. It was a stunning show of statesmanship.

The chief of elven intelligence and the head of the goblin secret service were chatting like old friends.

And they were doing their chatting on a pirate ship.

I smiled. Peace talks of questionable legality, to plan actions of dubious sanity, held on board a ship that wasn't welcome in any port anywhere.

It was perfect.

Though Markus and Imala could negotiate an alliance all they wanted to over stolen wine, still there were those like Carnades Silvanus and Taltek Balmorlan, elves whose hatred and greed blinded them to anything but the desire to destroy their enemies. Or goblins like Sathrik Mal'Salin and Sarad Nukpana, whose raw lust for power was insatiable.

Elves and goblins didn't need a stone of cataclysmic power—or an excuse—to slaughter each other. Dad had hidden the Saghred for hundreds of years, and wars went on just fine without it. Hate and greed and lust for power will always find a way. I had to find a way to destroy the Saghred.

And for my next trick, I was going to help put a Mal'Salin on the throne.

The lower hells must be freezing over.

Mychael and Tam had moved to stand on either side of me, and Tam was watching Imala and Markus with a mixture of pride and disbelief.

"We're watching history, you know," Mychael murmured.

I looked up at him with some disbelief of my own. "You realize that after we watch history, then we have to go out and make it."

Tam laughed. "I'm ready to make some history. How about you two?"

I just smiled and shook my head. "Conspiracy and treason are the ultimate games for goblins, aren't they? And for chips, you gamble with your lives."

Tam grinned, slow and wicked, his black eyes glittering in playful anticipation. "It's not treason if you win."

About the Author

Lisa is the editor at an advertising agency. She has been a magazine editor and writer of corporate marketing materials of every description. She lives in North Carolina with her very patient and understanding husband, one cat, two retired racing greyhounds, and a Jack Russell terrier who rules them all.

For more information about Lisa and her books, visit her at www.lisashearin.com.

THE ULTIMATE IN FANTASY!

From magical tales of distant worlds to stories of those with abilities beyond the ordinary, Ace and Roc have everything you need to stretch your imagination to its limits.

Marion Zimmer Bradley/Diana L. Paxson

Guy Gavriel Kay

Dennis L. McKiernan

Patricia A. McKillip

Robin McKinley

Sharon Shinn

Katherine Kurtz

Barb and J. C. Hendee

Elizabeth Bear

T. A. Barron

Brian Jacques

Robert Asprin

penguin.com

M12G110